THE
CHARIOT
AT
DUSK

THE TIGER AT MIDNIGHT TRILOGY

The Tiger at Midnight

The Archer at Dawn

The Chariot at Dusk

THE
CHARIOT
AT
DUSK

SWATI TEERDHALA

KATHERINE TEGEN BOOKS
An Imprint of HarperCollins Publishers

Katherine Tegen Books is an imprint of HarperCollins Publishers.

The Chariot at Dusk
Text copyright © 2021 by Swati Teerdhala
Map by Adam Rufino
All rights reserved. Printed in the United States of America.
No part of this book may be used or reproduced in any manner whatsoever without
written permission except in the case of brief quotations embodied in critical articles
and reviews. For information address HarperCollins Children's Books, a division of
HarperCollins Publishers, 195 Broadway, New York, NY 10007.
www.epicreads.com

Library of Congress Control Number: 2021933140
ISBN 978-0-06-286927-2

Typography by Carla Weise
21 22 23 24 25   PC/LSCH   10 9 8 7 6 5 4 3 2 1
❖
First Edition

TO THOSE WHO DREAM OF BETTER WORLDS

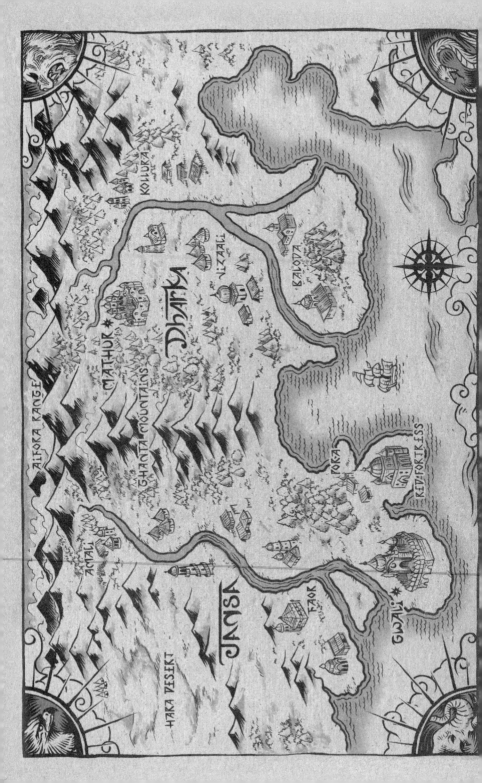

For their love was not a light, but
a dusk. Not darkness, but twilight.

—From the Tales of Naran and Naria

CHAPTER 1

Esha was in charge of this great, big, *quiet* palace. She turned the corner out of the throne room, the light tinkling of her anklet bells echoing across marble tiles.

The palace had become a makeshift home for those alive after the coup at the Winner's Ball. The Blades had taken over the western wing with the Scales, an uneasy peace settling between them. The Senaps who still resisted, well, the palace had become a prison for them.

And she was here.

Tasked with making sure everything didn't crumble down around them.

King Mahir had left to protect Dharka, Harun was captured, Vardaan had disappeared in the jungle beyond, and Kunal had betrayed them and fled with Reha.

It was a wonder that anything had gone right since then. The one bright spot was that the citizens outside believed the story they had woven and spread through the streets. The city was placated, at least for now.

She reached the open balustrade of the main hall and looked out into the fading red of the sunrise.

The drought had finally reached Gwali. Fishermen who would've risen at dawn and gone to the river now blocked the streets that went west to the ocean. Fights had broken out between deep ocean trappers and river fishermen. Only yesterday she had arbitrated a disagreement, feeding them false promises that things would be better soon. As for the merchants and food sellers, they were no better off. Many had reduced their wares and the shipments they had started from Jansa were slow and far between.

People were suffering.

A rustle at the door caught Esha's attention. A short man with a long mustache stood in the entrance looking curiously at her, and then beyond her.

Alok had appeared in the side entrance, talking in hushed tones with a younger Blade as he walked. His curls had grown out, framing his face in waves that would've made many a noble lady jealous. Esha patted her own mess of curls, trying to remember the last time she had brushed her hair. The man by the entrance perked up and waved a hand at Alok, who looked perplexed but smiled in return.

It was amusing to watch, but she had no patience for the man's incompetence in identifying the person he had come to meet. She had little patience these past few weeks since they had taken over the palace from Vardaan.

Esha swept around the staircase and walked into full view. If the man knew what was good for him he'd notice her now. He had been summoned to the palace to meet with Princess Reha, after all. The man threw her the bread-crumbs of a glance before he turned back to Alok—the only potential for power in the room, apparently.

Perhaps he believed the princess too busy to deign to be involved in these matters. The note the man received *had* been signed by a Lord Mayank, which might be cause for his confusion. But that was probably too generous to assume. The short man walked over to Alok, who wrapped things up with the Blade and dismissed her with a nod of his head.

The man bowed low.

"I received your note, your excellency."

"My note?"

"A bit late, but I rushed over here. I *have* heard news. And I came to the palace straightaway when I heard of it. I received the summons just as I was leaving my house." His words had an oily taste. The man straightened and faced Alok with a slippery smile. "But it was hard to come by, terribly difficult. And I have people to take care of in my guild, especially with the drought fast approaching."

Esha suppressed a laugh. He didn't even bother to play the game. Another setting and she may have even admired the man's gall.

"Are you . . . asking to be compensated?" Alok said. "For information that could save the city?"

"Oh no, my lord. I would never ask for that. But a little

help would be welcome," the man said.

This was where Esha should step in, but she felt compelled to stay back, keep watching.

The citizens of Gwali had believed their story, that the Yavar had attempted to invade the palace, that Princess Reha had defended them by alerting the Senaps to the attempted insurgence. That Vardaan abdicated in her favor out of gratitude. Most of the citizens were loyal, but there would always be a few who would be eager to take advantage of the turmoil that always followed a change in power. A strong story made that more difficult.

Alok gave him an absentminded nod and Guildsman Gugil's grin was unmistakable. The guildsman had yet to understand that Alok gave that nod to just about everything, mostly to stall a decision. To Esha, it was a fatal flaw. A good businessperson must always know where the power lay in a room, and if he didn't, it was his duty to figure it out.

Pity for his guild. Esha knew now with certainty why they were in such dire straits.

"I'll have to ask our leader, of course," Alok said, drawing out the words and casting a look about.

Esha emerged from the shadows like a wraith. The man jumped back. But then he peered closer and, seeing a woman, seemed to decide she was no threat. His mask of deference dropped and there was an upturned slant to his mouth, a gleam in his eye. He turned his back on Esha.

Bad move. Her hand went to the whips she now wore on her waist sash.

"Of course, your excellency. But aren't you the leader now, Lord Mayank? I got a note from you."

"Oh no," Alok said, laughing. "I'm not the leader of anything, unless it's how to get the chef to make more of those fluffy rice cakes. Our leader's behind you."

Esha enjoyed this part, where they turned and looked at her with new eyes. When they realized that she had the power, they transformed. Most men were smart enough to change tactics, accept the new norm. A few were still unwilling to see her, a woman, as the one to make a deal with. Their idea of a princess, of a woman, wasn't that of a leader.

Perhaps they had bought into the rhetoric Vardaan had spread; perhaps they had always held such beliefs in their hearts. Hard to tell and Esha did not care. Those men were difficult, but Esha had found a way to deal with them.

Esha clutched the ruby-encrusted hilt of the sword she now wore, the darkened eagle sigil apparent from the way she wore it. Vardaan's old sword.

Anyone worth their salt recognized it and bowed.

The man was not worth anything, as evidenced by his reaction. His eyes narrowed and his mouth turned cruel.

"Is this a joke? Or a test?" The man whirled back around to face Alok.

"Why would we do that, good man?" Alok asked, his confusion genuine. He was still learning this world of shadows and deals. Every emotion of his played across his face.

"Why indeed? I've been the picture of grace. I came here and I offered—"

"You got a summons from the palace to offer the information we need, the dire information your own country needs, on a condition. You asked for an exchange, a payment, a bribe, of sorts," Esha said. "Not really the picture of grace, Soham Gugil."

"I am Guildsman Gugil," he said, puffing his chest up. "I was asked to come as a representative."

"You were asked to come because I heard you have information that is vital to the security of Jansa. Now if you do, I'll consider not throwing you into the dungeons. If you don't, well, you're testing my last bit of patience."

Alok cringed. Esha liked Alok, truly liked him and enjoyed his company, but he was more like Kunal, more like that *soldier*, than not. There was no room for softness in this game.

"But I heard the princess was no more than a useless fop—"

Alok groaned. "Oh no."

Esha raised a hand and casually snapped two fingers. Two Blades dressed in the armor of the Senaps, painted Crescent silver now, ran up to her side. "We have another resident for the dungeons."

The two Blades each grabbed an arm of Guildsman Gugil, whose eyes threatened to bug out of his face. He finally realized his mistake, but Esha was already finished with their conversation.

"I have it, the information!" he said.

"Good. I'll come visit you later and you can tell me all

about it," Esha said sweetly, walking up to the guildsman. She ran a finger down the side of his face. He'd already started sweating. Why were the ones who blustered the most always the first to break? "Until then, you can spend some quality time alone with your thoughts."

"But my guild—"

Esha grabbed the man's chin and locked eyes with him. The disbelief that had turned into anger was now shifting into worry and confusion. He didn't know where to put her.

She liked it that way.

"Your guild will be taken care of. I do not punish people for the stupidity of their leaders. I'll send some Blades to your guild this afternoon to assess what they need," she said. "If it's dire enough that you'd trade this information for help, then you should've come to us days ago."

She let go of his face and wiped her hands on her waist sash, taking care not to mess up the delicate fabric of her peacock-blue silk sari. The Blades hefted him away, and the guildsman at least had the presence of mind not to scream the entire way, unlike some of the others. He did shout a bit, though.

Esha turned toward Alok, who was shaking his head at her.

"Another one? You can't keep them all in the dungeons."

She sighed and lifted her eyes to the ceiling. "Not this again, Alok. You know it's just to scare them. They won't accept me as a leader if I'm kind. As a woman, I have to be more ruthless, inspire more fear, engender more respect.

I'm setting up a country for Reha. When she returns, she has a country to rule and a city that believes in her power. It's enough that there are wild stories going around the city."

"Yes, I know, but—"

"What is the 'but,' then? Did the general not do worse, to his own soldiers?" she said, exasperated. She was tiring of having this conversation. Would Alok be protesting if she wasn't a woman?

"I understand what you're doing, even why. But it's a dangerous precedent to set," he said quietly.

"And I'm aware of that. I only keep them in the dungeons for a day," she said. "But might is still right to these men, and until I show my might, I cannot accomplish what we want to. I won't be able to find Vardaan, rescue Harun, save us from this drought."

She heard the way her voice caught and Alok gave her a soft look. He had heard it too.

"And Kunal?" he ventured.

Instantly, a vise squeezed her heart, stopping her breath for one aching moment. She hated hearing his name. Hated what it did to her.

"The soldier is none of my concern."

"But Reha?"

"Bhandu is on their trail. He's still sending regular reports. We have a few days until the solstice," she said.

Alok's shoulders sagged. "One piece of good news. If Kunal is able to renew the bond with Reha, it will be one less thing to worry about."

"If the soldier is able to do that, we will still have a fracturing country, a loose tyrant of a king who will come back for his throne, and"—Esha swallowed roughly—"and we will still have to find my friend Harun. My prince. Before the Yavar realize we have renewed the bond or are close to it. Who knows what they'll do to him if that's the case."

Alok's face turned ashen, and he nodded. "I know. I'm just trying to look on the bright side."

Esha smiled. "It's why I keep you around. How's Farhan's research going?"

Alok returned the smile, but it was for a different reason. One that had more to do with the boy than the research. "It's going well, I think. It's hard to tell. Sometimes he's close to tearing out his hair and others he seems absolutely absorbed in the work. But I'm sure we'll find what we're looking for."

"Good."

"About Harun," he said slowly, carefully. "I might have a lead."

"Two leads in one day?" she said.

"If it's any good." Alok's voice was cautious, but Esha had already begun to move, signaling at some of the Blades nearby to join them.

"Any lead is a good lead, Alok."

He looked hesitant. "And what about any leads about Kunal?"

The smile left her face. "Send those to Bhandu and Aahal. I want no part of that unless it's directly related to Reha."

"Esha . . ." Alok tried to reach out a hand to her but thought better of it and saluted instead. "I'll be back in a few hours, hopefully with some answers."

"My favorite words," Esha said drily.

Alok and two Blades walked out of the room, leaving Esha in the towering, cavernous hall. She sagged against the staircase as soon as they turned the corner, their footsteps echoing behind them.

If only Harun was here. But he was gone. Stolen. And she was alone, trying to figure out how to lead the Blades, and the country, by herself.

She let it all drop from her shoulders for a moment, all the burden of power and leadership, and her entire body quaked. She slid onto one of the stairs and leaned her head against the cold marble railing.

One step at a time.

Esha would solve this, one step at a time.

CHAPTER 2

The harsh wind of the mountains buffeted Kunal as he pushed forward. The rock underneath him was scraggly with no place for a proper foothold, let alone any room to stand and rest. Earlier on in their trip they had been able to change between flying and walking but not anymore. Not since Reha had started shifting uncontrollably.

In the beginning, it was the slightest thing. Claws sprouting from her fingertips when they had stopped to get more rations from a market, her wings shortening as they flew over the low hills of the northern region of Jansa.

But then she had stopped shifting and started doing something else entirely. Kunal glanced over at her shivering form as she carefully picked her way over the rocks. Her feet were now made of hooves, like a mountain goat's, her body adapting to the latest environment.

It had been like this since they had hit the Aifora

Mountains. At first she had shifted into a feline without her knowledge. Kunal had assumed she'd shift into a jungle lion, as was customary to her Himyad blood, but instead, she had become a snow leopard. It was as if the first change in the climate had triggered something in her that cast aside both her Himyad and Samyad blood.

Since then, she hadn't stopped shifting, no matter what exercises or breath training that Kunal did with her. Reha was handling it better than he might've, but he wasn't oblivious to the distress that lurked in her gaze. They had both realized Kunal's knowledge had reached its natural limit. He was unable to help her.

Kunal grunted under the thick wool uttariya that was wrapped around his face, nudging Reha and pointing toward a flat area of the mountain pass. Reha followed behind him, and they pulled into the small crevice tucked into the side of the rock. If nothing else, it gave them a short respite from the steadily falling snow, which blanketed the slate gray landscape in a light, ethereal white. Kunal reached a hand out and let a snowflake melt on his fingertip, marveling at the intricate beauty of it, the whorls of ice and spirals of silver embedded in each.

Snow at this time of year. Kunal had heard of it, but to see it in person . . . He felt a smile curl at the edges of his face. He imagined Esha's look when he told her that he actually—

The smile faded as reality hit him. He swallowed hard and turned to Reha.

"We're only a half day away by my estimate." His voice

was muffled, but Reha nodded.

"We've made good time," she said.

"Your new modifications have helped. Helped us find food back on the mountain pass."

"Oh yes, I'm so enjoying being in a new animal body with new desires every day. Really invigorating," she said.

Kunal couldn't help but chuckle. He was learning that Reha, despite everything that had happened to her these past few weeks, had a good sense of humor about her. He wasn't sure that if he was in her position—discovered that she was a royal and her family was alive, that she could never return to the Scales, that she was the only key to saving the land, and now, that she could barely hold on to her human form—he would be quite so levelheaded about it all.

"The breathing techniques you showed me are helping," she offered.

"I'm glad to hear that." Kunal tugged out their dwindling ration supply and handed her a dried fig. She started nibbling on it, her mind elsewhere.

"I just wish I could control it. Understand it. If we go by what the physical evidence indicates, my mixed blood doesn't just give me the ability to shift into a Himyad lion or a Samyad eagle but into any animal."

Kunal would've been terrified by the realization. Reha only seemed intrigued.

"Or it could be because we're approaching Mount Bangaar," Kunal said. "It's known to be the birthplace of magic and where the gods used to reside. It could be causing unknown changes in your body."

"Your powers haven't changed."

"They have become a bit sharper," Kunal admitted. "For example, I can sense there are two hares about half a league away from us, under the rock. It could be hitting you harder because you only just started controlling your shifts."

Reha peered up at the mountain peak looming above them. "Maybe it is the mountain. We are about to pass through the Golden Mist."

Kunal glanced up at the fading sky. Above, a few leagues ahead, a brilliant copper-and-gold haze perched upon the top of the mountain, beckoning at them. The Golden Mist. It was rumored to be the birthplace of the spirits, once the home of the gods. Many a story he had been told as a child had started in those hazy peaks.

Reha continued on. "While it's been an exciting few days, I'd like some semblance of control over my body."

Kunal sighed. "If it's the mountain, it'll get worse before it gets better. But we might find some answers in the temple."

"Sanapat Temple," Reha said softly, her eyes lighting up. "I read about it as a child. Carved into the mountain itself."

It was the temple that the royals traveled to every year for the renewal ritual of the *janma* bond. It had been over a decade since the renewal had been performed correctly, with blood from both lines. With the Samyad queens gone and the blood ritual unfulfilled, the land had begun to die. Now, with Reha's blood, they finally had both bloodlines they needed to renew the ritual and revive the land. To save everything.

A flutter of hope, one he had been carrying close to him since Gwali, rose in his chest. This was it; this was why he had left everything behind. A chance.

An image of dancing eyes and curls appeared, and he pushed it away. It was easier to not think of Esha's reaction, to hope for the best. That she'd understand why they had left. Kunal hadn't had much of a choice, but there was no way she'd know that.

Reha cocked her head suddenly, and a half a second later, Kunal heard it too. He pulled the younger girl farther into the crevice. Whispers filtered through the air, and Kunal couldn't be sure of the direction. A crunch of feet, one hundred paces away.

"We have some friends," Reha whispered.

His heart thudded in his chest. "Three, by the sounds of it."

"Four," she said.

Her eyes widened. "More than four."

"We need to keep moving, then," he said.

Reha nodded, hefting her pack and securing her wool uttariya over her long-sleeved tunic. "Should we try to shift again?" she asked.

She bit the side of her lip, looking out to where the sound

had come from. It had been only a week since they had started traveling together, but he was beginning to grow fond of his cousin. She was ruthless and she was strong. He had promised her his help when he had left with her.

"I don't know," Kunal admitted. "It would be the fastest way to the temple, but with your shifts the way they are. . . ."

"Kunal, cousin dearest, if we heal the cursed *janma* bond, maybe I will stop shifting. But then again if we don't shift now, we could get caught here by soldiers skilled enough to have followed us up here." She paused and gave him a tired look. "In this situation, perhaps shifting is a bit of a necessary evil, don't you think?"

He frowned but gave in with a nod. "Fine, let's do it. But be careful."

"Aren't I always?" she shot back.

It wasn't the first time Kunal had heard that phrase. But the thought of it, and the woman who usually spoke it, made his heart constrict.

Kunal closed his eyes and thought of his tether, the song of home—bronzed skin and bright eyes, curls that tickled his nose—and matched it with the animal song of his blood.

And in seconds he was in the air, soaring behind Reha, up to the top of the Aifora Mountains.

———◇———

Esha didn't think the dungeons were as bad as Alok said.

They were quite comfortable compared to the cramped hole Esha had been tossed into at the citadel during her time there. The palace dungeons were far cleaner and larger. Even in prison, nobles were treated better than common traitors and conspirators. Still, it was a rather convenient area for her purposes now.

Esha dragged her hands over the metal bars of the open cell in front of her. A cot, sunlight, and, at least, nothing *too* foul smelling. Back in the dungeons of the citadel, she had realized she had to escape if she ever wanted to be able to use her arm again. To this day, her right arm wasn't as strong as her left after her torture. She'd certainly never forgotten that.

The man she was looking for was near the end of the hall. When she arrived at the front of his cell, he jumped up.

"Master Gugil?" she said quietly. "I thought I'd come visit you again, see if you might have changed your mind."

Gugil scrambled to his feet as much as he could. His right ankle was clamped to the ground and only let him come as far as the front of the cell. He still wore his clothes from the day before, now crumpled. Other than the dark circles under his eyes, Gugil looked fine. But perhaps a night hearing the moans of other cellmates, courtesy of Aahal, might have helped him to change his mind.

He clasped and unclasped his hands.

"My lady—I mean, Your Highness."

Normally, Esha would object to the honorific, but she wasn't feeling very generous this morning.

"I regret my words from yesterday." The man cleared his throat. "I was, perhaps, a bit too hasty. I didn't mean to give the impression that I wasn't committed to our country's safety. It was shock—just shock."

"At?"

Gugil shifted uncomfortably, tripping over the chain. "I had been expecting . . . someone else."

Esha smiled, razor sharp. "I'm sure you were. Now tell me, Master Gugil, what information do you have?"

He took in a breath, glancing nervously at her. "King Vardaan—a few of my men spotted him outside the Hara Desert, on the western border."

She gripped the metal bars. "Was he alone?"

"No, he wasn't." The guildsman shifted his weight, looking uncomfortable. "The only reason my men recognized the former king was because of his shifting. There were sounds of a lion at night, unnatural sounds. A wounded animal, which is unusual for the Hara Desert. There are typically no lions in the surrounding hills, at least not for many miles. My men went to look around and one swore on his mother's pyre that he saw the former king as he shifted back. Alongside ten or so armed men."

Esha took a sharp breath in. "Mercenaries, probably."

This was good news, the best news she'd had in days. She nodded at the man in front of her and motioned at one of the Blades to come over.

"Thank you, Master Gugil," she said. "Now, that wasn't so hard, was it?"

"No," he said, gulping.

Only a night in a cell and he was already breaking easier than the sugar crust of her favorite mango custard. He'd never have lasted in the citadel.

"If you hear anything else, you will come straight to the palace," Esha said to the man. She played with the hilt of the sword at her waist, and his eyes darted to the flash of steel. "And if I find out that you've told anyone else, I can personally guarantee that you won't live to see the next solstice, let alone the next full moon."

Her voice was softer than silk. "Am I clear?"

Gugil bobbed his head up and down. Esha was about to turn and leave when the man spoke up again.

"I'd be remiss if I didn't mention it, Your Highness. The tanners' guild also had reports of another wild feline at night by the upper hills, near one of their outposts."

Esha was about to snap at the man that she had larger concerns than the fears of middle-aged men, when the guildsman's words fully landed. She inhaled sharply.

"Is something the matter, Your Highness?"

Esha didn't respond.

"See that Guildsman Gugil is taken back to his guild," she said to the Blade at her side. There was a relieved exhalation from the cell, but Esha was already halfway out the door.

If this guildsman's reports were true, they echoed those of a report she had skimmed last week. And two coincidences were no longer chance.

Esha picked up her sari skirt with one hand, racing up the stairs to find the others.

If she was right, and she hoped she was, they had a location.

She knew where Harun was being held.

CHAPTER 3

A small puff of air floated in front of Kunal, moving in and out with his breath as he trudged up the steep incline that would take him and Reha to the top of Mount Bangaar. The royals normally took the carved-out road on the other side of the mountain, but it would be too dangerous and exposed for him and Reha.

Reha's powers had given out about half a mile ago, after they had shaken the group that was following them. Kunal had shifted and caught her in time, forced her to take rest. She still shivered by his side, fighting as he was to get to the top of the mountain. He wanted to wrap her up in his uttariya but any coddling would earn him a glare and a verbal bite from his cousin. He'd learned that pretty quickly.

"Just a bit farther," he said.

"If you say that again, I will hurt you," she said. Sweat

beaded down her forehead even in the chill, and Kunal had the distinct feeling that she was hiding from him the full physical toll of her shifts.

Kunal sighed. "I'm just trying to be encouraging."

"Well, go be encouraging elsewhere."

"What happened to the sunny Reha of before?"

"She didn't fall fifty feet and almost break her neck," she said. Reha tugged her uttariya a bit tighter, her eyes skimming over the remaining cliff they had to walk. Her now-human feet were dirtied and banged up.

"Let me shift and carry you up," he said.

"No," she said immediately. "I have *some* dignity."

"Would you prefer your dignity over your body?"

"Are you always this self-righteous?"

Kunal quirked his mouth. "Yes, I think I am. At least, according to Alok and Esha."

Reha didn't notice the way his smile fell. "Tell me more about them."

He would've protested, but she needed a distraction.

"Alok—he's my best friend—and I met when I first came to the Fort. He took a chance on me when everyone else avoided the general's nephew, the new recruit. Laksh joined our group soon after," he said.

"Laksh?"

"We're not friends anymore." Kunal didn't say anything else, and they climbed up the craggy rock for another few seconds in silence.

"Esha," he finally said. "Ah, well, she's a whole other story."

"So, you were the secret lover she kept sneaking notes to? You know how much trouble I went through to get those clothes for you for the *Chinarath* festival?" she said.

Kunal sputtered, cold entering his mouth. "I'm not— we're not *lovers*."

"You are a horrible liar, Kunal."

His shoulders dropped. "I've been told."

"She'll be mad, won't she?" Reha asked, her voice quieting. "That you left? Without any explanation?"

Kunal's heart thudded against his chest. He thought back to the notes they had sent each other, the fight they had, the words he had said when claiming he wasn't and never wanted to be a Blade. The silence since.

"I'd be lucky if she's only mad. No, I think it will go deeper than that," he said.

"Deeper?"

"I may have said some things. Some harsh things before the Winner's Ball. I took them back and apologized, but it was our first fight. It was about you, or the idea of you, the lost princess. And now I've left with the lost princess, everyone's last hope."

It was the first time he had admitted it. Given space to the feeling in the corner of his soul where he knew he had changed things between them with his decision.

The rest of him refused to believe it.

"But it'll be fine," he finished. "Mad or more than mad, I will fix it. I'll win her back."

"Definitely lovers," Reha said. She bumped into his shoulder and smiled at him. "For what it's worth, it's clear she liked you."

"Sure," he said.

"You don't believe me?"

"I believe you just fine. But it doesn't help that you were lying to Esha the whole time."

"Everyone gets so upset over lies. They're just a little bending of the truth," Reha said. "Now, I didn't harm her, did I? I actually liked Esha."

The last part came out quieter, but Kunal understood. Reha was also worried about their return.

Kunal caught up with Reha and patted her arm. When she didn't bite his hand off, he carefully put it around her and drew her in, despite the cold. "We'll figure it out, cousin."

"Figure out what?" She peered up at him. "Is that the first time you've acknowledged our blood ties out loud?"

Kunal ignored her. "We'll figure out all of it."

Reha gave him a look as if he was being odder than a moon-touched trader, but Kunal also sensed her body relax.

She was just a girl still. That's why, more than anything, he had come here with her. Esha would have to understand that.

Wouldn't she?

Reha straightened, pulling Kunal's arm off. She cocked

her head to the side, some of the color returning to her face. He heard it too.

"Water," she whispered. "An underground river."

They had arrived at the top of Mount Bangaar.

———◄◦►———

Esha snuck into the Great Library from the secret side entrance she had discovered a few weeks earlier. The last thing she needed was someone watching her and questioning why she and a large number of Blades were going in and out of the Great Library every morning and evening. Especially with the number of Scales around, not to mention Laksh and Zhyani.

She trusted Laksh as far as she could throw him, which wasn't very far. Still, he had been by her side since the palace takeover and Harun's capture, and even convinced Zhyani and the other Scales to back off and partner with them. If nothing else, Esha knew that her and Laksh's interests were aligned, which meant that, for now, he could be trusted. And Zhyani followed wherever Laksh was these days.

She also knew Laksh wanted something else from her: information on Arpiya. It was cute, in a way.

But if she could say anything to her friend Arpiya, she would tell her to be careful with soldiers. Then again, just because things had turned out a mess for Esha didn't mean Arpiya was doomed to the same fate.

Arpiya had almost sobbed when Esha told her she had turned down being queen of Dharka, even though she had eventually said she understood Esha's decision. That had been weeks ago, and Esha didn't know if she felt the same way, or if Harun was even still open to her.

She didn't know what she wanted anymore.

The rest of the team was already there, scattered around the room in their usual spots, a lively discussion already under way.

Alok paced past Esha as Farhan tapped his mouth thoughtfully with a piece of chalk, leaving a white streak across his lips. Arpiya tugged the chalk away right before Farhan could accidentally eat it. Aahal's long legs were draped across the seat of a chair as he took over the better part of the table in front of them.

"The Hara Desert? We already combed through it," Arpiya said, shaking her head.

"They spotted Vardaan near the desert," Esha corrected as she walked in. "But we heard reports of these wild animals at nights near the hills as well, which can't be a coincidence."

"Technically, they could be," Farhan said.

Aahal gave his twin an exasperated glance. "There is no such thing as a coincidence; isn't that one of your lovely phrases?"

"Yes, but—"

"How about we don't try to rain on the collective parade, brother?" Aahal said. "I'm willing to go check out any lead."

"We can't have our best squads go out on a greedy guildsman's word." Arpiya looked mutinous at the thought.

"We're not going off on the word of anyone," Esha said.

"We're going off a pattern."

She tugged out a sheath of parchments she had spent the morning collecting, reports and patrol movements. Esha swatted Aahal's long arms off the table and spread out the papers. "These reports mentioned the same thing as the guildsman. And then look at these patrol movements. Troops were moved away from this garrison just days before the Winner's Ball. Someone had secured the area."

"It still seems unlikely," Farhan said. "And why would the Yavar keep Harun down here, on a border they don't even control? Unless the Western Lands have decided to break their neutrality?"

The front door of the warm room flew open and all four of them nearly jumped out of their seats, their hands going to some weapon at their hip or hidden in their waist sash.

Laksh held his arms up as he entered the room. "You're a jumpy bunch, aren't you?"

Zhyani followed in after, wound as tightly as a kite string. She wore a disapproving expression.

Esha rolled her eyes and relaxed her stance. "I can't imagine why we'd be that way." She turned to the man entering behind Laksh. "Can you, Lord Mayank?"

"No idea at all." Mayank grinned back at her, his eyes crinkling. He glanced at the table. "Planning something, are we?"

"*We* are," Alok said, crossing his arms.

Mayank hadn't quite won over Alok, though Esha didn't really know why. The others had no outward problem with him, and, in fact, Aahal looked up to him a bit. He had even started wearing his hair the same way as Mayank, echoing the current fashions of the Jansan court.

Esha waved Mayank and Laksh to her side. "We might have a lead on where they've taken Harun. The others think it's shaky"—two nodded heads and one glare from Alok—"but we don't have much else to go on."

Mayank sifted through the reports. "I heard what the guildsman said. From Aahal."

Aahal had the decency to blush a little under Esha's sudden gaze. "I have some House Pramukh soldiers in the area, and I can send them ahead to scout," Mayank said.

"And if we're right, and Harun is being held there? Won't scouts tip them off?" Esha asked.

"Are you indicating my soldiers aren't up to the task?"

"I'm saying that we still don't know what the Yavar want. If we make a move, we're inviting war. Right now, the country is unaware and unscathed. We need the utmost secrecy in rescuing Harun before anyone finds out, which means we use your men only if you know you have their trust to keep this a secret. If not, we can't send them, even if that means I ride on horseback to every town in the western hills by myself."

There was a strangled noise from her right, but Esha didn't look at her team. They had to understand how important this was to her. She'd go to the ends of the earth to get Harun back. It would be only half of what he'd done for her.

And the way she had left their relationship before he had been taken. . . .

Esha shut that door viciously before the stab of pain reached her heart. She missed Harun fiercely, and she needed him back here, by her side.

Mayank sighed. "They're loyal men, but after that speech, I'm not so sure it's enough. How can you judge loyalty of that kind?"

"Look around here." Her voice was quiet. "At these people."

"Then no," Mayank said, his voice resigned.

"We scout ourselves," Esha said.

Aahal looked a bit too excited, straightening in his chair and almost knocking Arpiya over. Farhan frowned, but Alok nodded at her, whispering into his ear.

"It's too dangerous," Zhyani said, shaking her head. She didn't wear a sari, and instead was clad in a dhoti and a short silk tunic. The one thing Esha had learned about the woman was that she was adaptable—and had a few too many opinions. Especially on how Esha should run the palace.

"It was always going to be dangerous," Esha said back.

"Are you sure about this?" Laksh asked her as she turned to him. He wore leather armor, which meant he must have been down in the training courtyard earlier today. Esha had put him in charge of rounding up potential soldiers who could be of use—or might be willing to turn to their side. He had put together a small group of soldiers and had taken

29

to running drills with them in the morning. Once a soldier, always a soldier, she supposed.

"No. But I don't have much of a choice, do I?"

Despite her best effort to suppress it, the note of desperation that had hidden in her heart since that day, weeks ago, rang out. Mayank walked over and took her hands in his own. Though she made a face, Esha didn't pull away. She was glad for the comfort. It was different offered from him, someone who she didn't have to look after and wasn't responsible for. Alok made a sputtering noise to her side.

"You're not alone in doing this," he said.

"I know. But it's not on them like it is on me," she said, her voice quieting so the team couldn't hear.

"Because you're their leader?"

"Because they're not at fault."

"And you think you are?" Mayank asked, his mouth curving into a frown. "Esha, you can't believe that."

"You'd be surprised what one can believe, especially when it is the truth." Esha pulled away, and Mayank let her go, shaking his head.

"If you're at fault, then I am as well. So is everyone. How could we have seen this coming?"

"I don't know, but somehow, somewhere, I failed."

Esha thought back to her first meeting with Yamini, how the Yavar princess had charmed her, how she had picked out a sari for her to wear. The hundreds of little instances where Esha could've picked up on her true intentions.

But maybe it had started back even further. Back in a forest with a soldier who had eyes that called to her, armor that was destined to break her heart and tear her family apart.

Esha gritted her teeth. She was the Viper. Whatever heart she had left was captured somewhere with her friend, her prince.

"That face is telling me that I won't be convincing you otherwise," Lord Mayank said. "But let it be known, I think you're wrong. And if you try to go running off into trouble because of some misplaced guilt, I will tell on you to Arpiya."

Esha burst into laughter. The others snapped around, stopping their bickering to stare at her. Aahal's eyes brightened, Farhan smiled, and Arpiya almost fell over in surprise.

Had it been that long since she'd last laughed?

Her team, her family, looked lighter than they had in weeks.

"Esha, if we're going to pursue the lead, we need you to stay behind. We need a leader in the palace," Alok said, moving between her and Mayank.

Esha looked between Alok and Mayank. "Then I leave the troops and the palace in the care of Lord Mayank. I have to do this myself. This is a task for the Viper, not a full squad. We'll be too noticeable."

"Esha—" Farhan started.

She held up a hand. "I know what I'm doing. Lord

31

Mayank has navigated this palace and its politics for years. He'll lead in my absence."

Mayank's eyes widened, his brow furrowed, but he gave her a quick, eager nod. "Whatever you need, I can do."

The team looked a bit apprehensive. Zhyani and Laksh exchanged a loaded glance. But Esha had decided.

"Now, if you do anything to jeopardize my people or this city while I'm gone, I will kill you myself," she said simply, facing Mayank. Alok, who had been glaring at him, finally looked a bit more placated.

Mayank was unfazed. "Noted, Viper. Don't worry, my sense of duty is almost as developed as my sense of self-preservation. I'll do my best, if only to make sure I stay alive when you return."

"Smart man." Laksh chuckled.

"Aahal, Laksh, we'll leave tomorrow," Esha said. "To find Harun."

And bring him home.

CHAPTER 4

The river under the mountain was magnificent. It gushed over the deep crevice that cradled it, splashing onto the rocky banks and soaking the edges of Kunal's and Reha's sandals.

Kunal and Reha stepped down into the subterranean cave, an otherworldly light filtering through the cracks in the rock to illuminate the temple below.

They walked farther inside, crossing the tiled border between the old weatherworn cave and the ancient temple. A strong wind filtered through the cracks above, and Kunal tugged his wool uttariya closer, exchanging a nervous glance with Reha. There was something unsettling about the cavern.

Kunal didn't know what to expect. All he knew about the ritual was that he was to recite the sacred words, and Reha would offer her blood at the right time. King Mahir had said that was what the royals had done for centuries to maintain the *janma* bond, their gift from the gods and their connection to the land. With that, they would save their land, both of their lands.

And while it certainly hadn't been easy getting to this point, Kunal couldn't help the feeling prickling against the back of his neck since they had entered the cave.

Something was off.

The sixth sense that had carried him through his days as a soldier hadn't led him wrong before.

But nothing happened. And so he continued on. It was probably just nerves, anyway. Anytime he had been about to finish a mission or enter a battlefield, he'd get a similar feeling. Kunal ignored the small part of him that whispered that this wasn't a normal mission or battle. This was life or death for his entire country.

They dropped their packs by the edge of the water. Kunal pulled off his wool uttariya and the top layer of his clothing, indicating at Reha to do the same. She removed the turban that had been covering her hair since they had left the palace and her straight black hair fell to her waist. It was matted and dirty after weeks of travel, much like Kunal's.

Reha wrapped her arms around her shivering frame. "What now?"

"We start the ritual once it's sundown," Kunal said.

"We did it," Reha said quietly. "We got here before the solstice deadline. We're going to fix this."

Kunal stepped into the river, his body seizing up in

anticipation of its chilly currents. Instead, the water was gentle and warm. Kunal sank deeper into the water with each step until he was in up to his waist. Reha stepped in after him, her nose scrunched as she touched the water, her face blooming in pleasure as she also discovered the water's pleasant temperature.

Streaks of dark stained the cave ground as the sun began to dip outside. It was nearly time.

A splash of water hit Kunal in the eye as he turned. "Hey!"

Reha grinned and splashed him again. "Don't tell me soldiers aren't allowed to have fun."

"This is a holy river," Kunal said seriously.

"And we're here for holy reasons. But that doesn't mean I can't have a little fun," she said. "Don't be such a bore."

Kunal sputtered. "Well, if I'm a bore, I'm a bore who got you safely to the top of the mountain—"

"You did do that," Reha said.

"And betrayed everyone around me to do it," Kunal finished. His shoulders caved in with the weight of the unfinished ritual and the tension that he had been carrying since he had left Esha behind. He had been trying so hard to ignore it.

Reha's eyes widened. She looked unsure about what to say to his outburst.

"Just so you know, I did the same thing," she said. Her voice was gruff but quiet. Kunal wanted to protest, but he knew she was right. And she had little choice.

The light flickered lower, and they both glanced at the slatted windows of the cave temple. Reds and purples painted the sky, exchanged for the brilliant blue of before.

"Let's get started," Kunal said.

Kunal began to chant, low and steady, just like King Mahir had shown him. It was the prayer to the Sun Maiden, the first one they were ever taught as kids. A beat after, Reha began the prayer to the Moon Lord. They chanted together, the syncopated rhythms clashing and harmonizing at turns. At every eighth beat, they'd dip, cupping water into their hands and pouring it over their heads to cleanse their bodies.

The river began to hum and glow a brilliant iridescent gold. Their chanting bounced off the temple walls and echoed to fill the entire cave.

Kunal motioned Reha toward him. She stretched her arms out, crossing them at the wrists. He unsheathed his dagger and cut her forearm to provide their offering to the Sun Maiden and Moon Lord.

Their voices crescendoed and he poured the vial of blood she had stolen from Harun over her arms. It pooled together in the cradle, mixing with Reha's blood before slowly dripping into the water below.

The river hissed as red mixed with the gold of the water. Reha looked worriedly at Kunal. He shook his head. Everything was going as King Mahir had described.

Kunal finished out the chant, letting the last of the blood fall into the river. It hit the water and spread into a thin layer of red on top of the gold. A whirlpool formed where the blood had hit the water, steam rising fast, fast enough that both Kunal and Reha stepped back and exchanged a nervous glance.

And then, nothing.

The entire river stilled.

Kunal held his breath and reached for his knife, as if it would help him if the river rose up. It didn't. In fact, the river gave a low gurgle and returned to normal, the now-blue water gushing over itself as if nothing had happened.

That couldn't be right.

Kunal pushed forward against the current, but Reha was one step ahead of him. She pressed the cut on her forearms again, wincing as droplets of blood dripped from her arm into the river.

Still, nothing happened.

The water did not hiss or still or acknowledge the offering in any way.

It was silent.

The walls of the temple shook ever so slightly and Kunal snapped to attention. A tremor? But no, the room stilled and they were confronted again with that deafening, mocking silence.

Kunal and Reha exchanged wary glances. This was not how King Mahir had described the ritual. This was wrong.

"Should we try again?" Kunal said. His heart thudded so loud he could hear it.

"I just did," Reha said, her voice stuttering. "I just did, and nothing happened."

"There was that tremor. Maybe its—"

She turned to face Kunal. "Kunal, nothing happened," she said again, her voice rising to a shout.

He put a bloody finger to his temple. They had done everything right, so what had happened? Could the king have been wrong? He had been adamant that all they needed to do was the ritual of old. But maybe it wasn't enough.

"Is nothing supposed to happen?" Reha pressed again.

"King Mahir said the gods would be invited down into the temple. The temple would glow and we would commune with the gods." Kunal glanced up at Reha, his head suddenly feeling much heavier. "He also mentioned it had been harder and harder to get their attention recently."

"But we have the blood." Reha shook the vial. "*Had* the blood. We only have two more drops of the prince's blood now and the ritual didn't work. After all this time and all this effort. What do we do now, Kunal?"

Kunal wondered the same thing. It couldn't be true. This had been what they had been working toward for moons. Reha, her blood, the ritual at sundown at the temple on solstice day.

He was left with only one thought. The *janma* bond was close to dead, and perhaps the gods wanted it that way. The river had glowed gold and accepted the offering, but to renew the bond fully, the gods needed to accept it as well. And that hadn't happened in ten years.

The gods must no longer be honoring the ritual.

They had taken too long, taken too much from the land without giving in return.

Kunal staggered back, sitting roughly on the banks of the river. He raised his hands to cover his face.

"I don't know, Reha," he said, trembling. "The gods haven't accepted our offering. I don't know what to do next."

"Maybe you should give someone else a chance," a voice said from the entrance.

———◦———

The fields surrounding the low western hills of Jansa were a pale watery beige, nothing like the vibrant gold and orange they had been a few years ago when Esha had been on a mission in the area.

That had been her last full mission with Harun, at the edge of the Hara Desert. She didn't enjoy the irony that this was where she'd find him again.

Her hands tightened and loosened over the hilts of her whips. As the group drew closer to the small town, Laksh kept glancing over at her. She ignored him.

Aahal had gone ahead to lay the groundwork for their arrival. They were to act as merchants looking to supplement their recent grain yield with trade. Aahal would charm the soldiers first and then artfully direct the conversation to the recent reports from the village.

He should be almost done by now. By the time Esha and Laksh arrived, Aahal would have their lead assessed and ready. The rest was easy.

Esha had no problem breaking a few skulls on this mission. Laksh looked over again, his eyes raking over her hands and their continuous movements.

"Spit it out," she said without turning in her saddle.

Laksh raised an eyebrow. "Are you sure you're ready for this?"

At least he was being direct. For that, she gave him a real answer.

"I should say yes, but I'm terrified of what we'll find. If Harun will even be . . . Harun. I've been captured before. Tortured and chained."

"I'm sorry to say it, Viper, but as a royal, he's a more important catch than you were. He'll be safe. At least from anything extreme. They'll want him in one piece for the trade."

"There is more to torture than just physical," she said quietly. Her hands clenched again. Laksh reached over and grasped her reins, pulling them both to a stop in the field, the village walls now visible.

"Look, Viperess—"

Esha glared at him.

"What? I liked Bhandu's term. It's catchy. Would you prefer 'our little Viper' instead?"

"Are you trying to get hurt?" she said.

Laksh placed a hand to his heart and then to his temple, where there was still the faintest hint of purple tendrils on his skin from the poisoned knife she had thrown at him in the forest moons ago. "I think we can leave the hurting in the past."

Esha tugged at her reins and he tugged back.

"All right, little Viper—"

"I'm *not* little—"

"Your prince will be fine. Maybe a bit bruised and beat up." Esha stared at him stonily. "But nothing that can't be fixed with the palace healers or a bit of time with you."

She shot him a withering look. "You're really quite annoying, you know that? It's a good thing my knife is tucked away. It can easily slip when I'm around people who talk too much for their own good."

Laksh grinned, unfazed. "You feel better, though, don't you?"

She did, but instead of admitting it she sent him a haughty glare and rode on ahead.

It was odd being around Laksh. All of it was odd. How Alok, Laksh, Zhyani, and Mayank had become part of their team in these past few weeks. How she'd almost had Laksh killed but stopped when it came to light how misled he had been by Reha. How Zhyani had almost killed them all when she heard they had lost Reha.

How it was all a tangled mess now.

A figure rode straight at them, coming from the city gates. Esha pulled on her reins and her horse whinnied at the sudden change. Aahal met up with them, his turban falling off his head and a panicked expression on his face.

"We were right," he said. "The servants gave it away. The animal sounds stopped being reported, even though no soldiers were dispatched, because they were paid off. And from the sounds of it, they're moving camp again."

"Where?"

"I don't know," Aahal said. "We have to catch them tonight."

Esha nodded. "Then that's what we'll do."

She shaded her eyes as she looked over the fields of wheat ahead of her, the low, jagged red hills that surrounded them like looming giants.

Now to make their move.

CHAPTER 5

Kunal had been surprised more times in the past few moons than in the year before. And he was getting rather sick of it.

He blinked a few times as soldier after soldier jogged into the small opening to the temple, blocking the already-meager light. At the front was a striking young woman with a stern expression and long black hair braided down to her waist. She was flanked by guards draped in furs and leather, spears pointed outward.

Yavar, all of them. And the girl, she looked so familiar.

The girl spoke again. "It doesn't seem like you've succeeded."

That voice . . . he'd heard it many times at the numerous Champions Balls he had been forced to attend during the Mela.

Lady Yamini, heir to Seshirekh, the current Yavar

43

chieftain. A low growl ripped out of Kunal's throat, a nod to the feral animal lingering under his skin, at the ready.

She stepped forward, exposing a slash of light to the inner temple.

Kunal jumped back into the water, brandishing his knife in one hand and a longer sword in the other. Reha's hands immediately went to her weapons as well. Yamini held up her hands, revealing that she was weaponless, at least as far as Kunal could see. He listened in closer for the telltale rustle or slide of metal against leather. Nothing.

That alone made him more suspicious than anything else.

Yamini looked past Kunal at the girl half hidden behind him. "You're a popular girl, Princess Reha. I've been looking for you. Your friends have also been looking for you, especially after you left them in such a bad position back in Gwali. They were not open to working together. I don't hold it against them—not really, at least." She paused for a moment. "I'm sure they'll find our gift in the desert soon enough."

Kunal stiffened, unsure what that meant. Yamini's sharp eyes noticed, her own narrowing in interest. "You don't know, do you? What your choices made them give up? Interesting. Anyway, we found you without them."

"Who are you?" Reha said with a disdain that would've made any royal proud. She jutted her chin out, her eyes flashing a burnished gold and garnet.

"I'm Yamini," she said simply. "Daughter of Seshirekh,

Yavar chieftain. Your friend seems to have recognized me." Yamini gave him a thoughtful look, tilting her head. "You're the Archer. Kunal, was it? In the chaos after the Winner's Ball, no one noticed their prizewinner missing. Wonder how long that will last."

Kunal didn't know what game she was playing. Her face was surprisingly open, her words direct. It confused him after moons with the Blades and Scales, dealing in shadows and verbal sleights of hand.

"I think it's time you leave," Reha said, tilting her sword over her shoulder, the sharp tip pointing straight at Yamini.

Yamini smiled. "I can't leave. I need you. But we can do this simply, without any mess, if you come with me now. The Archer will be free to go. We only need you."

"Why?" Reha asked, moving backward. "Sorry to say, but you don't sound like a great option right now. It always worries me a bit when someone says they need me. *Need* is a funny term. Do you need me to choose between two saris for your next party? Or do you need me for a sacrifice? Neither really sounds like much fun, though I will tell you that fur is not really your color."

Reha's ability to talk—and inability to know when to stop—still confounded Kunal. He began to move with her, putting the force of the river in front of them as a shield.

"I need your blood," Yamini said. "You are the only true heir to the Himyads and Samyads."

Reha let a short laugh out, harsh and sharp around the edges. "You came too late. The ritual didn't work," Reha said. "My blood didn't work for the ritual."

Yamini narrowed her gaze, glancing at the still-fresh cut on the girl's arm.

"Impossible," she said.

"I thought turning into a bird would be impossible for me, but look where we are now," Reha said.

A slow smile curved up Yamini's face like one of the moon cat's of folklore. Almost as if she had wanted them to break the *janma* bond.

Bonds were meant to be broken. Isn't that what Kunal had overheard Esha talking to King Mahir about? Was it possible—

"Regardless, we need you." Yamini grabbed a nearby guard's spear and thrust the iron tip forward. She looked as if she knew how to use it. "Come to us willingly and we won't have to shed any blood."

"I'm okay with a bit of blood," Reha said, holding up her arm. Yamini glanced at Kunal and Reha caught it. She jerked a thumb back at him. "And I know he can take care of himself."

Yamini shrugged. "Let the gods know I tried to avoid this."

She slashed her hand forward and two guards from her sides ran toward the river. The others circled around the mouth of the river, blocking one of their two exits. The soldiers tried to race into the river, but the water surged forward to meet them.

Kunal and Reha glanced at each other and pushed back

through the water, running as fast as they could. The water moved quickly out of their way.

They had almost reached the exit at the opposite bank of the river, when two guards rushed at them. Kunal and Reha tried to turn around, but another pair of guards blocked them.

Cornered like animals.

Yamini came from behind the two guards closest to them, wading into the river. The water didn't give way to Yamini, nor did it fight her as it had the other soldiers. Reha stared down at the river, giving the lifeless water a dirty look. "Traitor," she muttered under her breath.

Kunal didn't disagree.

Yamini approached them slowly even as Kunal and Reha backed away.

"I don't want to hurt you," she said.

"Why does it feel like there's a *but* coming after that statement?" Reha said.

Kunal grabbed Reha's hands, squeezing them and hoping she'd understand.

She nodded. Kunal dove deep into his blood song, searching for the notes to shift, but—

Nothing.

There was only silence in his blood. An emptiness he had never felt since he had discovered his powers.

Terror creeped up Reha's face as she discovered the same thing. They inched toward each other, looking back and forth between the different banks and the approaching

Yamini. Kunal racked his brain for any sort of tactic or trick that he could employ to get them out, but he came up short.

He'd never been in an ancient cave temple, fighting off Yavar clansmen in a magical river. And he hoped never to be here again. None of this was supposed to have happened, certainly not in this way.

Kunal raised his sword to his chest. They would have to fight their way out. Reha looked over and set her jaw.

Yamini reached out with her spear, suddenly lunging toward Reha. Kunal rammed into her. Her left side collapsed against his and he felt the briefest touch from her fingers before she fell into the water with a loud splash.

That seemed to grab the attention of the soldiers nearby. They raised their spears and released deafening cries.

Reha screamed back, her shorter frame carrying the weight of the cry with ease. She thrust her sword above her head with a fierce expression, revealing arms corded with muscle and dotted with small white scars. A life's worth of struggle was written on her skin and Kunal saw her for who she was.

A warrior.

Kunal raised his sword, ready to charge, ready to fight till death, when the strangest thing happened.

The cave entrance began to vibrate in a steady thump. It grew more and more frantic, until the stone shattered. A team of Crescent-silver clad fighters stormed through the door, surrounding the Yavar and immediately engaging them.

And in the front, a familiar face.

A familiar, red, furious face.

Bhandu.

He roared and rammed into the soldiers nearest him, shoving them aside. Kunal went for another soldier, sweeping his feet from under him and pushing him under the water. Reha, quick as lightning, landed blows that were as brutal as they were effective.

The Yavar in his hands had stopped struggling and Kunal threw him onto the riverbank instead of contaminating their holy river. Yamini was on the riverbank, her shivering frame struggling to her feet. Even in her apparent defeat, she didn't look cowed.

"This isn't over, Princess. We won't give up this time," Yamini said, her voice as resolute as the mountain that surrounded them.

Before Kunal could respond, two scarred hands grabbed him by the collar and dragged him out of the river. Reha was already on the riverbank, soaked to the bone and sputtering.

"You two, come with me," Bhandu said, pointing at a small crack in the stone that neither of them had noticed before. Another exit.

Two of the Yavar soldiers were wading through the water, just paces away, and behind them Yamini was shouting orders. The sooner they were out of here, the better.

"Bhandu, it's good to see you. Thank—"

"Save it, cat eyes," Bhandu said, his expression hard. "Move."

Kunal and Reha obeyed, sprinting out of the cave behind him.

———◄◊►———

The soldiers didn't move until early morning.

Esha stretched her limbs, rolling out a crick in her neck after being cooped up in the fields all night.

She was about to signal to Laksh and Aahal when voices filtered into the open area. Laksh and Aahal picked up on them as well, and they began to move into position.

They crouched forward, making sure to stay low for cover as they split up and each took their own direction. Esha sped to the left, hurrying through the fields. The sun was only just peeking its head over the horizon, casting a reddish-orange glow over the fields, mixing with the pale wheat stalks to create an ocean of yellow.

She blended in perfectly. It had been a good idea to steal these clothes last night.

The left flank of the caravan was exposed as Esha approached. All was quiet, only the faint breeze whistling in the distance. But Esha took care not to assume that meant the camp was still asleep. She stepped forward, crossing over a low fence tucked among the wheat stalks. It was higher than Esha expected and she stumbled on her descent, landing heavily.

Directly on a branch. The crack was loud in the cool silence of the morning.

Immediately, a Yavar clansman dashed out of the caravan, his curved spear at the ready. Esha cursed and took out her whips, lashing them against the ground in warning.

The caravan had been a trap.

The Yavar didn't stop running toward her. He lunged, thrusting his spear, and Esha danced out of the way, trying to use her whip to encircle and pull away the end of the clansman's spear.

But he was too fast. He kept spinning his spear around, pulling back and then lunging in a rhythm that Esha was struggling to follow.

She had to change the dance, then. Esha dove to the ground, and the sudden movement startled the clansman, giving Esha enough time to lash her whip around his left arm. She pulled him toward her even as he pointed his spear forward with his free arm.

Esha dodged out of the way, pulling harder. But the man wrapped her whip around his arm and dragged her closer.

She'd either have to let go or be stabbed.

Esha didn't let go at first, not until she had tugged out the knife in her waist sash. Her whip went flying in the air and the man staggered back.

Esha ran forward and kicked at the wooden spear, sending it flying in the air. The moment of distraction was all Esha needed, and she grabbed the spear and smacked him between the eyes.

He went down.

No one else came out of the tent, and Esha staggered forward, blood on her fingertips as she brushed her arm. A flesh wound. She tore off a piece of her turban and tied it around her arm, wincing as she cinched it tight.

Esha crept into the first tent. It was empty. As was the next.

Her heart began to drop.

Were they too late? Had she been wrong? Too reckless?

Esha set her jaw. Wrong or reckless, she had followed a lead to the best of her ability. And she didn't think she was wrong. She refused to let doubt plague her now.

She snuck into one of the last two tents. It was dark, unlike the others, and the ground was covered in furs. This tent had been lived in.

In the corner of the tent, a flap was loose, and Esha strode over to it. She had only managed to lift the edge of the canvas when something large rammed into her side. She tumbled to the ground, groaning as she made contact.

Esha barely had a moment to recover before she was lifted off the ground by a very large man. She sputtered as the air was choked out of her, unable even to cry for help. She looked around and glimpsed metal. The sword at the man's hip. Esha struggled wildly, thrashing her limbs while there was still energy in them. Only a bit closer and she could grab it.

"Stop struggling, little bird. It'll be over soon," the man said in a wide toothy grin. "We don't want to harm you or your friends. Not yet, our lady says."

"That—isn't—very—encouraging," Esha said. She rocked against the man, and her fingers grazed over the top of the sword. She put all her strength toward reaching down and yanked the man's sword out of his sheath, kicking at him.

The movement was enough to startle him, and he dropped her.

She whirled around, facing him with the sword now in her hand. Esha lunged forward and dove, slashing him across the leg. He slowed down. Esha stabbed him in his side, his arm, and then across his throat.

She didn't bother to wait for him to fall.

Esha dashed through the open flap of the last tent and there, in the corner, was Harun. Blue-sapphire cords were still wrapped around his hands and feet and his face was paler than she had ever seen it before. Purple smudges hung under his eyes, his cheekbones pronounced. It was as if every angle of Harun had been sharpened so that he was no more than muscles and sinew.

Curse Yamini for keeping the blue sapphires on him. Esha couldn't even imagine what the long-term consequences of such poison would be to Harun—to any royal. She prayed they wouldn't have to find out.

Still the relief at the sight of him dug deep into her. A flood of emotions rose to her throat and threatened to spill out, but she kept it in. Harun didn't need to see her blubbering.

"Esha?" Harun's voice was harsh, dry.

"Harun."

"Why are you here?"

"To rescue you, Your Highness." She fell to her knees by his side, yanking at the blue-sapphire cords. Her knife was one of the sharpest steels in the land, but the cords held firm as she sawed.

"I don't like it when you call me that," he whispered. His eyes began to close, and Esha shook him awake.

"It'll only be a few more seconds." The sleep Harun seemed to be drifting into didn't feel right. "Your Highness, don't fall asleep."

His eyes fluttered open. "Harun. I'm Harun."

"Your royal, pompous Highness."

"Esha . . ." His eyes widened a bit as the first hunk of blue-sapphire cords fell off. "Esha. Why are you here?"

"I already answered that, my prince." She tried to be as gentle as possible, but getting through the cords was tougher than she had expected. Sweat beaded at her temples and she shook her hair away.

"It's a trap," he said.

"I know. We'll have to find Laksh and Aahal after this and make sure they're safe." Harun didn't look any less concerned, but an element of confusion entered the mix. "I'll explain later. We knew it was a trap, Harun."

"And still you came?" Harun coughed, a trickle of blood sliding down the corner of his mouth.

"Don't ask me stupid questions," Esha said. Another cord fell to the ground. One more to go.

Color was slowly coming back into Harun's face, though

a haunted look remained. Esha moved faster, putting every last ounce of her strength into sawing. The last cord came apart, and Esha finally sagged in relief, her knife falling to the ground.

She rushed to help him, pulling Harun out of the remnants of the cords and to his feet. He wobbled, and she wrapped his arm around her shoulders.

Esha ran her hands up and down his torso as gently as she could, checking for broken bones or injuries of any kind. No external bleeding was visible, but she didn't know what the impact of the blue sapphire could be. He was all bones, lankier than she had ever seen him.

"Hmm, that feels nice," Harun said. "It's been a while since you touched me like that."

Esha gave him a stern look. He chuckled lightly.

"Did they hurt you?" she asked.

Harun shook his head but then paused, his eyelashes fluttering against his skin. "I don't know. There are parts of days I don't remember. There are parts of days I was very lucid. Esha, I—" Harun's voice cut off, and he stared up at her with wide eyes.

He pulled her into a hug, and Esha's heart fluttered. She wrapped her arms around him, holding him close, finally relaxing for just a moment.

They had him.

Even if she had to fight her way out through twenty men, they had him. She wouldn't be alone anymore. Her prince would be safe and whole. The future of her country.

Her friend.

She pulled back, knowing they had spent too long in the tent. Aahal's signal, a long sharp whistle, sounded through the air. The sound of two dozen wild horses trampling the ground came next.

Esha grinned. Laksh had done his job. The Yavar would need to refocus their attention to the horses that were currently running wild or lose their livelihood. And now they had the perfect opportunity to slip out, unnoticed.

She tugged at Harun, and they exited the tent together.

CHAPTER 6

They made it halfway down the mountain before Bhandu even bothered to look at Kunal.

"Your powers?" he asked.

Kunal shook his head slowly. Bhandu's jaw tightened before he looked away. Kunal's senses were still failing him right now, flickering in and out like the flame of a temple lamp.

Bhandu slashed away some vines to reveal underbrush just inches from the cliffside. A precarious place to rest but likely the only one for leagues. Bhandu heaved at the vines one final time and they fell at his feet, no match for the size and strength of his arms. The cave inside was dark but Bhandu pointed at it and then them.

"In," he said.

This was the least amount of words Kunal had ever

heard Bhandu say in the span of five minutes. He also wasn't peppering every other sentence with an emphatic "cat eyes," which normally would have pleased Kunal. He knew the reason for Bhandu's frigidity was his own fault, yet he had hoped for better. It was a preview for later, and he didn't much like it.

Reha looked uncertain, but she walked inside, Kunal close behind.

"My squad will find us soon, but until then we can't have any large fires," Bhandu said, looking out of the small dark cave.

Kunal's eyes quickly began adjusting to the dimness. Reha's eyes sharpened, turning those russet-gold and blue colors that they did before she shifted, but this time the change seemed under control. Their powers were returning, though apparently very slowly.

"Did the offering work? Is the *janma* bond saved?" There was a note of hope in his voice. With Bhandu's face covered in the darkness of the cave, they could see only his silhouette, a guardian against the light.

"Why were you watching us? How long have you been on our trail?" Kunal asked. He could hear his own voice shaking. No response followed. So Kunal finally answered him. "It didn't work. After everything. It didn't work. The *janma* bond is still broken."

"What? Why?"

"We don't know," Reha said. Bhandu tossed a look back

at her and narrowed his eyes.

"Your blood wasn't enough? How is that possible? We've been looking for the lost princess, savior of the land, for moons. Years," he said, almost as if to himself.

Reha stiffened, turning to watch Bhandu. It was clear she wanted to ask more, but she was struggling to find the words. Or to go against the life she had once thought was hers. Kunal understood. It still felt like a betrayal to his uncle to ask or be curious about his powers or his mother and father.

Bhandu's shoulders slumped, his expression turning bleak.

"Bhandu—" Kunal started.

"No," he said, cutting him off. "You don't talk. You don't talk to me at all, cat eyes. Not until I give you permission to. The girl will speak for both of you."

"We need to go back to the river on Mount Bangaar, Bhandu," Kunal said, shaking off Reha. "We have to try again."

"The girl will speak for both of you," Bhandu said, his voice becoming dangerous.

Kunal's brows knitted together, and he reached for Bhandu, but it was Reha who stopped him, pushing his arm back and shaking her head at him. Reha's grip held firm. There was so much he needed to say to Bhandu. So many questions that lingered on his tongue, waiting to be asked. What had happened? Why hadn't it worked?

And more he needed to get out, thoughts that swirled in his mind. Was Esha okay? Was she angry? How angry was she?

"All right," she said. "How did you find us? Why are you here?"

Bhandu finally turned, his silhouette half shrouded in moonlight that licked over his skin like white fire.

"To hunt you down."

Bhandu moved faster than a blink of an eye, two clicks sounding in the shallow space of the cave.

Kunal looked down to see shackles on his wrists, and similar ones on Reha's.

He had gotten his answer as to how angry Esha was.

———◆———

Esha and the others made camp in the rain forest, finding a cleared area. It wasn't anything like the jungle back home, thicketed and labyrinthian, but it would do for the night.

Yamini should've discovered Harun's disappearance by now. But Esha hadn't seen any sign of the princess on their trail. That was concerning, but Esha focused instead on the fact that they had Harun—even if it had seemed a bit too easy.

She glanced back at him, where he lay atop a makeshift cot. He had immediately passed out after they regrouped with Laksh and Aahal. By the sound of his breath, Harun was deep asleep now, still occasionally mumbling her name.

Laksh had raised an eyebrow at that, but Esha didn't think Harun was acting like a lovesick man. She had the feeling he was trying to tell her something. Once he rested some more, she would determine exactly what was making her prince whisper her name over and over.

A part of her wanted it to be about her, Esha the girl. She hadn't forgotten what he had said to her in the palace, the love he had finally declared. In fact, it had become all she could think about since the soldier had left, half her heart with him.

Harun had asked her why she had come, but didn't he understand?

Love didn't disappear. It faded, ebbed away, but the edges of it would always remain. She would always care for Harun, and when he had been taken from her, she had to go back into those depths, dive past the walls she had put up to prevent herself from getting hurt, and what she found there—it confused her.

Even more so after the soldier had left. Around the others, it was easy to act as if he no longer existed or mattered. But . . .

Esha shut that away. And yet that door kept inching open. The cursed soldier would never give her peace. She should've killed him in the forest ages ago.

Maybe she still would.

"I don't like that smile," Laksh said.

"Then you're a smart man."

Laksh grinned and looked as if he was going to respond, when a tremor shot through the jungle, almost tossing the both of them to the ground.

Esha grabbed hold of a tree as a second tremor hit, shaking the jungle floor so hard that she thought it might cleave itself in two. She braced herself for a third, but nothing came.

What in the Moon Lord's name was that?

She turned to ask Laksh that very question, but a low growl filled the air around them. They both whipped around, weapons out, before Esha realized it was coming from Harun.

His eyes flashed wide open, and the shift happened too quickly for Esha to react at first. It had been awhile since she'd seen him transform, and it didn't land easily. Something about his eyes unsettled her, and without notice, he dropped to his knees, his hands to his head.

A faint blue light pulsed from Harun's skin, as if his body was purging it from his very pores. Harun flickered in the tent, his body shifting rapidly. The only time she had seen this was when Kunal had first discovered his powers, and then all Esha could do was stand back and let him go through it.

"Esha," he said stiffly, his head hanging. "Move."

She had barely stepped aside when Harun burst into blinding light, a large royal lion now in his place, shaking his mane. Harun didn't even look back at Esha before charging off.

Esha stood there for a second, the breeze rippling through her clothes. Laksh shouted at her, but she waved him away as a smile came over her face. She ran off to follow Harun, leaving behind a confused and sputtering Laksh.

Harun was clearly tired and weak, his pace slower than normal. Soon, she caught up.

This wasn't the first time they had done this. When a younger Harun had been learning his shifts, Esha used to run beside him every night in the jungles nestled into the mountainsides outside of Mathur.

He burst across the plains, and Esha cut a path near him. Harun's yellow eyes acknowledged Esha, and he slowed his pace to allow her to follow him.

Esha tossed her head back and laughed into the jungle sky, the moist air settling onto her skin like a familiar song. The sun above them was only a sliver of light through the thick jungle canopy. Her feet began to tire, and Harun started to limp, but they kept going.

Eventually she reached out a hand to Harun's mane as they slowed, her tiredness causing her to trip a bit, her stubbornness preventing her from stopping.

Harun nudged her with his head, trying to catch her as she stumbled over the tangled roots of the jungle, but the stress of the past few weeks caught up with her and Esha fell to the ground, dragging Harun down as well.

He shifted as he fell so that the body that landed on top of her was very human and all Harun. Harun caught her neck in his hand, lowering her head gently to the ground before rolling over and collapsing onto the damp jungle ground.

Their breaths, the heavy gasps of exertion, filled the air around them. Esha rolled over onto her side. Harun's eyes were closed, his chest racked with huge pants, his fingers still shifting from claws into the callused fingertips she knew so well. She cupped his jaw, tracing a delicate fingertip over his skin. He grabbed her wrist, bringing it down to his lips and brushing a kiss over it. Esha shivered.

She leaned forward. "Harun?"

His eyes were still closed, his breath still ragged. His runs usually exhausted him, but this seemed different.

"You ran with me," he whispered.

"Of course."

Something wasn't right. Esha grabbed his arm, which had dropped from her face. It was ice-cold, and that same faint blue light began to shine around him. He began to convulse, and terror slipped down Esha's spine.

"Harun?" she repeated, growing frantic.

His eyes flew open. "Esha," he panted. "You need to know—"

"Harun, what do I do? I don't—"

"You need to know—I—"

Esha grabbed his arm and shook him again. His breath slowed, stuttered, then picked up.

"What? Harun?"

But the only noise left in the jungle air was the sound of her repeatedly crying his name.

———◄◊►———

Bhandu refused to take the shackles off despite Reha's constant demands. They had been traveling for a week, and Kunal had stayed silent for most of it, even as Bhandu's squad of Blades met up with them and pushed them farther into the northern towns of Jansa.

The adrenaline from before had faded, and all that was left was the deep, gaping maw of guilt and failure that threatened to swallow Kunal whole.

"We need to go back," Kunal said, his shackles clanging along after him, as Bhandu knelt to make camp. Reha sent him a warning look from her seat a few spaces over, where she was trying to make a fire. She had resigned herself a few days back, informing Kunal that she knew when to take a punch and when to fight back.

They had failed. It was time to take the punch and make a new plan.

But Kunal had put so much into this. Taken this risk at the expense of losing Esha and everything else he had so recently found.

"If you take off these shackles, Reha and I can fly up there in a day and be back. We have to try again. We need to try again. To save—"

"*We* don't need to do anything." Bhandu spun around, his face murderous and yet also filled with an emotion

Kunal couldn't identify. It was the first time Bhandu had spoken to him in a week. He had dutifully ignored him at every turn, walking around him, passing things across him, talking to Reha instead of him. "We *could've* done so much if you had only told us that you had this harebrained plan to go off to the mountains that night. Do you know what your decisions cost us?"

"No," Kunal said, throwing up his hands as best as he could with the shackles. "I don't. You refuse to talk to me. You won't even tell me how Esha—"

Bhandu was in his face in a second, his scarred hands grabbing Kunal. The fury on his face was a living thing, hot and unforgiving.

"Don't you dare even say her name. You've put her through so much—"

"Has something happened to her?" Kunal froze, his entire heart stopping.

Bhandu blinked. "No. Nothing has happened to *her.*"

He let go of Kunal, shaking him off like an itchy cloak, but not before staring at him long and hard.

"You have no idea, do you?" Bhandu said finally.

"I know she's angry. But I can explain, Bhandu. Reha said this was our best option, and we were so close. She would've left alone and untrained. I didn't have a choice."

Bhandu looked sharply at Reha, who was calmly watching the whole scene.

She shrugged. "It's true. I threatened to leave and make

sure no one would find me. The dramatics really worked on him."

Kunal frowned at her even as Bhandu snorted. He turned back to face Kunal, cocking his head.

"She's not just angry, cat eyes."

Bhandu told them then, the entire story of what had happened. The Scales infiltration, the pile of bodies in the Great Hall, the arrival of Yamini, Vardaan's escape, and Harun's capture.

Kunal sagged against the nearest tree.

He hadn't known. It was the only thing he could keep telling himself.

As if it absolved him.

Even Reha's face had turned gray, the sticks she had been using having fallen to the side as she stared up at Bhandu in horror.

"The Yavar have my brother?"

Bhandu looked as if he wanted to snap at her, and Kunal could hear the words in his head. If she had cared about her brother, her father, any of them, why had she run off with Kunal? But she hadn't known either. They had been trying to save them, save the entire country.

Instead, they had failed miserably.

"Esha has a lead on his location," Bhandu said. "I haven't gotten an update in days but . . ." Reha picked up the sticks and started rubbing them together frantically, turning away from Kunal and Bhandu. "Esha has never failed in a rescue before."

"Bhandu, I—" Kunal started.

Bhandu whirled around and pointed a finger at him.

"Whatever the reason, you chose to leave us behind. You made a decision, *alone*; you went off to be a hero, *alone*." Bhandu took a breath, his hands clenching into fists. "We invited you in. And Esha. She watched over you when you were poisoned, she saved your life, and this is how you repay her? If anything happens to Harun, if even a hair on his head is harmed when we get him back, it will be your fault, cat eyes. Yours *alone*."

The young man moved to leave, but Kunal caught his arm.

"I had no choice, Bhandu," Kunal said.

"You keep telling yourself that."

"What would you have done in my shoes?" Kunal demanded. "Would you have let our one chance at saving the land slip out of our fingers?"

Bhandu dipped his head. "I don't know. But if you think that's going to be the problem when you return, then you have a lot to learn about Esha."

"What do you mean?"

Bhandu looked at him with pity. "She blames you for everything that happened."

"But I had no idea—"

"Our Esha, you met her as the Viper. You broke through that mask, and she let you see the real her. She trusted you." His voice caught, and he coughed it away. But Kunal had seen the flash of pain on his face. "We let you in, and you broke that trust. And it's clear from your actions that you never trusted us."

Kunal let Bhandu go, a whirlwind in his heart. He couldn't even think of Esha now, but the team . . . He hadn't thought of them. Serious Farhan, laughing Aahal. Arpiya, who had been the first to give him a chance back in Mathur. And Bhandu, who he had grown to see as a comrade in arms, a friend.

Was Bhandu right?

Had Kunal made the wrong choice?

CHAPTER 7

They had rushed Harun home, after pulling him from the hill camp, almost a day ago. He'd been asleep since he had awakened and run into the jungle as if the gods themselves had possessed him. Even now, his eyes were closed, his skin emitting a faint blue light.

Esha wanted to go into his skin and purge the cursed blue sapphires herself, but all she could do was sit there and wait for him to wake. Helpless.

Farhan had spent all night and morning in the library researching blue sapphires, but there was little about their poisonous effects on royals. Even the scholars were clueless. She'd sent a note to King Mahir, deciding the truth was more important than the worry of frightening him. And she still couldn't ask Harun what he wanted to tell her.

But what worried her the most was the earthquake they

had felt. Esha hadn't imagined it. By the reports, tremors had torn down the countryside at the same time she and Laksh had felt them. The Rusala region was the worst hit, with a nearby dam cracked and threatening to break. The water there, in the Rusala Dam and the nearby step wells, was some of the only left in the region. Esha had already sent a squad of Blades and Senaps to the Rusala Dam to assess the damage and decide on any next steps needed to prevent catastrophe.

It also didn't bode well for Bhandu's mission. She had immediately sent out scouts to the mountains to catch Bhandu and his squad. If they completed the ritual it would be one less thing for them to worry about. Then they could put the country back together and find a proper form of government.

Esha had already started the process of reopening the local tribunals and city councils. They had yet to announce a new government or ruler, so until they did, it had to be done quietly. Once Reha was back, Esha would gladly hand back the reins of the country. Take her prince, go home. Be rid of this cursed palace filled with soldiers.

A cough came from the bed, and Esha lunged forward.

"Harun?" she whispered.

His eyes were milky at first, but then they focused on her. "Where am I?" he croaked.

She moved closer, and he flinched.

Esha waited, fighting back the wave of worry, and

moved closer slowly. She would tear Yamini apart if she saw her ever again.

"You're safe," she said.

"Home?" His voice was a soft croak, hopeful.

Esha shook her head. "The Pink Palace. But we're in control of it."

He was too weak to hide the disappointment on his face.

"Harun, do you remember what you were going to say? In the jungle?" Esha asked quickly. She didn't know how much time she'd have before he exhausted himself.

"In the jungle?"

"You said you had something you had to tell me."

Harun flushed, color rushing into his cheeks. "Um, I think I told you everything I had to in the palace." His voice was quiet, a bit remote.

Esha coughed, the tension suddenly so thick in the room that it was suffocating.

"No, not that. Though . . . we should talk about that. After you shifted, you told me you had something to tell me. It sounded like a warning."

Harun's face pinched in thought. "Oh," he breathed, his eyes blinking in recollection. He spoke slowly, his voice thick as jaggery syrup. "Yes, the warning. I heard things, possible information, while I was held captive. I can only remember bits and pieces right now, but the Yavar, they came to the Sun Mela for a reason. And I think they might have had someone inside the palace. It's a hunch. I don't know for sure. They knew too much for it to all fit otherwise."

"I trust your hunches."

She could still feel the rage inside her at the idea of Yamini hurting her friend, but now it was colder, deeper.

A person on the inside could mean anyone—a servant, a merchant who did business with the palace, a soldier, a Blade. And it could also be nothing. A plot by the Yavar to sow discord. Let the captive prince overhear a lie. But Esha had seen enough betrayal in her past to not immediately discard the idea of a mole in the palace.

"I wish I remembered more—" Harun began.

"It's okay," Esha said softly. She placed a gentle hand on Harun's forearm, rubbing into the tense muscles. He began to relax, and he gave her a small, almost nervous smile. This was the boy she had met after the coup and the Night of Tears. Quieter, unsure, vulnerable. Before the world had asked him to don armor and hide himself. She had the sudden urge to pull herself closer, to lean in and take away his pain in the best way she knew how.

Instead, she let her hand only linger, long enough that Harun glanced up at her with warm, and confused, eyes.

"We have Blades stationed at every exit and entrance," she said, clearing her throat. "We'll start to give two sets of information to confirm if this inside person is one of ours."

"One of ours? Esha, that's a big conclusion to jump to."

"It'd be stupid not to consider it after everything that has happened." He didn't have anything to say about that, only a purse of his lips.

"Anyway, the Scales have agreed to work with us against

the common threat of Yamini and the Yavar." She glanced to the sitting room outside, where Laksh and Mayank were sitting and talking. "For now. Laksh helped rescue you. I believe they're acting in good faith. But we'll be careful, especially with this new news."

Harun tilted his head in a slight nod. "I trust your judgment," he said quietly.

Emotion choked her throat, and she reached out to run a hand through Harun's damp hair. Harun tried to catch it, but he was too weak.

"Don't. I'm a disgusting mess," he said.

"You are," she agreed, which earned her a short laugh. "But I don't mind. Don't act as if I haven't seen you at your worst. Remember that night when you and Bhandu went out drinking? He challenged you to a bet as to who could drink more? One of your stupider decisions. I'm pretty sure Bhandu could outdrink an inn full of fishermen."

"Hey—"

"And then I was taking care of you for the rest of the night so your father wouldn't find out. You know Bhandu had baited you into it, right?"

Harun pursed his lips. "Why do you think I accepted? I have honor."

Esha shuddered. "Please, let's never use that term again." Amber eyes haunted those words.

"Honor." Harun looked up at Esha, who made a face. "Pride, then. I was young."

"Why do you say that as if you're not young still?"

"Younger, then. More foolish. I felt a need to prove myself at every turn," he said, straining to get up from the bed. Esha moved his pillow and helped him sit. She handed him a glass of water.

"Isn't there a maid who could do all this?" Harun asked.

"Not one I trust," Esha said with a scowl.

Harun raised an eyebrow, and Esha sighed, giving him a detailed account of what had happened the night of the Winner's Ball, including the betrayal from Aditi—or Reha or Dharmdev, whatever name she decided to go by. Esha had trusted the maid who had deception in her heart from the first kind word exchanged.

Esha had been pretty stupid.

She wouldn't be anymore.

"It's not your fault," Harun said as she finished. "I want you to know that."

"Laksh said something similar," Esha said. "It's a nice thought, but *I'm* the one who let my guard down."

"And what about the rest of us? Your need to martyr yourself takes away our free will. We made the choice to trust the soldier too. I do trust him, even still."

"What?" Esha pivoted in the bed to face Harun full on.

Her old friend was still handsome even when sickly. His cheekbones were pronounced, his face more angular than before, but he still held that power in him. Harun reached and captured her hand in his, drawing it into his lap. It was comforting to feel the warmth of his skin, the calluses of his fingertips.

How had she ever thought she'd be able to get over Harun? He had never left her behind. Even now, weak and disheveled, he could make her body heat in memories. She leaned into him.

"He betrayed us, but he also left to save the country, if our reports are accurate," Harun said, reminding her of her own words.

"He left us in a lurch; he took the only key to saving Jansa and he fled. He is the reason we couldn't trade for you."

"Which is perhaps a good thing. Reha is far more important than me," he said reasonably. Well, Esha wasn't feeling in the least bit reasonable. "And did Kunal do that knowingly? Somehow I doubt his cursed sense of honor would allow him to leave me behind, even despite our obviously loving relationship."

"Humor is a good sign," Esha said. "That means you're healing at least."

"Don't change the subject."

"Color is coming back too."

Esha put a hand to his throat and then head, checking his temperature. It put her a few inches from Harun, and their eyes caught. She glanced at his lips. Harun groaned, shaking his head.

"What?"

"You always know how to distract me," Harun said. "Which means talking about this is more important than I thought."

"You don't even like the soldier!" Esha crossed her arms. "And when did you become a talker? If memory serves, you were just as happy not talking before."

Harun ignored the barb. "Kunal isn't my favorite, but I don't have to like him to understand him. Esha, there was always the chance he'd choose his honor over the team. I tried to tell you."

Esha sputtered. "What?"

"You were blind to it because of your . . ." Harun swallowed. "Because of your feelings."

Esha blushed. She didn't want to discuss her feelings for a soldier with Harun. Not after his profession of love to her. It made her feel like an even bigger idiot than she was.

"You didn't see it, but I did. I tried to tell you," he said.

"Are you really trying to prove how right you were?"

"No, I'm merely saying—"

"There were edges to this I didn't consider. I know," she said. The fire had left her, and she drooped. Anger was easier than the roil of emotions that had taken up residence in her soul. Her voice quieted.

"It's not your fault," Harun repeated. Esha knew he was being kind. Six moons ago and they'd be having a huge fight over this, but they'd both changed since then.

"Look, he must have left because it was the only option for saving Jansa," Harun said. He looked as if the words pained him. "Does that mean he was right? Time will tell. If he was a Blade, I'd have him whipped. It was a direct refusal of orders."

"Exactly," Esha said.

"But he wasn't a Blade, Esha," Harun said.

And you knew that.

Harun didn't say it, but he didn't need to. She had staked her heart, her reputation, and the safety of her entire team on this soldier. Of course she had been let down.

The bronze would always show through.

A servant knocked on the door. Esha straightened and adjusted her sari, putting space between her and Harun.

"Come in," she said.

The servant came straight to her and handed over a scroll. "Sorry to interrupt, my lady. This came from the hawk you had designated us to watch."

Esha nodded at the servant, who disappeared quickly through the door. Harun gave her a questioning look as she unfurled the note.

"It's from Bhandu," Esha said. "He found them. And he's on his way back."

"That's good," Harun said. He seemed to reconsider at the frown on her face. "Isn't it?"

"It is."

But at the end of the note:

The ritual didn't work.

CHAPTER 8

Despite their brutal pace, it was another week before they reached the Pink Palace. Reha was tiring, had been tiring since the last town, but she was the sort to grit her teeth and bear it. Kunal kept an eye on her for no other reason than that she had no one else. She was his family now, at least until they got back to the palace.

Bhandu had received a note that Harun had been brought back to the palace, though he was unwell. He had also let Kunal know that it was the only reason he wouldn't be immediately fed to the vultures that lived on top of the citadel once they entered the city.

At least he was talking to him now. Even if the man was sniping at or threatening him at every other turn, his conversation meant there was a chance Kunal could win him back.

He hoped the same of Esha.

The closer they got to the palace, the more Kunal started to believe it had all been for nothing. Drought loomed over the land like a greedy specter. Bhandu's squad members had collected water from the mountain rivers and were distributing it wherever they could after the tremors. But it wasn't enough.

Now, because of what happened at the temple, the people of Rusala could lose their dam filled with precious water. Some of the towns they had passed were being rationed to six buckets of water a day, barely enough for families of four. Others, only two buckets.

Kunal's heart had ached at every stop, as that familiar feeling of helplessness from his first trip through Jansa washed over him. This time it was mixed with something else—the knowledge that he had failed. And he had no idea what to do next. Apparently, when he made his own decisions, they were disastrous.

They reached the walled gates of Gwali. Kunal didn't recognize the Senaps that were on guard. He peered closer at them, trying to determine where he had seen them before.

"They're Blades," Bhandu provided, drawing his horse up next to Kunal.

His eyes widened. "And the actual Senaps?"

"Those who came to our side are safe and posted elsewhere. The others . . ."

Kunal blanched, and Bhandu chuckled.

"Where are you taking us?" Reha asked wearily. Bhandu glanced back at her, frowning. He pulled back until his horse was alongside hers.

"The palace," Bhandu said. His voice softened, and he glanced at her shackled wrists. Bhandu had taken a liking to Reha, if only because she was Harun's sister. At first they had been standoffish, until Bhandu had called Kunal a "cat-eyed, boring, no-fun lump of clay" and Reha had laughed. That seemed to break the ice and absolve her of actually being Dharmdev, which Kunal thought was a bit unfair. *He* hadn't framed Esha. But he wasn't about to bring that up to Bhandu, not when he had a knife on him.

"Harun will be there. Your father wrote saying he wanted to come, but we couldn't allow him," Bhandu said to Reha.

Kunal noticed the way Reha's jaw tightened. "Of course. He is the king, and we are in uncertain times," she said.

Bhandu nodded, though he looked disappointed. "He can't leave the capital when Vardaan is still on the run. He's readying the Dharkan army, just in case. He said he hopes to send troops and supplies as soon as he can."

"Makes sense," Reha said, nodding. She rubbed her shackles absentmindedly in a gesture that Kunal had come to recognize as worry.

Kunal pushed his shoulders back, straightening his spine. The palace meant that they would be brought to Harun. The prince would be glad to see his sister, no matter what chaos she had caused. Not so for the Fort soldier.

"Does he know?" Reha asked quietly. "That I was Dharmdev?"

"I don't think he'll hold it against you until we hear your story," Bhandu said.

Kunal grunted at that.

"Something to say, cat eyes?" Bhandu asked, turning in his saddle.

"How forgiving we are of someone who orchestrated the framing of your dear Viperess. Almost had her killed," Kunal said.

Bhandu paled a bit. He hadn't quite put that together, had he? Kunal cared for Reha—it was hard not to after weeks teaching her how to shift—but she still had a past that was unaccounted for.

Reha glared at him. She squared her shoulders, much like Kunal had done moments ago.

"I take responsibility for my past actions," she said. "But they don't define my future."

Kunal glanced wearily at her. If only he could feel the same way about his own.

———◈———

Kunal searched for Esha in every corner, convincing himself he saw a glimpse of her curls, her bright eyes, the minute they entered the Pink Palace. Bhandu led them through the eastern gate, away from the center of the city. Kunal couldn't help but wonder if she'd even look for him.

Esha would see him. She knew him. She knew that he

wouldn't have ever left her, not unless the world was at stake.

He held out that hope until he and Reha were tossed into the throne room. The towering eagle throne of the ancient Queens of Jansa dominated the space, demanding attention.

Reha looked around in openmouthed awe.

Even Kunal took a step back to take it all in. He'd never been in here, even when on patrol as a Senap. It had been off-limits when Vardaan had been king, and now it seemed haunted.

He glanced over at Reha. This would be her throne one day. She started picking at her shackles again. There was fear in her eyes, but Kunal knew she had given up much to be here. She had left it all behind and made her choice.

Kunal had just never realized he had too.

The door to the side creaked open, and a man in an official-looking turban bustled in, two Blades in Crescent silver armor not far behind. He caught sight of them and then stopped in his tracks.

"Kunal?"

Alok looked different from before, healthy and flush. Leadership suited him. He strode over to Kunal and had him wrapped in an embrace in seconds.

"You're safe," Alok whispered, tears at the corners of his eyes. "It didn't work?"

"No, it didn't," Reha said to his side.

Alok looked up and over at her, his face impassive. "Princess Reha, I presume?"

"Just Reha for now," she said. Reha waved around her

shackles. "Are these necessary?"

"It was ordered." Alok looked chagrined.

"By who?" Kunal asked. "Can we talk to them? Is it the prince?"

Who was in charge? If he could tell their story, perhaps he could ease over Reha's path, maybe even his own. Esha had always said stories had as much or more power than brute strength.

Alok hesitated. "I'm not sure they're going to be so amenable. I know your heart was in the right place, Kunal, but . . ."

Even Alok thought he had made a bad call.

"Ah, well, you'll see," he said. Kunal gave him a pleading glance when the door flew open again.

And Esha walked right in.

———◦———

Esha was rather annoyed after her meeting with the Scales. Laksh and Zhyani were demanding to be let in on the meetings she was holding with Mayank and some of the city councilors and guild leaders. She had tried to delicately point out that they were already having difficulty giving the appearance that nothing was amiss in the palace and having all of them in a simple trade meeting might arouse suspicion. Servants loved to gossip.

Most of the city believed that Reha was here. And that she was in charge. Esha thought she played the role well enough, especially with the help of strategically placed uttariyas and veils. It was just that she didn't want to play it.

Once they had Reha back, they could talk about their inclusion into meetings. And that day was today.

"Bhandu," she said. "Please stop hovering." Esha affected her kindest but sharpest tone, like that of a schoolmaster. Bhandu had been trailing after her since he had returned, as if she needed a bit of extra care. He moved maybe an inch away and held the door open for her to enter the hallway to the throne room.

"I've been gone for a few weeks, and I come back to you looking as if you haven't slept in days. Weeks," he said.

"I haven't slept," Esha said, "since we rescued Harun. I've been watching over him."

"By yourself?"

"I have to," she said. "I can't trust anyone else."

Bhandu looked as if he was about to object but then gave a short nod. "Maids."

"Exactly. I can't get rid of the numerous ones we have, but I have no idea how loyal they'll be. Until Harun is back on his feet, it will be me and any other Blades. If news gets out that Harun isn't well, it will cause turmoil. We already have one throne's succession in question. We can't make it any easier for the Yavar."

"Is that what they want? To invade?" Bhandu's brow furrowed at the idea.

"I don't know," she admitted. "Harun . . . might know more, but his memories are hazy. I can't help but feel that

Yamini let him go on purpose."

"The Yavar caught up to us, so perhaps they let him go because they found Reha," Bhandu said. "But then, why Reha?"

"Exactly." Esha rubbed her temples. "I wish I had more answers."

She had spent every waking moment buried in books about the ancient magic and rituals of the Southern Lands after getting word the renewal ritual for the *janma* bond hadn't worked. It was frustrating work, despite having Farhan as a companion. But it was a good reminder—even as her entire world fell apart—that the sun still rose, fiery and gold.

The sun and the moon waited for no mortal.

Bhandu waved a hand in front of her face and she snapped to, realizing she had stopped in the middle of the hallway to the throne room.

"Are you all right? Should I send for Arpiya?" His voice was worried, soft. Even Bhandu had changed in these past few weeks. He smiled less, and there were creases on his forehead that hadn't been there before.

Esha shook her head. "I'm fine. Take me to Alok."

"I could've sworn I left him here," Bhandu said, perplexed. They both noticed the throne room door ajar at the same time. Bhandu's eyes widened, and he tried to move in front of her. Esha looked at him as if he had grown a third head and waved him aside. When he didn't move but just stood there sputtering at her, she sighed and walked around him, pushing him aside.

"Honestly, Bhandu."

"Don't—Esha—"

Esha strode into the throne room. "Once I finish this off with Alok, I want you to take me to the girl. Just her. You can bring her to—"

She turned around and spotted Alok, who was talking to a man in unfamiliar clothes and with what looked like thick silver bracelets on his wrists. She was about to wave to Alok when her entire body went numb.

The soldier.

He was here.

Esha didn't want to acknowledge his presence, give him the satisfaction of an ounce of her attention. But she did look up. And her heart and soul flew out of her to lay themselves at his feet without hesitation.

Kunal was in a simple cotton uttariya and dhoti, the dark green of both making his amber eyes shine even in the dull light of the morning, cloudy and gray as it was. He was as handsome as ever, so much so that her heart squeezed in pain. She knew not to trust that soft mouth that curved in a smile at her. Not to fall in love again, even a little bit.

Especially not with him.

But still, the sight of him made some traitorous part of her bloom. Her pulse quickened at his broad shoulders, the memories of those hands on her skin. She could deal with that. That physical desire between them would probably never subside.

This deeper feeling, however, it had to die.

And so Esha marched over to him.

"Esha," was all he said. And it was all she needed to hear to know that a part of her would be lost to him forever, never to be recovered.

Fury rose in her throat, raw and red. It sharpened to ice as it left her mouth.

"If you were going to steal away our only bargaining chip, you might've at least succeeded in your mission," she said.

Esha glanced at Reha, who was next to him, looking chagrined. They had been cleaned up, but both bore the marks of having traveled. Scratches and bruises trailed Reha's limbs, and she had lost weight. Her eyes were different too, a multicolored hue that left Esha feeling unsettled.

Both were changed and yet the same. A specter hung over them. Failure? Or the knowledge of what it had cost to get there? Esha didn't know if she cared.

"We didn't know," Reha said.

Kunal seemed to have lost his voice. He stared at Esha, a war raging across his face. He still hadn't learned to control his emotions or perhaps she just knew him well. What she'd give to trade that information away now.

She could say something kind, anything to ease the grief she saw in his eyes. To give him hope.

Esha turned her back to Kunal and walked to the opposite corner of the room.

"Save your story for someone who cares," Esha said, turning to Bhandu. "Call the others. We have much to discuss."

There was little kindness left in Esha.

CHAPTER 9

Esha drew a finger over the dust on a side table in the war room. The last time she was here they had been negotiating for peace and she had sat in the farthest corner of the room. Now she pushed back the tall chair at the head and sat down. It was a massive rosewood table, constructed to make everyone else in the room feel small. Here was where queens had plotted wars, negotiated trade, protected their kingdom. And now here sat Esha.

Neither Jansan nor a queen.

The others soon arrived for the meeting, with Aahal trailing close behind Laksh. Mayank was noticeably absent, stuck in meetings with the army who refused Esha's—or Reha's—command. A problem for another day.

Bhandu walked in last, his new charges following him into the room. She looked away and focused instead on the papers in front of her.

She knew this was a haphazard group of allies. Almost immediately after noticing Laksh was in the room, Kunal tensed and backed away. The others, her team, they looked tired.

They were all tired.

That Esha understood in her bones. There was no precedent in their history for the ritual not working, not after the Blighted War—and the era before that they knew little about. Added to that was the unsettling news they had received in the decoded messages from the Mathur scholars.

Esha turned her gaze to the girl on her left. So this was the real girl behind the mask. Reha's shackles clinked together as she took a seat, the only sound in the uneasy silence that had spread over the room. There were echoes of Harun in her face, in the sharp upward sweep of her cheekbones, the dark eyebrows.

This was their lost princess, their savior. This was Dharmdev, the thorn in their side for the past moon and earlier, the girl who had framed her. Who knew the name of her parents' killer.

Esha shut that door in her mind as quickly as she could. Her focus on revenge had nearly cost them everything. It might have been the reason she hadn't caught on to Reha earlier.

The others' reaction to the presence of Reha was a spectrum: Aahal jumped to his feet and introduced himself, saying he was sorry that Harun would be her big brother, before Bhandu dragged him away by the collar. Laksh's ever-smiling mouth turned tight, and Farhan barely seemed to notice, his nose stuck in the scroll from the Mathur scholars. He had been researching what might have gone wrong since Bhandu had sent his note about the failed ritual. Alok hovered over him, though he glanced up once at Reha. Kunal, though, wasn't looking at Reha.

He was looking at her.

Esha's gaze skimmed over him before turning toward the group. That familiar heat, tinged with a dark rage, lingered beneath her skin at the sight of him. It was better for both of them if he wasn't in range of her whips.

Laksh came over to her side of the throne while Farhan and Aahal lingered near the seats. Bhandu paced the floor, watching his two captives, who didn't move a muscle.

"I'm glad to see you both decided to join us," Esha said.

"We didn't have much choice," Reha said. Bhandu and Aahal exchanged looks.

"True."

"We would've come back," Kunal said. "Even if Bhandu hadn't shown up." Reha's brow wrinkled, but she stayed silent.

"Good to know," Esha said. "What's your report, soldier?"

Kunal looked up at her, and there was a softness in his gaze that she had all but forgotten existed between them.

"Your report," she spat out angrily.

◄◊►

Kunal hated the way Esha was looking at him, like she barely knew him. As if he were one of the many nameless chess pieces working under her command. Part of him whispered that he deserved it, all of it. He had gone all the way to the mountain and failed.

Kunal rubbed his brow, fighting his developing headache, and his shackles clanged heavily against each other.

"Can we at least take these off?" he said.

"No," Esha said. She gave him a hard stare.

"Given that we both were there to see the ritual fail, we have more knowledge than anyone here," Reha said. "Let's start this off on a good foot." She looked down at her chains and then at Esha's hard stare and winced. "A better foot."

Esha looked furious, but she didn't protest. Kunal knew any hatred for him wouldn't trump her skills as a strategist. "Fine. Bhandu, remove them. But if either of you shift and try to run off, I will gut you both. I don't care if you're royalty, a princess, or Dharmdev." She leaned in closer. "You're in my house now."

"I thought—" Kunal started.

"Who do you think has been playing the role of Princess Reha here? Who has kept this charade running while you two were off on your vacation to the mountains?" she said, her teeth gritted.

"It was hardly a vacation," Reha said.

Bhandu came and took their shackles off. Kunal rubbed his wrists, his skin chafed where the shackles had been.

"The ritual didn't work," Kunal said finally.

"Oh really?" Laksh asked idly. "I'd wondered why the river is still dry as a bone outside."

Kunal shot him a look. "Lovely to see you haven't changed, Laksh."

"Why would I change when I'm perfect?"

"Everything else has," Kunal said.

"Does the honorable soldier finally see that there might be more than one side to a story?" Laksh said in a singsong voice. His voice was cruel, but below it, only because Kunal knew the man, was a note of hurt. The thing was, Kunal supposed Laksh was right.

They both put their country and duty first, but still, Kunal hadn't almost killed his best friend. He hadn't chosen pain.

"Perhaps, but I still think the side of attempted murder is the wrong one."

"I never tried to murder you—"

"No, you tried to murder Esha—"

"What?" Bhandu exclaimed from the corner. He whipped to face Esha. "Why is he not in chains, Viperess? Why is he here?" He moved toward Laksh, but Esha held him back with a hand. She watched their whole interaction with a cool eye.

"Let him be," she said.

"So, he can be forgiven after trying to capture and kill you?" Kunal said bitterly. He didn't care that everyone else could see his resentment. He hadn't realized it would be so keen until Esha had turned away from him.

"We're getting off topic," Esha said. There was a clear tension in her jaw. Even with the rankling feeling in his chest, Kunal realized he wanted to talk to her. What had she been through here in the palace? Would she ever tell him? "Not only did the ritual not work, it broke something in the land as well, sending tremors throughout the countryside that almost destroyed the Rusala Dam. We need to focus on that."

"My aunt's farm was destroyed," Alok said quietly. Esha's face softened, and she gave his hand a light squeeze. "Her entire livelihood gone, in an instant."

"Alok—" The rest of Kunal's words choked in his throat. How could he ever begin to apologize for that? Alok would never blame him, but Kunal couldn't help but feel responsible. His failure had hurt someone he loved.

"Soldier, you're right," Esha said, though she looked pained saying the words. "Things have changed. The Scales, and Laksh, have been quite helpful the past few weeks as we tried to piece together a plan for the government. We're working to ensure that the land—all the Southern Lands— doesn't descend into chaos."

Reha leaned forward, clearly shocked. "The Scales are working with you? Zhyani?"

"You're passing judgment after you kept me in the dark?" Laksh said.

"You didn't— Did you tell—"

"No, *Princess Reha*, I didn't tell anyone about your

identity." Laksh looked almost insulted by the insinuation. He folded his arms across his chest and leaned back in his chair. "We had a plan. You were the one who backed out."

"Laksh offered a truce. An alliance," Esha said, continuing on.

"And the others? Malik? Ishaan?" Reha interrupted again. She looked at Laksh, question in her eyes. He stared back, his face impassive.

"You can ask them yourself."

Reha didn't look excited at that.

"They're trusted as allies now? After everything they've done?" Kunal said. He couldn't help the strain and confusion in his voice. "And I had to beg to have our shackles removed?"

"To answer your question, soldier"— Esha gave Reha a stern look—"Laksh and the Scales have proven themselves to be allies recently. Even Zhyani has proven useful, despite everything. Reha is a known liar. And you? You weren't a simple ally. You were part of our team. And you left."

Finally, a note of emotion in Esha's voice. Even if it was fury.

"We didn't know the Yavar had taken Harun," he said, quieter than before.

"I knew they were after me, and I refused to be taken captive, so I left," Reha said. "And we tried to fix the ritual ourselves. Nothing we did was wrong." Reha tilted her chin up in defiance, but Kunal saw the wobble that threatened at the edge of her lips.

"If we had known . . . ," Kunal started.

"And if you had? You wouldn't have left?" Esha demanded.

Kunal and Reha exchanged a look.

"That's what I thought. Don't expect me to favor your hero complex and credit you. Heroes die alone. We work as a team," she said.

"We weren't trying to be heroes—" Reha said fiercely.

"We were doing what was right," Kunal said.

"Good of you to decide what is right for all of us," Esha said.

"This isn't helping," Farhan said from the corner. His voice was quiet but carried through the throne room, echoing up into the cold marble corners of the ceiling. "What happened when you did the ritual?"

The tension was thicker than fog. Esha's hands were gripping the edges of her seat as if she was coiled to strike.

"What's done is done. Farhan is right. What happened with the ritual?" A look of weariness seemed to flit over Esha for a moment, but she hid it away quickly, only noticeable in the way her index finger kept tapping the wooden table.

"Nothing," Reha said, growing exasperated. "Cursed nothing. We did it exactly as King Mahir taught Kunal."

"How did you—?" Kunal asked.

"Why do you think I asked you? I knew you were getting training from the king. Being a servant had its benefits."

Esha grumbled something under her breath, and Laksh put a hand over her twitching hand, whispering something low into her ear.

Kunal's blood rose, and his nostrils flared. He wanted to break that hand.

"Laksh has been mooning over Arpiya." Alok's whisper jolted Kunal. "Esha and he are just friendly. Stress of betrayal and all. It's Mayank you have to look after," he said darkly.

Kunal sputtered. "Mayank? Not Harun?"

"Harun?" Alok looked shocked and then thoughtful.

"Alok," Farhan said patiently, a schoolmaster gently scolding a child. Alok straightened and mumbled an apology. "Kunal, what was supposed to happen in the ritual?"

Kunal cleared his throat. "The river was supposed to accept the offering, and the spirits of the gods would be called down, ringing the bells and lighting the lamps that dotted the cave temple. The river accepted the offering, but nothing else happened. It was as if it simply gave out," he said. "Like the gods demanded more to fulfill the ritual. What we gave wasn't enough."

Farhan looked thoughtful while he tapped a finger against his chin. "My guess is that it's like a decaying mechanism, one that has stopped working. After a decade of misuse, it makes sense," he said. He looked at all of their confused faces and sighed. "Think of an iron farming machine. Without care and the proper materials, it will rust over and become useless. The only thing to do would be to bring in new parts."

Aahal piped up. "Are you suggesting we find a new temple?"

Farhan shrugged. "I'm not sure."

"And your books haven't told you anything better than 'I'm not sure'?" Bhandu asked.

"It's slow going, all right? It's not as if the ancient texts anticipated this sort of catastrophe," Farhan snapped.

"Well, then, perhaps books are useless," Bhandu said.

Farhan gasped and held a hand to his heart.

"Boys," Esha said in a commanding voice. They snapped to attention, both looking mutinous but vaguely guilty.

"Actually, the ancient texts might have anticipated something like this," Kunal said. Six heads whirled to face him. "King Mahir mentioned that the original ritual included artifacts that had been lost to time. He had been searching for them as a backup. He believed the ritual would work, that it was the best way forward. But clearly he was wrong."

"Artifacts? But the ritual only requires blood." Farhan's brow furrowed.

"Not according to the history of the royals."

Kunal quickly filled them in on the story King Mahir had told him of how humans grew corrupt and careless, taking advantage of the land. How the gods withdrew their blessings after the Blighted War, until the two royal families banded together and made a new deal, removing the magic from all so that only a few became its stewards, passing the burden to the royals. That the original Ayana, the first ritual, had been done with ancient artifacts of the Sun Maiden and Moon Lord.

"If we can find the original artifacts, we might have a chance," Kunal said. "They might fix the rust, so to speak."

He'd been thinking about this since the journey down the mountain, after he realized that they had failed and that everything he had done was for naught. He had to find a way to change the future, make up for his mistakes.

"You're saying our only chance is with mythical artifacts that we don't even know exist? Even King Mahir thought they weren't the best option. He wouldn't have taught you the ritual otherwise," Laksh said. "Are you sure the trip down the mountain didn't addle your brain, Kunal?"

Kunal glared at him. "No more than poison did yours."

Alok unleashed a beleaguered sigh, pinching the bridge of his nose. "So very mature of the both of you. Really representing us well here."

"If it's any consolation, I feel the same way about them," Aahal whispered to Alok, pointing a thumb at Farhan and Bhandu.

"We know they exist," Esha said quietly, her expression lost in thought. "If King Mahir has been looking for them, he'll have information. Harun would know."

"Then bring him," Reha said. Her voice was cool and collected, but Kunal could hear the undercurrent beneath it. Anticipation. "Where is the prince?"

"Harun was captured and tortured because of your selfish choices." Esha turned to face Reha. "Your brother is recovering now."

Reha shut her mouth quickly and stepped back. "Recovering?"

"He'd been bound with blue-sapphire ropes for weeks.

It's still purging from his skin," Esha said. Kunal noticed the way her hands curled into fists, the fierce set to her jaw. Whatever had happened to the prince still worried her.

"We can send a scroll to King Mahir," Aahal suggested.

"Already on its way," Esha said. "And the note from the Mathur scholars, it confirms that the bond could theoretically be broken. It was attempted once before, leading to the Blighted War. We should find out if the artifacts were used then." She paused, her voice tremulous. "If the artifacts were used to create the *janma* bond in the first Ayana, then it goes to follow that they could be used to break it as well."

"I can dig into the archives. Now that we're looking for artifacts, I can scan the texts more specifically. I've been spending my time trying to find everything about magic and rituals. This, this is a direction at least," Farhan stressed, looking less defeated than before.

"It is something," Esha agreed. "We need to figure out what those original artifacts were, how many, and where they could be. Retrieval is next."

"How can the Scales help?" Laksh asked softly. Kunal wanted to step over there and bodily insert himself between them, despite what Alok had said. He didn't know this Mayank, but Laksh was a threat Kunal understood better than anyone else here. At least the prince was asleep somewhere.

"There's something that doesn't make sense," Reha said quietly. "Why are the Yavar after me? And why did they stop following us?"

"They were looking for the temple too," Kunal said, realization hitting him. "They had come to stop the ritual when we were there, but it had already failed. There's only one reason they would have captured Harun when they already had Vardaan in their pocket. It would've been easy to pull the strings behind him if they wanted to open up the country for them to take."

"You're seeing things where they aren't, soldier," Esha said, gritting her teeth. "They were looking for power, plain and simple. Why would they care about the ritual? They gave up the rights to the land and the ritual centuries ago."

"Perhaps that's changed. Perhaps there's something we don't know. The Yavar failed in their invasion thirty years ago and maybe now they're trying another tack."

"Or they're looking to strike when there's discord here."

Kunal shook his head. "No. Why follow us to Mount Bangaar, then? Why capture the prince only to let him go after they had found us and the temple? They know something about the ritual that we don't." As soon as Kunal said it, he knew it with certainty. He recalled the way Yamini had walked into the temple with purpose. "They want something. Not just chaos. Something for themselves."

"Remember what Vardaan said?" Laksh said to Esha. "In the throne room?"

Esha's face shifted from indignant to ill.

"That the Yavar want to reset the bond," she said quietly. "Is it possible he wasn't lying?"

"The soldier is right," a deep voice said from the front of the room.

Harun stepped out into the throne room, leaning heavily on a cane. Still, he managed to look like the arrogant prince that Kunal had first met, commanding even in his weakness. Arpiya followed him in. Her short hair had grown out so that it reached her shoulders, and her normally bright smile turned down at the edges.

"That's exactly what Yamini wants. And we don't have much time to stop her."

CHAPTER 10

Esha rushed to his side, wrapping an arm around his waist. Harun gave her a grateful look and leaned on her instead of the cane.

"What do you mean?" Farhan asked.

Harun chuckled lightly. "I don't think they truly understood the extent of my powers. My hearing, for one. I heard a lot of things, even in the tent I was in. Hard not to when you're in a small camp. It was the only thing I could do, so I listened. Once the poison haze of the blue sapphires cleared, I remembered more. And it's worse than you might think." He paused to cough, and his entire body shook.

Harun looked more uneasy than usual. "She's trying to rewrite history. The stories we were told as children aren't true. Vasu the Wanderer didn't choose to give up his connection to the gods willingly. He betrayed Naran and Naria, and the Yavar have been cursed ever since. Yamini is trying to cleanse her people of the curse and bring back their connection to the land."

Esha didn't like the sound of that.

"She believes it's their right to reclaim the bond, but I think she also knows it's a smart move to consolidate her power as heir. She needs to win over her people. And if she accomplishes this, she'll have won the clans' loyalty for life—if not longer."

"She's looking for these artifacts, then?" Arpiya asked.

"She didn't say as much, but she's looking for something," Harun said. "She has resources and scholars. She came to the Pink Palace for a reason, beyond just finding Reha. If my father had found out about the artifacts, she will soon, if she doesn't know already."

"Especially since Reha is now here," Farhan said.

"Reha?" Harun's eyes widened, and he jerked his head around, searching for her. She was immediately noticeable, the only unfamiliar face in the room. He walked over to her without Esha's help, limping ever so slightly. "Reha."

Reha's face was set at first, closed off, but as Harun came closer, she glanced around as if looking for an exit. Kunal squeezed her hand quickly.

Harun stopped once he was in front of Reha, grief and joy warring across his face. Reha looked as uncertain.

"Do you remember me?" Harun said before frowning. "Of course you don't."

If she had, they wouldn't be here.

"I remember pieces," Reha said hesitantly. "I knew I

wasn't from Gwali, but I thought my family was gone. And when I told the other kids in the quarter that I had family from the palace, they laughed at me. Told me any family would all be dead."

Harun opened his mouth and then snapped it closed, a look of uncertainty on his face that was incongruous with his normal attitude.

"I hate to interrupt this touching moment," Laksh said, actually looking a bit uncomfortable. "But perhaps we can postpone this family reunion for later? We need to figure out what to do next. If what Harun said is true and Yamini is looking to rid themselves of their curse, it could be at the expense of our own people's *janma* bond. If she fulfills the ritual, who knows what disaster will befall the Southern Lands." He shivered. "I don't know about you, but I don't want to find out."

"Oh, we're the Southern Lands now, are we? Not Jansa and Dharka?" Kunal said softly.

The former friends exchanged a look, and it reminded Esha that Laksh and he had been in contact all through the Sun Mela, maybe even from the moment they had set foot in Gwali. There was weight between them, one that spoke of a longer story. Yet another reminder that while Kunal had asked for trust from her, he had been hiding his own secrets.

"It won't matter if there's a Jansa or Dharka if neither of them exists," Laksh said.

"How do we even know what the Yavar want is possible?" Aahal said, shaking his head. "The bond is unbreakable."

"The scholars in Mathur disagree with that. After my first conversation with Zhyani, I asked them to look into it, how it would be possible. And King Mahir confirmed it as well. Breaking the bond has been attempted before, by the human who started the Blighted War, which means that we have to assume the worst. Good, bad, broken, unbroken, it won't matter if Yamini discovers the artifacts," Esha said. "We'll need to find them first. If there's an inkling of truth to the story of their power, we can't delay."

Harun drew out a small scroll from his waist sash, holding it uncertainly, like it might bite him. "My father gave this to me before the Winner's Ball, in case I ever needed it. He said it was past his time to hand it over to me, and to us." He shook his head. "I had no idea what he was talking about then and I can barely make out the script, but he mentioned something about the artifacts. He had been looking for them, and this was all he had been able to find. That this scroll, the copper scroll, would help—"

Farhan's head shot up. "Copper scroll? *The* copper scroll?" He jumped up from his seat and rushed over to Harun.

Esha looked around, bewildered. No one else seemed to know what Farhan was talking about either.

"I can't believe it's real," Farhan continued. "Can I touch it? I've been spending so much time researching the history of the ritual after the Blighted War, but I hadn't even thought to look for scrolls from before that time."

"Farhan," Esha said gently. "Care to explain to the classroom?"

"Ah, yes." Farhan stepped back and laced his fingers behind his back as he spoke to the room, a lock of his long hair hanging over one eye. "The copper scroll is said to be the first written account of the tales of Naran and Naria. It accounts for the first Ayana and the quest that they undertook with Vasu. It was lost during the Blighted War, but many say it was only hidden and that it contains untold knowledge. Some even whisper that it leads to the treasures of the gods, to a city hidden during the Blighted War."

Harun looked down at the scroll in his hand with more delight than Esha had seen in moons.

"Send another note to my father. Let him know the copper scroll is in play and we need any information that he's gathered," Harun said.

Esha stepped up to his side. "As for us, we have work to do. Farhan, we'll need you to decipher the scroll as best as you can, find the locations of the remaining artifacts. Aahal, get us the supplies we'll need for an extended mission, just in case. As for the others, we'll help Farhan research and then split into teams for the mission itself. Soldiers"—she looked at Laksh and Kunal—"you'll be accompanied by Bhandu and Arpiya. Reha will stay back with me and Alok."

Esha inhaled deeply. "We have to get to the artifacts before Yamini."

There was a beat of silence surrounded by blank faces. A moment later, the room was filled with noise.

"Happy to volunteer," Laksh said just as Kunal said, "Are you sure?"

"I won't be going on any mission with a Scale, even a former one," Bhandu said. "Former soldiers are bad enough as it is." There was a short nod of agreement from Aahal, though it was cut off with a look from his twin. Arpiya shrugged while Reha looked at the window, clearly wishing to flee again.

Esha couldn't help but agree with Bhandu.

The last thing she wanted to do was work with Kunal. It spoke to how broken their relationship was that she would prefer working with Laksh, who had once held a knife to her throat. At least with Laksh she knew to keep herself on guard. Better a knife to the throat than a knife in the back.

Esha looked at the group in front of her: old enemies, former friends, long-lost siblings, unwanted family, potential lovers. An uneven mix—volatile, even.

They were the best chance at finding those artifacts before the Yavar.

Gods help them all.

———◁◦▷———

The room quieted, falling victim to Esha's domineering stare. But Kunal wasn't done.

"You're going to put Laksh on this mission?" Kunal said, approaching Esha as everyone began to get up and leave. "He'll steal the artifacts and give them to the Scales."

"And why would he do that?" Esha asked, terse.

"Has anything he's done before indicated that he wouldn't?"

"I think if we have to worry about anyone running off

and doing things on his own, it'd be you, soldier."

Kunal winced. He knew she wasn't going to let it go anytime soon, but that she wasn't even hiding it? Not a good sign.

He stepped closer to her, and she breathed in sharply. Farhan, Aahal, and Bhandu were discussing something in the corner, too far to hear. And Harun had already found Reha, who looked scared and expectant at the chance to speak to her brother.

"Esha . . ."

"What?" she said, turning around to face Kunal. She seemed to realize her mistake—she was just inches away from him now.

"I've been trying to talk to you, alone."

"That's a bad idea, soldier," she said. Kunal reached out and lightly grabbed her elbow. The skin on skin contact felt like the first sparks of a fire, and judging from her response, she felt it too. He moved closer, drawing a finger down her skin. For a moment, she let him.

"Esha, we need to talk. I need to explain—"

"Save it, Kunal," she said shakily. A storm flickered behind her eyes, and she pulled her arm away from him. "I've no use for pretty words."

She walked away before Kunal could form a reply. A deep sigh tore out of him.

"It'll take time," Alok said from behind him. Kunal turned to face him. "Everyone will need time to get over it."

Kunal slumped against the wall. "I was just doing what I

thought was right. She's being unfair, unreasonable. Every-one else has been forgiven for their mistakes except for me."

"I know. But doing the right thing is seldom the easy thing for others," Alok said softly. Kunal looked up at his friend: the kindness in his eyes and the set of his jaw, which indicated power, self-possession. This was a new Alok. He had taken to the Pink Palace like a fish to water.

"Look, Kunal. If there's one thing I've learned about Esha, it's—"

"This I have to hear," the prince said. In possession of his cane, he moved quite quickly. Reha had left with Bhandu, so the prince's attention was fully on them. He looked happy, buoyant almost. Meeting your sister after a decade could make even the worst sort tolerable, Kunal supposed.

"Your Highness." Alok stiffened.

"No need for titles. Call me Harun." Harun laughed a little, raising an eyebrow at Kunal, who didn't bother to change his expression or demeanor. There was a moment of pause between them that lingered unkindly until Harun cleared his throat.

"I have you to thank for keeping my sister safe and bringing her back in one piece. I know, very well, how little control I have over the women in my life." Kunal caught Harun's glance at Esha and resisted the urge to hurt the prince, especially as he was being pleasant for once. "So their safety is a gift."

"You're welcome," Kunal said. Alok nudged him in the ribs. "And I regret that my actions led you to be . . ."

"Kidnapped and tortured?" the prince supplied.

"That," Kunal said, heaving a sigh. "It's all cowshit. Yamini, Vardaan, all of it. If I'd known, I wouldn't have gone."

"That's a lie," Harun said. Kunal's body tightened, but the prince didn't have any malice on his face. "It's not in your nature to play politics or to understand the consequences of your actions. It's what made you a good soldier."

Kunal flinched. It was a harsh but true assessment.

"It also makes you a good man to have on our side," Harun said. "We need more people like you, though it pains me deeply to admit it."

"People who run off and don't tell anyone what they're doing?" Alok looked confused, and Kunal sent him a glare.

"People who question. Have an opinion on what the right thing, the good thing is. From the stories my father told me, he was quite like you back during the War. 'The Arrow of Dharka,' they called him."

Kunal flushed, pleased. It wasn't a bad thing to be similar to the king he had grown to admire. If he were to follow in the footsteps of an uncle, King Mahir was the one he would choose, especially over the general.

Harun leaned unsteadily on his cane, his growing exhaustion apparent.

Kunal couldn't imagine what the prince might have been through since Kunal had been gone. And he certainly didn't know how to broach the subject or treat the kindness Harun was showing him.

"But my father fought a different war. We're not dealing with such an honorable enemy," Harun said. He walked past Kunal and stopped, turning to look at him. "I've always known you for what you are, Kunal. You're not a Blade, you're Jansan, and you have worn the bronze armor of the Red Fort. That is an asset to us and our cause. But don't let it be a liability."

He didn't need to finish the threat; instead, he walked away and held up his hand to signal the team to gather around.

"I rather like him. He's a bit scary, though. Reminds me of Esha," Alok whispered into Kunal's ear. Then he gasped. "Oh, is that why you brought him up?" Alok gave the prince an appraising look.

Kunal frowned. They weren't that similar.

—◦—

Esha snapped her fingers to get everyone's attention. "We'll meet again tomorrow after we've started researching, but we have our basic teams. We've already gotten reports that Vardaan has been spotted, so it's safe to say it won't be long before he comes back for his throne. If you have a problem with your team assignment, don't bother talking to me. We don't have time for squabbling if we're to get this done."

Harun walked up and put a hand on Esha's shoulder. Kunal frowned, his eye shifting between the two of them. "What she's trying to say is—we've not all gotten along. By any stretch of the imagination. But this threat will require everything of us. We need to put away the notion that we are Jansan or Dharkan, Blade or Scale or soldier. We're only going to succeed by working together. Yamini's soldiers are well armed and well trained, and they're looking to regain their honor and bond to the land. They'll do it at any cost. So we have to be willing to do that as well. For all the Southern Lands."

No one looked particularly happy, but they nodded in unison.

"I'll help with this, but then I'm gone." Reha's voice was quiet at first, quiet enough that Esha thought only she had heard the words. But Harun stiffened next to Esha.

"Nothing personal, but this wasn't the plan." Reha's gaze flickered to Laksh. "I'm better off alone."

Whatever Reha was, it wasn't a lone wolf. The Viper was one, and even she needed her team, but Esha remembered a time when she had thought being alone was better, easier than having to worry about others. A flicker of understanding lit in Esha, a clue to the puzzle that was the girl in front of them.

Harun didn't seem to have gotten the same message.

"Reha, we need you here. This is your home," Harun said, his brow creasing.

"That's not my name," she said.

"Aditi, then?" Esha asked. Reha flinched a little. Good.

"No."

"Then what?"

"I don't know. I was given a name by the Thieves, but

it never felt right. But Reha, that's not me. Not yet. I'm no princess and I'm no savior."

Esha crossed her arms. "No one here is asking for a savior."

"For now," Reha said. "But I know how this goes. Take the title of princess and I'll be captive in this palace, never free again. I'm not meant to be a caged bird."

Harun looked unsure what to do, whether to push back or to let her be, so Esha stepped in.

"All right," Esha said. "We'll be grateful for your help on this mission, but you're free to go after. We won't hold you."

Harun's head snapped up, and Esha shot her hand out to grab his, squeezing it tight.

Trust me.

"I can work with that." Reha's jaw tensed but only for a second. Then her shoulders fell into an easy shrug before she sauntered off.

Harun turned to her, accusation written all over his face. "You let her go."

"You don't know how to talk to her."

He made a strangled noise. "Clearly! Last time I saw her was when she was a child."

"I know her type."

Harun didn't look convinced.

"I'll take care of this," Esha said, putting as much confidence into her voice as she could.

Her first instinct was to let Reha go, give her time to see

what life at the palace was like, the power, the privilege she would have. This was a girl who risked herself to try to save the land, even if it failed. She was more like that soldier than she let on. A hero.

But a kernel of doubt lodged into her mind as Reha walked away. She knew how to play these games, but Reha had once been Dharmdev—a master puppeteer.

Esha only hoped she hadn't just been played.

CHAPTER 11

It took Farhan only a few days to begin decoding the copper scroll, especially once the hawk from King Mahir arrived. Esha was glad for Farhan's speed, especially as she couldn't shake the feeling that they were running out of time. The scholars in the Great Library had been pulled into the research as well and given as little information as Esha could get away with, merely that the matter they were researching was of the utmost importance. It had surprised her how effective that had been.

Esha spent the day in the library helping Farhan as much as she could or out in the most dangerous streets of Gwali, searching for information or old texts that spoke of the copper scroll and the secrets within it. Everything she found she would deposit back onto the large wooden table Farhan had made his home for the past few days, to the point of having the servants send meals to it.

Aahal would accompany Esha on some of her excursions. He was rather good at speaking to the maids and Esha was good at getting things out of men. She found she enjoyed being back in the Viper's skin, even for a short time. It allowed her to forget everything else, to become someone else, return home in a way, even when she was stuck in Jansa. Disappearing into that old skin seemed even more necessary nowadays with the amount of time she was forced to endure the soldier's presence.

Kunal had become a fixture in the library too, which made Esha leave on more of her excursions than she cared to admit.

She could tell he was angling to get her alone again to talk to her, but she was sick to death of talking. Perhaps his story would change her mind, but she knew it would take a lot longer for her heart to change.

Something broken wasn't easily put back together.

Esha was in the library that morning, tracing her finger along a condensed line of old Dharkan, when Farhan's head popped up and he made a loud noise, startling the sleeping Alok and making Esha jump.

It took Esha a second before she realized it had been a sound of joy. She rushed over to Farhan's side.

"I think I've found something. Maybe figured this translation out," Farhan said. He poked at Alok, who looked up sleepily at him, eyes blinking. "There are two!"

"Two?" Esha prompted. If she didn't edge him along, Farhan would get caught up in the intricacies of his research and findings, never to surface again.

"Two artifacts. The ancient text speaks of two artifacts. A conch for the Moon Lord and a lamp for the Sun Maiden," he said. Then his face dropped into a frown.

"What's the matter?" Kunal asked, coming over from his spot at the end of the table.

"They say *what* the artifacts are . . . but not *where* they are. All it's saying is that the artifacts always make their way back home, but it doesn't mention where those homes might be."

"It's progress," Esha offered. Farhan had been taking a lot upon himself and even with the help of Kunal, who was surprisingly adept at translations, Farhan was showing signs of tiring. He only got like this when he was deep into research, and he hadn't been given an opportunity to do that since the Vizak Operation a few years ago.

Farhan had been interested in intelligence first and foremost, but he had followed Esha into the field to get more experience. Unfortunately for him, he had excelled in the field, so Harun and Esha had kept him there whenever they could. But here in the library, he was back in his element.

Kunal came closer to her side of the table, so that he was only a hand's width away from Esha. She inhaled sharply, her body instantly warming.

That rage still simmered underneath, but it was cooler after the soldier and Reha had given their report. Not because Esha forgave or trusted him, as both would be stupid. Despite all her current misgivings, she knew in her heart they needed him for this mission. Logic made her realize this, but it didn't change the pulsing, raw core of betrayal she felt inside her chest.

She shifted back to Farhan, who was scribbling something and muttering under his breath. He shoved a scroll of notes out of his way.

Kunal picked the scroll up and examined the underside, his eyebrows rising. Esha fought back her instinct to reach out to him. Even her own body was traitorous.

"I know this symbol," he said slowly. "I've seen it before."

Farhan looked up sharply at him. "You have?" He motioned to a scholar nearby, asking him to bring the prince over. Harun and some of the others from the team were in the corner, poring over their own piles of scrolls.

Harun appeared a minute later beside the scholar. Arpiya followed behind him, Reha in tow. The other boys were out gathering supplies and Laksh was in the city, trying to get as much information about the copper scroll as he could.

"You called me?" Harun said, coming to her side.

"I did," Farhan said. "We made a bit of progress."

"I was telling them that I recognized this symbol," Kunal said. He traced the pointed flower inscribed in the corner of one of Farhan's scratch scrolls.

"I copied this down from the copper scroll, unsure what it meant. Good thing I did," Farhan said.

"Can you remember where you've seen it before, soldier?" Esha asked. Kunal looked up at her, his amber eyes shining in the low light of the Great Library, and her chest did that annoying thing again.

"At the temple," Kunal said. Harun looked confused. "The temple your father took me to. The royals' temple on the outskirts of Gwali."

Recognition alighted in Harun's eyes, and Esha looked between him and Kunal, frowning. Another secret.

"Where in the temple?" Harun asked. "I haven't been to that temple in many, many years. Not since the coup. But I do remember the carvings in the inner temple."

"I'm not entirely sure where. It could be a clue, or it could be nothing," Kunal said.

"No, no. Every lead is a good lead in these sorts of scenarios," Harun said, almost more to himself. He leaned the cane against the table and walked over to the copper scroll, unrolling it with careful hands. It was a delicate thing, an old thick scroll of papyrus woven through with gleaming copper threads. The inscriptions on it were half chiseled, half painted on.

"There," Kunal said. He pointed to the corner of the scroll, where a series of symbols trailed up the outer edge, almost like a border. "The rest of this section is empty, like someone forgot to finish it."

"Unlikely." Farhan snorted. "The scholars of the Age of Gods were said to be the most meticulous. They invented the sun stone, modern arithmetic, astronomy. Any science we have today originated from them. If there's a gap, there's a reason."

Esha squinted at the scroll, turning her head. "From

this angle, that gap in the scroll—doesn't it look a bit like an inverse map?"

Three heads turned to look at her and then turned sideways to look at the map.

"Huh," Harun said. "I can see that."

"Where's this temple again?" Esha asked.

"On the outskirts of the city," Kunal said.

Esha nodded. The sun was still high enough in the sky that they'd be able to make a trip there and back if needed.

Reha spoke up from her uncharacteristic silence. "Isn't this all a bit much? Copper scroll of bygone eras. Magical scholars who leave blank spaces for maps."

"Scientific scholars," Farhan corrected. He frowned. "Though I suppose they did study the arcane then too." His expression grew thoughtful and curious.

Reha walked over to where the rest of them stood and peered over the table. She wore a light cotton sari, but her waist sash was heavy with the scabbard of at least three knives, and she kept unconsciously playing with the tassel of one. "I repeat, doesn't it all seem . . ."

"Reha," Kunal said. "You spent the better part of our trip up to the mountains shifting between every known animal on this earth."

She flushed. "Fine, point taken."

Harun looked perturbed at this recollection. "Seriously? Are you all right, Reha? Father and I wondered if something of the sort might happen. We spent years gathering texts and figuring out how to train you. I mean—we hoped to—"

"You know how to fix me?"

"I think so," Harun said. He hastily added, "Not that there's anything wrong with you."

Esha had never seen Harun like this. Jumpy, uncertain. It was endearing. But she supposed he had never been in this situation before—trying to convince his long-lost sister to stay to get to know her family and take up her mantle as queen.

"I have time tonight. Or tomorrow morning. If you want to try training," Harun said.

"Yes," Reha said immediately. She bit her lip. "That sounds . . . fine. Kunal's training wasn't all that helpful, actually."

Esha thought she heard Kunal mutter something under his breath. She looked up and he caught her eye, making an exasperated expression at the two siblings. Esha rolled her eyes and grinned before she remembered. She looked away quickly, steeling her face back into a mask.

"Great plan, you two," Esha said. "Though I have to admit I'm curious to see just how many animals Reha can shift into, we have only so many hours before sundown. Let's gather the others. We have a small trip to make."

———◄◦►———

Kunal hacked through the brush of overgrown vines till the marble facade of the royal temple was visible. The others trailed dutifully behind him like ants. He hopped over overgrown vines and ducked under massive arches, making his way into the inner temple. The outer structure loomed over the rain forest floor, not even bothering to blend into the foliage around it. It stood out like a sore thumb on its small hill, nestled between two larger hills that vied for attention.

"Here it is," Kunal said, climbing up the last steps. "The hidden temple of the royals."

"Wow," was all Alok had to say.

In the midday sun, the entire temple was cast in shifting streams of light. Only half the murals were aglow, the others dim, and yet they conveyed a magic and age that none of them had truly seen before.

Kunal understood their awe. The temple was still as stunning as when King Mahir had brought him here. It was a living jewel nestled in the jungle.

He walked through the entrance chamber by three gold basins, each holding water to cleanse its visitors before they entered the inner temple where the gods lay. They all stopped, everyone taking a few seconds to wash their hands and feet with the water from the basin before entering.

"I remember seeing the symbol on the scroll somewhere here," Kunal said once they were inside the main arches and in the inner temple.

Harun nodded. "Then let's search for it."

Despite Esha's protests, the prince had insisted on coming, claiming fresh air would be good for him. And it seemed he was right. There was a new color in the prince's face, and his steps were slow but sure.

They split off into pairs: Laksh and Arpiya headed off

to the west, Alok and Farhan to the east. Esha looked at the remaining people, grabbed Harun, and went to the north. That left Kunal and Reha to take the south.

He motioned at Reha to follow him, and they began to go through each mural on the southwest corner of the temple.

Her hands kept straying to her knives at first, but after a few minutes of uninterrupted, silent companionship, her shoulders dropped and her hands relaxed. She had been the same during their first few days on the trip, always looking over her shoulder. Kunal didn't know what had happened in her missing years to make her that way, but he found himself angry on her behalf.

He knew more than anyone the injustice of fate, but in Reha's case, she had a family somewhere, lost to her. That they hadn't been able to find their way to each other for years—it ripped apart his heart, made him want to reach out and protect her. But she'd likely break his arm if he tried. Reha was like Esha in that way.

Reha waved him over. The murals that danced over the walls and ceilings here were inlaid with glittering topaz, rubies, and emeralds. Scattered around the jewels were deep pockmarks revealing that a few jewels were missing—or stolen. But Reha was pointing at something else, an image within the mural. "Does this look like something to you?"

"It looks like a scroll," Kunal said, squinting at the image. He hadn't noticed it during his trip with King Mahir.

Reha pointed to the corner. "I think that's the symbol.

This could be a depiction of the scroll itself."

"Could be. What are they doing, though?"

Kunal stepped closer and ran a hand down the wall, carefully touching the intricately wrought image.

The mural depicted a story of Naran and Naria, two similarly tall and brown-skinned figures fighting side by side, a scroll grasped between their hands. The interesting part was that the scroll was unfurled in the image and the space it took up almost matched the size of the copper scroll. Inlaid rubies dripped from the hands that held the scroll and onto the faded image of the scroll.

There was an empty fissure in the wall to the left of the scroll, in the shape of a teardrop. Kunal peered closer at it, noticing that there had once been a ruby inlaid, but it seemed to have been wrenched out. There were flecks, tiny glittering shards, left behind in the hole.

He traced his finger over the mural gently, tapping the rubies. One of them sparked under his finger and he jumped back.

"What was that?" Reha said, eyes wide.

"Magic is still alive in this temple. It was part of the reason King Mahir brought me here during my training. He said it held secrets untold, sacred to the royals. What if—"

"What if?"

"Does that indentation look like a droplet to you?"

"No, it looks like a random indentation," Reha said.

"Humor me."

"Then yes, it looks vaguely like a droplet." She tilted her

head. "Kind of like a droplet of blood, though that's a bit macabre for my taste."

Kunal nodded. "There was something in this teardrop before. A ruby, perhaps?"

Reha leaned over and traced the outline of it. Almost immediately, she yanked her hand back, cradling it against her chest.

"It shocked me." But she stepped closer, examining it. "I think it wants to show us something. But how do we unlock it?"

Kunal thought for a moment. "Blood? It seems to be the key to everything else. And if we're in this temple, then it's royal blood it'll want. Yours is the strongest."

"Not strong enough to renew the ritual," she said. Kunal gave her a look. "But all right. Not like we have anything to lose. If it tells us anything about these artifacts, it'll be worth it, though I'd rather not be bled dry by the end of this whole escapade."

Reha drew out her knife and pulled a thin line against her fingertip until it pooled into droplets of blood. She pressed it against the mural and then stepped back.

The mural began to pulse and radiate a spectrum of colors. And then as that subsided, the tiles began to rearrange themselves, shifting in a concentric circle around the now-blood-filled teardrop, shaping themselves into a textured, colored layer on top of the open scroll.

Slowly, the tiles coalesced into scrolling lines and swirls of a long-forgotten script, punctuated by illustrations.

"A poem," Reha said.

"A poem?" Kunal repeated. He squinted at the text. "A map to the location of the artifacts hidden in verse. Of course."

His voice carried in the curved ceilings of the inner temple, and he heard a gasp from behind him. In seconds, the others were at his side, staring at the lines of ancient poetry that had been revealed to them, hidden all along in the wilds of the jungle.

"Good work, soldier," Harun said, clapping him on the shoulder. Kunal was so pleased at his find that he didn't shrug him off.

Kunal could only hope it would lead them to the artifacts before Yamini.

CHAPTER 12

Esha had stayed with Farhan for the better part of the evening, watching as he tried to decipher the copper scroll's poem. They'd left the temple hours ago after copying it down and since then, he had been at work. Kunal and Harun were helping with the translation, aided by a few smart remarks from Reha.

"My lady?" A voice pulled her out of her thoughts, and Esha rose from her seat in the corner. The Blade who entered the room was a few years younger than Esha but had quickly taken on a leadership position after the coup. Laya was one of the few Esha entrusted with sensitive information anymore. "A note for you."

Esha unfurled the scroll, reading the missive as quickly as she could, her mouth slanting into a frown. She resisted the urge to fall into the seat nearby, knowing it would worry the others.

It was from King Mahir—there had been an attack on Mathur. And she hadn't been there.

She knew the king was quite capable of defending his own country, but Mathur was her home, and she wanted it to be her home after all of this.

The only spot of good was that it was an unsuccessful attack by a small force. The focus of the attack seemed to be on the prisons. Normally not a huge concern, but the prisons near the center of Mathur were where most of the Jansan prisoners of war were kept. It'd be the perfect place to hit if someone were looking to build a small army of loyal soldiers. Someone who had been recently ousted.

Vardaan had to have been behind this attack. First he had recruited mercenaries and now criminals.

He was smart. A head-on offensive attack would've prompted a large outcry from civilians. But a smaller attack, even if unsuccessful, would breed distrust and fear. Esha knew, deep down in her gut, that this was going to be the first calculated step of many from him. Unless . . . unless they were able to catch him first.

It was another worry thrust onto her, on top of the existing search for the artifacts.

Esha swept into the next room of the palace, tucking the note away in her pocket to show Harun later. The list of things to do around here waited for no one, and if she was being honest, she wanted to delay delivering bad news to him and the team. Let them celebrate finding the map for the rest of the afternoon.

She had a few minutes until Mayank was supposed to meet her, so she took a moment to walk over to the marble balustrade and look out over the city of Gwali. The once-vibrant city was diminished, the rising temperature oppressive and dry. The river was nothing but patchwork now, even this close to the ocean. More fights had been breaking out between the various guilds, between the guilds and merchants, and now even between the citizens and merchants.

The slow return of the local courts was helping, allowing certain groups, like the guilds, to work things out among themselves. Esha had sent a Blade representative undercover to each of those courts to keep an eye on things, and despite the heat in the air and in people's hearts, order was being kept.

But they needed a leader, one who could defend them. Esha couldn't take on that role publically, and truth to the gods, she didn't want it. This wasn't her country to lead. She wanted to bring balance, not lead a nation. Certainly not a nation that wasn't hers to lead.

"Gold coin for your thoughts?"

"I see the price has gone up," Esha said with a smile.

Mayank chuckled, taking the spot next to her. His face was impassive as he looked out over the city, but Esha knew there was an ocean beneath the surface. Mayank and his house had been key in consolidating resources for the towns most stricken by the drought. He'd corralled troops, bargained with foreign trade officials, and all without any skin in the game or his formal title bestowed to him.

"It was my mistake in the beginning to ever think they could be worth any less," he said courteously. Esha raised an eyebrow. He had always been good at the court speak, which Esha never trusted, but still, the compliment lifted her spirits in a small way.

"Buttering me up, are you?"

"Whatever for?"

"There's always something," Esha muttered.

"It has been an interesting couple of weeks here." His voice took on a serious tone. "But things are looking up. Reha is back, and we've been able to open up trade with the west until we find the artifacts. The queen in the west is new and eager to show her power. Our timing was right, despite everything."

"It's all being held by a thread." She sighed. "But none of this would've been possible—taking control of the palace, everything since—without you."

Mayank gave her a short bow. "Happy to serve, Your Highness."

"And there's that. I'm no 'Your Highness,' but I've been playing the role as we've needed it. I think it's time you are bestowed your birthright, Mayank. And since I'm acting heir and leader right now, I formally bestow the title of Lord of House Pramukh to you."

Mayank didn't—or couldn't—say anything for a minute. Instead, he took her hand and bowed deeply over it.

"Thank you," he said finally, his voice trembling. He coughed and covered it up quickly. Esha pretended she hadn't noticed.

"The papers are being drawn up, and Reha is going to sign, so it will be official. I also want to name you my acting general," Esha said. "And none of that bowing nonsense. Get up, Lord Mayank."

Mayank straightened. "No, that's too much—"

"Nonsense," she said, waving a hand. "What have you been doing this whole time but keeping peace and maintaining relations with our neighbors? Perhaps not the traditional duties of the army, but we haven't had need for those. What is proven is that when we do need those, which we will soon, you can handle the responsibilities. And the army will listen to you."

"I'm not so sure about that," he said.

Esha nodded firmly. "I am. And as my acting general, if you will accept, I'm informing you that Vardaan attacked Mathur just two days ago. I'm about to mobilize scouts to check the surrounding areas and to go deeper into the mountain borders to look for signs of any other troops or gathering armies. We'll need to keep an eye on this."

Mayank stared at her for a moment, the gratitude in his eyes making her uncomfortable. "I will. Accept, that is." He swallowed. "It would be an honor."

"You don't look so well," she said, peering at him.

"It's a lot, Esha." He shook his head, as if he still didn't believe it. "To be finally handed what you've wanted for so long, and more? Especially when you never thought yourself deserving of it?" he said.

She had never been in the same situation, but Esha thought she understood. Though Mayank had kept a happy face on, being denied your birthright by the king for reasons out of your control would take a toll on anyone. No wonder he had become so good in court speak. He must have been fighting for years for what little scraps Vardaan deigned to give him.

Esha took Mayank's hands in her own and squeezed. "Curse those people who let you think you were anything but capable. You might have been born into your house, but you've *earned* your place here, in the Pink Palace of Jansa. Don't let anyone take that from you."

Mayank gave her a tight nod. "I have out a few scouts of my own; let me write notes to them, inform them of what has happened. And tomorrow, I'll speak to the acting citadel officer and the acting Senap officer."

He bowed to take her leave, and she let him go, the excitement and purpose almost radiating off him.

Esha smiled to herself, happy to have done one thing right.

◄○►

Kunal turned into the large room, sneaking in before the others saw him. He was supposed to be going over the poem and the scroll with the others, but he was tired.

Exhausted. And it wasn't only because he had just seen Esha with Mayank, alone.

He needed a second to himself, that was all. The team had barely let him out of their sight since they had returned from the mountain. Kunal leaned back against the cold wall of the room, the darkness soothing around him. He hadn't expected what it would be like, coming back. It wasn't as if he had imagined anything.

That wasn't true. He had imagined himself coming back a hero having saved the land. They would've been welcomed home with honor. Esha and the team would have been safe in the palace and grateful to see the lost princess again. Happy to see the land whole.

Without a single life lost. Certainly no fractured dam or a threatened city. Zhyani had said that there was a casualty, that someone who had been trying to fix the crack in the dam had fallen and injured himself.

And the way Esha had looked at him, as if he didn't even exist to her anymore, he wouldn't forget it for a hundred years. It would stain his heart if he couldn't change it.

He would find a way out of this. He would fix this.

Like you fixed the bond? The tiny voice in his head was vicious, unflinching.

The need to escape overwhelmed Kunal, but the sudden presence of an eagle shooting out of the residence wing of the palace would surely beg questions. Kunal walked over to the table in the corner, grabbing hastily at the tray of water goblets that were arrayed there from the previous meeting.

The entire tray went flying as he reached for it. Kunal lunged for it but was too late. The metal clattered uselessly against the marble floor, filling the room with tinny echoes. Kunal suddenly felt bone weary, like someone had reached inside him and wrung out his organs.

Feet rushed into the room, whips unsheathed. Kunal didn't even have to lift his head to know who it was. Her face was fierce, worried, burdened.

Kunal felt a stab of pain in his chest. He had done that to her. Her shoulders dropped when she saw it was just him, alone in the room. She quickly lit the torches and turned to him.

"What happened?" Esha said, her whips still in both hands. She looked uncertainly at him—was that worry?

"Nothing." Kunal rose to his feet and tried to regain a semblance of composure.

"Are you sure? There should be guards in this room. I had them posted to this wing."

"I told them to leave."

"Why?" she demanded, immediately suspicious. He hated that she glanced at the windows, scanning them for their locks.

Kunal shrugged. "I needed space. A moment to myself."

"That wasn't your goal when you fled from the palace?"

"No," Kunal said, angry at the brutality in her tone. "Though I suppose I deserve that."

"That and a lot more," she said. Esha twirled her whips

into loops and tucked them back into her waist sash.

He pointed at her waist. "I see you're using them again."

"Hard not to when you're in a palace full of Scales and Senaps."

She turned to leave, but he held out a hand to ask her to wait. It was as if he had struck her. Esha curled away from him, her entire body turning in on itself. And yet, she didn't stop him when he approached and cupped her face.

Esha glanced up at him and he could see the flutter of her eyelashes, the short inhale of breath in her chest. Feel her pain.

"Don't go," he said softly.

They stood there for a long moment, and Kunal was merely happy to be close to her again. Inhale the scent of night rose from her curls, feel the silk-soft touch of her skin. And it gave him hope. That she stayed, that she even spoke to him again.

"I would've said the same to you," she said. There was no venom, just the soft, tired truth. And it struck him deep.

"Esha . . . ," he said, drawing out her name into long syllables. "How do I explain?"

"I'm not sure you can, soldier." Her armor was coming back, piece by piece, link by link. Kunal rushed in.

"I wanted so desperately to do something right. To prove I was supposed to be there, that I had a purpose aside from being a soldier. And to make up for even an inch of the pain I had caused on my campaigns. And if I could do that without putting you in harm's way, why wouldn't I? Don't you see?"

His voice was desperate, and he pulled her closer, holding her in his arms. Esha put her head on his chest for a brief moment.

Then she pulled away, putting space between them. Unwelcome distance.

"Maybe I would've," Esha said, shaking her head. "But there were too many things unsaid, too many decisions made without me for you to claim that you thought of me. What about with Laksh?"

"Why do you think I hid his return and his blackmail? You know how I felt about him," he said.

"I know you were hurt, but you still thought there was good in him. I could understand why you'd go back to him and the Scales—"

"I didn't. He threatened you. He threatened Alok."

"And you didn't tell me about it?" She laughed. "I have a whole rebel army at my disposal. I would've been fine."

Kunal shook his head. "It would've jeopardized the entire mission if he had revealed your identity."

Fury snapped at her face. "And what would you know about jeopardizing a mission, soldier?"

"I'm not just a soldier," he said vehemently, despite the burning feeling in his chest that wondered if he ever could be more. "And you set me to follow orders blindly, after everything that had happened with my uncle."

Esha's volley stopped for a moment. Kunal felt a perverse sense of victory.

"I didn't treat you differently than I would've treated anyone else," she said.

"I wasn't a Blade," he said, gritting his teeth. "I was your soldier, your lemon boy. I wasn't your recruit. I could handle myself. I've killed dozens, I've led campaigns across this land, expeditions into other countries, and you treated me as if I couldn't even handle the inner workings of a coup."

Kunal breathed heavily, staring at her. Her eyes were wide. This truth had been in him all along, deep and festering. A cord of anger wrapped around his heart, one twisted with guilt and betrayal of his own. He had made a huge mistake, but Esha hadn't been faultless either.

"Perhaps you're right," she said quietly. "Perhaps I misstepped. But I wasn't wrong to worry about whether you could be trusted with sensitive information if the first thing you did with an asset was to run off with her to save the world by yourself."

Kunal didn't have a second to respond because Esha rushed forward, poking him hard in the chest.

"I was the first to trust you, Kunal." The rawness of her voice, the fury and grief, almost bowled him over.

"I know. I never meant to break— What do I have to do?"

Esha stepped away from him, backing into the darkness of the room. Her mouth was set, her expression turning to stone.

"Nothing. I want nothing from you."

Kunal's heart threatened to stop.

"I believed you. I listened to you. I forgave," she said. "And now my parents are still unavenged and Vardaan is gone. I should've killed him, but I saw your cursed face and I didn't. I had him in my—"

Esha grasped at the empty air, turning desperate eyes on him.

"I didn't lead you astray. You did the right thing," Kunal said.

"You lied to me, even after everything. Even now, I can't trust you."

"You can," he said. "Why do you think I did any of this?"

She laughed. "For me? Do you really believe that?"

Kunal closed the gap between them so that they were almost nose to nose, but he stopped before their bodies touched.

He knew Esha and the way she held herself, and the stark mask of the Viper she put back on made him pause.

Made him question. Hope.

"You can trust me, Esha. We want the same thing. Peace for our lands. Balance and the return of the bond. You know I'll do anything to achieve that."

"Clearly."

Kunal winced. "I did what I thought was right."

"I know, Kunal. It's why I allowed you back into the palace. It's why I'm entrusting any part of this mission to you. And I can even forget the error in judgment you made. Perhaps even see why you made the choice to run away with Reha and try to renew the ritual."

A spark of hope burst into Kunal's chest, expectant.

"Good," he said. Esha stepped backward, out of his reach and into the open area of the room.

"I can look past all of that. I know you can be relied on to see this mission through." A laugh burst from her lips, cold and short. "That's the only thing I know."

Kunal felt that there was something more she wasn't saying, but the more he thought about it the less he wanted it to be true.

"That's all you know?" he asked softly.

She didn't flinch from him this time, but neither did she move. Marble had taken over Esha, so that she resembled the columns near her more than the girl of blood and fire he knew.

"What are we to each other, Esha?"

She hesitated for a tantalizing moment. Her eyes flickered at him before she looked away. "We're allies. I'm grateful you brought Reha back. And now, we have a mission to finish."

"Nothing more?"

Perhaps Esha heard the hope in his voice, but perhaps she didn't care.

"Forgiveness is the only thing I have to offer, soldier. I would take it if I were you."

"This isn't forgiveness, Esha. This is . . ."

"Did you expect everything to return to the way it was?" She turned to look at him, her gaze cutting. "That will never happen. Things have changed. I've had to lead this palace and find a way to rescue my prince. I've had to send my own friend to hunt down the boy I might have loved, if he had ever given me his trust. And now he's back, asking to return to the way things were. Now tell me, why would I want to return to that? To lies and split loyalties, to hiding? I've always been great at deceiving others, soldier, but it seems the best con I've ever played was on myself. Now, I'm happy to have you remain in the palace and help us find the artifacts, but beyond that . . . I just can't help you."

"Esha—"

"You asked me a question, soldier. I gave you your answer. We're allies." Esha moved to turn away. "Nothing more."

He reached for her at first but then let her go.

"Fine," he said.

Esha stopped in her path. Kunal couldn't tell if she was unsettled that he had agreed with her or that he had let her go.

But even he had his limits. Out of all the people in this great, staggering palace, she should have known him. After everything they had been through together, the chase through Jansa, the Sun Mela, the secrets they had revealed to each other—the hopes, the dreams, the fears. She should've trusted in him, believed in him. Given him a chance for forgiveness.

Kunal had always known that Esha was as fierce in her hate as she was in her love. He had guided her to forgiveness every time, chosen to fight for her soul over her anger. And still, he was given no inch from her.

"That's fine by me," he said, anger and frustration coating his tongue. "Have it your way, Viper. That's what we are, then. It's clear you enjoy believing the worst of me. Allies and nothing more. Nothing more at all."

For the first time, Kunal understood what people meant when they said they had lashed out. He felt his words strike out like a whip.

But Esha stood still as a statue, tall and proud, directly diagonal from him across the marble. She glanced away so that her face was hidden. In that moment, Kunal thought he might have seen sadness. Grief.

Esha gave him a short nod and left, leaving him alone again in the vast room.

CHAPTER 13

Esha found Farhan in the same spot in the Great Library a day later, crumbs from his last meal scattered across his tunic. She gently nudged his shoulder, and he flew out of his seat.

"Been here long?" Esha asked, gesturing at his tunic. Farhan glanced down and brushed away the crumbs.

"Since I woke up," he said. "It's driving me crazy, trying to figure out this poem."

"And he's been driving us crazy," Harun said, coming up to her side, looking in better health today. His cheeks had begun to fill out again. His beard had been trimmed, and he wore a deep blue dhoti, foregoing any jewelry today. He threw her a wink when he caught her staring.

"You've been here the whole time?"

"Just the last hour. I've been trying to help, but Farhan

hasn't been very collaborative." Harun leaned in, lowering his voice to a whisper. "I think he prefers Alok as his research assistant."

Esha chuckled, but Farhan ignored the both of them. "It's a combination of ancient Jansan and Dharkan script; that's all I've been able to figure out," Farhan continued.

"That's something," Esha said. "A start."

"But there's enough that I don't understand. I'm not a scholar of languages. We could ask Kunal," Farhan said. Esha felt herself frown. "But I don't think this is something we can do alone."

Esha and Harun exchanged a look. "I have a translator I think we can trust. She used to be a scholar at this very library, before the Night of Tears. She helped me when I was on the run from the Fort a few moons back." Esha turned toward Harun, who was standing behind her. Close enough for her skin to tingle at his warm breath. "What does it say? My ancient script reading skills are rusty."

"Nonexistent, you mean," Harun said.

"Oh, is that how you want to start your first day of full health? Getting a beating from me?"

Harun grinned impishly, the corners of his eyes crinkling with joy.

"Is that what you're going to call it? A beating? Don't threaten a lion, my little viper."

"If I remember correctly, the last time I threatened you I had *my* whip around *your* throat."

Esha moved her hand closer to his, linking her pinkie with his. It was an unconscious movement at first, old habit. But then she didn't want to move. Harun's eyes trailed down to their hands.

"Oh, I remember," he said, his voice catching at the end.

"Um, is this a bad time?" Alok said. He stood near the doorframe, his eyes darting between the two of them.

"It's a great time," Farhan said. "Harun is in enough good health to be flirting again, and Esha is less grouchy than normal."

Two heads swiveled to glare at him.

"What? If you don't like the truth, don't parade it around me."

Alok coughed uncomfortably and walked over. Harun looked as if he was going to pull away, but he glanced up at her. Esha hadn't moved her hand.

For the first time in weeks, she was right where she wanted to be. Here, with him, with her team. Even Alok, though he didn't seem to return the sentiment at the moment.

Esha didn't miss the flicker of happiness that crossed Harun's face. And the wariness that followed. Even after what she had said the night of the Winner's Ball, Harun was holding out hope. They might banter like normal, but she was closer to the precipice with him than ever before.

All Esha could feel was a certain happiness that at least this hadn't changed. She and Harun could—and would—always be this. In this they were practiced, hiding away their feelings.

It was just that Esha no longer knew if she wanted that.

"It's a good time. Come on in, Alok," Esha said. "We just realized we're going to need a translator. We'll need to split into two teams, one focused on the lamp and one focused on the conch, to make the most ground before the next full moon."

Farhan nodded. "The solstice has come and gone as our initial deadline. The scholars in Mathur agree that Reha's blood held back utter catastrophe. But the Rusala Dam is indication that it won't last forever. More disasters will strike. These rituals can only be done on sacred days normally, full moons or solstices. I'm not sure we can wait till the next solstice."

"Makes sense. Full moon it is," Harun said.

Bhandu's and Arpiya's loud and insistent voices floated in from the hallway, announcing their imminent arrival. Harun leaned over, tracing his finger over the scroll they had copied the temple poem down on.

"Wait." A frown creased his brow. "Does it seem like something's missing to anyone else? Like there was once a symbol here? Look at the blank space there. It reminds me of something. Something familiar."

"Missing?" Farhan rushed over to Harun, almost knocking over a small box of chalk. "No, it didn't." He peered closer at the scroll, grabbing it so quickly he almost smudged away the edges of the copied poem.

"Here," Harun said. "These few lines seem to be about the lamp. I recognize that symbol: it's similar to the ancient Jansan symbol for light that's on the altars in the temples in Mathur. But then there—" He pointed at a break in the text. "That seems to be a different script. Almost like a break in the text."

"That doesn't mean something is missing." But Farhan examined the text closer, his eyes tracing over the lines preceding and following the text break.

"If we follow the pattern," Esha said slowly, catching up to Harun. "Then there should be another symbol here, just like the one for light." She traced the blank space. "But there's nothing. Not as if on purpose but as if broken. There should have been a conch here, if the drawing was complete."

"And if you look closer, there's a hanging edge to the scrollwork on that *re* symbol there," Kunal said, leaning over the table from the other side.

Esha jumped, as did Alok and Farhan. Harun merely nodded in welcome at Kunal.

"You'll get used to it," Harun said absentmindedly. "The superhuman speed. I heard him coming down the hall a minute ago."

"You never snuck up on us like that!" Esha protested.

"I had training," Harun said with a shrug.

Kunal muttered a quick "sorry" right before Arpiya and

Bhandu arrived. Harun caught them up quickly. Esha didn't miss the way Arpiya raised an eyebrow at her closeness to Harun or the way that Alok tried to distract Kunal.

"Soldier," Esha said quietly. "What did you mean before, when you said there was a hanging edge?"

Kunal hesitated and gave her a heavy look before he walked over. He stopped before approaching the table. Esha tilted her head in permission, noticing that there were circles under his eyes that hadn't been there the day before.

Kunal traced his finger over the edge of the last word of the stanza. "This curve. It doesn't belong to any other letter here. I can't be sure, but it looks as if it's the start of another stanza."

"I was right," Harun said triumphantly. Farhan looked sour for only a moment before curiosity took over.

Esha seemed to be the only one who was considering the weight of this discovery. A missing stanza meant that they still didn't have a clear idea of how to find the conch. Even the path to the lamp was shrouded in mystery and old text.

One step forward, two steps backward.

"We must have missed something in the temple," Esha said. She shook her head. "We'll have to go back before it's dark. We can't afford to lose any more time."

"I'll go," Harun said. "And I'll take the soldier with me."

Esha didn't like the sound of that.

———◆———

A thick silence lay between Kunal and the prince as they cut their way to the temple. It seemed as if their excursion just a day ago hadn't made any difference—the jungle had grown back.

"Over here," Kunal said. "Let's look for that hanging curl that was on the tracing."

Harun nodded, surprising Kunal. He had always seen the prince as arrogant and unbending, but he had been pleasant on their journey so far, almost too pleasant. He'd told Kunal to lead the way, hadn't brought up his excursion to the mountains. The only thing he did press on was Reha—he was infinitely curious about Reha, combing over every detail Kunal offered.

Of course, neither of them had brought up Esha. That would certainly demolish their tentative peace.

He didn't want to think about Esha or her stubbornness. Kunal steeled himself, thinking of what Reha had said. It wasn't fair to fault him for a bad outcome. His decision had been in earnest, and if Esha couldn't or wouldn't see that, well, it said more about her than him.

He kept that fire around him. It kept him from sinking into the darkness that lay underneath the thought that he may have ruined things. That he shouldn't have agreed to break what had been between them.

Kunal shook his head, returning to the task at hand. He approached the mosaic-studded wall. The poem had faded, leaving only a hint to the words that had been emblazoned on the stone just a day ago. Reha's blood was only a pink smear on the white of the marble.

Harun was to his right, waving over the far right side of the wall the camphor light they had brought with them. The sky outside was tinged with purple, the first sign of the Lord of Darkness's approach. They'd have to make haste.

Kunal traced the stone, feeling the grooves for any sign of the second stanza. The stone was smooth, the only cracks in it from old age and weather. This part of the temple would be exposed to the elements outside, the jungle only a wingspan away. Water from the monsoons would have worn down any jagged edges over the years.

But there—

Kunal spotted a fresh crack in the stone, scuff marks visible to his heightened eyesight. This was the work of a chisel, not the weather. Chipped-away stone flecked the uneven line between the stones, and as he peered closer, Kunal saw faint pink smudges. Blood.

"Prince—"

Harun was already next to him. "Blood." He sniffed the air, his eyes flashing gold and yellow. "I know this scent. It's only a few weeks old."

"A few weeks?" Kunal thought quickly. "Someone must have come for the second stanza. Stolen it away from others. Maybe to get the artifact for themselves, certainly to make sure no one else got it."

Harun swore colorfully, as rough as a Jansan fisherman.

"It's got to be Yamini," Kunal said. "She found us at Mount Bangaar. She wants the artifacts."

"I don't know." Harun paused and sniffed the air again. "Don't you smell it, soldier? It's familiar. It's not the crisp white snow of the North. It's home. It's earthy. It's silt and ocean."

His eyes widened.

"My uncle. Vardaan has the conch."

Now it was Kunal's turn to swear.

———◄○►———

Esha slammed the table hard enough that a goblet nearby tilted over.

"Moon Lord's fists," she said. "Of course Vardaan has it."

"It's possible he doesn't have it yet. Harun said it was a few weeks old," Arpiya said from her seat in the windowsill. She sat cross-legged, which didn't look comfortable. "And we've had eyes on him for a while. Maybe he just has the stanza. Maybe he hasn't even deciphered it."

"He knows where the conch is," Kunal said.

Esha turned her full gaze on him. There was still fire when their eyes caught, but it was brimstone and ash instead of the warmth of the hearth.

"Vardaan would always require us to cover our tracks during campaigns, especially after diversionary tactics. My guess is that he knows. That's why the stone was chipped off. That's why it was made to seem as if it was weather. Vardaan covered his tracks. Perhaps he doesn't have the artifact, but he knows where it is."

Harun leaned against the wall nearest Esha. They were gathered in the kitchens, away from prying eyes. The scent of ghee and spices permeated everything, the cooking fires nearby adding a layer of warmth that had most of them sweating. Bhandu and Aahal were prepping and gathering supplies. Farhan was still poring over the old texts, attempting to pull more from the unwilling ancient scrolls.

"So you're telling me Vardaan is our only way to get to the conch. The conch, the second artifact that we absolutely need to prevent another catastrophe, is in the hands of the Pretender King who put us in this situation in the first place?"

Kunal pursed his mouth, looking confused as to whether to answer.

"Don't say anything," Alok advised. "No one likes the bearer of bad news."

"Too late," Esha snapped. She moved toward the window, massaging her temples.

Arpiya was curled up in the corner of the windowsill now, looking as forlorn as Esha felt.

First the attack in Mathur and now this? Esha had done her best before to stay levelheaded, but it was becoming harder.

Vardaan would never help them—and yet, Esha remembered how he had warned them in the throne room during the Winner's Ball. How adamant he had been in preventing the Yavar from winning. Perhaps they could use that.

"For what it's worth, my uncle is only human," Harun said. "He has a weakness: his pride. It's what drove him to leave Dharka in the first place. He was never content to be second."

"Right," Esha said. She took a full breath, an idea growing in her chest. "Harun, you're right."

"Can I get that in writing?"

"We got reports of Vardaan in the hills near the western border. If Zhyani's continued reports are correct, he hasn't left. And I bet he won't leave. He'll be back, once the dust settles. Vardaan's pride drives him, and pride will be his downfall."

Harun's eyes gleamed in recognition. "Are you thinking—?"

"Yes."

"I hate when they do this," Arpiya said from the windowsill.

Kunal glanced between Harun and Esha with narrowed eyes.

"Someone care to enlighten me?" Kunal drawled in a perfect imitation of Laksh.

"We're going to take Vardaan prisoner," Esha said.

"Oh, of course," Kunal said.

"I like it. Solid plan," Arpiya said. Esha thought she heard a half snort from Kunal. "I volunteer for the first watch of the prisoner." Her smile was razor sharp.

"We'll need to split up, though," Esha said.

Harun nodded. "We'll need half the team to meet up with your translator, the one who can lead us to the lamp."

"Now, we fight for the conch," Esha said.

And make a deal with a monster in the process.

CHAPTER 14

Kunal heaved a heavy sigh as he tucked his uttariya into his waist sash. He turned around and patted the pack behind him on the horse. They'd been traveling for almost four days now.

The silence from Bhandu was the worst. It also seemed to be a struggle for Bhandu. Being silent was not in his nature, and only a half hour into their journey, Kunal understood what kind of trip he was in for.

Laksh and Arpiya had fallen behind them, talking to each other in low voices, their horses lingering together. The only reason Kunal was vaguely comfortable with this situation was because it prevented him from having to interact with his former best friend.

There was too much there for him. Laksh was a reminder of the hurt of betrayal. And what Kunal himself had done to Esha. It didn't help that she had forgiven Laksh and not him.

Bhandu held up a hand as they arrived at the next town. It was barely more than a few huts strung together, but it had a trading market and would offer them the supplies they'd need before they ventured into the mountains and jungle. Kunal had insisted on more rations. With the land the way it was, they couldn't rely on the magic in the jungle to still be full and whole.

Kunal had a copy of the scroll in his bag, the only concession from the team that they didn't wholly mistrust him. Farhan had given them landmarks to look for, assuming that Kunal and the others would be able to recognize them when they saw them. It left Kunal nervous.

All they knew for sure was that they were looking for a set of temple ruins hidden in the jungle. That's where the lamp was supposed to be.

"You look horrible. Are you eating?" Laksh asked, peering at him from across his horse. "And your hair, it looks as if it hasn't seen a comb in years."

Kunal rolled his eyes. "I've been busy. And it's not like the mountains and being yanked back across Jansa by chain really helped."

"You had time at the palace for a shave, at least," Bhandu said, appearing out of nowhere.

Arpiya came from behind him, forcing Kunal to do a double take. "Don't listen to him. But I do have a comb in my pack if you'd like it. I'm always quite good with giving shaves."

"I'd watch her hands, though. Some of those shaves

ended up with dead men," Bhandu said menacingly at Kunal.

"Stop it." Arpiya sighed. "I'm never forgiving Esha for putting me with you three," she muttered under her breath as she walked away. Laksh clapped him on the back and followed after her.

Kunal turned to Bhandu, stopping the burly young man.

"We can't go the entire trip like this," Kunal said.

"Like what, cat eyes?" he said. "And I can go along any way I please."

"I'm sorry," Kunal said, realizing he should've said it earlier. "I never meant to leave you behind."

Bhandu narrowed his eyes at Kunal but finally heaved a big sigh. "I know you're sorry. And it is getting tiring having to be so angry at you. I've never done it before. Really takes up a lot of energy."

He paused. "You did promise to take me flying again. When you left, that's what I was most angry about," he said.

"Not stealing away with Reha?"

Bhandu shrugged. "You've always been an honorable, stupid man. Once I got over the initial shock, I held out hope that you had just taken her to the mountain. But you have to understand. None of us knew. It was easy to imagine the worst of a soldier who had only just come into our lives. You could've taken her to bargain with yourself. You could've been working with Vardaan. My mother always said never to trust a man with cat eyes."

Kunal stepped back. "What? I would never—"

"That's what we decided too, the rest of us. Then all that

was left was the hurt. We trusted you."

"I know," Kunal said, his voice quieting. "That's what I'm most sorry for."

"I know," Bhandu said. "I accept your apology."

"Really?"

"Don't make me take it back, cat eyes."

"Too late. Can't take it back now."

Bhandu squinted at him. "Have you developed a sense of humor?"

"Never too late, I'm told," Kunal said.

Bhandu guffawed and clapped him on the back. Kunal let him push him toward the stall full of maces and listened as Bhandu droned on about the benefits of the smooth domes over the metal-tipped spikes, happy to be included again.

———◄◊►———

The small mercenary outpost was exactly as reported. Esha made a note to send an extra bushel of mangoes to Guildsman Gugil's people. However annoying he was, his information was proving to be valuable.

They approached the outpost, tucked into the valley between two hills, on foot, having left their horses behind half a league away. Esha's footsteps were quiet and Harun's almost silent. She'd always thought she would be a formidable warrior with even an ounce of his supernatural senses.

Esha still wasn't sure Harun was ready for this mission, but his entire body seemed brighter, lighter, since he had a purpose again. And he'd always been a good field asset. It was just his misfortune that he was also talented at speaking the honeyed language of courtiers and money.

Harun glanced at her, noticing her stare. He had tied a thin uttariya around his head to keep his hair and dust out of his eyes. It disguised his features, but Esha wasn't sure anything could remove the regal tilt of his chin or the sharpness in his gaze, so similar to his uncle's.

"Are you sure you're feeling fine?" she asked in a low whisper.

Harun sighed. "Esha, you don't have to keep asking me. The answer is the same as it was ten leagues ago and at the palace and at the market in Onda."

"If you're sure . . ."

"Better question is are you? Feeling fine?" He said it casually, but Esha could tell by the practiced way he said it that he had been holding back the question for a while.

"Better than ever," she said, revealing a wide grin. And she meant it. They were steps from dragging away the Pretender King in chains. What had she ever wanted more than this?

Harun's hand brushed her own and warmth shot through her limbs. He squeezed her hand and let go.

Oh. That. Once she had wanted that more than anything.

Today was a day for the past, then, the past she had tried so hard to put away. Esha decided today she would put her ghosts to rest for once.

They found a large rock and crouched behind it. Two

men to their right at the entrance of the small camp. Two to the left. Mercenaries surrounded the main entrance to Vardaan's makeshift camp.

Good thing they weren't going in through the front door.

She waved two fingers at Harun, pointing to the back of the camp. He nodded and followed behind her, as low to the ground as she was.

At the back there was only one guard, but he was the important one. The one with the keys to the camp. Vardaan had set up a perimeter of locked wooden gates around the center of his camp, where his tent lay.

To get in, they needed those keys.

They stopped half a league away from the southern side of the camp, hidden by the low brush of the saffron-colored hills nearby. Normally, the meadows would be filled with stalks of wheat that climbed up the base of the hills. They were sparse now. Poor cover. So Esha and Harun stayed behind the shadows of the hills instead of making a direct approach.

Esha stopped and turned to Harun, glancing down at her disguise. "How do I look?"

"I never know the right way to answer that question."

"Radiant is always a good one. Luminescent. Incandescent."

"Beautiful."

"That's pretty standard," Esha protested.

Harun leaned closer to fix the hem of her uttariya, pinned

to her hair and blouse in the way of the local townspeople. Her yellow cotton sari was simple, with a small border and small diamond-shaped mirrors sewn into a checkered pattern.

"I quite like this look on you," he said softly, brushing away a strand of her hair.

"Oh really? Village girl?"

"Village girl, village boy. Other lives." He pointed at himself. The uttariya around his eyes, the thin cotton dhoti, the twined ropes around his biceps instead of gold armbands. He looked different without any adornments. Harun had always dressed simply for a noble, but this was different. He was right. This was another life.

"Boring lives," Esha said, though one look at Harun told her that they both knew her dismissal was false.

Why were they doing all this—risking their lives, trying to prevent civil war, the destruction of their land—if not for these so-called boring lives? They were the truth in all this. And it was what they wanted, at the end of this conflict.

"After everything, I hope we all have boring lives," Harun said.

He held her gaze, his fingers still tracing the outline of her jaw. He had held back since their conversation at the Winner's Ball. Waiting. Part of her didn't want him to. She wanted the old Harun, she wanted the old fire between them that she had doused in search of . . . what? Bronze-colored lies?

"Me too," she said finally.

A snap of wood drew their attention. The first perimeter they had laid had been crossed.

It was time.

———◄◦►———

Esha pulled her uttariya over the right side of her face, holding her other hand out as if shielding her eyes. She stumbled a bit, making sure to be as loud as possible.

"Halt! You there," a voice said.

Esha raised blinking, bleary eyes to face the mercenary's voice. He wore only leather armor, and his turban was tied to the side, like many of the mercenary guilds chose to do. He'd be more difficult. Soldiers at least wore the veneer of duty and care for the people. Mercenaries were only in it for the coin, though there had to be another angle at play here. Vardaan didn't have the deep coffers of the crown anymore and yet they followed him.

"I'm so sorry, sir. I was told to come this way," she said in a trembling voice.

Esha cowered, one of her hands wrapped tightly around her basket, the other stretched out in protection. His reaction would determine her approach.

"Explain yourself," the guard snapped. He had a long mustache and cold eyes that darted between her face and her clothes. He was assessing her, and Esha sent a prayer up to the Moon Lord again for Harun's quick thinking with their disguises.

"The town council wanted to send a gift," she said shakily.

He blinked at her, a wolfish grin across his face.

She stuck her arms out before he took a step closer, thrusting her basket full of mangoes toward them. He frowned at the basket—before he saw the fruit inside.

"Mangoes!" he said, his cold veneer slipping for a second. "I haven't found any in recent months."

"It's not the season, sir. They're not as ripe or plump as they should be," she said, eyes cast down.

"A fine gift, still," the man said happily. He took the basket and put it down on the ground behind him. He was clearly a mango connoisseur, which made Esha a bit sad about what was going to come next. "Wait, how did the council know we were here?"

He narrowed his eyes at her, his fist closing tight around her wrist. She went as limp as she could without giving up ground. Let him think her weak.

"I don't know, sir. I'm just a villager. I can't speak for the council. . . ."

His suspicion didn't dissipate.

"The boss told us to keep an eye out for pretty, dangerous girls. I thought him paranoid, but here you are." He peered at her. "You certainly are pretty, but you don't look that dangerous. Though last time I thought that, I got this scar." He pulled his collar to the side, showing a puffy, ugly scar that traced his throat.

Moon Lord. Only one weapon caused that sort of scarring.

She unconsciously dropped her free hand down to her

waist sash, where her whips were nestled. The mercenary didn't miss the movement, his eyes alighting in recognition.

This was what happened when the Viper left men alive. If only Kunal were here now, to see the truth of it, he might not have judged her so harshly before. She could still play it off, though. Esha pulled out a small figurine of the Sun Maiden and clutched it in her hand, whispering in prayer. The mercenary dropped her hand and grabbed the figurine from her.

Esha tried to move away, but he grabbed her around the waist, reaching for her waist sash.

"Better to be safe than sorry," he said. A cruel grin split his lips.

Esha held back a curse. She could either fight back and give herself away or let him grope around and find her whips. Either way would draw too much unwanted attention.

"Falguni!" a sharp voice called out.

Esha and the mercenary froze. She was wrapped in his arms, but not in any sort of pleasant way, and she had just maneuvered her elbow to connect with his jaw.

Harun strode into view holding a huge wooden stick in one hand, fury written across his face.

"There you are, Falguni. I see you've found a new toy. A soldier is it, this time?"

Esha looked at Harun as if he had drunk the trader's herbal drink.

What was he doing?

"I'm not good enough for you? I thought we had fixed our problems, Falguni." Harun still kept the menacing stick raised high, but his face dropped into a morose expression. "But now I find you here, in the arms of a . . . fierce and scary-looking man. A soldier. Of course you'd want a soldier."

The mercenary was so confused that he didn't seem to notice that Harun was closing the distance between them.

"What? I don't even know her—" the mercenary started. He was eyeing the large stick in Harun's hands and the size of Harun himself.

Esha finally caught on and let herself fall against the mercenary's chest, tilting her elbow away from his jugular and her chin up at him. She batted her eyelashes at him before turning to glare at Harun.

"At least he doesn't take me for granted, Arun!" Esha threw back. She snuggled up to the mercenary, looping her arms around him and slowly lifting his sword out of its sheath. "He's a *real* man. Willing to be vulnerable and tell me how he feels."

Now the mercenary truly looked bewildered, but he was beginning to shake off the first haze of confusion.

"Well, it's harder for some people to speak about their feelings, Falguni."

"Well, how was I supposed to know that, Arun?"

Esha almost had the mercenary's sword out of its sheath. Which was good because he had finally managed to unravel from her embrace.

"Because you knew me, Falguni! I showed you how I felt about you every moment we had alone."

Esha wasn't sure they were playacting anymore.

"What in the— Who are you two? What are you doing here?" the mercenary shouted. "I thought you were the—"

Harun was a few paces away now. Esha spun around and kicked the mercenary in the chest. He sprawled to the ground, and she pointed his sword at him, one of her whips now in her other hand.

"Viper," the mercenary spat.

He tried to get up, even with the point of his sword squarely in the center of his chest, but Harun was behind him in seconds. He had him tied and trussed up, a gag in his mouth, before he could let out even a whimper.

"You were always good at that," Esha said in appreciation.

"Nice acting," he returned.

Esha coughed. "Same to you."

"Do we leave him here?" Harun looked down at him and then at the camp nearby.

"Let's move him, just to be safe."

Esha nodded, and they dragged him under a thickety brush, the shadows covering him. Harun knocked him out with the mercenary's sword and claimed it for his own.

"You were talking about us, weren't you?" Esha asked, unable to help herself.

Harun brushed dirt off his hands and straightened,

sliding the mercenary's sword into his waist sash. "I didn't mean to," he said.

"Ah," Esha said.

"Ah, indeed."

"Should we . . . talk? About . . ."

Harun winced. "We really have the worst timing. You need to go before someone notices the guard has disappeared."

Esha reached over and thumbed through the man's pouches, pulling out a set of keys. When she stood up, Harun was only a few inches away.

Worst timing of the century. But perhaps it was for a reason. Harun's words kept playing in her mind, an endless song of mistakes.

"After, then," Esha said.

Harun moved closer and closer still when he saw that Esha didn't back away. He cupped her face and kissed her with a fire she had never quite forgotten, one filled with memories.

"For all the times I didn't," he said, pulling away. "Good luck."

She heard the words in between, the words they had never said.

Good luck. Come back to me. Be safe.

And she saw that Harun wanted to say them, that they were on his lips, but at the last second he only nodded at her.

She turned to go, hefting her whips, but Harun's voice rang out, surprising her.

"Come back to me, Esha. In one piece, please," he said wryly.

She saluted him. "Of course, my prince."

———◁◦▷———

Esha wrapped the blue-sapphire ropes around her wrists and forearms, entwining up her arms like the gold snake jewelry she used to wear.

She crouched low and approached the wooden gates that had been linked and set up around the center area of the camp. They were taller than her and heavy, indicating that Vardaan wasn't taking any chances.

The gates also told her that even though these men were his, there was only so far that he trusted them. That she could work with. That was the key information they needed for later.

For now, Esha got to work with the mercenary's keys, unlatching the locks on the fenced gate. It took longer than anticipated, and Esha realized she was running short on time. They had paid off a villager to monitor the lights of the camp, which meant she now knew she had only a few minutes before Vardaan would send out guards to protect his tent and shift into a lion to sleep.

And since she had no desire to fight a lion, Esha moved quicker.

She felt along the edges of the back cloth of the tent. Even the best-made ones had a seam or two that she could rip through. They all had a double flap in the back as protection against the winds here.

Esha cut through the back flap and used the second one to hide her shape as she got a glimpse of the inside of the tent.

A tall shape moved near the far end. She heard faint sounds, clinks of metal against wood as he removed his jewelry. His sword stayed at his side. Esha noticed he had gotten a new one, not as ornate as his old one she had worn but just as fierce, with an exacting edge and a lion crested on the hilt.

Esha burst out of her hiding space and ran full speed toward Vardaan.

Vardaan whirled around, his sword out, before she even reached him. Anyone else and she would've had her whip around their throat before they even realized she was in the room—but Vardaan wasn't just anyone. She had counted on him hearing her coming.

Esha ducked under the sword and slid to the ground. She lashed one end of blue-sapphire ropes around the bare skin of his ankle.

He growled and almost sent Esha flying. But she whipped the rest of the ropes around him, wherever she could make contact with bare skin. She held on to the ropes and tugged.

Vardaan fell to his knees in front of her, eyes flashing between yellow and brown. He was trying to shift.

"Viper," he spat.

Esha tightened the ropes, whirling around him to knot and tie the blue-sapphire ropes. As a finale, she dug out a collar especially made for Vardaan and adorned him with it.

She thought he looked spectacular, the blue diamond at his throat particularly beautiful. And the only thing that could hold back the man in front of her.

Vardaan had stopped trying to shift. Or no longer could.

"You found me," he said slowly, with difficulty. Blue tendrils crept up his temples like hungry vines. "Now, what are you going to do with me?"

Esha smiled.

CHAPTER 15

It was harder to find the translator's house than Kunal anticipated once they arrived in Amali. They ended up knocking on a number of doors to cross or confused faces, enough that even Arpiya was getting twitchy by the end of it.

"Did Esha give us the wrong information?" Kunal murmured to himself.

Not quietly enough, though.

"Esha would never," Arpiya snapped at him, snatching the scroll away. "More likely that you can't read," she said.

Kunal sighed. Just as he had gotten back on Bhandu's good side he had found himself on Arpiya's bad side. He hadn't determined yet which one was worse, but at least being on Bhandu's bad side had been quieter.

He didn't put up a fight as Arpiya took control. It gave him a moment to take in the city of Amali—the diamond of the North. He thought it more like a dim topaz.

The sun had come down to perch upon the city's shoulders, bathing everything in an orange glow. It didn't help that any hints of green in the land had almost entirely disappeared. Women and men crowded near the wells, jockeying for the best place in line.

The one thing in their favor was that the Lady of the Parvalokh region was firmly on their side. She had never bowed to Vardaan, keeping this area as separate as possible. The bigger question would be if being so far north and so far removed from the capital had forced the region to make another alliance.

But this part of the country had fought in the War in the North, had been the first line of soldiers to prevent the Yavar's excursion into the rest of Jansa twenty years ago. It was unlikely they would ally with the Yavar, but Kunal wasn't sure he could trust those old instincts of honor anymore. What he could trust was the pain of the past.

The main roads they wound through were changed from his last visit over two years ago. The smuggler caravans were less hidden, the desperation more obvious. Esha had mentioned that she and Harun had sent supplies through to Amali and it showed, to some degree. The city was doing better compared to the other towns they had traveled through, which wasn't saying much. When had having a continuous source of water become a measure of success and not a given?

Kunal took in the city like he had taken in all the other

sights on their journey up here—with a heavy heart.

"Oi, cat eyes, what are you daydreaming about?" Bhandu said.

"Peace," Kunal said. "An end to this."

He couldn't help the note of sadness that slithered into his voice. This is what he had hoped to stop. This suffering. But here they were, on another wild monkey chase to try and fix a problem they hadn't started.

A meek voice whispered in his mind, one that was getting stronger, wondering if, maybe, there was no solution to this problem. What then? If their land was dying and they alongside it, what could they do?

Everything. A fiercer part of him spoke.

Arpiya rose her hand to halt their small company. Kunal's horse reared back, and he rubbed his neck to calm him down. He would have to be more careful about guarding his feelings around the animals. He was learning that they could sense them, take them on. An interesting revelation and one that Kunal wanted to explore—when there was time.

They dismounted and tied their horses to a post. A few houses down they stopped in front of a house with a wooden door. A huge crack scarred the outside.

Arpiya knocked softly.

The door swung open, a moon-faced woman behind it.

"I'm looking for a tailor," Arpiya said hesitantly, and then with more confidence. "I caught my hem while on horseback."

The woman craned her neck to look out at all of them. Bhandu knocked into Laksh, his mace clanging against Laksh's armor. Kunal jumped back in time to avoid another collision.

"It's going to be tight," she said.

———◄○►———

Kunal picked up one of the many scrolls in the scholar's house and squinted at it, trying to figure out what ancient script it was in.

Arpiya and the scholar were discussing the stanza in the corner of the small house. Bhandu and Laksh were perched like two uncomfortable birds of prey on stools near the front of the house. Scrolls poured onto every surface that seemed available, from the shelves to the main table to the small chairs in the back. Kunal could get lost in them for hours.

Translation and ancient scripts had always been his favorite lessons. The stories that accompanied them had fascinated him back then and still did—stories of another world, hidden in scrolls and waiting to be found.

"Kunal." He didn't move the first time, absorbed in what he thought might be a record of tax collection from before the Blighted Age.

"Kunal." This time Arpiya appeared in front of his face and snatched the scroll in his hands. She rolled her eyes. "Of course Esha would go for a dreamer."

"What—?"

"We need you here." Arpiya didn't sound happy at having to admit it.

The scholar had spread out the scroll and traced a copy of it. She was separating the words, trying to match letters to ancient scripts. So far, she had done an excellent job.

Kunal read over her shoulder.

"The songs that are hidden,
The prayers that are spoken,
The light that is bidden,
Will come to all."

The scholar's lips were pursed in thought.

"What in the Moon Lord's name does all that mean?" Bhandu asked.

"I'm a translator," the scholar said. "That's my trade, so I could be wrong on this, but I feel like I've heard something like this before. The flow reminds me of an ancient poem. If only I could remember—"

"Ask Kunal," Laksh said, a bored half smile curving up his cheeks. "He used to read those musty old poems during campaigns. I thought he used them to put himself to sleep until I realized he enjoyed the things. Memorized a few too, I believe."

Kunal flushed. "Just for that competition."

Arpiya's eyebrows rose. "Competition?"

"Kunal painted watercolors that went along with the old poem about the Chariot at Dusk," Laksh said, his voice light and slightly teasing. "It was the talk of the Fort."

"Isn't that the story of the Lord of Darkness's tragic romance with the Goddess of Light?" Bhandu said.

Arpiya shrugged, the ends of her hair swishing around

her face. "There are two endings. In Mathur, it's not so tragic. We're less interested in a dutiful, honorable death or whatever nonsense stories that you Jansans drink as your mother's milk."

"My version wasn't so . . . tragic." Kunal frowned. "Or I don't think. It's hard to remember."

"Either way, the general boxed his ears when he found out Kunal had entered the competition, said painting and art weren't becoming for a soldier," Laksh said. The mocking tone in his voice faded. "Another reason I hated that man."

"I didn't know you cared," Kunal said.

Laksh gave him a look.

"Cat eyes, do you have anything in that brain of yours that might help here?" Bhandu asked.

Kunal mulled it over. "It sounds familiar, like you said." He nodded at the scholar. "Similar cadence and words as the . . . 'Temple of the Hidden Song.' That's it." Kunal almost jumped in delight. He had always loved that poem.

"Huh?" Bhandu said.

"It's an old poem about a hidden temple of the ancients, though now that I know more about magic and blood songs, I think it was probably an abandoned temple of the royals. Hidden, obviously."

"Okay, secret temple of the royals . . . That tells us what?" Laksh said.

"It will have to be in a jungle. Think of where the temple King Mahir showed me was," Kunal said. "It was sun stone and jungle. Can you all think of any other place that will have what's needed for both?"

Bhandu squinted at him. Laksh and Arpiya exchanged a glance and shrugged.

"The Tej rain forest?" the scholar guessed.

"Great guess, but I don't actually think so." Kunal shifted uncomfortably. "I . . . visited a few moons ago and the surrounding area is probably too wet."

"So we're talking deep jungle?" Arpiya said. Kunal tilted his head to tell her to go on. Arpiya's face was soft in thought, hinting at another side to the fierce girl. Then she began to jump up and down.

"Oh, the jungle near the Mauna Valley!" she almost exclaimed.

Bhandu sighed, mumbling to himself in a frustrated manner about how she always got to answers first.

"Yes," Kunal said, smiling. "Great job."

Arpiya grinned back, until she realized who she was grinning at. Her face quickly changed to a scowl.

"Looks like we're going to the Mauna Valley," Laksh said.

Kunal recalled the last time he had been there, when Rakesh had attacked Esha and he had been shot by a poisoned arrow from the Blades. At least this time, no one would be after him—or so he hoped.

"Before we go, we have something we wanted to give you," Kunal said, coming around the table to where the woman stood.

Arpiya nodded, pulling a small scroll from her pack. "A

gift from the Viper. She hopes you remember her fondly."

The scholar stood up, straightening the pleats of her sari. "Of course."

Arpiya handed her the scroll, which the woman unrolled quickly and read. The change on her face was that of night to morning, clouds to sun rays.

"Really?" the woman whispered.

Arpiya nodded, trying to act solemn but her bouncing foot giving her away. "It's real. An official welcome back to the Great Library. You can continue your life's work, Pooja."

Pooja darted forward with surprising speed and wrapped both Arpiya and Kunal, the two closest to her, in a hug. They stumbled back in surprise.

"Thank you," she said. "Thank you. You've returned my life to me."

Kunal glanced at Arpiya over the woman's head and saw an opening.

"Sorry," he mouthed at her, before wincing. The scholar was strong.

Arpiya didn't meet his eyes for a few seconds. Finally, she mouthed back, "Fine."

They still had a long way to go to find the temple and the lamp within, but Kunal couldn't help but feel a glimmer of hope at seeing the happiness in the scholar's face.

They'd return the world to rights. Bit by bit.

———◇———

The musty scent of damp wood greeted Esha and Harun as they entered the dungeons of the citadel. The very stones themselves creaked and moaned, something that Esha had never forgotten. Those sounds and these smells had been Esha's constant companion for a torturous month.

Esha's fingers clenched into fists, an unconscious movement, one that said her body remembered this place all too well. If she had a choice she would have never stepped foot in this miserable hole again.

But she was here for the man next to her.

Harun's face was composed, but a muscle under his jaw kept twitching. His tell. Esha reached out and interlaced her fingers with his.

The twitching stopped.

This wasn't easy for either of them. To be back here with Vardaan, to be with this monster of a man. To remember.

But it was necessary.

Vardaan had demanded to see his nephew after his capture, when he had been dragged here and thrown into a cell. Harun had decided to grant his uncle's request and asked her to accompany him. It made sense for her to be there as the de facto leader of the palace at the moment, but Esha knew it was more personal than that.

Harun didn't want to face his uncle alone.

Esha didn't know what she might do to Vardaan if she did see him alone.

Going together would ensure that they got the information they needed. Harun was skilled, but he had too much history with his uncle, and it was a history Vardaan wouldn't hesitate to exploit. Esha was still surprised that Vardaan had agreed to help them, which added to her uneasy feeling. There wasn't a single good reason for Vardaan to help, not one without a catch. She was going to find it before it undid them all.

They turned the corner and came to the cell at the end of the row, separated and isolated from the rest. There was Vardaan, Pretender King of Jansa.

In the darkness, he was nothing more than a slip of a man, a curve of light. They stopped in front of the tall metal bars and waited. Vardaan took his time coming to the front of the cell, dragging his chains so slowly that the screech of metal against the stone floor filled the entire room.

Even now, Vardaan had to make an entrance.

"Hello, nephew," he drawled. "And the Viper, what a pleasant surprise. I did ask to see my nephew alone, but I suppose you couldn't help yourself. You know, I had the pleasure of making an acquaintance with one of your people some time earlier."

"Oh?"

"Yes. They were quite willing to tell me almost everything they knew. Even switch to my cause, our cause."

Esha snorted. "Your cause is only yourself."

"Now that's a bit harsh, don't you think, nephew?"

Harun stayed silent, but he stepped closer to the bars.

"None of our Blades would be disloyal," Esha said, glancing at Harun.

"Are you sure, little Viper?" Vardaan's smile was a silvery gleam in the shadows.

No, she wasn't sure, but she sure as cursed all wouldn't admit it to him of all people. Rage rose in her throat at the thought before Esha realized. He wanted her angry. Angry people made mistakes; they were easy to manipulate. And she had almost walked right into a trap.

Perhaps he was right, perhaps he was playing her like the old veena she had been toying with in the palace music rooms. But she wouldn't reveal any weakness now.

"I am as sure of my people as I am of your fate, Vardaan," she said.

"Ah, we've dispensed with the titles, have we?"

"King, Prince, murderer, traitor. Vardu," she said, sneaking in King Mahir's nickname for the man, the name he had hated. "Take your pick."

That earned her a flash of real emotion. Anger. She hid her smile.

"I'm helping you, am I not? Perhaps you should be kinder to me, Viper," he said, menace lurking behind.

But he was here, behind bars of immovable steel. Hidden under the pillar of the city, the citadel. For once, they were at an advantage.

"Kindness is a perception, King," she said, using the title like a curse.

"You should muzzle your Viper, Harun."

"I'm sorry, uncle." Harun stepped forward and placed a gentle hand on her elbow. "I'm sorry you feel aggrieved by the truth. I would never presume to tell her what to do."

He glanced at her: the ramrod posture, the way she was

gripping her sword. *Not anymore.*

Esha kept her posture, but something in her began to crumble at his words.

"That's what it is?" Vardaan looked contemplative. "I thought she and the— Intriguing. A love knot." There was an understanding in Vardaan's words that Esha didn't appreciate.

Vardaan straightened, as much as he could with the numerous chains bound to him. The entire cell filled with the sound of clanking metal.

"I find myself tiring." He let out a wide yawn. "Ask your questions quickly, children."

"Where is the conch?" Harun asked.

"Straight to it, are we? I've hidden it." He paused for a moment, the silence weighing down the room. He was certainly dramatic. "In Mathur. In my favorite place as a child."

"That's it?" Esha asked, her voice nearly a growl.

"Should be more than enough. You have your memory, nephew. I took you there a few times, even. Your father would know too—that is if he remembers anything about our childhood."

It was said simply. But there was a discordant note, a minor key of sadness—or regret. Here was the human in the monster. Here was why she so often underestimated him.

"And once we're there?" Esha said. "What then? You send us on a wild monkey chase and have a laugh back here?"

"No. I'm sure you'll set a number of your Blades to

monitor my every breath," he said. Vardaan raised his shoulders into a lazy shrug, the metal creaking as he moved. "It's not a wild monkey chase but believe me as you will. I am in *your* power. What could I possibly do?"

She narrowed her eyes at the innocent tone he used, and he grinned at her. A slanted, cunning grin that took her in whole.

Harun stiffened next to her. They would have to send scouts, keep the team on alert.

"So we find this place and then? You're only of use to us if you talk, uncle." Harun let the words linger, his own threat coloring the air.

"You'll need a ship," Vardaan said. "That's my only clue. I have to make you work for it a little, don't I? A good uncle teaches a boy how to fish, doesn't just hand it to him. That's what your father would always say to me."

Esha snorted dismissively. "We're a bit past being a good uncle."

"Then I have time to make up for. You'll need a ship to get to one of my favorite places, where the conch has been hidden. I have faith in you, Harun." Vardaan winked at him.

Now the question was if they could have faith in the Pretender King.

CHAPTER 16

Esha barged into the small anteroom, waving a note in the air. Three pairs of heads popped up to look at her. The anteroom they had chosen for today's meeting had the bare minimum of what they needed: a table, a few scattered chairs, and privacy.

"Good news," Esha said. "King Mahir responded. He has been looking for the artifacts without the map. He had some insights into the copper scroll."

"What's the good news?" Alok asked impatiently. He twisted the ring on his finger, the only indication that the stress of the last few days was getting to him.

"He also has some thoughts on his brother's favorite location. He mentioned they used to travel south a lot as kids, for the winters. Vardaan always loved the rivers near the coast of Dharka," Esha said.

Farhan nodded and scribbled something onto a scroll.

"That helps immensely. Vardaan will have to have kept it near a place of magic. Let me think. . . ."

Esha thought to the team that had left a few days before: Kunal and Laksh, Arpiya and Bhandu. She shouldn't be worried and yet it never quite worked that way. Kunal and Laksh were volatile together, but Esha had hoped they would balance each other out. And Arpiya would keep an eye on them both.

As for her team, Esha quickly assessed who would be best on a quick mission. She'd have to take Reha, if only because she didn't trust the girl here alone, and Aahal. Perhaps Alok or Harun. Farhan was too valuable as a translator to endanger him, and he was making strong progress on the pile of scrolls they had gathered.

"That narrows it to . . ." Esha trailed off, hoping Farhan would finish the sentence.

Farhan traced his hand over the large map unfurled across the wooden table in front of him.

"The Jyos tributary. Or the Ruins of Varnika."

"Isn't the Jyos tributary just near the coastline?" Reha asked, peeking around Farhan. "I've heard about it a lot. Near the famous rice paddies of southern Dharka."

"There's only a small part of the coast that's referred to as the Jyos tributary," Esha said. "It's where the river splits before entering the ocean and was given that name because of the two colors of water that merge there. Harun, thoughts?"

"From what I've been able to read over Farhan's shoulder,

the Jyos tributary makes the most sense," Harun said. "The conch needs to be kept underneath the water, according to the old myths, though the myths also say it will only open to an unuttered truth."

"That's ridiculous," Esha said. "What does that even mean?"

"Couldn't we just drip more blood on it?" Alok said, his ring twisting having graduated to worried nail-biting.

Farhan shrugged. "That could also work."

"Good thing we have you around now, isn't it?" Esha said to Reha.

"Wonderful," Reha said. She looked a bit concerned.

"Anyway, the Jyos tributary rings a bell," Harun said. "My uncle used to always talk about it, the place where the two mightiest rivers of Dharka meet and battle it out for supremacy, before combining as one."

"If he hid it there, it sounds likely he hid it at the point of convergence for the rivers." Farhan looked disquieted. "We'll certainly need a ship, and it won't be an easy journey."

"Then we'll take a team to scope out the area and report back," Esha said. "Reha, Alok, you'll be coming with me. Harun as well. But Farhan, we need you here."

Esha put a hand on the boy's shoulder, and he nodded, though he looked a bit disappointed.

Keeping Reha here had been important as they put together the details of the coronation and the type of government after. And to her surprise, Reha had taken on the role better than expected. Though she and Harun had barely talked, she was willing to listen as they shuttled her to meeting after meeting, switching the veils so that when they introduced the princess Reha, it truly was her.

But Esha wasn't sure what Reha would do if left alone here. She was still close to many of the Scales, especially close to Zhyani. And while the Scales had been allies, Esha was still wary of trusting too many people.

Reha's eyes brightened. "I'll be able to leave?"

"For a bit," Esha said, raising an eyebrow. "You don't have to look so excited. We haven't locked you up, despite my suggestion. Dharmdev still has a lot to answer for."

Reha rolled her eyes. "I keep telling you I had only just gained the title of Dharmdev; it was passed from leader to leader. There were multiples, sometimes even at the same time. Do you really think one person could've fit all those stories?"

"I did," Esha said, the smugness apparent in her voice.

"Well, the Lord of Justice simply wasn't as good as the Viper. Is that what you want to hear?"

"It's a start," Esha said.

"I'm sorry for what they did to you," she said hesitantly. Reha tucked a piece of her hair behind her ear in a demure movement, a contrast to the direct way she stared at Esha. "I didn't order the mission that killed General Hotha, the one that you were framed for. I heard of it, but I'd only just gotten my pin, and then a few months later I was assigned to you. I was just doing my job."

That's what everyone said, wasn't it? Esha might have been one of those people too, following orders without thinking, doing whatever was asked of her, but Harun and she had been a balance to one another. Their power struggles had actually pushed them to never do things just because they had always been done. In that way, they had constantly challenged the past, despite Esha being unable to let go of it.

Even now, she felt the prickling of the knowledge that Reha held—who her parents' real killer was. She wondered if the girl would tell her. So far, she had been forthcoming with information, but Esha sensed a dark past behind Reha.

Perhaps the boat trip would be the time for them to speak honestly.

"I liked Aditi," Esha said. "I might like you too, Reha. I remember you used to hate mangoes and loved sums as a child. Is that still true?"

Reha looked at her, surprised. "Yes. I was the only one who could work the ledger for the Scales. And mangoes still give me hives."

"You don't like mangoes?" Alok said. "That's a punishable offense to Esha."

Esha chuckled. "To anyone else, maybe. You might not remember, Reha, but we spent much time together when you were younger. I remember it all. And I've fought for you every day since I helped you escape during the Night of Tears. Since I was captured and tortured for information about you. And since I became the Viper."

Reha's face scrunched up, and she looked as if she was going to say something, but Esha didn't know what.

"I hope you prove worth it," Esha said.

She hoped all of this was worth it.

———◁○▷———

After two days of endless jungle and rock that looked the same, Kunal came across a small river. It was unusual, not just because the land everywhere else was drying up, but because it was flowing in the wrong direction.

At the Fort they had studied ecological patterns, and Kunal had been a good student. With the wind going east and the slope of the land, the water should be running in the opposite direction.

He held up a hand to the others.

Bhandu almost ran into him, cursing under his breath. "What now, cat eyes?"

Kunal shushed him. He closed his eyes and tried to center in on the river and any animal life in the area. Normally, the jungle was a symphony of sounds, something he had reveled in even before he had been able to use the full power of his blood. But there had been little animal activity so far in their travels.

He got off his horse and knelt by the small river, putting a hand to the ground. The songs here were different, broken. Notes missing and discordant harmonies.

Wrong.

"I think I found something," Bhandu said.

"What?" Arpiya asked.

Bhandu pointed at the ground and reached over to pick up a small shiny shard of some sort of stone. "If we're looking for temple ruins, this might be a good start."

Laksh nodded, gathering the reins of Bhandu's and Kunal's horses and leading them over to where Bhandu stood. "Looks like sun stone, which they used for temples here in the jungle. It's the only stone that can resist decay in all this humidity and rain."

"Good find," Kunal said, nodding at Bhandu.

"That's it, then," Arpiya said. "We're close."

She bent to the ground, looking for other stone fragments. Kunal watched her, an idea forming in his mind as he looked between the river and her. There were more fragments and the others were picking them up as they followed the river.

The river must be a clue. Perhaps it was being pulled in the other direction due to a core of magic or something else powerful. They knew little about the artifacts, but two of them together in one location must have some effect on the land around them.

"I've got an idea," Kunal said slowly.

He motioned for them to follow and took off in a sprint up the hill, following the river.

◆◇◆

The water near the Jyos tributary, the confluence of the two tributaries of the Bhagya River, glittered like a thousand broken stars, a heavenly blue and green swirled together into one. Esha shaded her eyes from the hot sun as she gazed over the villages below from the hill they had stopped on.

Home was beautiful. Sweltering, sure, but beautiful. The dry sun of Jansa was nothing like this sticky heat. Her heart had felt lighter since they had crossed over the border to Dharka and part of her never wanted to leave. She inhaled the humid air and let out a loud, contented sigh.

Reha cursed to her left, swatting at a group of mosquitoes as Alok chatted good-naturedly at her. It appeared as if the girl didn't quite feel the same way as she about the weather.

"No one told me Dharka was filled with these annoying bloodsucking gnats," Reha said, continuing to swat unsuccessfully at the air around her. "Zhyani and Ishaan always made it sound like some paradise."

"Oh, that's a good sign," Alok said. "Means the land isn't so parched that it can't even produce humidity."

"I'd be okay with a little dryness if it got rid of these things," Reha muttered.

Esha tugged out the map Farhan had copied over for them and pointed at the lines he had drawn, with the supposed location of the conch somewhere in the middle.

"We need to get there to find the conch most likely," Esha said, squinting and pointing at a spot on the map.

"That's in the water," Alok pointed out.

"Precisely the need for a ship." Esha made a face. "At least he hadn't been lying about that."

Harun trotted up from behind, catching up with them. He had an uttariya tossed over his shoulders and a lightweight linen turban on his head. A simple outfit. Most people didn't know what Harun looked like here, or so he had convinced them.

The awkwardness between them had fully thawed since Esha had rescued him, but still neither of them had brought up the conversation they had before Vardaan's capture. They had agreed to talk, but it always seemed like more important things came up.

"Here," Harun said. He handed a small rag and vial to Reha. "It'll help with the mosquitoes. Drench the rag and put it on your pulse points. Should give you relief for a few hours."

"Thank you, Harun," she said. "That's kind of you."

"Mosquitoes are miserable creatures," Harun said, giving her a little smile. "Our father taught me this trick. I'd always be the one to get bitten first—well, until you came along. The mosquitoes always preferred you. Mother would say it was because you had the sweeter blood."

Reha's eyes perked up at the mention of their mother. "I think I might remember that, actually. She had long hair, didn't she? And it always smelled of jasmine."

Harun nodded happily. "It was her favorite scent. You'd try to braid her hair and fail miserably." He laughed, a small but joyful one. "It would come out a tangled mess that would take her hours to comb through."

"I'm still horrible at braids," Reha admitted.

They both grinned at each other, and Esha's heart lightened.

Esha cleared her throat. "We can charter a ship from there." Esha pointed at a small dock in the distance. "If this map is any indication, we'll need to be directly over the spot to find the conch."

"With a little bit of blood, right?" Reha asked wryly.

Esha chuckled. "It might be a lot of blood. And if that doesn't work, we'll need to ready our truths."

She had meant it in jest, but looking at the faces of her team, she realized that they all had hidden truths in them.

And if it was blood or her truth, Esha was pretty sure she'd pick the former.

CHAPTER 17

Laksh had some choice words for Kunal when he and the others caught up to him. Kunal had run up the mountain to follow the steep curve of the river as it pushed upstream, and his hunch had been right. Bhandu and Arpiya were panting as Kunal took a deep breath of air, his hands on his hips. He felt good.

"I preferred it when you only lapped me once," Laksh said. He dropped the reins of the horses and leaned a hand against the nearest tree to support himself. "Have I mentioned I'm not a fan of these new supernatural powers of yours? Mighty unfair."

"Wait till he takes you flying," Bhandu said, sending him a wicked grin.

Arpiya groaned at both of them and caught up with Kunal, who continued pushing forward.

"It is pretty unfair that you're not even slightly out of

breath after making us run up that hill," she said in greeting.

"Laksh was always a bit of a whiner," Kunal shot back.

"Is this the fun Kunal?" Laksh looked skeptical. "I'm not sure I like him."

Kunal shushed him with his hands. "You're all so loud."

"Ooh, he's doing that bird thing again. See how his eyes are flashing yellow and he's cocking his head? Like a bird," Bhandu said knowingly.

Perhaps being ignored wouldn't have been so bad. Kunal growled in frustration and pointed upward.

Arpiya picked up another stone, a larger one. "It looks like Kunal was right. The size of the rubble is getting larger. We're getting closer."

They carried on, trudging up the hill to follow the small river. They crested the hill and at the center of it were the ruins of an old temple. The jungle had claimed it, devoured it, made it its own. Vines grew within its tall broken doors; trees sprouted in the middle of the old courtyards, still apparent centuries later. The air smelled damp around the temple, warm and heavy like the air after a thunderstorm.

The ruins of the temple, shards of rock and stone jutting out at odd angles, shimmered in the midday sun with a luminescence that brought to mind the Tej rain forest or the ruby-red cliffs near the Fort. This had to be it.

Kunal pushed forward.

"It's got to be at the end of the river," he said. "Let's check there first."

The others nodded. The river itself flowed into the temple and they followed it to its end, climbing over huge cut boulders and rubble, stepping carefully from tree root to root to keep their balance.

At the end of the river, tucked into the back of the now-decrepit courtyard was a towering banyan tree pulsating with a light glow. And at the base of the trunk was the symbol from the scroll, the one for light.

"This is it." Arpiya's breath caught. "It can't be a mistake that the symbol is here again."

"Split up," Kunal said. Up ahead of them, past the tree, were two dimly lit corridors that led into the ruins of the temple. "Arpiya, you're with me. Laksh and Bhandu, you're together. We'll search the left hall."

He thought they might object to his orders, but all three nodded and split up. Arpiya and Kunal tread carefully, noticing the foliage grew denser and sharper the closer they were to the temple, almost as if the ground wanted to keep them tangled there.

The light faded as they drew deeper into the temple's crumbling halls.

"Where would a lamp be kept in an ancient temple?" Arpiya said. "That's where we should start." She turned to face Kunal.

"Why are you looking at me?"

"Come on, we all know you're a teacher's pet. You were clearly the only one who listened during school lessons as a kid."

Kunal sighed. "Let me think." They crept farther into the darkness. "A conch was always blown and a lamp was lit at the beginning of old prayers to call the gods down, invite them into the house before offering them food, water, and milk. So, if I were to guess, they should both be on opposite sides of the main altar where the priests would pay their respects and perform the rituals."

"On it. Altar," Arpiya said, clapping her hands together.

The corridor they were in opened into what had once been the main hall. It towered above them, huge chunks of stone missing from the left side of the ceiling, cascading into a waterfall of stone that held up part of the room. Kunal didn't like the looks of it.

The rest of the hall was kept up by massive marble pillars, similar to those in the temple that King Mahir had taken him to in Gwali. Kunal looked for the altar, which would normally be in the northern part of the room.

"There," Arpiya whispered.

Kunal followed her lead, his eyes adjusting to the darkness. He had no idea how she was seeing so well herself, but she made a straight line for the north end of the room. A large multicolored stone mosaic stood at the front, cracked in three.

The closer they got, the more it seemed like the light was being sucked out of the room.

Something bumped into him and Kunal jumped back and drew his knife.

"Cat eyes! It's just us," Bhandu said, stepping out from

the dark. Kunal relaxed. "We looked for the lamp in the last corridor to no luck. Laksh mentioned that we might want to look for the altar."

"Right, the altar is our best bet."

Kunal and Arpiya approached the left of the altar. She reached forward, touching the stone lightly and Kunal did the same, searching for notches or anything that might indicate a hole for a lamp.

There.

Kunal felt a rough engraving under his fingers, different from the rest. He pushed at it and stepped back as the whole block of stone in front of him groaned. Arpiya scrambled back as well. A similar groan of stone resounded from their right, where Laksh and Bhandu had found the other side.

The stone opened up to reveal a small cube of dark, empty space.

"Are we supposed to reach our hands in there?" Arpiya shook her head. "Not happening."

"I'll do it." Kunal transformed his hand into a talon and reached in, ignoring the initial prickings of fear. He felt nothing at first, then, slowly, the smooth shape of something. He pulled the lamp out carefully, taking care not to bang it against the sides.

He placed the lamp in the center of his palm. It was made of ceramic and, by the sparks of light that glimmered into the dark hall, what looked like sun stone.

"We found it," Arpiya called over. "We cursed well found it."

Kunal was so glad he could kiss the ground.

He tucked the lamp into his pack, nestling it within the softness of an old uttariya.

"Let's move," he said to the others. "We've just stepped into a centuries-old temple, one that's crumbling, and I don't want to wait to see if we're to be the last ones to ever step foot in it."

Laksh looked around. "I agree. Let's get out of here and celebrate where our voices might not bring two tons of stone down on us."

They crept silently out of the main hall, away from the altar, moving as fast as they could without disturbing the ruins. Kunal came out into the old courtyard before the others, the mild sun blinding after being encased in darkness.

Kunal stopped there, listening for the others, and sagged against the sturdy marble pillar near him. A shuffling sound of feet, heavy and uncertain, came at him.

"I'm over here. If you need help or need to slow down, you can just say it," Kunal said to the others.

"Shut up, Kunal," came Laksh's voice from down the corridor.

Kunal grinned, feeling lighter than he had in days. They had found the lamp, and it was safely in their possession. Things were looking up.

A rush of relief flooded through him, stronger than he had anticipated. He hadn't realized how much all of this had been weighing on him, the ritual failing, the hunt for the artifacts.

Nearby, a flock of sunbirds landed all over the uneven stones, cawing and chirping insistently. They looked familiar. There had been so few animals on their journey here that it wasn't hard to remember. Something poked at his memory. Hadn't there been a flock of sunbirds at the supply outpost too?

Laksh soon tumbled out of the corridor, rubbing his temple and casting a dirty look toward Kunal. His lanky frame was covered in a white film of dust, and he had a small bruise on his upper arm.

The footsteps continued, even as Laksh came to a stop in front of him.

Kunal sprang to his feet just as a sword sliced through the air, exactly where he had been leaning.

It was an ambush.

CHAPTER 18

The ship Esha and the others had chartered was small and somewhat rickety, but it served their purpose. The captain had thought they were moon touched, but once he had seen the bag of gold they had to offer, he changed his mind. Still, he refused to come with them, which was fine by Esha. One less person to worry about.

The four of them crewed the boat themselves. They didn't have far to cross, but for all her adventures and all she had done so far in her short life, Esha wasn't one for boats.

She leaned over the railing of the small boat, letting the wind caress her skin and toss her hair about, and focused on the horizon. It's the only way she could deal with the toss and turn of her stomach as the boat caught the waves.

Silence hung peacefully between the four of them as they rode into the middle of the Jyos tributary, turning their boat in a direction that none of the others were going. The wind caught them and guided them along, no sign of Yavar ships on the horizon. They had arrived here first, before Yamini. A small blessing from the Moon Lord.

Alok waved a hand in the air to beckon the group over. Esha left her spot near the edge of the boat and gingerly walked over, making sure to hang on to the railing as much as she could. The boat lurched unsteadily now that they were in the center of the Jyos tributary, where the two rivers clashed and melded.

Esha chanced a glance over the railing. The green and blue streams of water mixed together in a way that was spectacular and otherworldly, a combination of the gods. Had the land been more like this before the wars the humans started?

Esha could imagine it. The sharp, bursting colors of life that had filled the land. Magic, and yet not magic at all. A gift. One humanity had treated with thoughtless abandon.

Perhaps this was a punishment they deserved. Perhaps this was the way of the gods.

Esha snapped out of her bleak thoughts. Whether humanity deserved it or not, it was her job to change things, even if they had to call down the gods themselves. She wouldn't let Yamini set the terms of the land for her people.

"Woolgathering?" Harun tapped her on her shoulder, and Esha turned.

"Can you blame me?"

"It's been a long few weeks," he said softly. He reached out an arm to her, and Esha took it gratefully. He helped her the rest of the way, allowing her to lean on him. "I forgot that our little Viper hates boats."

She glanced up, frowning. "I'm not sure I approved of this nickname."

Harun chuckled. "I like it. Makes the idea of the Viper a little less scary."

"The point is to be scary, Harun. To drive fear into the hearts of my enemies," she said fiercely. Then she leaned over the railing and hurled everything that had been in her stomach.

"Yes, yes. You still do all of that," Harun said. He had held back her hair and let it down as she straightened. He offered her his waterskin and she took it gratefully.

"Never mention that to anyone. On pain of dismemberment," Esha said, wiping her mouth.

Harun nodded solemnly. "Of course, my little Viper."

Esha made a face at him.

To their right, Alok jumped up and down. "We're here, and I see something."

They joined him, Esha glancing back nervously at Reha on the prow. How did the girl know how to ride a boat? There were depths to her that would take a while to unravel.

"Guess we didn't need my blood after all!" Reha shouted over. "But make it quick. The tide is picking up."

They leaned over the railing, and at the seam of the two rivers was a tall jagged rock at the bottom. It jutted out and would have appeared commonplace, except for the dotted stars etched around it, similar to the symbol they had seen on the map and in the temple.

"It can't be that easy," Esha said.

"How is this easy?" Alok said. "One of us will have to go get it."

Esha blanched.

"I'll go," Harun said.

Esha shook her head sharply.

"I've always been a strong swimmer," he said.

"No. Harun, you cannot—"

Harun stripped off his turban and uttariya and without a glance behind, got up on the rail and jumped into the water. Esha and Alok shouted, exchanging terrified looks.

"I cannot go back and tell the king that I lost his only son and heir to a river!" Alok said frantically. "And Farhan! He would never forgive me!"

"What are you talking about? King Mahir will have *my* head," Esha said.

"You're both overreacting," Reha said from behind. "It looks like my brother is doing quite well."

Alok and Esha both looked over. Harun was swimming against the current, his strong body carving through the water with powerful movements. He *was* a good swimmer.

Harun reached the rock. "What now?" he yelled at them.

"Perhaps we should've discussed that before you jumped in the water!" Esha yelled back.

Harun only grinned back at them, one precarious arm wrapped around the rock.

"Try your blood," she said.

"Or a truth," Alok said.

"How in the Sun Maiden's name does one offer a truth?" Reha muttered from behind them.

Harun tried cutting his forearm on the rock first.

Nothing happened.

When it stayed the same after a few minutes, he leaned forward, looked around uncertainly, and whispered something into the center of the symbol on the rock.

Within seconds, the rock began to glow and shake, almost tossing Harun off. Esha let out a scream and rushed to the edge of the deck.

The water rose up and crashed down with terrifying speed. Esha tried to count out the rhythm—something—but it kept changing.

She tried to reach back for a rope, but Alok caught her.

"Oh, no you don't. Kunal would murder me if anything happened to you."

"I have to get to him," she said frantically. "The water—it's—"

"Esha, you can't help him. I know you want to tie yourself to the prow with the rope and jump in, but the water will hold you back."

Esha stopped in her tracks. "How did you know that?"

"It's what Kunal would've done," was all Alok said.

The mention of the soldier made her start moving again, faster and more frantic.

Esha lunged forward to the end of the deck, fighting against the wind gales from the water. The waves began to rise higher the closer she got, whirring into a deafening din of wind and water.

"Esha, wait! Look at what it's doing right now!" Alok yelled.

The water began to split around the rock, creating a small perch for Harun to stand on.

Esha took a step back, and Alok grabbed her by the arm, pulling her safely away from the edge of the ship.

Harun took an uncertain step before rising to his feet and reaching over onto the rock. He traced the symbol with his finger and stared at it a second before giving it a push. The rock vibrated and the central part of it broke free, show-casing a small wooden box that had been hidden. And in it was an ivory conch, shining and glowing as if it was the moon itself.

He reached in and wrapped his hands around the conch.

Esha ran over to Reha. "Pull us closer."

"I can't get that much closer," she said. "I'm already struggling to keep us steady."

"We need to get closer," Esha said. "Because once that water comes rushing back in . . ."

Reha tensed in understanding. "I need you to go to the sail. Pull it as taut as you can."

Esha ran over and, with the help of Alok, pulled the sail tight. The ship careened to the left, pushing them into the currents around the rock.

Harun's hands were still wrapped around the conch, but he hadn't removed it from the case yet.

"Don't!" Esha yelled. Harun tensed but stopped.

The ship pulled even closer.

Just another minute. And then . . .

"Now!"

Harun pulled the conch away and dove away from the water, close to the ship. Esha lowered a rope into the water. Harun was swimming closer, but the waves that had parted for him were now building into a small tsunami behind him.

He only needed to grab ahold of the rope.

Esha let the rope down farther, trying to guide it into the direction Harun was swimming. He was so close.

Harun reached out—and missed. Esha cursed, promising herself that she'd kill him herself if he didn't make it onto the boat.

Esha slackened and tossed the rope once more, and this time, Harun grabbed the end of it. He tugged on it, and Esha almost rammed into the railing of the ship, holding as tight as she could.

Her muscles ached with the strain, and her face was lashed by the salty sea spray, but she gritted her teeth and held steady. The river would not claim him.

Alok rushed over and helped her hold the rope tight as Harun climbed up it and Reha navigated them out of the way of the mini tsunami.

"Hold on," Reha said.

Harun crashed onto the deck, helped over by Alok. Esha fell into a heap beside him, both of them lying faceup and panting on the ship deck. Water streamed off them, seeping into everything nearby.

"Now that you're safe I can tell you in no uncertain terms that if you ever try anything like that again"—she coughed violently—"I will murder you."

"Don't. Worry." He sounded worse. "I think that was enough adventure for another few months."

"Esha's right," Reha said, collapsing back as she let go of the wheel. It stayed steady. "If you do that again, brother, I will help her murder you. You don't get to die before telling me that story you promised. You know, the one about how you escaped from that mob of monkeys near that temple. We had a deal."

Harun kept coughing, but he also hid a smile that Esha didn't miss.

CHAPTER 19

Kunal leaped backward, dodging the next swipe of his attacker's blade. To the left, Laksh dealt with his own assailant, his double swords out and swinging wildly. Sounds of fighting and a yelp came from farther down the corridor, where Bhandu and Arpiya had been moments before.

Kunal ducked the blade again. The floor of the temple ruins was rocky and strewn with roots, rife for him to trip over at any moment. He needed to go on the offensive.

But the knife at his hip would be no match for the heavy sword being thrust at him. Kunal leaped and rammed into the Yavar man, who hadn't stopped for even a second.

His attacks were relentless, and Kunal had to finally roll away to escape him. He unleashed his talons and slashed at his attacker's face. The man cried out and dropped to his knees.

Bhandu and Arpiya were facing off with their own

attackers, both Yavar by the looks of their furs and the method of their attacks: quick, darting blows that barely allowed their opponents a chance to respond, let alone recover.

Laksh was battling off two Yavar in the corner. Kunal hefted a block of stone and threw it at one of them. It crumbled on top of his head, crushing him below. Laksh took advantage of the moment to stab one of his swords into the side of the other Yavar, a tall woman. She went down with a furious yelp.

"That is an enviable power," he said with ragged breaths, looking down at Kunal's rock-dust-covered hands.

Bhandu and Arpiya had forced their two attackers to the edge of the uneven terrain, where the rocks dropped off a steep cliff. Arpiya sent one Yavar flying over the rocks. Bhandu caught his attacker and gave Arpiya a questioning look. She shrugged. Bhandu nodded and threw his attacker over too.

They ran over to Kunal and Laksh, temple dust mixing with sweat on their faces, and formed a tight semicircle.

"We should've expected it." Arpiya shook her head, looking out to the jungle in front of them. "I knew it was too easy."

Two of the attackers got back to their feet and shouts filled the air. Five more Yavar ran into the temple's broken courtyard.

"Spoken too soon," Kunal said.

Three more Yavar came from behind, and Kunal whirled around, his talons out, his knife clasped in one hand.

"An ambush would mean we had been waiting in hiding for you," a voice said. Yamini walked in front of the row of Yavar, a splendid silver fur across her shoulders. "You led us here."

"Popping out of the forest to attack us is about the same thing, Lady Yamini," Arpiya said.

"It worked, didn't it?" Yamini shrugged, twirling the spear in her hand. "We've been tracking you since you entered the jungle. Earlier in fact." Yamini glanced over at the flock of sunbirds, which were flying toward her and the little piece of cloth she had in her hand. She threw the cloth a few paces away and the sunbirds rushed to the spot.

"Ostra oil," Kunal said sharply. "How? When did you get it on me?" He knew he had seen those sunbirds before.

"Your scabbard." Yamini smiled. "The temple."

Kunal swore. He should've remembered that the Yavar used tricks in their warfare, like this oil that helped them track whoever they wanted. It had started as a way to keep track of their horses before there were fences, but it was widely used by some of the clans now to monitor their army's movements.

"Do you think we didn't know you'd be looking as well?" she said. "Especially after you took the bait and took your prince back?"

"A poor bait if we got what we wanted and you didn't," Arpiya said. She stood tall, inching away from the nearest Yavar and her spear.

"You have no understanding of what we want. The

prince was simply a tool, but we had no need for him anymore once we found your lovely princess." Yamini faced Kunal and held out a hand. "If you give the lamp to me now, I'll leave your friends alive."

"We've found nothing," Arpiya said, stepping in front of him. Her voice grew hot and fiery. "And it's not as if we'd give you anything even if we did. You'll bring chaos to this land, killing hundreds, thousands. Our lives are nothing compared to that."

"So you do have it," Yamini said, her face melting into a pleased expression. "Relieve them of the lamp."

One of the Yavar jumped forward and rammed into Kunal, knocking his pack to the ground. The lamp tumbled out.

"No!"

Kunal wasn't sure whose voice that was—all of them lunged forward at the same time, trying to prevent the inevitable. A wiry Yavar man got to the lamp first and swiped it into his hands.

Kunal rushed forward, but two Yavar blocked off his exit with spears pointed at his throat. He backed off, as did the others.

"Smart choice, Kunal," Yamini said, backing away.

One of the Yavar tripped as they walked, stumbling backward and dropping his spear.

Kunal took that tiny window of opportunity to shift, unfurling wings so large they could eclipse two men. He knocked down two Yavar and flew into two others, jamming them into the nearest tree until he heard a crunch.

He wouldn't leave here without the lamp.

Yamini's face froze, her eyes growing wide as Kunal turned and set upon her. Two Yavar jumped in and pulled her out of his range.

Arpiya slammed the hilt of her knife into one Yavar's head and hitched the soldier over her hip. The Yavar fell in a sprawl and then crawled back, getting to her feet and running away. Two others weren't so lucky and didn't catch their lady's retreat. Laksh ended one swiftly with a slash to the throat; Bhandu stabbed the other.

Kunal's eyes were on the retreating form of Yamini. He was about to run after her when a scream rent the air. Laksh and Bhandu were backed into the wall by the Yavar, in dire need of backup if the fresh wound in Bhandu's arm was indication.

But Yamini was disappearing into the jungle, with one of their only hopes at salvation.

Another choice.

Another decision.

"Kunal! Go after her." He heard Laksh's voice, but it sounded like an echo in his ears, a hazy memory. He should go, chase after Yamini, but his body didn't seem willing to move with him.

What if this was the wrong choice, like he had made before?

Was he even capable of making the right choice?

It was the split second she needed to make her escape. Thankfully, Arpiya didn't hesitate. She sprinted after Yamini and the lamp, a look of fierce determination on her face.

Kunal finally woke from his stupor and rushed after them, putting every bit of his strength into the chase, lifting off and soaring into the air. He quickly caught up with Arpiya, who was grappling with Yamini on the ground.

They were evenly matched. Yamini had her elbow at Arpiya's throat. But Arpiya had a knife at Yamini's side. She dug it in without hesitation, with precision.

The lamp dropped out of Yamini's hand as she twisted and yelped in pain. Kunal sped to catch the lamp, snatching it from the ground. Yamini snarled at the both of them before sprinting away, having realized she was outnumbered.

Kunal tried to run after her but a deep groan from Arpiya stopped him. And they had the lamp. Yamini would have to wait.

"She's gone," Arpiya said, panting. It was only then that Kunal noticed that she was injured as well. Arpiya held her left shoulder, stanching a wound with her palm.

"It doesn't matter. We have the lamp, thanks to you."

"My pleasure," she said, trying to salute but wincing instead.

"Let's get out of here," he said. "Bhandu's hurt."

Kunal glanced back before they left.

The space where Yamini had been was deserted, only a trail of blood left.

———— ◄◊► ————

They arrived back at the jungle at the base of the mountains, making camp as soon as they could.

Everyone's spirits were high, and no one mentioned the way Kunal had frozen, only the bravery that Arpiya had shown. Laksh had wanted Kunal to tell the story of Arpiya stabbing Yamini one too many times for Kunal's comfort.

But Kunal was in a good mood, and even went along with one of Laksh's jokes. No one had quite known what to do after that. Bhandu was in a corner under a copse of trees, fast asleep, his wound patched up. He had been pretty happy at the possibility of adding another scar to his collection. Laksh and Arpiya had drifted off to sleep, far too close together for Kunal's taste, but he let it go.

Kunal tried to sleep, but it evaded him. He decided to take a patrol, though with his hearing and the traps they'd set up, no one really had to take patrols regularly. But a restless energy pursued him.

He cut through the thick jungle. The maze calmed him, forced him to focus on only what was in front of him. It was so different from his first time in a jungle, back in the Tej rain forest. Then he hadn't known of his powers or heritage, had merely been trying to fulfill a mission, honor his uncle.

How much had changed since then.

A noise sounded in the brush, steps away from him.

"Who is it?" Kunal asked.

A figure, draped in furs, walked into the light. Yamini.

Kunal instantly went on guard to attack. He rushed at her, but she neatly dodged and knocked him down with the flat of her spearhead, the tip slicing into the skin of his arm. Pain seared through Kunal, bursting across his vision like a blue haze.

He tried to get to his knees, but his body wasn't listening anymore.

"Hello, Kunal," she said, looming over him. He dragged out his sword and held it threateningly in front of him. Yamini didn't step closer than a few paces.

"What do you want?" he said. His lungs felt on fire. "And what in the Sun Maiden's name did you do to me?"

Yamini stepped forward, tilting her head in question. "What do you mean? Oh, I found a way to embed blue sapphires into my spear. A sound measure, it seems."

"If you were looking for another bargaining chip, I will be useless," he said, gritting his teeth as he rose to his feet. He stayed out of range of her spear. "They won't trade for me. There will be no rescue."

"I doubt that." She looked past him, into the dark jungle behind him. "But I'm not looking for a bargaining chip. I wanted to talk." Yamini held her arms wide open, sweeping her arm across. "And I'm alone. No tricks. Not this time."

Kunal didn't ease his posture, keeping his sword where it was. Instead of lowering it, he raised it to her throat. "Then talk. But know that if you're looking to find the rest of them, I won't lead you there."

Yamini blinked. "Ever the consummate soldier. I see why Esha liked you."

Now it was Kunal's turn to blink rapidly.

"Kunal, you're a soldier. A practical man, even if you're a royal. I've heard reports of what the past ten years in Jansa have been like. Harsh for the common folk, especially those in rural areas. The land has become unforgiving due to an ambitious king—"

"—who you helped—"

"—and a relentless, ancient bond that in all honesty is more like shackles. Demanding blood from the two most arcane and depleted houses? The entire land depended on the royals to flourish, and so did the people. Don't you think that's a bit unfair?"

"Yes," Kunal said. Yamini's brows rose in surprise at his agreement. "I do think it's unfair. To both sides. But do you know why it happened? The people once had a direct bond with the land but were poor stewards. The gods almost took away our connection to the land, but the ancient royals stepped up and took the burden of the knowledge and the magic to ensure the land for all of the people."

Kunal caught Yamini's surprise. She hadn't heard the full story before.

"Perhaps that is true, but that's more reason that the old bond should be broken," she said.

"That could be a catastrophe for all of us. Look at what happened when we failed to renew the bond. Chaos for all of Jansa. We're in uncharted territory."

"Uncharted territory could mean a new start," she said. "You of all people should want that. It's clear you care about your country. And the deal that the ancient royals made may have worked back then, but it doesn't work now. You know what the Yavar speak of? A horrible choice that was once forced on Vasu the Wanderer. He betrayed his truest friends, Naran and Naria, and was banished to walk the land for eons as punishment. Our lives are not punishment. The Yavar *have* thrived. But I want more for my people. I want a new world order, not one determined by people centuries ago.

"I want us to start again. All of us as equals."

The idea rang true to Kunal, to the part of him that had always felt unmoored by the current status quo. He didn't know what horrible choice Vasu the Wanderer had to make, but Kunal understood the pain, the agony, of doing what one thought was right. Even now, he wondered if he had made the right choice by leaving behind his newfound friends before.

He and Reha had failed, but did that make him more wrong to have chosen so? He knew that the success of the mission wasn't what had turned Esha from him. It was his choice.

And he didn't know if he would've made a different one.

"Equals? How could we trust that?"

"The way a soldier trusted a rebel," Yamini said.

Kunal shifted in place, tightening his grip on his sword. "It would be chaos," he said.

"Is that such a bad thing? A new world order demands change."

"I agree that the curse on your people is not fair," Kunal said. "Generations shouldn't have to pay for the misdeeds of a few. But the gods are not meant to be kind. They are all knowing."

"We are meant to shape our own destinies. Think on it, Kunal. There's a chance for a new world," Yamini said. "That's all I want—not power or glory or an empire. Just a chance."

A noise startled them both, and Kunal whipped toward it. By the time he turned back around, Yamini had faded into the night.

CHAPTER 20

Kunal took a deep breath before pushing open the door to the meeting room. They had returned to the palace a few days ago. Everything had gone well on their mission, and yet, he was nervous to be back. It had all felt so simple when he was searching for the lamp, but now he had to face the decisions he had made.

He inched the door open, trying not to make any noise. Only Esha and Arpiya were in the room, both of their heads bent low as they chatted. Esha let out a laugh and Kunal almost smiled. She was radiant.

He didn't know when he'd be able to get her to smile like that again, if ever.

Kunal had noticed a slight softening of her position toward him. Esha glanced at him now and again, when she thought he wasn't looking. He felt torn between remorse and a hot rush of indignation at her. It was cursed unfair that he was left here worrying about their every interaction, pretending and failing at not caring. He noticed the very way she breathed.

Kunal frowned, feeling the edges of it carve into his cheeks. Maybe he had been too hasty to push her away, but his pride held him back. She had been the one to withdraw her hand first, to judge and accuse.

"Brooding again, are you?" Alok said, coming up behind him. He clasped Kunal on the shoulder.

"Again?"

"You've been doing more of it recently." Alok looked pointedly at Esha. "I think I might know why. Give it time."

"That's what everyone's saying." Kunal let out a small growl of frustration.

"Then everyone's right."

"You don't know her like I do. She doesn't take to forgiveness easily."

"Then maybe you shouldn't have done something to forgive?" Alok's friendly gaze showed a flash of something steelier.

"Not you too," Kunal said. "I know. I get it. I've heard it every single way from almost every single person in this room. I didn't murder anyone." Kunal's voice rose, and Alok had to shush him, dragging him into a corner of the room.

"Harun was captured," Alok said in a low tone.

"I didn't know! And I've made up for it since. Did we not bring back the lamp?"

Alok sighed. "Emotions don't work like that. That's why I said to give it time."

Kunal growled. "I'm sick to death of that. Bhandu has moved on. Arpiya is fine. It's only her. And she acts as if she had no part in it. She's being so . . . stubborn."

"Oh yes. Stubborn. Esha is the stubborn one. Of course," Alok said.

"I can't grovel forever," Kunal said, voicing a thought that had been becoming stronger.

"Can't or won't?"

"She's being unreasonable."

"She's hurt."

"Well, that makes two of us!" Kunal said with more force than he intended. Alok merely blinked at him. Kunal could've sworn he was trying to hide a smile, or a sigh. "It . . . doesn't feel good that she immediately assumed the worst of me. That even now she won't even try to hear me out. How do you build a future off that?"

This time Alok did sigh. He patted him on the shoulder. "Everyone has been on edge for so long, and now with the threat from Yamini . . ."

Kunal groaned. "Speaking of Yamini, we need to act quickly. We have a lot to discuss."

He motioned for Alok to shut the door just as Bhandu and Aahal walked through it, resulting in a loud bang and a yelp from Bhandu.

Esha's head shot up in alarm before she sighed and got

to her feet. It was hard to tell if she'd noticed Kunal. He'd come to expect some sort of reaction, even if it was simply her ignoring him as best as she could.

"Are you all right, Bhandu?" she asked.

"Yes," Bhandu grumbled back, shooting a dirty look at Alok. His wound had healed up nicely, though Bhandu still winced a little as he moved his arm.

Alok whispered, "Sorry," and put his hands up, backing away from the door and the angry young man rubbing his shoulder. They began to bicker, with Aahal and Arpiya taking sides and adding commentary.

"Are you going to stand in that corner all evening, soldier? Come into the light," Esha said. She stood near a tall chair, next to the window.

Kunal started. She had noticed him. He smiled before he could help it and quickly worked to change it into a frown. Esha didn't miss a beat, though.

"I'm not sure a smile is warranted, soldier," Esha said softly. She didn't walk away as he approached this time, even though Bhandu, Alok, and Arpiya were fighting still. That meant the two of them alone.

That tiny ember of hope sparked, as it always did.

"You came back, though, which is an improvement," she said. "You did well with finding and retrieving the lamp. It all went rather well, I hear, despite the ambush. Though . . . I also heard that we might have had a chance to capture Yamini. Arpiya had to run after her. You'd think, with your wings and all those powers, you might've gotten there before her."

Kunal looked at her in question before realizing. "Bhandu already sent you a full report, did he?"

"I heard you hesitated. Are you reconsidering working with us, soldier?" Esha asked lightly. Still, Kunal didn't miss the steel edge to her question.

Had he? Hesitated?

"No, I'm not, Viper," he said. "And I didn't hesitate."

And if he had, could he be faulted? For the longest time all he wanted to do was follow his duty, and when he had discovered how much wrong he had allowed in the name of that duty, he had committed himself to doing better. Doing whatever it took. But even that had been the wrong choice, and now it seemed as if, no matter what Kunal did, he'd never be able to right the wrongs in his past. That he was doomed to keep making mistakes.

He kept trying and he kept failing.

So what if he had hesitated? His indignation rose, comforting and welcome, to mask the shame under his skin. It was clear he couldn't rely on his instincts.

"You hesitated," she stated flatly.

Kunal jerked away from her. "You can stop your insinuation that it's because I've made a new alliance. I haven't." Kunal swallowed roughly. "I was trying not to be rash. My team was there, and I couldn't make the decision for them."

Esha walked around the chair till she faced him,

searching for something in his expression. Her tone softened. "I see. So you're saying you didn't act and you let Arpiya run after Yamini. For your team?"

"They were outnumbered. I heard Bhandu scream," he said. Kunal hoped Esha hadn't heard the waver in his voice, the uncertainty that sat below. "And I did catch up to Arpiya and Yamini, once I made sure the others would be all right."

Esha raised an eyebrow. "Fair point. Are you really telling me you hesitated for your team? The team full of highly trained and capable warriors? For Bhandu, who treats wounds like things to collect? And you're saying it had nothing to do with your own fear?"

"What?"

She tilted her head up. "You heard me, soldier."

"Kunal."

Esha shrugged.

"I don't have time to do this. Believe whatever you want about me, Esha. You always do."

"You're deflecting," Esha said, though she flinched.

"And why do you even care?" Kunal said, his words clipped. Something rose in this throat, that pressure he had felt near the temple when he had paused and watched Yamini disappear. It felt like it would drown him under its weight. It whispered of all the things he might do wrong, had done wrong.

He didn't want to talk about this.

Esha came closer, close enough that the scent of night rose washed over him, memories close behind. It only added to the suffocating feeling he felt. There was another weight he didn't know if he could ever escape from.

"It's okay to be scared," she said. Her tone was softer, kinder, than he had heard in weeks. "It happens to everyone."

Kunal looked up, and Esha's gaze was resting on him, her head tilted to the side and her lips pursed in . . . what? Concern?

It punctured the suffocating bubble around him, and instantly the air between them changed.

Thrummed.

———◦———

Esha noticed the change in Kunal almost immediately. He had seemed burdened before, trapped, even. And then his eyes flickered to hers and that spark between them—the cursed annoying feeling that would never go away—returned. And now he was looking at her like he had once, raw and vulnerable . . . and all too much.

"Esha, I—" he started.

She cut him off quickly, her heartbeat racing. "I just want to make sure hesitating doesn't become a standard practice for you." Esha kept her tone as formal as possible.

"It won't," he said, matching her tone. "It didn't." Kunal's cheeks flushed, and he crossed his arms. "Anyway, that's rich coming from you."

"Me?"

His face grew stony, his gaze sharp and pointed in a way she hadn't been expecting. Like he saw her, all of her, and she was left wanting.

"You're scared too," he accused.

Esha laughed at that, mostly because she didn't know how else to respond. Of course the minute there was a return of their old relationship, she had run away. She couldn't trust in that. Better to keep the distance, be safe rather than burned again. But Esha couldn't deny that she felt a pang of loss when his tone had turned to anger.

"Of course. I'm scared of us never getting the ritual done properly. I'm scared that Reha will leave this country with no real leader and a power vacuum for moons or even years. I'm scared Vardaan will find his way back."

"Not just that," Kunal said. "You're afraid you might actually forgive me, see things from another perspective. You're afraid you won't be able to use your anger as a shield anymore. That you might get hurt. Well, Viper, we all have scars. We all have wounds, hidden ones, open ones, but you don't see us hiding from the world."

He was wrong.

A smaller part of her whispered of how right he might be. Fear was a living thing, shifting and changing to fit its host.

"Is that what you think this is? You think I'm afraid to forgive you?" She laughed. "No, I'd love to. I can't."

"That's your choice."

"You're saying it's my choice? Certainly not what you said on the night of the Winner's Ball."

Kunal hesitated at that.

"Don't stop, soldier. This is the most honest you've been with me in a while. Why do you even care if I'm this person you've depicted? Afraid. Weak." She heard her tone sharpening, looking for a victim.

"I never said you were weak." Kunal shook his head. "Being afraid doesn't make you weak. Courage isn't the absence of fear. And you, Esha, are one of the bravest people I've known."

That stopped Esha cold. She hated it when he did that, held her close with his words, saw through the veils and masks she donned.

How did one even respond to that?

"Which is why I know you're scared, and no one else will tell you." Kunal stepped in, so close she could feel the rough texture of his uttariya against her skin. "But I have nothing to lose. We're nothing to each other, right?"

The latent fury in his words nearly took her breath away. She wanted to say she hadn't expected this, but it would be a lie. Kunal and she were more similar than she cared to admit. Pushed too far, even Kunal wouldn't back away.

Esha coughed. "I'm not— You . . ."

Kunal cocked his head in a very Viper-like manner. "You? You're not the only one with something to forgive, Esha."

The sound of clapping broke through the cocoon of their conversation, and Esha immediately stepped away, looking toward the noise.

Alok was clapping his hands and doubled over in

laughter, a pleased-looking Bhandu next to him. Aahal stood to the side, shaking his head as he covered his face with a hand. He brightened as he caught Esha's gaze.

"Can we get started?" Aahal said. "I've had about enough of these two."

Esha cleared her throat. "Of course. We'll be traveling to Mount Bangaar together, as a team, to try the ritual with the artifacts. Here are the assignments. . . ."

Esha didn't glance back at Kunal as she took her place at the head of the table. It wouldn't matter. It wasn't like she ever forgot where he was in a room and now, more than ever, the distance would be good.

And if Esha kept telling herself that she might actually believe it.

CHAPTER 21

Esha rode with Harun to Mount Bangaar with as much haste as possible. The artifacts were securely in their possession, and for the first time in weeks, she felt a sense of relief. They were one step closer to finishing this, for good.

Esha had become more accustomed to travel by lion than she was happy to admit, and felt a a pang of loss as they stopped on a cliff near the top of Mount Bangaar two days later. If only she had been gifted with such powers. Though Esha wasn't sure she'd ever want to be royal, having seen enough of Harun's struggles over the year, she thought she would have been a fearsome creature if she had been able to shift.

Arpiya and the others were waiting for them. Kunal and Reha had flown the rest of the team to this meeting point and they would go up the rest of the way together. The Blue Squad had been stationed nearby at the base of the mountain for backup.

Harun tilted his head upward. "The others are here. Bhandu's got a very distinct tread."

"Early," Esha noted, though she wasn't displeased. Always good to know her team still ran well without her. They climbed the final rocks and emerged on the top of a huge flat cliff, almost one hundred paces long and wide.

Harun appeared next to her, holding out a hand to help her jump over a slew of slippery rocks. Esha turned her head toward the towering mountain in front of them and leaned back, trying to take in its majesty. This was Mount Bangaar, home to the Golden Mist and spirits and gods of yore.

Their potential salvation.

◄O►

From his memory Kunal led the group through the pathway. His last trip up here was imprinted into his mind, whether he liked it or not.

They had intercepted the others—Reha, Laksh, and Aahal—farther down, and he could hear them whining behind him. It mostly came from Reha, who was not happy to be here and was shifting violently again. Esha was doing her best to distract her, but it was really Harun who was helping his little sister ease through the transitions—while also keeping her in a good mood. A difficult feat, which he knew personally.

He glanced back at Esha, and she quickly looked away.

"You know, it's funny." Laksh drew up next to Kunal so

that they were shoulder to shoulder. Kunal glanced at him and sighed. He was too tired not to take the bait, and he could do with a distraction.

"What is, Laksh?"

"I was just thinking about how you ran off here without telling anyone and how it led to so much chaos," he said simply, as if discussing a lovely morning.

"I thought it was the right thing to do," Kunal said again, for what felt like the hundredth time.

"Oh, I don't care," Laksh said. Kunal knew Laksh did care; otherwise he wouldn't be here, badgering him. "But it is interesting. You were so rigid in your hatred of me. Your dismissal of me. Dishonorable, disloyal, blah, blah. It's not all so simple now, is it?"

"I never hated you," Kunal said quietly.

Laksh cocked his head. "No? It seemed like hatred."

"I never could've hated you. I loved you as my own brother, Laksh. I was hurt. Deeply hurt and betrayed. But hate?" Kunal shook his head.

"Is that your way of telling me that there might still be a chance for us to"—Laksh paused— "once again be friends?"

Kunal turned to face his old friend. "You can only feel betrayal if you once cared deeply. There will always be a chance, Laksh. Perhaps we can do it right this time. No secrets."

Laksh shifted and looked away, but Kunal saw the flash of a smile. When Laksh turned back, his face was neutral. "I would like that. Seems a bit of a waste to toss years away."

"If only that was how everyone felt," Kunal said before he could stop himself.

Laksh's expression softened, and he put a hand on Kunal's shoulder. The touch felt comforting, and he realized how keenly he missed the way Esha would hold his hand, like it was hers to protect and care for. "Like you said, there can only be hurt and betrayal if there was feeling before. Don't lose hope."

Kunal nodded tightly, clasping his old friend on the shoulder.

He didn't know how to tell him that he wasn't sure if there was anything left between him and Esha, if he wanted it anymore.

But right here, right now, he was glad to put a small piece of his past back into place.

———◄◊►———

The temple entrance was unassuming, a pile of moss-covered stones stacked in uneven heaps, unusual for this high in the mountains. There were no signs or sounds of wildlife up here, only the soft rush of a river. Esha picked her way through the small opening to the cave below, stepping as carefully as she could.

Inside the cave's mouth were hidden heights. The outline of a stone temple flickered in the shadows. Esha stepped closer. The temple of the ritual was carved directly into the mountain, an incredible feat of mastery. It was streaked with gold, glinting in the twinkling, dimmed light of the glowing river inside.

Esha kept hopping and tripped on one of the rocks. An arm encircled her waist and pulled her back quickly into a hard chest. She glanced up.

"Saving me, are you?"

Harun grinned. "We have to change roles sometimes, don't we?"

Esha chuckled, turning in his arms and pulling away.

Reha was ahead of them, hopping along the terrain with those goat hooves of hers.

It had been unusual to see at first, but Esha had quickly seen the advantages of having Reha's powers. Though with two royals, Esha was now the slowest one in their group, which she was not happy about. She patted her back again, ensuring the artifacts were there.

There was a huge crack in the stone ahead of them, and Harun jumped ahead, landing nimbly on the ground below and offering a hand to her. He had taken to this mission, and though she had checked for every sign of continued blue-sapphire poisoning, he was recovering well. He still stumbled, but something about the fresh air here seemed to be renewing him.

Or perhaps it was all the magic. The temple teemed with it, and yet Esha could imagine a time when the magic had been even more vibrant.

They gathered together at the bottom of the temple, near where the river carved through it. Kunal, Bhandu, and Laksh stood on one side of the river and Esha, Harun, and Reha were on the other.

Esha took out the lamp as Harun took out the conch. They moved the artifacts closer to the river, waiting for the glow of the water to shine within the artifacts as well.

Reha ventured forward. "The conch to awaken the gods. The lamp to illuminate the dark."

Esha's eyes were drawn to the fading sun. "We don't have much time," she said.

Harun nodded and motioned at Reha to follow him. They walked into the water together and began the ritual, cleansing themselves and starting the chant. Reha followed in the chant a second behind Harun, but he waited patiently for her as he finished each stanza and step. Kunal watched them both with interest, and Esha realized that he had never seen it properly done.

Neither had Esha. It felt like a secret, one not for their eyes. An ancient tradition beyond any of them.

Esha took it all in with hunger, the beauty of the movements and the rhythmic intonation of the chants. Harun and Reha, brother and sister, united in their purpose.

At the end they cut their palms and offered up their blood into the river. It splashed into the blue waters, sparking and turning a deep vibrant gold.

A bubble of elation rose in Esha's throat. They had done it.

Through moons of searching and fighting and loss, they had finally found a way to save the land and rebuild it. She could fight a thousand battles if she knew the people of the Southern Lands would have food in their bellies and water to nourish them. That their spirits would remain whole.

Jubilation rushed through Esha, threatening to overtake her.

But the cave wasn't done with them yet.

The floor began to rock, and a steady thrumming resounded across the stone walls of the cave temple, rising to a high, keening pitch. The earth itself began to hum, and Esha stepped back in alarm.

The others looked around for the source of the sudden commotion. Esha pointed to the top of the river, which originated from a huge obsidian stone in the center of the temple. It had stopped glowing and was slowly splitting down the middle.

Moon Lord's fists.

She broke into a run and yelled at the others to follow. Bhandu had already begun to mobilize.

Esha narrowly missed a huge stalactite as she dove toward the river, grabbing for Harun and Reha. She splashed through the water and pushed them both down just as a rock crashed to the ground. Reha struggled under her grip until Esha realized she wasn't struggling but shifting.

She burst out of the water as a gorilla, holding both Harun and Esha in her arms. Reha threw them onto the left bank of the river right as stones came crashing down where Esha had been.

"Go, get Harun out of here!" Esha yelled at Reha and Arpiya. Harun was coughing, looking around for her, but she pushed him forward. He stumbled but got to his feet.

Bhandu rushed back to help her, but she waved him

away, pointing ahead. "Make sure we have a path out of here. I'll get everyone," she ordered. He looked unhappy but nodded.

"If you're not outside in two minutes—"

"Bhandu, go!"

A bellow shot through the open cave, crashing out into the air beyond like a conch had been blown within the cave. All Esha could hear was silence—and below that, the steady thrum of her heart.

She rose unsteadily, brushing off the dust and crumbling rock that covered her body in gray.

The artifacts.

Esha ran for the spot on the left bank with the two artifacts. The stone was cracked in a circle around them, like someone had taken a sword to it. The artifacts themselves were whole. She was about to grab them when a hand shot out and held her back.

Esha whipped around and faced a dusty Kunal, blood streaking down one side of his face. She reached forward instinctively to check for a head wound.

He brushed his fingers against hers. "A flesh wound, no more. Wait," he said, holding her arm.

The ground shook between them, slivers of stone falling to the ground all around them.

"Leave them. The ritual's not complete."

"Not complete? It didn't work," Esha said. "We have to escape."

Kunal shook his head, his face insistent. "No, it's just not done. It can't be done." He didn't move, keeping his body in between her and the artifacts.

What was he doing? Had he lost his mind?

This was not the time for theatrics or hero antics, not when their lives were at stake.

"We have to leave, soldier."

"I can't," he said, shaking his head. "I'll finish this out and then I'll shift and catch up."

He almost seemed to believe that was possible, despite the entire temple crumbling around them. There was no time for this discussion.

"We can leave with or without the artifacts, but I'm definitely not leaving without you," she said with finality.

And she realized she meant it. No matter what had happened between them, she didn't want to see Kunal dead.

"The ritual didn't work," she said, pointing at the fissures in the rock below. "The cave is about to collapse; the temple has already fallen."

She didn't want it to be true either. She didn't want to see all of their work engulfed in stone and dust. But something had gone terribly, terribly wrong.

Bhandu had snuck back and was moving toward the artifacts, signaling to her. She wanted to leave the cursed things behind, but they needed them. Esha grabbed Kunal's hands and yanked him forward with all her might, drawing his attention away.

"Kunal." He looked at her, a look of utter defeat written across his face with a deep rawness.

He never was good at hiding his emotions.

Those emotions would get him killed if he didn't move in that instant. Esha knew it with a certainty that made her bones ache. If she left right now, he'd die, standing right here.

Esha did something stupid then. She reached up and kissed him, pulling him to her in all the rubble and ruin. It broke whatever spell he was under. He gave her fire back to her in their kiss and a feral life came back to his eyes.

At first it had been to give Bhandu time to grab the artifacts, but the connection between them sputtered and sparked to life, as demanding as ever. Esha let herself fall into him.

Suddenly, wings engulfed her as the temple ceiling fell around them. But the stone didn't hit them. Instead, Kunal and Esha flew out a narrow hole in the stone ceiling just as the temple fell in on itself and crumbled into a pile of rubble.

They hit the ground and rolled down the hill, only coming to a stop when the ground flattened. Esha struggled to her elbows, dragging herself as up as she could, searching for her team.

They were scattered across the mountain base. She did a quick count and breathed a sigh of relief. Everyone was accounted for, including Bhandu. She wouldn't be losing anyone today.

Esha let herself fall back, breathing heavily as she lay on the dirt.

There was an intense pounding in her head, filling her to the brim with a sensation she had felt in only one place before: the Tej rain forest, the most magical in the Southern Lands.

It was only then that she noticed the land was different.

What was once brown sand was now a vibrant green, mixed in with moist dirt. And the air. It was how a rain forest was supposed to smell: vibrant, dewy, alive.

The last thing she saw before she passed out was in the far distance.

A spot of blue and the roar of rapids coming to life.

The river.

Magic had returned to the land.

CHAPTER 22

Kunal still couldn't believe it, even days later.

The worst had happened. The bond was broken, shattered beyond repair. Reha's blood had failed, as had their second chance, the artifacts. Every option they had tried had led them here, to the *janma* bond broken.

And yet, catastrophe hadn't yet arrived. He had fought to go back and try again, had demanded they finish the ritual, but that was before they all realized the truth. They hadn't saved the bond.

Worse, they had gone ahead and broken the bond for Yamini.

The crumbling of the temple should've told them everything they needed to know about the state of the bond, but it wasn't until they had gotten to the bottom of the mountain that the three royals had been able to confirm it. Magic was rampant in the world again and it felt like a tilting seesaw, unbalanced and dangerous.

It was a feeling deep in his bones. He knew the prince felt it, too, the chaotic instability in this new world. Already they had gotten word from hawks about the dangerous shift of the land. It was green again, but the magic threatened to overflow. Another earthquake had struck, close to the western border. Without the bond, the magic had no tether, no balance.

And yet, it was beautiful.

The landscape as they traveled back was vastly different, greener than he'd seen in a decade. The Bhagya River flowed again, though it now gushed erratically over the tops of the mountains and into the dried-up ravines in the northern Jansan towns they passed. The wildlife was slowly returning as well, hoots and chirps and whistles filling the air all around them.

It didn't take long for them to realize that everyone could feel the changes—not just those of them who could shift. Laksh sensed that there was a stream nearby only a few seconds after Kunal had earlier that day. He could still picture the confusion and then wonder on Laksh's face.

There wasn't much they could do now but collect information as they traveled back and regrouped. Uncertainty showed itself in all of them.

Esha and Harun talked in hushed tones, Arpiya and Bhandu play-fought louder than usual, and Reha kept to herself. Kunal tried his best to engage the young princess in conversation and not dwell on what exactly Harun and Esha were discussing. The overall mood was somber. The worry seemed strongest from Esha who, despite her best efforts to be cheery with others, couldn't fool Kunal.

He had tried, once or twice, to talk to her about the kiss. She avoided him at every turn, but Kunal knew it for what it was. She hadn't given up on them. Not truly. And he was realizing he hadn't either, despite his frustrations.

But he couldn't wait to return to the palace.

There, he could get Esha alone to talk.

There, in the Great Library, might be answers about the broken bond.

He hoped.

It was their best chance to stop Yamini.

◄◦►

There was a welcome party at the gates of the Pink Palace as Esha and the team arrived: a smattering of Blades—and one very angry Scale in the form of Zhyani. If Esha had learned anything about the woman so far, it was that she did not enjoy being left in the dark—and that was exactly what they had done here.

It was clear that, while news of the bond breaking had not formally reached the city, some of its more well-informed residents were already aware of the changes occurring around them.

Zhyani waited till Reha was inside the throne room to unleash the torrent words that were built up inside her. Esha might have felt the same way if she were in Zhyani's position. It never felt good to be the last one to know, or even the second to last. And there was clearly a history between the two of them. Esha winced, thinking about how she had lied to Harun about Kunal's parentage.

This might not be fun. She considered escaping but found herself too curious to see how Reha would react. Esha walked over to help a servant unpack their supplies, all the while keeping an ear to their conversation.

Zhyani cornered Reha in seconds. "What did you do?" she said, a barely contained fury in her voice.

Reha's face dropped into innocence, though she snuck a look at Esha, who pretended not to hear. "Us? Nothing."

"The land is green again," Zhyani said, as if it was the worst outcome possible.

"The merchants' guild found a new way to fertilize crops?" Reha said weakly.

Zhyani ignored her. "It can mean only one thing. You went behind my back with those . . . Blades. I told you I didn't trust them."

"Look, you should be happy," Reha said. "The land has returned to its former glory. Why do you care how that happened? It's not a big deal that you didn't know."

Zhyani almost growled. "I'll decide what's a big deal or not."

"You're overreacting."

"You don't get to tell me that. First, you run away to the mountains with the Archer, of all people. Second—"

Reha stifled a laugh. "Is that what you thought?" Silence. "Wait, that's what you thought? Zhyani, I would never—"

"Just stop. You've been lying this whole time."

"Why are you so angry?" Reha said, pulling herself up to her full height. "Isn't this what you wanted? Didn't you want the land returned?"

Zhyani glanced at Esha quickly before lowering her voice. Esha didn't bother to look away this time.

"Not like this," she said. "Not by these foreigners. This should've been our doing. Who knows what those Dharkans have done to the bond? Perhaps they severed it for themselves."

"Zhyani. Be reasonable. It wasn't just Dharkans there. And we didn't plan for this to happen."

Zhyani wrenched away. "Why would you help them?"

"They're our allies," Reha said. "Why have you stayed here if you didn't feel the same?"

"Fine," Zhyani scoffed. "Allies they are, but that's all. And that doesn't answer my question."

Reha hesitated, running a hand through her hair. "Zhyani—I'm going to stay."

Esha held back her surprise, even as it eased the tension in her heart.

"Here? In the palace? Why in the Sun Maiden's name—"

"I'm the lost princess."

Zhyani laughed, a full-bellied one. "Good one."

Reha sighed in a manner that reminded Esha of Harun.

"Zhyani, haven't you wondered why the princess hasn't gone out into the city yet?" she asked. "I only found out before the Winner's Ball, right before we left for the mountain. When I got back I said I'd help them with the bond, but now that it's broken, we're sitting ducks here. Jansa is at risk and I can't leave now. There's too much to do."

"And you're the right person just because you have a title with your name now?" Zhyani said with a sneer.

It was hard to miss the venom in her voice. Reha flinched.

"No," she said. Reha reached out to Zhyani, wrapping her arm around her elbow and drawing her closer. Zhyani wrenched herself away.

Fingertips grazed Esha's own arm and she looked up into amber eyes. "Let them be," Kunal said. "They have things to discuss." His voice was soft and Esha knew he was right, but he had to tug at her elbow to pull her away.

They walked out of the main wing in silence.

"It's not going to be easy for her, is it? Staying here?" Esha asked quietly.

"No, I don't think it will be," Kunal said. "But she's staying, and I can't deny I'm happy about it."

"Me too," Esha said, and she realized it was true.

Somehow, somewhere, the girl, her old maid, her unseen enemy, had become a vital part of their team.

Maybe she had been too harsh on the young princess.

Maybe.

◄○►

Kunal finished his training as early as he could that morning. He was desperate to do something today, something that would move them forward. He hated all of the waiting they had to do, so he instead buried himself in research with Farhan at the Great Library. It let him feel useful without having to face the others.

For some reason, he had held back from the rest of the team. He couldn't stand the despondent faces of the people he had grown to care about, especially when he had no solution to offer. No new plan of any sort.

Esha had been cooped up in meetings with Mayank and the acting Senap commander for the past two days, trying to assess what the resurgence of magic meant for the land. Kunal had been invited, but something had prevented him from going. A hesitation that had put him here in the library, where he could be more useful.

And where he wouldn't have to make any more decisions that could ruin the entire land.

The only small spot of good was that this time, none of it was his fault. He had done his best to fix his mistake and the others seemed to acknowledge it now.

He nearly ran into Esha when he turned to walk into the library antechmanber.

"Soldier," she said, surprised. Esha stepped back. "Why weren't you in the meeting? Even Reha was there and you know how much she hates them."

"I thought I'd be of more help here, with Farhan," he said.

She narrowed her eyes at him. "You'll be at the next meeting. If I don't see you there, I'll get one of the Scales to drag you in. I know how much you'll enjoy that."

"Esha, I'll be of more use here," he repeated more firmly. Their demeanor to each other had changed since their kiss. It was unsure yet friendlier than before. Having magic back in the land opened up an uncertain world for them all.

"You can't avoid them forever. And I expect you to bring your ideas to my meetings. Not all of them are horrible, soldier. I mean, the last one, but other than that. . . ."

He reached out and grabbed her wrist to stop her and she jumped at the contact, her bangles clattering together. Her eyes darkened and she glanced down at his hand on her wrist and up at him.

"Esha, we should talk—"

"I have to go, but tell Farhan I'll be back later for a report," Esha said quickly, avoiding his eyes. "Arpiya will lead the meeting now since it'll be heavily focused on redrawing that map."

Kunal let go and felt as if his skin had been scalded. "I'll be here."

She nodded curtly before disappearing around the corner.

"Tell me again why we're all here," Bhandu asked. Esha pointed at his feet, which were on the table, and at the scholar who was watching him with a pinched expression.

"Feet off the table first," she said, and then sighed.

"We're gathering information again, trying to see what we may have missed."

Esha had come back to the Great Library, mostly out of a need to do something. She much preferred action to idle thought. But in their current situation, action did nothing. An underlying air of tension sat on top of their meeting today, everyone slightly at odds, uncertainty of the future tainting the atmosphere.

The sun barely peeked over the hills outside the open windows of the Great Library. The faint smoky smell of incense drifted in from the early-morning prayers held by the priests below. Many of the team were yawning and rubbing sleep from their eyes. Farhan had slept here, of course.

"Farhan?" she asked, stifling her own yawn.

"I still don't have a working theory," Farhan said. He looked up from his scroll at Esha, who frowned back at him.

"That's helpful," Esha said.

Farhan shifted in his seat. "I'm trying to figure out why it didn't work out, same as you. And you only asked me this last night. It takes time!"

"I'm sorry. You're right," she said, properly chastised. Farhan's shoulders inched down from his ears and he gave her a short nod. "I'm on edge. The magic is back and unstable. We don't know quite what to expect. This is not only an opening for Yamini but an invitation for every other nation who has been eyeing our lands. We're sitting ducks here."

"We're all on edge, Esha." Farhan ran a hand through his long hair.

Esha took a better look at him. He was right. The normally-put-together Farhan was disheveled, his cotton uttariya untucked and his hair sticking up in the back into a cowlick.

"We did everything right," he said. "Even King Mahir was of the same mind. The texts all say that the original ritual had two artifacts that were used."

Bhandu nodded. "It looked like we had done everything right. We had the artifacts. The right blood. And it was done at Mount Bangaar."

"The home of the spirits, most holy place since the Age of Darkness," Esha said, agreeing. "I keep going in circles about what might have gone wrong. We had everything. It was as if it still wasn't enough for the gods."

"Wait . . . ," Farhan said. "Repeat what you just said?"

"We had everything?"

"Not that. Before."

"Home of the spirits, most holy place since the Age of Dark—"

"That's it." Farhan lit up like a spark and shot to his feet. "That's it."

"What is it?"

"Location. Locations change throughout history, everyone knows that," he said as if it was the most obvious fact. Esha got to her feet, compelled by his excitement.

"They do?" she said.

"Capitals, borders, city boundaries." Farhan flitted around the room like a bird. Esha tried to follow him, but he was moving too fast, speeding around the library and collecting scrolls from various sections.

"I don't understand," she said.

"And you know how our little Viper hates not understanding things," Bhandu said from his seat.

"Grab me that one, with the brass handle." Farhan pointed ambiguously to the shelf of scrolls to his right as he contemplated a row to her left. Esha looked around in confusion. The whole row of scrolls had brass handles.

"It has a purple mark on the side," Farhan clarified, his voice growing more distant.

"Did you find something? Do you know why the artifacts failed?" Arpiya said, clearly having lost her patience.

Esha grabbed the purple-marked scroll and walked over to find Farhan poring over a mound of half-opened scrolls. A little bubble of excitement grew in her chest—she tried not to let it rise too high.

"No," he said. Farhan glanced over at Arpiya, finally answering her question. "But I might have an idea."

Well, that was better than what they had before. Esha nodded quickly.

"Tell me what you need."

"First, I'll need—"

The doors to the library banged open and two Blades rushed in. Laya held a small scroll tied with a red ribbon and she jogged over to Esha. The other stood at the door as guard.

"Esha, an urgent note," Laya said. Esha accepted the scroll and unraveled it, curiosity speeding up her actions.

Her heart plummeted at the first words.

"We've spotted an army, my lady," Laya said, repeating the message on the scroll. "From our reports . . . we think it's Vardaan's."

"Impossible," Esha said. "He's been in our dungeons this whole time."

The minute she said it she knew it could be possible. They had underestimated Vardaan, again. They should have decimated his camp when they had captured him.

"What kind of army?" Esha asked.

"Mercenaries, from the looks of it. Criminals from the prison break. Soldiers from before who remained loyal to him. We've alerted the border squads and we're awaiting your orders."

"Double the guard on Vardaan in the citadel. Monitor every person who goes into that level. Move all prisoners from that level to two levels above. We need to take every precaution. Somehow he is communicating with the army from his cell."

The mole. Esha couldn't ignore the thought now.

But who?

Laya nodded. "I'll make sure of it. He won't be able to sneeze without one of us watching him."

Esha grasped her shoulder and squeezed. "Thank you, Laya. And the report on the other thing?"

The young Blade shifted a bit. "Nothing confirmed. I will keep you updated on the daily reports of the river, but nothing on that yet."

"Please do. And find the prince and Lord Mayank; we need to convene." Esha paused. "Invite Reha and the soldier—Kunal—as well."

Laya saluted and left.

Esha turned to the other Blade, who still stood guard. "Give Farhan everything he needs and let me know how it goes. You know where to find me."

She left the room, hurrying back to the war room.

There was a way through all of this, Esha knew it.

She just had to find it.

CHAPTER 23

Esha rushed past him so fast that Kunal barely had time to register it was her. Her hair was loose, her curls escaping their haphazard braid, and her neck was unadorned. Typically, Esha loved her jewelry. And something was worrying her, as evidenced by the way her arched eyebrows were knitted together. He would never say it to her face, but she looked . . . frazzled.

"Esha?" She didn't stop. "Esha!"

"Kunal," she said in a clipped tone. She blinked rapidly, almost as if she had just noticed him.

"What's wrong?" he asked immediately. Esha was lost in thought and she had called him by his name. Something was clearly very wrong.

She looked down, her hands busying themselves with the ends of her waist sash. Kunal noticed she had forgone the fashionable brocade sashes for a simple, sturdy silk one.

Another thing he had missed.

"You can tell me," he said softly. "We're . . . friends."

"We are? I thought we were nothing to each other." She said it in a dead voice.

"You said allies," Kunal said, refusing to take the bait. "Aren't allies friends sometimes? And anyway, lemon boy and demon girl have a history. Friendship comes in many forms."

"I still can't believe they called me demon girl," she said, though she failed at keeping her face stern. A grin escaped.

"Lemon boy is more flattering, I suppose. But demon girl? Now that's someone to watch out for."

"True," she said. A little laugh escaped from Esha, surprising both of them. "All right, lemon boy. You're going to find out tomorrow morning anyway during the emergency council, but Vardaan has gathered an army. And now I've heard Mayank won't be back till tomorrow evening. We're losing an entire day to respond to this new threat."

"Ah," he said. "That is bad."

Kunal tried not to show his reaction on his face. He didn't need to add to her concern.

"I've been trying to think of a plan, anything, but I'm drawing a blank."

"What about Reha?" Kunal asked. "She is the future queen. Could she drum up support? In the city?"

Kunal wasn't good at these political games and it was a grasp in the dark, but a spark lit in Esha's eyes. She tapped a finger to her lips.

"That's an idea. Do you think you'd be open to taking Reha on an excursion tomorrow?" she said.

Kunal nodded quickly, if only because this was the longest and most amiable conversation they'd had in a moon.

"Soldier, lemon boy. All labels," Esha said thoughtfully. Some of her frantic energy had dissipated. "Do you think you'd be ready to take on another one again? As the Archer?"

This time Kunal's nod came slower. He wasn't sure he liked the gleam in Esha's eye.

———◄o►———

The moment Esha entered the dungeons she knew it was a mistake. The damp stench assaulted her, forcing forward memories she had spent years burying. Having Harun nearby had kept them at bay, but without him, they ran rampant in her mind, hungry and restless.

The faint tinkling of metal against metal drifted through the long corridors, filling the air with a simmering menace.

Esha steadied herself with a deep breath and pulled herself together. Showing her seams in front of the Pretender King would be reckless. And dangerous.

Vardaan's beard was longer, his hair mussed, and yet he managed still to remain regal. It was the thing that had always annoyed her about Harun. Looking good on long missions was never as easy for her, not without her kohl and hair comb.

"Hello, Viper," he said. He sat against the wall, his eyes closed. He opened them slowly. And smiled.

She didn't bother to ask how he had known it was her.

By her second week in the citadel, she had known the different footfalls of every guard.

"Vardaan."

"I'm not even afforded my title?"

"King? That one is false. And Prince?" Esha stepped closer to the steel bars. "You abandoned that the moment you abandoned your country."

Vardaan shrugged, unconcerned. There was a coiled tension in his body, one that Esha noticed immediately. He might be captured now, but this man would never be captive.

"Have you come to berate me some more, Viper?" he said. "Or have you finally discovered your mole?"

"The one that you claim exists? I'm supposed to go on your word, am I? I know it would please you to see us tear ourselves apart." She tried her best to look bored. "Hard to rely on that."

"The Blades have always been an annoyance to me. Never my opponent," Vardaan said dismissively. But she saw the corner of his mouth twitch. The flare of his nostrils.

"Of course. The brave king protecting us from the Yavar. That's who you'd like to be known as, isn't it? I wonder what the city would think if they knew you had made a deal with them years ago."

Vardaan lifted an eyebrow, finally deigning to look up at Esha. "Everyone wants to be the ideal, moral hero. Some of us resign ourselves to being the hero that is needed."

"And you think this is what Jansa needed?" she asked.

Esha could hear the heat in her voice, feel the way it slithered up her throat.

"Why are you here?" Vardaan asked.

Esha stilled, fighting for her composure again before she spoke.

Vardaan suddenly stood, his face breaking into a dark, knowing smile. "Did my gift arrive?"

"If you mean your ramshackle group of murderers and criminals pretending to be an army, then yes," she said.

"People can surprise you, Viper." He chuckled. "I've learned that very well over the past years. They took a garrison, did they not? I think that rather proves their worth."

Esha gritted her teeth. How did he know that?

"It's easier than you think to hear things," Vardaan said, reading her mind. He began to pace—or prowl—his small cell. "Or perhaps it's because you didn't listen to my warning. You have someone in the palace who is not so loyal to you."

Esha scoffed, shrugging her shoulders. "That's not such a bold statement to make, Pretender. We've a palace full of fake allies and former enemies. Anyone could be working at cross purposes," she lied.

The first thing she had done was to vet every remaining person in the palace. The nobles she had sent home early, except for the ones who called the palace court home.

"If you say so," Vardaan said.

Esha kept her face still, only letting a hint of a smile show. "Though I thank you for your concern, *Prince*, I think we both know why I'm here."

"You're wondering if my army is acting of their own accord. Yes, I did leave them with certain instructions." He came to a stop near the slat that let in light to the cell, too small to be called a window. "But really, they've outdone themselves. I'm quite pleased. The pupils have become the teacher."

Something felt off, but Esha couldn't put her finger on it beyond a feeling. This wasn't the first time she had been goaded, not by a long shot, and Esha knew to listen for more. She noticed the hint of pleasure in his voice, as if he were getting away with murder.

Vardaan was smug.

"You're lying to me," she declared.

"I haven't lied to you yet, Esha. Look at how much I've helped you. I led you to the artifact."

"That's only because you want the quarrel to be just between us. No Yavar."

Vardaan smiled. "Very true. I see why you've been such a formidable opponent. There's quite a sharp mind behind those beautiful, cold eyes."

"Everything you've done has only served to help yourself," Esha said, ignoring the barb. Let him think her unfeeling and frozen. It would serve her purposes.

"And what about my warning?"

"Of a mole? You seek to sow discord." Esha laughed, low in her throat. "And even if it were true, why would you reveal that?"

"Perhaps I want to give you an equal chance," he said evenly.

"At what?"

He paused. "Now that you'll have to figure out yourself."

Vardaan leaned back against the wall again, clearly done with their conversation.

Esha bit her lip, frustration growing in her belly. "How? How are you running the army from this cell?"

"Am I? Am I doing that? Or have I just planned better than you, Viper?"

Esha had no answer for that.

She snapped her fingers and the guards returned, their spears glinting in the dim light of the dungeons.

"We'll see," Esha said.

His laughter echoed down the hallway as she left.

<hr />

The streets of Gwali were overflowing with people—and fish. Different kinds of carp, tilapia, and catfish were heaped onto wooden pallets strewn across the market. Reha pinched her nose as they approached.

Kunal took a deep breath, choosing to look at the overabundance of fish, and the subsequent smell, as a good sign. Sure, the unwieldy magic had led to surges in the water levels, nearly drowning ride paddies in Dharka and overflowing dams in Jansa, but now there was fish.

He couldn't remember the last time there had been fresh, plump fish sold in the markets in this quantity, enough that every single man, woman, and child could have a whole fish to themselves.

"I know I should be happy about this," Reha said. "But I can't help but worry what's to come next. I'm as excited as the next person that we have a source of fresh food again, but isn't this . . . a lot?"

Kunal wanted to deny it, but he understood her concern. The fishers were smiling but looked exhausted. They had ridden massive uncontrolled waves to achieve these results, which was both incredible and unsustainable. This was a land that had to be tamed again, that may never be tamed again without the bond. As it was now, life would be a daily struggle. Right now the magic gave, but what if its ebbs were worse than its flows?

The gods gifted humanity the bond to give them a steady, balanced connection to the land. This was the opposite of balance.

Kunal shook his head. "Honestly, I don't know how this will play out. I see nothing but uncertainty on the horizon. Without the bond, we're at the mercy of the land and the magic. I don't think our ancestors grasped that, nor the king."

"Former king."

Kunal colored. "Old habits, my queen."

Reha gagged at the title. "I am not ready for that word."

"You realize that we're walking into the city square, don't you? Maybe refrain from making retching noises about leading Jansa in front of your subjects? I think that would be best advised."

"You know I don't mean it that way," she said quickly. "I love our people—my people. It's just, no one likes clipped wings, right? Who wants to be caged the way a queen is? And nothing I've learned in my time at the palace has truly convinced me otherwise. Not yet. I'm here, but I don't particularly like it."

Kunal shook his head at her.

"What? I'm honest," she said. "Isn't that a virtue?"

Kunal only sighed.

They strolled through the edges of the market, to the corner where the podium and small stage rose from the ground. Reha had demanded that the soldiers guarding them trail behind them and they were doing so, though Kunal could hear every shuffle and step they took. Reha probably could too, but if it helped her feel normal and more at ease, so be it.

"Reha, no one's trying to clip your wings."

She shrugged and shielded her eyes from the sun as they came to a stop. Only a small smattering of people gathered around the stage, most still too occupied with the abundance of fish. Kunal noticed that she didn't object to the use of her name anymore. She had donned it, taken ownership of it like she had most other things.

"Time to dance," she whispered. Laksh had arrived across the way.

Kunal patted her hand. "It won't be that bad."

"You could at least try to sound convincing." She made a face and stepped to the side.

Kunal adjusted his armor and unwrapped the uttariya that covered his head and torso. Instantly, whispers began to punctuate the air, murmurs about the Archer. Despite not being in the public spotlight anymore, the Archer had taken hold as a symbol to the people of Gwali—to Jansa.

Laksh had informed them of this after their return, but Kunal had resisted doing anything with the knowledge. Even now, it was only because Esha was right: they needed support.

Kunal had no idea what he could do, but he was willing to give it a shot. The crowd began to swell, the whispers growing. The only thing Kunal was grateful for was that it gave Reha more cover. His limbs froze, a nervous smile overtaking his face.

A touch at his elbow almost made him jump out of his skin. Laksh.

Laksh's jagged scar brought Kunal back to the present and back into his body.

"What's wrong?" Laksh whispered. "You look like you did when your uncle discovered your secret stash of poetry." Kunal only shook his head. "Well, try to act like the famous Archer, all right?" To the crowd he bellowed, "The Archer has returned!"

Kunal nodded faintly, just as the crowd broke into an answering roar. Even Reha stepped back at the noise.

Laksh hustled him to the front, Reha left to the protection of the guard behind them.

Kunal shook his head in disbelief. "All of this? For the Archer?"

"For you," Laksh said. "I told you that you've grossly underestimated your popularity. You have a chance to do something good here, Kunal."

Kunal swallowed. He had been trying to do good for the past few moons. And he had failed. Why would now be any different? How could Laksh trust him to be this Archer? He barely knew who Kunal was anymore.

Laksh must've caught the change in Kunal's mood because his expression softened. He placed a hand on Kunal's shoulder and squeezed.

And then pushed him onto the stage.

Kunal stumbled at first before quickly finding his footing. The sun shone directly into his eyes at this angle, making it difficult for him to make out the individual faces of everyone in front of him. It helped and yet . . .

He cleared his throat and moved to the front of the small stage as the shouts of the crowd muted to a hushed, expectant quiet. The swirl of thoughts from before threatened to storm down on Kunal, holding his voice and body in a vise.

But then he caught sight of a familiar face and long mustache.

Raju—he could never forget his name.

The merchant in Ujral who had been secretly teaching his daughters in the back of their tent and had made fresh lentil cakes for Kunal, even as a soldier. Another lifetime ago, before the Mela, before Esha, before . . . everything.

Yet there he was. Raju's basket was overflowing, and he held the hand of a small girl. He wasn't sure if Raju recognized him until he stepped forward. The man beamed at him, radiating happiness as he whispered to the woman next to him that he had met the Archer once, that he had been an honorable, kind young man. One who reminded him of his son.

It was what Kunal needed to snap out of it.

He raised his hand and placed four fingers against his chest, the sign of welcome in Jansa. The crowd returned the gesture, a few even bowing.

"My people," Kunal started. "I know that the past few years have been tough, almost impossible, and that you have suffered greatly. We all have. I was born nearby, in the hills to the west of Gwali on a tea plantation. I came to the Red Fort as only a child, desperate to see good in everyone. And since then I have been on a journey, from soldier to man to—"

"The Archer!" someone cried from the back.

"To the Archer. A title I do not deserve. The Archer in the old tales was noble and virtuous, wise and strong. I am only human. And the one thing I've learned is that our strength in this country comes from the people. We are fighters and we will continue to fight until our city is safe. Until the entire land is safe."

266

A deafening roar crushed them from all sides.

"We will continue to fight and strive for this land, the land that the Sun Maiden gifted to us. Our blessing. That is why we will need every one of you. Our city is under attack from a man who claimed to have its best interests at heart, who broke our sacred bond, our divine covenant, with the gods. Who threatened the future of our home. Now, we must defend it at all costs."

Kunal took a breath. A string of nervous energy pulled through him, threatening to overtake his voice, but there was a stronger cord nearby, one of calm and surety. He grabbed for that and turned to face his people, outstretching a hand.

"Will you join me?"

The wooden roof of the stable nearby shook with the answer.

"Will you join *us*?"

Kunal stepped back and let Reha walk forward. She was frozen behind him, her face pale and devoid of the typical smirk that rested on her lips.

He squeezed her arm, like Laksh had done for him, hoping it would bring her back into herself.

Finally, Reha moved. She shook out her hands and took a few tentative steps to the front of the small stage.

"Your princess—and future queen," Laksh announced to a wide-eyed, captivated crowd. Gasps peppered the air, alongside murmurs and wonder. The princess had returned.

It was not a myth, a story, or a lie.

"Your humble servant," Reha said. "I have been a lot of things, but, most important, I am your humble servant. Princess only in name."

Her hand still trembled, but she hid it with her commanding voice. Reha was meant for the stage, even if she did not love it. The people watched her in awe, enraptured by her every word.

Kunal smiled and stepped back.

CHAPTER 24

T he sun set with a vicious brilliance from the windows
of the Great Library that day, purple and pink slashing across the sky. Esha had been there since sunrise, buried
under letters and reports. She had just managed to tunnel
her way out, giving her only a half hour to get some fresh air
before she had headed to the war room for their emergency
council.

Kunal was supposed to be returning soon from taking
Reha into the city to speak to some citizens who might be
eager to see the faces of the Archer and the future queen.

Esha turned the corner from the residence wing of the
palace back to the academic wing, where the Great Library
lived. Farhan had sent her a note to meet him in an hour's
time, but she had decided to arrive earlier and take the time
to peruse those scrolls again. She had that feeling again, that
she was missing something right under their noses.

If only she could figure out what. Esha sighed and pushed open the small door from the outer ring of the Great Library to the main hall, sneaking in before anyone could spot her. She wanted privacy, time alone with her thoughts and worries.

She immediately heard hushed voices in the main area. She crept forward and stayed to the shadows, listening. Kunal and Reha were in conversation near the stacks of scrolls of ancient poetry and mythology.

"You promised me," she said. "You said it would be no big deal and yet there were scores of people. Not the small crowd of fishers you promised."

"Reha, I'm sorry. I didn't know how many people would arrive. But doesn't that say something about the depth of feeling the people have for their would-be queen?"

"It's enough I've lost everything I knew before and now I have to pretend to be someone I'm not? And these cursed trainings." Reha's voice was low, worried, tired.

"I thought you were enjoying your magic trainings with Harun," Kunal said.

There was a pause. "I am. My . . . brother has been perfectly lovely. I just have so many questions."

"Have you talked to Harun?"

Reha hesitated, crossing her arms. "I don't know how to. He's been asking so many questions about my past life, but I've been avoiding them. I've just earned his trust, and while I hate everything else about this stupid palace, I don't hate that. He won't like the person I've been and I'm not sure I can be the person you all need. I've thought about it, you know, just flying away. I'm bad at these things, sticking around, being useful, following orders."

"You wouldn't get very far."

"Thanks for reminding me." Reha rolled her eyes. "I don't have to be here. Neither of us do. You mentioned Farhan is making progress on finding the right location for the ritual? Why don't we just go now and scout? I know I said I'd stay, but I hate being cooped up here."

"No, Reha," Kunal said. "First, we don't know the location yet, and second, we'd be walking into a potential ambush. We'd need backup. We don't know if Yamini will be there or what she truly wants."

Esha could tell Kunal was trying to use logic, but it didn't seem to be what Reha was looking for.

"Come on, we were a good team," Reha said, nudging him in the side. It was a familiar gesture, as if she had done it a number of times. He swatted her away and nudged her back.

"Except for the failure part."

"How were we to know it wouldn't work?"

Kunal made a strangled noise. "I don't know. Any sort of caution or planning? Maybe we could've figured it out, Reha, if you had agreed to wait."

"Waiting is boring," she said petulantly. Her tone sobered. "You knew the conditions. I thought the Yavar were there for me. I didn't know it'd be Harun they'd want in my place. I thought if we left they'd come after us."

"Maybe it would have occurred to you if you had given me a moment to discuss it. Instead you threatened me with the safety of our country. And I betrayed everything for it." Kunal's voice had the blaze of fury and Reha stepped away a pace.

Her voice quieted. "I'm sorry. I just thought—"

"You were scared." He said it matter of factly. "You were about to run."

"I almost did." Reha didn't elaborate, but Esha could hear the layers of pain that surrounded that statement and for the first time, Esha understood.

How would she have responded if her entire life had been torn from her? Her identity, her past, her future? She certainly wouldn't have tried to save anyone, let alone try to fix a problem that wasn't inherently hers.

And Kunal . . .

It was the first time she heard not just regret but anger. Did he regret that he was forced to choose? The room where Kunal and Reha had stood was quiet now and Esha realized Reha must have left.

For the first time, Esha saw what Kunal had seen.

A scared young girl, full of power, the key to their salvation. Two choices, neither good, one full of potential.

Kunal would've never said no to someone in need, or a land in need. Hadn't he left his post the first day they'd met? For a girl he'd never see again. Something in her heart opened up, just slightly. A door to before and a passage to after, if she was willing to take it.

Kunal was still standing there when she turned the corner, his head hung low. He rubbed a spot on his shoulder as he stared out the tall window, lost in thought.

Esha approached him before she could overthink it.

"There really was no good option for you, was there?" Esha said quietly. Kunal's body tightened as he turned to look at her, his pale amber eyes heavy in their gaze.

It was the first time she had realized it. There was a line that she'd never cross, but Kunal wasn't her.

He held his honor and duty in him like metal fused to his bones. They gave him strength, and it spoke to his commitment that he was willing to sacrifice everything to save them all. He was honorable to a fault. But isn't that what she had loved in him? He pushed her to be better.

"I would say no, there wasn't, but I've been rethinking and replaying what happened that night over and over," Kunal said finally. "Maybe there was and I was too stubborn to see it. But in that moment, I thought I was being offered the best chance of saving the land, ending all of this. Without more bloodshed, without more strife." His voice lowered to a whisper. "I'd keep you safe and wipe the blood clean from my hands."

He hung his head, the white scar that cut into his full mouth curving with his frown. This wasn't the soldier she had met, the warrior she knew.

This was a man haunted.

"You're an idiot, you know that?" Esha said. She heard her voice rising. "You tried to play the hero, but no one asked you to. You're not the only one with blood on your hands." Kunal flinched, but Esha pushed on. "No one asked you to be the hero because the burden shouldn't be on any one person to save us all. Did you consider disarming Reha and holding her till we came? Or convincing her to stay?"

"I did," he said. "But she could shift and she threatened to leave."

"I suppose."

"And I didn't know Yamini had turned, or that Harun's life was in danger," he said, a little bit louder, a bit more assured. "If I had known, I wouldn't have done it."

Esha smiled, a sad one. "That's not true, Kunal. I think you would've. And if I'm being truthful, perhaps that would've been the right decision. You would've come back just to play right into Yamini's hands. As your leader, I came to understand why you had decided to go off alone."

She dropped her hands, dropping her gaze as well. "But as your friend—as more than your friend . . . You left. Without a word. Without a goodbye or an explanation. We could've always found the girl again. But losing you?" Esha turned to move. "That killed me."

A low shuddering noise came from Kunal.

"And I will accept that," Kunal said. "But you kept things from me. I didn't know if I agreed with you, so I made the call that I thought was best. I did what I had never done before. I acted. I protected. And I was wrong and I've lived with that every moment since. But I at least tried. When

I spoke to you about my concerns, you brushed them off. Running off to be a hero wasn't the right answer, but . . .

"Our trust was fraying long before I left," Kunal finished softly.

The next moment hung in the air, paused and expectant. The lights in the library had dimmed, casting shadows around Kunal, highlighting the small white scars that dotted his skin.

Once a soldier, always a soldier. But did she believe that anymore?

"So where does that leave us?" Esha said.

"Where do you want that to leave us?" Kunal asked.

"I don't know," she said quietly. "Friends? Lemon boy and demon girl are too important to give up on. There's too much history to abandon."

Kunal nodded slowly. "Friends, then," he agreed.

She smiled at him, the first in a long time. Esha told herself it felt right, that being friends was the best they could've hoped for between a soldier and a rebel.

She had forgotten how good she was at lying to herself.

CHAPTER 25

It was by the early-morning light that Esha caught Zhyani and a cadre of Scales leaving, their horses packed and at the ready. Esha had taken to these walks since they had returned to the palace two nights ago. Her dreams had been plagued by worry and dread since she had received the note about Bhandu's excursion and these walks had been her only solace.

Esha emerged from the shadows to come up behind Zhyani.

"Going somewhere?"

Zhyani turned to look at Esha, tilting her head. "Bit early for you, isn't it, Viper?" She hid it quickly, but it seemed Esha had taken Zhyani by surprise. She had been planning to sneak away.

"Not at all. I thrive in the morning," Esha said.

Zhyani made a noise. "I thought you were a creature of the night."

"I'm comfortable in many situations," Esha said, smiling. "Why are you leaving?" Her tone became more serious. "Reha won't be pleased."

She hoped Zhyani understood what she wasn't saying.

Reha would be heartbroken. The girl already thought she had lost her entire life to this newfound identity of hers and now that she had decided to stay, to do the right thing, she would need more support than ever.

"I—I can't stay right now." Zhyani looked away with a sigh. "I'll be back soon. But we're going to go out. Get more information on Vardaan's army. We'll send regular reports."

"And when will you be back?"

"Soon," was all Zhyani said.

"Is it because she's the princess? She ruined your plans? She's your friend. She needs you," Esha said, her voice turning to ice. "Or do the Scales have no loyalty?"

Zhyani stepped closer, anger written across her face. "How dare you? Reha is more than a friend. She's—" She stepped away, her fingers clenching over the horse's reins in her hands. She quickly found her composure again. There was a new rawness in her voice when she spoke. "Be careful with her. Reha. She's too good at goodbyes. And don't miss me too much. I'll be back soon."

"Seems a bit on the nose, doesn't it?" Esha said, a hint of spite lacing her words.

Zhyani didn't respond. Esha didn't expect her to.

She glanced at Esha before raising a single gloved hand in signal to the other Scales. They mounted their horses in unison, a few of the Scales looking back at Zhyani with what Esha thought might be unease. So it wasn't a unanimous decision.

Esha stepped back so as to not get trampled, though a part of her wanted to charge after them and drag them back into the palace. She wrapped her arms around herself in the light chill of the morning, letting the low chirps of the morning birds echo in her ears.

She's too good at goodbyes.

What had she meant by that?

In the maelstrom that was her brain, Esha could only hear the whispers she had ignored since she had dragged Vardaan back. Whispers about a mole in their midst. Why else had Reha stayed back when she had been so adamant about leaving before?

Esha straightened her spine. Reha had shown little to earn her distrust, and she wouldn't doubt her now.

But the seed remained, nestled into her heart. Reha, or Aditi, had fooled her once.

Zhyani nodded at Esha before taking off with the Scales, down the ramp of the Pink Palace and back to the city that had made them.

◆

The minute he was down in the damp, dark mustiness of the dungeons, Kunal regretted the impulse that had brought him here. No, not an impulse. A summons.

The king, his once sworn leader, had written to him, demanding an audience. Though in not so many words.

Kunal shivered. There was a slight chill in the dungeons, tucked away from sunlight and made for torture. The latter was evident in the care and shape of the cells. Thick metal bars, small slats for light, keeping prisoners in constant suspension between day and night. All the hallmarks of a military prison.

He approached Vardaan's cell, stopping a few paces away. It still struck him to see the king, to see Vardaan, here.

Esha wouldn't like to hear it, but he had a command to him that rivaled the Viper's. It became clear to Kunal how so much of the damage to his country had happened. Charisma was a weapon sharper than any blade when wielded right, and it was on display in front of him.

Vardaan was thinner than when Kunal had seen him last, his face hollow but not gaunt. There was still an energy that suffused his body, like he wasn't quite done with the world yet.

That's what worried Kunal.

Esha had filled him in on how Vardaan had helped in finding the conch and the other moves he had made, even while behind bars. She seemed to have shifted her attention back to other pressing needs, particularly with the army, but Kunal wasn't sure it was the prudent move.

Kunal wasn't sure it would ever be smart to forget what the man in front of him could do.

"The Archer, isn't it?" a deep, rumbling voice asked. Vardaan assessed him with a cool gaze. Kunal had to resist the urge to straighten and check his weapon placement. This wasn't an army inspection. This wasn't his king anymore.

"That is what they call me."

Vardaan chuckled and got to his feet, his shackles and chains clanking against each other in a discordant song. The resemblance to Harun was striking at first, until Vardaan came closer. There was a cruel set to his mouth, a tightness.

"It took me a while to figure out that the Archer, the legend reborn, was actually my best friend's nephew. I had meant to look for you after his death, but when I sent a note I was told you were out finding retribution for your uncle's murder," Vardaan said. "Avenging his honor."

The words sent a shiver down Kunal's back, a memory from the past.

He could still taste the way that desire had felt, like smoke and ash and steel. A memory of his uncle flashed across his mind, the first time he had led Kunal through the tall arches of the Red Fortress.

He had never thought he'd be here, even a year ago.

"Honor is beginning to take on a new meaning for me . . . sir," Kunal said.

He still couldn't find it in him to let go of those old habits. The anger that Esha held in her heart for Vardaan was something Kunal understood but didn't share. That hatred.

But when he thought of the ravaged, barren land that Jansa had become, that he had discovered on his travels,

Kunal thought that, maybe, he could feel a flicker of hatred in his own heart.

"You must be wondering why I asked you here. Let's not mince words. I know you are working with the Blades. I know you deserted your position." Kunal winced, but Vardaan continued. "But many things have changed and I'm becoming an old man."

Vardaan came closer to the bars of steel that separated him and the outside world. He looked tentative, nervous. "I simply wanted to see the man you've become," Vardaan said finally, his voice lowered and tremulous. "It's been over a decade now since Setu found you, hasn't it?"

Kunal wondered if it was real emotion that choked his words or if he was a better actor than even the Viper. Doubting others was not in Kunal's nature, but he had grown to see it as wisdom now. Protection.

"Setu would have wanted to see you too," Vardaan said.

A bitterness rose in Kunal's throat and he reacted before he could stop himself. "I doubt that. What would my uncle say if he saw me now?"

"Setu was always contrary. I never knew what he was going to say or do," Vardaan said, chuckling. Vardaan glanced up at him, kindness in his eyes, as if he was sharing in remembrance with him. Kunal hadn't known that part of his uncle, but he did remember the few times he had taken his side or shown him kindness after failure.

"Your father, on the other hand. He is entirely different."

Vardaan's eyes shifted, regaining their sharp edge.

Kunal almost stepped back at the transformation.

And at the clarity in Vardaan's words.

Not *was*.

He is entirely different.

Was this why Vardaan had brought him down here?

Kunal was in his face, his hand wrapping around Vardaan's throat through the bars.

"My father? What do you know? Do you have him?"

Vardaan dared to laugh. "Have him? Gods no. I would never force myself to spend time with that man. I always wondered what sort of woman would tolerate him. His utter tedium. I suppose our dear Viper has that answer. I never took her as a woman who would go for a soldier."

A few of the guards near the end of the hall shifted, unsure whether to come closer and unsure who to help.

"A prince is more her style, don't you think?" Vardaan grinned. "I saw her with my nephew, you know. As long as he's around, you'll never have a chance."

Vardaan's words were the slap in the face Kunal needed.

He had once had those thoughts, it was true, but Kunal was beginning to understand who he was now. What he offered. Who he wanted to be.

And he wouldn't let Vardaan rile him.

It was clear to Kunal now that the summons was about getting information on Esha. Vardaan thought by goading him, throwing him off balance, that he might betray her.

He let go of the man and stepped back, putting as much

distance between them as he could. Harun had mentioned that he should limit his visit, keep metal between them to ensure that Vardaan wouldn't recognize his blood song.

At least Vardaan didn't know about his mother, even if he knew about Esha.

"It would be a mistake to believe anything you say," Kunal started. "That I should've realized. But the biggest mistake I made was ever believing you were a man to follow. A king of any kind. You, Vardaan, are nothing and will be nothing but a bad memory."

Kunal would make sure of it.

He hurried out of the dungeons, leaving behind Vardaan and his previous life.

———◁○▷———

Esha waited for Harun in the small corner of the palace gardens, resisting the urge to check the sundial once again. He was usually never late. They had a standing meeting to go over battle strategies in the war room, but this morning she had woken up to a note from him asking to meet here, at this time.

So where was he?

Footsteps sounded behind her and Esha turned around, ready to berate Harun. First he changed the time of their meeting and then he was late.

The words dried up in her mouth when she saw Harun.

He wore a russet-red dhoti, a cream uttariya thrown over one shoulder. He had taken to wearing leather armor guards since he had returned and the ones he was wearing held more than a few nicks. Her prince was getting his training in.

He looked . . . different. There was a resoluteness on his face that she hadn't seen in moons. He looked that way only when he had made a decision and he was unhappy with it.

"Harun, why—"

Without warning, Harun wrapped Esha in his arms and kissed her. And when she returned the kiss, he deepened it into a searing, soul-searching kiss that left her breathless. He pulled away a moment later, clearly shaken.

"Harun."

He stopped her. "I wanted one last kiss. One last time."

"Last— Harun, what are you talking about?"

He stepped away from her, drawing his hands together in front of him. He took a ragged breath, his dark eyes searching for something in her own. "I saw you with him earlier. Kunal."

"Harun, it didn't mean—"

"Whatever is between you isn't finished." He chuckled, but the laugh was as dry as sand. "It's clear as daylight to anyone else but you two."

"There is nothing left there," she said.

"I wish that were the truth," Harun said quietly. A gentle breeze ruffled his hair. "A part of me will always wish that I had never sent you on that mission in the first place. But then we wouldn't be here, closer with every step to saving the land."

He stepped closer and cupped her face, his thumb drawing small circles at the edge of her jaw. "I want all of you, Esha. I always have. I was just too stupid to realize it before. But I can't turn back time and I think . . ."

Harun sighed, his shoulders drooping. "I don't want to be second."

"That— You were my first choice." Esha's voice sputtered and sparked, even as she tried to figure out the truth in her words.

He flinched. "I was?"

"You *are*—" Esha hesitated. He was, wasn't he? A flash of amber eyes, of bronze against a night sky made her heart clench.

"It's okay." He gave her a wry smile. "You deserve to have a chance with him, like you said before. I deserve . . . something."

"Everything," Esha whispered.

Was this really it? She wanted to scream, yell, cry, shake him back to the time when they had a chance. But Harun was standing up for what he wanted.

Even now, Esha believed she could fix this.

She could find the right words, slip back into his arms and discover that old passion together. But the funny thing was, she did love him. And so she would never do that to him.

"I wanted everything with you," Esha said.

"You don't need to explain," he said, his voice suddenly harsh. Harun straightened and gave her his brightest smile.

It was marred by the shadows in his eyes. "I'm just telling you, as your friend—that chapter isn't over."

"And if it is?"

"Close the book and come back to me," he whispered, something in him finally breaking. Esha moved toward him, but Harun stepped back, shaking his head. "But I'm not sure I'm willing to wait to find out the answer."

Esha wrapped her arms around herself. Finally, she nodded.

"I understand," she said softly. She cleared her throat. "Does this mean you don't want to see me again? Should I find someone to take my place?"

Harun turned sharply and gathered her up in his arms. "No. Never. I mean, do I want to see the soldier around for the rest of my life? Not particularly. But you? Of course."

"Really?"

"I might need some time. But I made a promise to you when you found me in the caravan after the Night of Tears. Do you remember it?"

"You said I would never have to worry again. That I had been found," she whispered.

"Mathur is your home. The palace is your home. It will always be open to you."

Esha noticed that he had evaded her question. Ever the prince, ever the courtier.

Even now, she wasn't sure if Harun was right. She didn't know if she believed there was another chapter for her and Kunal. They were friends, that was all.

But hadn't she said that about her and Harun?

Harun stepped away from her, a poor attempt at a smile on his face. She gave him her own, hardly any better. A facade.

The years of dreams and hopes she had tucked away threatened to tumble out at her feet. They whispered of cool nights in the palace under the twinkling stars of Mathur, dual thrones shadowed by blue marble, kisses caught between missions, dreams to save the world. Harun's retreating back was the only thing that gave the whispers pause.

Esha let him go.

CHAPTER 26

Esha came back to their emergency meeting with a headache of epic proportions.

The last few days had been a trial, from her conversation with Harun to new unanticipated complications with the Jansan army, and finally, to their desperate need for recruits.

While it had seemed like a good idea at first to invite everyone to their meetings, given how vitally they needed help, she hadn't anticipated how much fighting there would be. She wasn't innocent—she fought as hard, if not harder, than some of the others. Harun's newfound desire for more conversation and conflicting opinions had seemed smart at the start, but Esha was doubtful now.

It would be much easier to have everyone listen to her without any argument.

As it stood now, they had decided to keep an eye on Vardaan's troops rather than to take any immediate action.

Esha had recommended going on the offensive, as had Lord Mayank, despite not having enough troops right now. A strong front was needed. But Harun and Kunal had fought for more caution. Reha had remained silent.

So, of course, they had decided to take a break and reconvene. Esha took a sip of her chai tea and sighed, rubbing the bridge of her nose in thought.

Now they had to contend with Vardaan *and* the mystery of the broken bond. Esha had put teams of Blades and Scales to discover what they could. She had also worked with Reha on setting up a hidden council of town leaders and elders to gather reports on what was happening around the country, for more grassroots information.

Most people were joyful, excited about the return of the river. But most of them also attributed it to the bond being renewed. Esha was working with Laksh and Reha to carefully seed out the information that the bond might have been broken entirely, just to see how the reaction would be. So far, it was middling.

People were terrified by the idea that there was no bond anymore, but some were hopeful and many others didn't care. The land was everything to them. The fear didn't worry her—Esha was confident that the people would come around. The random cases of magic did trouble her.

She had only felt it once, that unworldly presence of magic. She had gone off path during her daily walk and edged into a nearby garden. The difference had been staggering. It was as if the ground itself was alive, pulsating, teeming with an unbridled energy that she realized now was magic.

No wonder Harun had been so worried. Even Esha could tell there had been no balance to that energy. One tip the wrong way and it could engulf them all whole, which was a sobering thought.

She finished the last dregs of her tea as Lord Mayank came back in. He took a mango cookie from the tray on her table and nibbled on it.

"Yes, please. Have a cookie," she said with a frown.

Lord Mayank smiled and took another bite. "How do you think it's going?" He inclined his head toward the door. "I saw you included the soldier. And the new princess. Not what I expected."

"People are never really what you expect, in my experience."

"I would love to hear more about this experience of yours sometime," he said casually. Had Mayank been a budding rebel? A fan?

"One day," Esha said. "When Vardaan isn't breathing down our necks."

"I mean, you must have met the Viper." He sounded excited by the idea, even a bit pining. "A legend."

Esha hid her smile behind a cookie. "I cannot officially say whether I've met the Viper. But there may have been a mission."

Mayank gave her a knowing look and winked. "Ooh, a mission? Sounds far more interesting than life here."

"It was fun," she admitted. "It was also lonely and terrifying and hard." Esha put her feet up on the chair in front of her. "Palace life is much easier."

"But just as deadly."

"That is the truth." She nodded. The night before they'd gone over all the various Houses and their current loyalties with Reha. Even Esha's head spun after all of it, and she enjoyed games like that. "But in a much less obvious way."

"Do you really think we should go on the offensive?" he asked. Mayank pointed at her feet. Esha removed them from the chair and he took the seat next to her.

"I think it's better than waiting for Vardaan to make his first move. The more time we give him, the bigger his army. I don't believe we should underestimate the Pretender King."

Mayank nodded, looking out of the window to their right. "I agree. But I also worry we'd be putting troops in danger for no reason. What if he's trying to draw us out to easier terrain, where his smaller numbers won't matter? We have the advantage in Gwali."

"It's possible." Esha shifted in her seat, unsure how much to tell Mayank about their trip north. She decided this was no time for secrets. "I'm sure you've noticed magic has returned to the land. The entire city is whispering about it after that scene at the fish market."

"I might have noticed something," he said, his eyes alight. He had clearly been waiting for her to bring it up. "It's good news. The bond. You succeeded."

"No," she said. "We didn't."

The confusion on his face was clear, but Esha paused, unsure how exactly to explain all that had happened. Finally, she told him everything.

"It's *broken*? How is that possible?" Mayank rubbed his temples, looking as if there were a million things suddenly on his mind. Esha understood that keenly. "And the Yavar . . ."

"They're going to do everything in their power to forge a new bond, one in their favor," Harun said, reentering the room with Kunal. His glance was heavy and lingered on her. She hadn't fared much better since their talk. It had been the right thing and yet . . . the right thing was rarely easy.

And Kunal. Despite their currently nonexistent relationship, she had thought Kunal would at least try to get her alone once they were back in the palace. Especially after that kiss. That stupid kiss. Yet, he had barged out from the room the moment the break from their meeting had been announced.

"Farhan confirmed it. We missed something," Kunal said as he reentered the room. He held up a scroll as he got to the front of the large wooden table. His lips pursed at the sight of her and Mayank so close together. Reha took that moment to rejoin them, arriving with leaves in her braid and a new knife in her waist sash.

The scroll itself was larger and older than any she had seen in the library in their recent searches. It reminded her of scrolls her father had pored over when she had been young, ones that had been tucked away in the back, hidden away from the regular visitors to the famous Great Library.

"We had everything right—except for the place." Kunal unfurled the scroll and pointed to an old and worn-out section of it. "We assumed all that was needed were the original artifacts and everything else would be the same. It's been niggling at me and it was something Reha said that unlocked it. The ancients drew their borders differently. Gwali's walls were only built in the last few centuries after the Blighted War and certainly after the first rituals were performed. The mountains were then considered sacred but only used for pilgrimages."

"What does this mean, then?" Esha asked.

"The first ritual, the Ayana, wasn't done at Mount Bangaar. That's why the temple crumbled. It couldn't handle the magical resonance of all that energy. It wasn't built for it. The original artifacts came from an age of magic, where everyone had some in their veins. The lands pulsed with it."

"It's like that report of the rice paddies to the west," Lord Mayank said, scrunching his brow. "The old buoys and dam that had been built for the river were washed over. They couldn't handle the rush of the new river. The magic overwhelmed the ancient levees that had been built, even damaging the old temple on the river. It was similar to what you had described, Esha. Stones cleaved in two, as if someone had taken a sword to them."

Kunal nodded. "Exactly. I saw that report." Esha gave him a sharp look. How? He ignored her and kept going. "It's what gave me the idea. The stones cleaved in two—it can't be a coincidence. Magic is pooling in specific parts of the land."

"So then what?" Esha asked.

"This scroll corroborates my thoughts." Kunal pointed to the section and traced a line straight across to a small image. "A city of gold. That's what it says in ancient Jansan."

"'A city of gold, drowned by the sea,'" Reha sang quietly. "'A wreath of sorrow, no way to be free.'"

Esha snapped her head around. "Where is that song from?"

"A sea ballad," Reha said, nodding. "Common around here. But it comes from the tale of the city lost to the gods' wrath during the Blighted War."

"Does the song say anything else?"

She shook her head. "I can ask around." Reha looked as if she wanted to say something but didn't know how to. "We should wait. Vardaan's a danger, but he's not our main danger, especially since he's cozy down in our dungeons. If the Yavar reforge the bond on the full moon, it won't matter who's fighting who. We knew he'd come back before my coronation, anyway. I'm not eager for the throne, don't get me wrong, but we need to have a ruler on the throne before we declare war. The matter of ruling must be decided."

Esha looked long and hard at Reha.

She had changed since she had known her as Aditi, the past two moons weighing on her. Her round eyes were lined in kohl, the current court fashion, and she looked the part of a regal lady. Her training as a lady's maid had made that easy.

But there was a rawness to her that Esha recognized in herself. A willingness to do what needed to be done. It wasn't found in everyone. And her lack of desire for the throne made her the very queen this healing land needed.

"We should move up the coronation," Esha said. "Why wait?"

Reha looked like she had been slapped. "What?"

"Not a bad idea," Harun said. He rubbed his chin in thought. The other two men seemed to be considering it as well.

"If we get you on the throne quickly, we have power," Esha said. "We can build alliances under the rule of the rightful Samyad queen."

"In name alone—" Reha started.

Esha waved her concerns away. "No one is ever ready to be queen. But you are more ready than most. True, we'll have to find some way around the optics of you being part of the Scales, but we can work with it. The country is dealing with an uncertain time, even if they don't quite know it. And it'll be a move against Vardaan that doesn't require our military. Our currently useless military."

"Maybe we should take some more time to talk about it," Kunal said, glancing at Reha. The girl's face was pale.

"What are we doing now if not talking about it?" Esha countered. "A two-pronged attack. One offensive, one defensive. We crown Reha as the rightful queen and we search for this lost city of gold."

"Drowned city of gold," Lord Mayank corrected.

"Doesn't that sound so much more fun?" Esha muttered. "We can do both at the same time. A cover to distract Yamini or whoever else might be on the trail of the artifacts."

"We don't even know if we can find the city for sure," Reha said.

"That's what we're going to find out, aren't we? The soldier and Farhan seem to be sharing one mind, so I'm sure we'll have more answers soon. We can also put our best scholars on it." Esha grimaced. "On pain of death. It'll be important to keep this secret."

"You said I'd have a month," Reha said, shaking her head. Her hands were tight on the edge of the table and her shoulders tense. "I have my own business to square away here in the city. Do you think I can just—?"

"Reha, it's only a few weeks earlier," Harun said.

"A few weeks is a lot! I don't—"

Esha grabbed Harun's hand and he turned to look at her. She shook her head at the response she knew he was building to and nudged her head at the girl and the door. Harun nodded and walked over, putting a light hand on Reha's arm. "Let's go for a walk. I'll show you the jasmine bushes you were asking about before. We don't need to come to any decision now."

Reha looked as if she was going to protest, but they left together, Harun slinging a tentative arm around his younger sister. Esha knew the relationship was still uncertain and that they were both at the stage where neither wanted to disturb the waters.

It wouldn't last. Esha hadn't had any siblings, but she had enough Blades running around her to know that familiarity only bred more conflict. They were laying the foundation that would allow them to weather those storms—at least that's what she kept telling Harun every time he started to get that pompous, older-brother look on his face.

"I guess we're reconvening later, then?" Lord Mayank asked.

Esha sighed. "Let's make time tonight. Hopefully, Harun will have convinced her by then. We should put the other plans into motion."

Lord Mayank nodded. "I'll go ready the troops and see if we have any preparations needed before the coronation. I can also get a covert look at how prepared we might be for any attack."

"We're not attacking, though, are we, my lord?" Kunal said from across the table, looking at Mayank with an expression Esha couldn't place.

Mayank didn't fidget under Kunal's stern gaze. "No, we aren't, young prince. But best to be prepared, don't you think?"

"I agree," Esha said quickly. "I'll come stop by the barracks later, if that's all right."

Lord Mayank gave her a short little bow and left the door ajar behind him.

Which left her alone with Kunal.

"I don't like it," he said. Kunal walked around the table till he was on the same side as her. As always, he made her heart catch in her throat. He was dressed simply, but the palace servants had cleaned him up in a way that was befitting of his royal bloodline.

"Which part?" She arched an eyebrow at him.

He moved closer, and while she considered fleeing, her ego refused to let her.

"You know he likes you?" Kunal countered instead. He stopped a pace away from her, tracing the edge of the wood table.

"Who?" And then, "Everyone likes me."

Kunal chuckled, deep in his throat. "Can't disagree with that."

His smooth muscles were obvious under the thin, silk uttariya he was wearing. His arms outlined by the thick gold armbands around his biceps. And the green of his dhoti brought out the flecks of green and gold in his amber eyes.

"Mayank."

"Lord Mayank, soldier."

"Prince Kunal, Viper," Kunal said in turn, his voice low.

He had closed the gap between them, apparently encouraged by the fact that she hadn't fled the room like usual.

Esha thrust her chin out. "The title doesn't suit you. And he likes me as well as anyone else does. I'm good at what I do and I make a good ally. A good friend, even."

"Is that all it is?"

"Jealousy doesn't look good on you." She had been hoping to throw him off guard, put him on the defensive with her accusation, but he merely shrugged.

"I'm quite comfortable with it."

"Mayank is my friend. We had plenty of time to get familiar, what with the kidnapping, palace coup, and your absconding with the only heir to the throne. Mayank stepped in when I had no one else I could trust. He helped the Blades take the palace."

"Oh, and he did that for no reason? No motive?"

"He certainly did. He wanted his title back and I gave it to him. He earned it," she said simply. Kunal narrowed his eyes but said nothing.

They were close to each other again and Esha thought back to their kiss at the temple, and to the many before. She wanted this fire between them to be doused. She didn't want to deal with this confusion of emotions every time she saw the soldier, not when she had made up her mind. They were an impossibility. A myth. A warning for others.

"That was all?"

"You're being impossible."

"I'm not trying to. I'm merely observing," he said.

"Well, then, perhaps you shouldn't have left," she said, stepping up to him. She poked him hard in the chest and couldn't help but feel the nostalgia that washed over her.

"I shouldn't have," he agreed softly. "And if I could go back . . ."

"Don't lie to me," she threatened.

And tried her best to hide away her heart, just in case.

———◇———

There was so much to say, but Kunal didn't know where to start.

"See," she hissed. "You can't even admit it."

"What are you even talking about?"

"Just say it." Esha came up closer to him, her lashes fluttering as she glared up at him. Her chest heaved and his eyes trailed over her, down her turquoise sari and across the hand that was now poking him.

Sun Maiden's spear, he couldn't handle it anymore.

He pulled her into him sharply, kissing her with the passion he had been bottling up for weeks now. She returned the passion, digging her nails into his upper arm so hard that he gasped. Esha looked up at him, her eyes dark and twinkling with satisfaction.

She pushed him onto the table so that they were at the same height and his body reacted immediately. He knew this was a bad idea, knew they should be talking instead. But he wasn't strong enough to push her away.

Esha captured his lips, again and again, pushing down on him with a passion that made his blood rise in return. When she nipped his lip, he gave a little gasp, looking up. She glanced at the mostly closed door, seeming to come to a decision. With firm movements she tugged his uttariya off, her hands roaming over his bare chest. His hands curled around her hips, pulling her into him.

She grinned against his mouth, and when they broke apart, her hands twined their way down to his waist sash. He tensed up. Her eyes were dark, and he could tell that part of her wanted this.

But he also realized that if he answered her passion right now she would be his for the moment, but her heart might be hidden away from him forever.

"No," he said.

Kunal thought he could feel his heart shattering at the look on her face.

Esha paused, going still as death, and Kunal imagined he could feel the shock—and embarrassment—radiating from her. He caught her before she leaped up, pulling her into an embrace where she couldn't avoid his eyes.

"Not like this," he said gently. Her eyes shot up to his and he was caught in their fiery embrace. "Not here in the war room with everyone just paces away. Not when I can see the pain in your eyes, the Viper seconds away."

"The Viper will always be seconds away," she said, her voice low, pained. "And that's not pain; it's fury."

Kunal flinched. "Then even more so."

Esha tried to wrench herself away, but he caught her. He pulled her back to his chest, trying to show her that he wasn't saying no, just not right now.

He didn't want their first time, his first time, to be out of anger.

Not with Esha.

"Esha . . ." Kunal kissed her neck and for a moment

he felt her soften, but the edges of her anger were still too sharp.

She yanked herself away, fixed the pins in her hair and turned to leave.

She was a fool. An utter fool.

Her cheeks flushed and she fumbled with her hair, anything to distract herself from Kunal's rejection.

Kunal came closer to her and reached out to her. She didn't push him away and he cupped her cheek, pulling her closer to him sharply with his other arm. The heat between them rose with a roaring flame. He looked down at her with a heavy-lidded gaze.

"I didn't say no before because I don't want this," he said, making it very clear what *this* was. "But I want more. I want you, Esha. I want all of you." Kunal's voice was fierce, composed, but Esha detected the hint of desperation below it.

And she so wanted to say yes. To give him all of her, to give him her heart once again and hope that this time, he would handle it more gently. But Esha was no stranger to the pain that people could cause. How did she know he wouldn't turn away and leave this way again if his duty was called into question?

The uncertainty was too much for her, the potential cost too high.

"There's no more of me to give," Esha said. She stepped into his embrace, wrapping her arms around his neck, easing her fingers into his hair before she pulled him down into a searing kiss.

"This is it, Kunal," she said. "Take it or leave it."

Kunal looked down at her, eyes dazed. That she was good at, that she knew how to do. Esha smirked.

He opened his mouth to say something in his dazed state but then stopped and shook his head. When Kunal caught her gaze again, his eyes were sharp, clear, focused.

"No," he said, pulling away. "No deal. I'm not giving up. Not anymore and not on this. I've been wondering what I wanted to fight for since the day I turned my back on the Fort." Kunal's eyes flashed a dark gold. "This is it. I'm fighting for you."

A rustle sounded in the outer hallway and they broke apart.

I'm fighting for you.

Esha couldn't deny she wanted him to try.

CHAPTER 27

Esha tore into her cumin-encrusted flatbread, dipping it into the hot, spicy lentils and scooping them into her mouth. She resisted the urge to let out a sigh of pleasure.

Harun chuckled from her right. Esha cocked her head at him.

"Nothing," he said in response to her unspoken question. "That look on your face. How's the food?" Harun's tone was teasing.

"Can't remember the last time we saw that face," Arpiya said.

"When we found those extra bushels of mangoes downstairs two days ago," Bhandu said.

"Ah, yes," Arpiya said. "I heard about that one from Aahal."

Aahal looked up from his plate with large eyes, realizing he had been mentioned. He opened his mouth to respond, but all four of them looked at him and said in unison, "Finish chewing, Aahal."

Aahal gave them a grumpy look before returning to his food. There was a firm knock at the front door. Esha dipped her hands in the bowl of water to the right of her plate and then walked over to open the door to their room. Their team had taken to meals in the privacy of Esha's rooms more often recently, to seek respite from the rest of the palace's inhabitants.

A short girl with a tight, long braid and in training gear was at her door.

"What is it?" Esha said sharply. Not again. She was beginning to dread the sight of Laya, the young Scale in charge of her messages. They were never good. Didn't she deserve some good news, for once?

"I didn't have time to read, Viper," she said. Laya handed her the small note and Esha unwrapped it quickly.

Her jaw tightened as she read. "I was right," she muttered to herself. She repeated it louder. "I was right."

"You usually are," Aahal said helpfully from the corner.

"Care to tell us what's in the note?" Harun said, abandoning his plate to peek over her shoulder.

"Vardaan has taken a garrison of ours in the west."

There was a beat of silence in the room, a moment of heaviness that weighed on them all. His threat was real now. It couldn't be ignored, which would mean a rounding of troops, an inevitable war, and certainly lives lost. All of them had been children during the start of the War of the

Brothers, and they had barely survived through the long ten years that followed. No one wished to return to that life, especially not when magic was finally back.

Erratic and unreliable but back.

Esha continued on. "It was always likely that he'd take that garrison. The soldiers there are far west enough to give their loyalty to whoever has the largest amount of coin."

"Mercenaries," Bhandu spat out.

"Vardaan has those too."

"Why are we not more worried about this?" Kunal asked. Everyone jumped. When had he come in? Once again, Esha wished she had those powers.

Esha frowned. "I think we're perfectly worried. He's amassed a small army by now, especially if he's able to convince the soldiers at the garrison to follow his cause."

"They might not be given a choice, Esha," Kunal said.

Esha dipped her head. "You're right."

"If that's the case, should we offer an alternative?" Lord Mayank said from the side. He'd taken to joining their little impromptu meals. After gaining his title back, his presence had been more in demand than ever—mostly from people who wanted something from him.

Esha could see that the attention was weighing on Mayank. He had known what he had been fighting for when he had sought to get his title reinstated, but Esha supposed that sort of responsibility was difficult no matter how mentally prepared you were for it.

She could relate to that. Now that Harun was healed, he could take up more responsibility of the Blades. But the palace itself was still a shared problem between her and Mayank, with Reha's increasing help. Reha had proven herself to be more than capable to start to run the country. . . . It just didn't seem as if she was always that willing.

Of course Esha understood that discovering at sixteen that you were the next queen, after thinking you would rise to be a rebel leader, was jarring. But Reha would have to get over it. No one's life turned out exactly the way they expected.

That gave her an idea.

"Yes, we should provide an alternative," Esha said. "Offer them new positions here, in Gwali, or wherever they want to be posted. Whoever makes their way back to the capital will be rewarded, and any information about Vardaan's new army will be rewarded. Handsomely."

"Won't that cause worry among the citizens?" Kunal asked.

"Exactly." She turned to stare at Kunal. "Vardaan's made his move. The threat is real and we need to mobilize our citizens. Do you think anyone in Jansa wants to return to Vardaan's rule?"

"Actually, there are groups—" Aahal started.

Esha sighed. "There are enough that don't. Let's empower them to protect their own country. Mayank, notify the city councils and town leaders of the threat. Tell them to gather their militia and close their walls at night. We don't know where he'll attack next."

Lord Mayank nodded.

"You should attend to the military as well. Prepare them," Harun said.

Esha agreed, having already arrived at the same thought.

"I'd like to come," a voice said from the door.

Reha shut the door behind her. She wasn't a rare sight in their little gatherings, but Reha had friends in the palace and in the city, and Esha had been giving her the space she needed to come to terms with her responsibility. With a team of Blades watching her every move, of course. Especially after the little conversation she had overheard between her and Kunal.

She's too good at goodbyes.

Moon Lord, she would be an idiot to take her eye off their future queen, despite the successful speech Reha had delivered.

Kunal looked like he might protest, and Harun was eyeing his younger sister with curiosity. They had been spending more and more time together, and the fact that Harun didn't object or suggest that he should come along, aside from the fact that introducing the prince of Dharka to Jansan soldiers would be a nightmare, reinforced her decision.

Esha glanced at the girl. "All right. They'll need to answer to their queen one of these days. Might as well get them used to the idea of you."

Reha's face grew pale, but she had a decisive look in her eyes. Finally, she nodded.

———◆———

The barracks were stuffed with soldiers, overflowing with men at every corner. Many had clearly just run there, perhaps having heard that the acting general and the young princess were coming.

There was a heavy silence as they walked into the room. A few rows of the men immediately bowed with their palms together as Mayank crossed into the room. His men, most likely, though the numbers indicated that Mayank had won over quite a few to his side since his appointment. There was a scattered line of women too—fresh new recruits courtesy of Mayank, who had overturned the ban on women in the Jansan army.

Esha narrowed her eyes at the other men who took a few seconds too long to bow. One of the soldiers broke away and came forward.

"My lord," the man said. "What brings you here?"

"An announcement," Mayank said. He glanced over at Esha and Reha. Esha tilted her head in acknowledgment, pleased that he had deferred to her. She could get used to this amount of power, she knew.

Esha stepped forward, nudging Reha as well. The girl didn't move, though.

"We have news of Vardaan's movement in the west. He's gathered a small army of mercenaries and former soldiers." Esha emphasized the latter to indicate it would be the fate of any who decided to defect for Vardaan's cause. "And you know how the Jansan army treats deserters."

There were collective whispers from the men. Not all of these men were convinced of their cause, but she knew most were smart enough to acquiesce to the change in government.

"We'll need to prepare the gates for a possible siege and mobilize troops to protect our borders beyond Gwali. Lord Mayank has already informed me of—"

"Does she speak?" The soldier who asked the question was older, gruff in speech.

Esha merely looked down her nose at him.

"The girl? Is she mute? That's our princess?" he said again.

Some of the men around him murmured in agreement.

"That's no way to speak about your future queen," Esha said calmly.

He spat. "Future queen of nothing. She's a runt of a girl."

Lord Mayank stiffened beside her, but Esha reached out an arm and stopped him.

"I'd watch your tongue, soldier." Esha stepped forward.

"I'll say what I like, especially if it's the truth," he said. The heads around him were nodding. She'd have to address his insubordination quickly, before it grew. A mutiny would be a nightmare right now with Vardaan already on their borders.

"That's a challenge, isn't it, Vilas?" Lord Mayank said quietly. The soldier in question hadn't heard him, but a few of the men around him had and they began to back away. A few tried to stop Vilas before he spoke again, to little success.

"I won't be following her. She's barely out of her wet cloths," Vilas said, louder and more emboldened. One of the men, a friend by the looks of it, tried to grab him and get his attention.

"Definitely a challenge, my lord," Esha said, loud enough for everyone to hear. There was a momentary hush.

"I believe it is one. Vilas, are you prepared to make it official?"

This soldier, Vilas, would back down now. It wouldn't be worth it to him to continue the challenge, but Esha looked over at the soldier and his small cadre of men. She was wrong.

Vilas set his jaw and walked forward. She had misjudged either the strength of his ire at having to follow a girl or his own lack of self-preservation.

"Yes, I am," Vilas said, his hand going to his sword. A few of the men around them stepped back, not wanting to be tainted by association. The others remained where they were, curious at what would happen.

"Are you sure you want to issue a challenge?" Esha said quietly. Only Mayank seemed to heed the low violence in her voice. He stepped back a little, whispering something into the ear of a servant.

The soldier laughed and slapped his biceps. "I'll take you on any day, little woman." A slew of men jeered at his back, heartily enjoying the insinuation in his words.

Esha was glad Kunal wasn't there. He'd do something stupid. Harun at least knew to let her fight her own battles. Mayank seemed to recognize it as well.

"Remember," Esha said. "You asked for it."

Esha reached for her waist sash.

A hand shot out in front of her, holding her back.

Reha walked past her and stopped in front of Vilas, a hand on one hip. She played with the edge of her waist sash idly, but anyone worth their salt would look closer and see the two knife hilts that poked out above.

The princess was almost as tall as Vilas, but he still managed to sneer down at her. Reha took it in stride and looked the soldier up and down.

"I appreciate the help, but I can handle my own problems," she said. "A duel, then, Vilas?"

Vilas nodded, a slow grin coiling up his face, pleased that he had only a girl to beat. He motioned at his comrades to move back and they complied, forming a circle around them. A knife appeared from Vilas's side, glinting threateningly.

Reha responded in kind, drawing both of her knives.

She and Vilas eyed each other, and he had just opened his mouth to say something when Reha, without warning, slashed at the side of Vilas's leather armor with one of her knives. She stabbed the other into his arm.

He let out a strangled cry and rushed forward. Out of knives, Reha raised her fists and aimed a flurry of punches at his torso and one at his jaw before dodging away.

She was a whirlwind of brutality, aiming blows like Esha had seen in the fight houses of Gwali. And she was fast.

Reha didn't bother with niceties in real life and she certainly didn't in her fighting. She went for his weakest areas: backs of the knees, throat, groin.

Vilas punched back, more out of self-defense than anything else, but he didn't know how to respond to her style of fighting. Reha rammed the man down to the ground and wrapped her arms around his neck, squeezing as hard as she could. His body went limp and she let go of him immediately and rose to her feet, brushing off her now mussed and ruined sari.

She turned to face the others, triumph on her face when she was yanked to the ground.

Vilas had grabbed at her feet and was dragging her backward. Mayank moved forward, but Esha stopped him. She knew what he was thinking, that this was too much for a princess.

But Reha wasn't any princess, and if they let her finish this, she'd be a leader to reckon with.

More than anyone, Esha understood having to make your mark.

Reha flipped over and scrambled away as Vilas rose to his feet. He ran at her and swiped a knife at her face. Reha dodged in time, crouching low and jabbing into the soft side of his stomach.

"You . . ." The anger in his eyes was tinged with panic.

Perhaps he had realized he had just tried to stab his future queen. But men weren't particularly logical creatures in Esha's experience. He kept coming at Reha, who ducked and dodged with a neatness that expressed practice.

Reha kept her forearms up to protect her face and one of her exposed forearms caught Vilas's knife. She yelped and stepped back, blood welling in the long gash.

Vilas grinned, chancing a look at his fellow soldiers. Which meant he missed the low simmer of rage on Reha's face. Esha had seen it enough to know the shift was pressing on Reha, and Reha couldn't control it. Which might not be a bad thing.

Reha made a growling noise in her throat, staring at the back of Vilas's head with a feral rage that would have scared Esha if it didn't make her smile.

Her eyes flashed, green, gold, yellow, before settling on a russet-red color. Claws slashed through her skin and her body almost shimmered in the warm haze of the barracks.

"Finally," Esha whispered to Mayank, who looked a bit alarmed.

Vilas turned around, his eyes growing wide, his grip on his sword faltering. The soldiers behind him stepped back and some of them whispered in awe about Naria coming back to life. A few dropped to their knees, swiping four fingers over their chest.

Reha moved with such lightning speed that no one even registered what happened for a second. Vilas was standing, and then he was on the floor, blood spilling out of a wound to his side.

Reha's chest was still heaving and that ferocity was still in her eyes. Esha rushed over and put a hand on Reha. The girl grabbed her wrist at first, the strength in that one gesture enough that Esha was sure she'd be bruised later.

But Esha's touch on her skin seemed to bring her back into her body and Reha blinked up at her, her eyes returning to their normal light brown color.

"See to him," Esha said sharply, pointing at a few soldiers who were standing there, mouths agape.

Reha nodded at her and Esha removed her hand and stepped back. The princess stepped forward, holding her bloody knife at waist height.

"Anyone else?"

A soldier came out of the fray and held out his spear in front of him, pointing at Reha. He took two steps forward and then dropped to his knees, his head bowed.

"To the future Queen Reha," he said.

One by one the other soldiers followed until there were only a few stragglers. Queen Reha stood above them, her chin tilted proudly.

Esha turned away, smiling. "An army," she said to Mayank.

"An army," he confirmed, smiling.

The both of them stepped back and let Reha take the lead. She was now stepping from soldier to soldier, talking to them, learning their names and positions. Esha could sense

Reha's powers lingering under her skin, alive and coursing through her blood.

The powers in Reha went beyond what they'd seen before—what Kunal or Harun or even King Mahir could understand.

And if the soldiers were smart at all, they would have noticed that too.

CHAPTER 28

The Great Library was quiet in the early morning, despite most of the scholars being awake and bustling about. They moved silently and Esha almost wanted to grab one of them and ask them how they did it. It would be a great method for training new recruits.

Instead, Esha walked over to poke Farhan, who had fallen asleep atop a pile of scrolls.

"What?" Farhan shot upright in his chair quickly. He saw her and then brushed the hair out of his face. Esha raised an eyebrow.

"I made Alok get some sleep last night," he responded.

"Which meant you didn't. That is, until now, right?"

Farhan sighed. "Right."

"Have you eat—"

Farhan pointed at a mostly empty tray, with crumbs and some leftover yogurt. "Yes, I ate. Why does no one think I know how to take care of myself?"

Esha brushed a piece of flatbread out of his long hair. "Perhaps because you haven't proven it, Farhan. And we all know how you get when you find something to research."

"Speaking of that," Farhan said. "I think I've had a breakthrough in the location of the Drowned City of Gold."

Esha leaned in. "Show me."

"First, I had to go back and comb through the old texts. Something had gone wrong with the ritual for you to have broken the bond. I thought maybe there was another artifact but no. It wasn't that."

Farhan waved her over to the other side of the desk where there was a large map, with several thin pieces of parchment laid over, each with their own scribbles and drawings. One didn't look like his handwriting.

"Kunal's been helping me," Farhan said when he caught her peering at the new handwriting. "He's very adept at language translation."

"Of course he is," she said, a bit unkindly. She wasn't embarrassed by his reaction from the previous week, or so she kept telling herself. Esha knew Kunal had wanted her, that evidence had been clear, but he was too . . . *Kunal* to accept what was being given to him.

Farhan gave her a look but seemed to decide that it was better not to get involved. He moved past her to point at the edge of the map where Gwali lay.

"See how the other maps, when overlaid, all seem to point to something? I had thought the concentric circles were just to show how the original artifacts had been hidden, evenly across the land. But then—" Farhan pointed to the drawings of the Aifora Mountains on his map. "If you look here, you'll see that the mountains are entirely out of the range of these circles. They're not truly captured in the range."

Esha traced her fingers over the circles and then up to Mount Bangaar in the north of the Aiforas. "That's why the ritual didn't work? Because the mountain isn't part of the original map. But why should that matter? Why are these circles so important?"

"That's what I was wondering too," Farhan said excitedly. He shifted the overlying thin parchments so that the circles locked up together, ringing out across the lands of Jansa and Dharka. "And as Kunal and I began to map out where the artifacts had been found, we noticed a pattern. See here? If we work backward, the circles are emanating from somewhere. Here."

Farhan pointed to a small circle off the coast of Dharka, across from the port of the Red Fortress.

"There?" Esha said.

"There." Farhan gave her an apologetic smile. "The Drowned City of Gold."

Moon Lord's fists. Of course the *drowned* part of the title was literal. Things never got easier, did they?

"Are you sure?"

"Not at all," Farhan said confidently. "It'll take me another few hours to confirm that my calculations are correct and even then, it's a guess. But Kunal said he'd be stopping in. In fact, he's late. He should be here."

"Oh?" Her heart beat a little quicker.

"You could stay and help too, if you want to. Kunal promised me the morning."

Esha ignored the mention of Kunal. But she could stay. She'd already met with Mayank in the morning to go over coronation plans and helping Farhan now might mean answers sooner. Her desire to find the City of Gold was slowly turning to desperation after her chat with Vardaan.

"This is great work, Farhan." Esha squeezed Farhan's shoulder and he turned and looked up at her. He blinked rapidly and flushed.

"It was nothing."

"Not nothing. Our most brilliant mind. You found us the answer—"

"Only a potential answer. Don't tell anyone else yet." Farhan gave her a look. "Harun included."

"He's at the healers anyway. How about I help you?"

Farhan nodded happily. "We'll be able to move much faster if I have two pairs of hands."

Esha nodded. "Tell me what I can do."

Farhan beamed, laying out so many scrolls and papers and chalk scribblings that, ten minutes later, Esha had still only gotten through one scroll and was somewhat regretting her decision to help.

But she got to work.

———◄○►———

Kunal had found his way back to the library after another excursion into the city with Reha. This time, they had prepped in advance and he had made sure Reha was ready to receive the crowds.

The Archer still couldn't draw as big of an audience as the lost princess, that was for sure. And she was getting better at it, knowing who to talk to, where to spend time, whose baby to kiss. Kunal was proud of her, though he wouldn't dare to tell her that. Reha was the epitome of a skittish colt.

He had settled himself to the right of Farhan—Esha was to Farhan's left and Kunal was not going there right now. A pot of ginger chai and plate of almond-pistachio cookies had made their way to the center of the table and Kunal grabbed one of the cookies as he continued his conversation with Farhan. They'd been like this for a while, despite Esha's annoyed sighs. Farhan required somebody, or really something, to bounce his ideas off and Kunal didn't mind volunteering.

"No, look here," Farhan said loudly. "I think if we just move this . . ."

"Wait," Kunal said, grabbing the scroll back from Farhan, who frowned on cue. "There. Do you see it?"

Kunal traced his finger over the dot that landed squarely off the coast of Dharka near the rice paddies.

Farhan nodded, coming closer. "Where I had thought. This confirms it." He looked up in triumph. "The Drowned City of Gold. We have a location. Or an area, at least."

"How sure are you?" Esha said. It was clear she was

resisting the urge to grab the carefully laid plans. Instead, she came around and sidled up to Kunal and peered over his shoulder as best she could. He leaned back and smiled to himself as he heard the way her breath changed.

"Ninety-eight percent," Farhan said.

Esha's eyebrows rose. "That's high. Happy to hear it. We'll send out a team to scout ahead if possible."

"It might not be possible to send out a scouting team. The City of Gold was once the ancient capital of the Southern Lands, the meeting place of the gods when they still walked the earth. It won't be easily revealed to just anyone," Farhan said. "There might be barriers, a requirement to entry."

"Royal blood," Kunal asked.

"Possibly," Farhan said. "It was used to call down the other gods for their counsel. And it seems from these scrolls that the Ruby Temple inside the City of Gold is the first place the Ayana was done and the bond made. There's a chance we could try to do the ritual again there."

"And disturb the sacred?" Laksh said, appearing from the doorway, Alok close behind.

"It's not really disturbing them," Alok said, frowning.

"If we don't try and complete the ritual before Yamini, she could forge a new bond, one that could permanently change the Southern Lands and our way of life," Esha said. "Remember, Yamini and the Yavar are disgruntled that they've been cut out of the bond. If their story is true, Vasu didn't choose not to be part of the bond; he was *refused*.

This could be their chance to get revenge on the rest of the Southern Lands, to harness the magic into a bond just for their land. Then we'll have more than earthquakes to contend with."

Kunal had to admit that he agreed with Esha. He wasn't keen on this idea of finding a lost, ancient city of the gods, but it didn't seem like they had much choice.

"Yamini mentioned something else, when she found me in the jungle."

Esha whipped around. "And you're mentioning this only now?"

"I'm sure Kunal had a reason," Alok said, poking him in the ribs and nudging his head at the others insistently.

"A lot has happened, and I honestly forgot. And, let me just say, this is all getting a bit old," Kunal said. "Why would I have come back here if I were planning to betray you all?"

"Oh, to win back our trust, lull us into a sense of security, and steal the other artifacts," she said.

"And why in the Sun Maiden's name would I want to help the Yavar?" Kunal demanded.

Esha opened her mouth a few times like a fish before letting out a humph. "Fine."

"Would you like to hear about it? Are you done with your tantrum?" Kunal said. By gods she could be infuriating.

Laksh let out a loud cough, but it sounded suspiciously like laughter.

Esha narrowed her eyes at him but gave a tight nod.

"She found me, after that first attack in the jungle. She said she had just come to talk, so I let her talk. Yamini talked of a new world order and asked me if there was something so wrong in changing the world to become a better one," Kunal said.

"Like Vardaan was just trying to *protect* Jansa by overthrowing the queens and taking the throne?" Esha asked sweetly. Kunal winced.

"A new world order," Esha mused. "What could she mean?"

"The country isn't dying from drought," Alok said. He walked over to the table with a thoughtful look on his face. "What we thought would happen, absolute catastrophe, hasn't. Yes, there are political and economic upheaval to deal with, but the land? Magic has not destroyed it. It's replenished it, without the bond."

"Until humans can no longer help themselves," Kunal muttered.

"What?" Esha said.

Kunal sighed. "King Mahir told me the ancient history of the royals. Why the first bond was even made. It was to take away the burden, and power, from the people. In the ancient era, all humans had magic, but they quickly turned to using it for greed, instead of seeing it as a gift from the gods to ensure our connection to our land. It began to be abused. The gods threatened to take away humanity's connection to the land—the magic—which would have meant catastrophe, and the ancient royals convinced them to give the burden to them instead. Only the new version of the bond was able to keep it together."

The group was silent at that. None of them had an answer to Kunal's unspoken questions. How did they know this would hold? Was this the right option for their land?

"It's our best chance," Esha said quietly. "We have to get there before Yamini. She didn't happen to mention if this new world order of hers would only be for the Yavar, did she?"

Kunal shook his head.

"Didn't think so. For all we know, if Yamini gets there first, she'll forge a bond that lets the Southern Lands wither and die. Just as the magic has returned."

Esha didn't need to say what the outcome of that would be for their countries. Devastation. On another level. This bond magic wasn't to be trifled with. They were messing with the magic of the gods.

"As I was saying before, we can't just send out any scouting troops," Farhan said, inserting his objection before it could be forgotten.

"I'll go," Kunal said immediately. "I'll see if I can find the Drowned City of Gold." He needed to do something, anything, right now. The library was a start, but . . .

"You can't go alone," Esha said. "There's too much at risk." She left the rest unsaid, that letting Kunal go alone was not something she was willing to do, but it was obvious from her tone. Kunal bristled.

"We can't send a team," Kunal said. "The location is at

least a week's ride at this time of year with the winds. You'll have no choice but to make stops. Can Reha go—?"

"No," Esha said immediately, almost too quickly. "She's still in royal training right now. I know she'll jump at the opportunity to leave, so we're not going to give it to her. I can go alone."

"Then I'll come too. I can fly us there in under a week. The headwinds going east are much faster in Jansa," Kunal said.

There was an uneasy silence that settled on the room at his words.

Esha cleared her throat. "Fine, that is the most practical choice. Laksh, we could use you on the mission too if you want to—"

"No, no. Sounds like a great mission for two people," he said, emphasizing the word *two*. Laksh gave them both a too-wide smile. "Two people only. You two people."

"Okay . . ." Esha didn't look thrilled at the idea. "Alok?"

"Nope!" He laughed nervously. "While I'm dying to meet the Viper out on a mission, I have no desire to get between the two of you—I mean the incredible dynamic between the two of you. Didn't you both defeat ten Senaps together? So good . . ."

Esha and Kunal looked at each other and there was a flicker of a moment between the two of them where they recognized what they were committing to: days together. He tried to give her a smile, to show her it would be nothing, but his own body betrayed the sudden worry that flooded him.

"So glad to hear how eager you both are to not be on this mission," Esha said drily, turning away from Kunal. "Looks like it's just me and you, soldier."

"Till the end," he said, returning the dry tone.

She didn't respond to that.

CHAPTER 29

E sha cleaned her weapons as the last dregs of the night faded above the palace rooftop. Kunal would be meeting her here at sunrise, but she'd snuck up here early to get time alone, a precious commodity recently.

Harun had protected her from so much of the burden and monotony of running a rebel group—or a palace. And Reha . . . Reha was another problem, as if Esha didn't have enough already. Aside from her suspicions, Reha was having a rough go at her princess lessons. Esha knew she had told Harun she would get her to stay, but how did you convince someone to become a princess, a queen? Give up her life for her people, sacrifice her future for her land?

Not all of them were Kunal.

Even now, a small part of her admired Kunal, resented Kunal, for that honor. He looked his duty in the eye without flinching. Esha felt as if she were being dragged to hers, especially today.

The idea of days with Kunal left her feeling both hot and cold with equal measure. Their kiss after the emergency council was decidedly more than friendly. They were on a knife's edge here.

She shaded her eyes as she looked out over the rooftop and out to the waking city below. She'd been in Gwali for nearly two moons now, the longest she'd been on one mission in a long time. If one could call it simply a mission.

This was her life now.

She told herself that was the only reason she had agreed to scout the City of Gold with Kunal. Esha liked to think she had the ability to put the mission first.

A thud landed behind her.

Esha turned and lifted a hand in greeting before returning to her task, sanding the nicks out of her knives.

Kunal was in armor again, except this time, it was painted Crescent silver. It suited him, actually, a pleasant contrast to his dark skin. What had surprised her was the readiness with which he had agreed to wear it when only a moon ago he had bristled at the idea of even being called a Crescent Blade. Only a moon ago they had disappeared into the streets of Gwali to celebrate *Chinarath*.

Kunal walked over and crouched next to her, grabbing the sand to treat his own weapons. His hair was long now, longer than she had seen it before, and it curled softly at the edges.

Esha's body tightened at his closeness, memories flooding her skin. She hated that he looked good in this armor, that it reminded her of whispered words across a vast hall or stolen moments under darkened marble archways. She hated the angles of his jaw and the scar that attempted to mar the perfection of his lips and failed.

The impulse that made her want to reach out, trace the outline of the scar. Bring her face closer to his.

She coughed and rose to her feet quickly, startling Kunal, who looked up at her in question with those stupid amber eyes.

"We should leave soon, before first light is over."

Kunal nodded tightly and rose to his feet. "Agreed. The sooner we get there the sooner we can get back. Are you ready?"

His hand grazed her arm as he rose, as if he had forgotten that they didn't do that anymore, that they weren't *that* anymore. He pulled away, hunching into his armor.

There was a foot of space between them and Esha was already regretting her choice. That heat. It was already seeping into her bones and he wasn't even touching her. And when his fingers brushed her skin, Esha wanted to step back, to run away.

It was like a spark under her skin, hotter even because of all the unsaid words.

"Esha?"

She realized she hadn't responded to his last question, whether she was ready. She wasn't. Esha wasn't ready to be near him, let alone to be wrapped in his arms.

"I'm ready." She grinned, bright and too cheery. Kunal frowned at her. He knew her too well.

"It might not be like the last time we flew. And I'll have to touch you. . . ."

"Some of us are aware of the consequences of our actions, soldier," she snapped. Her mask went up, around herself and her heart, leaving only the heat. "Anyway, we were always good at that part. Just bad at everything else."

"Esha, don't do that," he started.

"Do what?" she challenged, stepping closer to him, her chin jutting out. This game she could play. Even if it felt like a hundred steps back, it was a comfortable dance.

"You know exactly what." Kunal reached out and pulled her close. Esha fell into him and he encircled her with his arms, his very skin on fire against her own. She looked up at him and her breath caught at the intensity in his eyes. It flickered with heat, desire, and something deeper, something that scared her.

Friends? She was an idiot. They could never be just friends.

In seconds they were in the air, the wind screaming at their back and gusting around them. Kunal held her tightly, and despite hanging on to him like a barnacle, she felt safe in his arms. She opened her eyes and marveled at him.

Man and supernatural. His eagle wings were as broad as four men and seemed as if they had always been a part of him.

"Amazing," she whispered in awe.

The training sessions with King Mahir had helped Kunal to control his powers, but they'd done something else too. Kunal flew with confidence, his powers now part of him instead of foreign. And she had missed it all happening. There were big secrets they both kept, but Esha wondered if somehow these smaller ones, these tiny changes, were worse.

Kunal grinned down at her. "You haven't seen anything yet."

"Try me." She was always up for a challenge.

"If you're sure."

He sped up until the wind was like a whirlwind around her and took her higher up.

"Open your eyes, Esha."

She opened one eye and almost gasped, only remembering at the last second that it was unbecoming for the Viper. Though in Kunal's arms she was never more than Esha, despite what she wanted. She wanted to hate him, so badly.

But here, in his arms, she had to admit to herself that she wanted to love him just as fiercely. If there was still time.

"It's beautiful," she said.

Esha reached out a hand into a cloud that passed them, its chill covering her fingers instantly. Kunal pulled her tighter against him as they sailed through another cloud, one filled with droplets of rain just barely condensed together. Esha was damp when they exited, but she didn't care. She laughed, a smile breaking free onto her face.

Kunal's wings slowed, and he looked down at her. Their faces were inches apart and Esha hadn't felt happier in weeks, months. Being up here made her think that maybe they should stay up here forever, the two of them, never to deal with the realities of the world below.

Perhaps here they could find each other again. Repair their wounds.

Her breath came in shorter and she considered leaning and closing the gap. What would happen if she kissed him, here, right now? Would he say no again?

Kunal and Esha hovered there, but she was the one to pull away, turn her head back toward the ground below. The Viper had no fear; except for the eagle, it appeared.

Looking down immediately made her dizzy but not enough to miss the look of disappointment in his eyes. "We're almost there," he said quietly.

The Viper was smart, cunning, wily.

But Esha?

Esha was only human.

———◄○►———

Kunal flew them to the ground. He put Esha down first and made sure she had a firm foot on the ground before he landed. He didn't remove the arm he had around her waist and she didn't make any sudden moves to run away from him, unlike earlier.

Finally, there was no reason for him to keep holding on. Of course, he could think of plenty of reasons, from the soft curve of her hip to the way her lower back fit into the palms of his hands or the way she fit under his chin.

All of those things that Esha didn't care about anymore. She always did that, switched to the physical, used the desire they both clearly felt as a weapon, a wall.

Esha brushed off her sari, coughing lightly into her fist. A film of awkwardness settled over them, which had never been the case before. Not when they were chasing each other, or trying to kill each other, or after.

It was a new equilibrium. Kunal didn't want it.

He heard rather than saw the change in her demeanor that indicated the moment before was over. "Let's go," Esha said. "There's no time to waste."

She checked her weapons and pack, her Viper mask coming back on inch by inch, and took off into the jungle, assuming he would follow.

Kunal bit back a sigh and took up the rear. He couldn't take his eyes off her no matter how much he tried. He told himself he was just savoring this, one of the last times they might spend together. He painted her in his mind like he always did, the determination in her jaw as she muttered to herself about what direction to go in, the way her hair seemed to defy the constraints of the braid she wore. The sway of her hips, the curve of her cheek, the way she licked her lips when in thought.

It was only this deep observation that allowed him to see the one thing that made the heaviness in his heart lighten. He saw when she turned around, casting a glance at him behind her.

For just a second.

———◁◦▷———

Esha stepped through the unruly, rocky terrain, hopping from flat stone to next. Kunal followed behind her, nimble for someone with wings cascading out of his back.

They had reached the hardest part of their trek, where Kunal couldn't carry them. The terrain was too uneven and he couldn't fly them for fear of being seen. His strength so far had helped them move quickly, as had Esha's ability to grin and bear his touch. Or at least, that was what she was telling herself. Sometimes it was easier to lie to oneself than to anyone else.

Her thoughts drifted to the soldier behind her with alarming frequency, especially after she had caught him staring at her. She would've felt self-conscious except that his attention on her seemed to give her confidence. Added a sway to her step.

They'd gotten by with as minimal words as possible since they had landed, except for a brief respite the night before. They had come across a banyan tree and spent the night there again and something about it—the memories of their first night in the Tej, the softness in his eyes as he asked if she needed water or if she was tired—it loosened the strings around her talk. They had fallen asleep talking, like before. At the memory now, Esha felt something relax in her. Maybe she was making this too difficult.

Esha motioned to Kunal as she maneuvered over a particularly tricky section, pointing to the instabilities in the rock. Finally, they got to the rock face they had seen earlier, the last obstacle.

She started the climb, Kunal to her left. He took to the climbing like a fish in water. Esha was unsurprised. Her lemon boy had always loved climbing to the highest turrets in the palace. Why would this be any different?

Esha glanced down and caught a glimpse of the jungle canopy below, green and gold, though dimmer than ever before. It was the last defense of foliage before the land gave way to the desert and the sand beyond.

She reached up, the rock above her holding firm as she tested, and then dug her hand in to pull herself up, the strain on her muscles welcome after weeks of being in the palace. Esha looked down for a second but pulled her head back sharply, dizziness engulfing her. The tops of the trees below felt as if they were leagues away and the change made her stomach suddenly drop.

She turned her attention back up, and soon, she caught up with Kunal. They both heaved themselves over the mountain ledge at the same time. Esha tumbled into Kunal, who was just getting to his feet, and they rolled over a few times before coming to a stop as they hit a fallen log. She ended up sprawled on top of him.

The unexpected contact made her entire body flush and a warm heat pulsate through her limbs. Did he have to be so cursed handsome?

"This feels familiar," Esha said under her breath, but of course, Kunal heard.

He turned his face up and grinned at her. "Very. All we need is sticky tar."

Kunal wrapped his hands around her as Esha moved to get up, preventing her from moving. He leaned forward and she thought he might kiss her, her heart seizing in terror— or want, she couldn't tell.

But he simply took the curl that had escaped her braid and tucked it back into the coils, or tried to. Her hair had a mind of its own.

Kunal pulled them both up in one swift motion and the moment he let go of her Esha scooted away. Or at least she was going to, but the soldier took hold of her hand.

"Stay close," he said.

"Do you think I need protection?" she said, scoffing. "I know these parts well."

"Oh no, I'm the one who needs protection," he said. Kunal tilted his head, his lips curving into a grin. "So you can't leave."

Esha snorted. "That's preposterous. You, with those huge wings?"

His wings flattened against his body, almost as if in response.

She grumbled and started to move but let him keep her hand, tugging at him to follow. A few minutes later, Esha and Kunal came to a halt. This mountain was the center of the circle Farhan had marked on the map.

Below them to their right, laid out on the edge of ruby-red cliffs, was the Red Fortress. They glanced at each other but didn't say anything. The memories said it all.

To their left was open coastline, and the possibility of the City of Gold.

CHAPTER 30

The wind buffeted Kunal's wings as he traveled over the coast of Dharka, past where Jansa and Dharka joined.

He had left Esha behind to do the legwork of scouting on land, knowing that flying would be far more efficient for the coastline. And far less dangerous. Esha might be the Viper, but the sailors of the Ilyasa Port weren't known to be friendly.

He eased into the nearest airstream and enjoyed the feeling of weightlessness that always followed. Kunal always did enjoy this part of flying. The freedom was unparalleled and nothing compared in his human form. In some ways, he had been searching for this feeling since he was a child. Perhaps he had known even then, on some level, what was in his blood.

Kunal wheeled lower to the ground in his eagle form, gliding along a low airstream near the coast of Dharka. He turned his attention to the strip of gold beach that separated the land from the blue below. The map indicated that the temple was right off the coast, near a jutting rock formation.

Kunal spotted a string of rocks that looked like sharp, taloned fingers pointing straight up into the sky. Esha had said this area was considered unlucky for sailors, and most traders and fishermen avoided it, which made sense to him now. If one got too close to those jagged rocks, it would be the end for their ship—or for them. But he was curious if there was something more to the warnings. Something supernatural.

The wind shifted and Kunal leaned in, letting the change in direction bring him closer to the rocks and the ocean below. He wasn't quite sure what he was looking for.

Kunal sharpened his hearing, picking out the sounds of seagulls above, the crash of waves below, the whistle of the wind, and listened for more. At first, there was nothing. But then—Kunal picked up the slightest of pulses, a deep, buried, watery song.

His eyes flew open just as a gust of wind blew him off pace and sent him soaring into the rock formation. He flapped his wings with all his strength and broke away as fast as he could.

There had been a song. An ancient, dangerous one. Buried deep beneath the crashing waves of water below, just out of reach of his hearing. He couldn't pinpoint where the song had come from, not without returning to get closer to those rocks, but he had heard it.

Perhaps the sailors were right, and the rocks were merely unlucky.

But Kunal had felt something when he had flown above those rocks, where the song was strongest.

A presence.

The Drowned City of Gold.

———◄○►———

They returned to the palace a few days later and called for a meeting immediately. Kunal reported back what he found as soon as he could, after corroborating it with Farhan. The location he and Esha had found fit perfectly with the map from the copper scroll and once they had overlaid the location as the center, everything fell into place.

"Be careful not to make any marks," Farhan said from his spot.

Laksh peered over Kunal's shoulder. "Didn't he say not to make any marks?"

Kunal jumped and turned to glare at the other man. "I didn't until you startled me."

Laksh snickered. Kunal rolled his eyes and turned back to his work just as Alok came into the room. Laksh's face brightened when he saw that Arpiya was close behind.

"Have I mentioned how happy I am that you two are speaking again?" Alok said.

"Once or twice," Kunal muttered.

While Kunal normally loved the company, he also was growing irritated by the increasing number of people streaming into and out of the Great Library when he was finally close to overlaying the map onto a proper scroll. With some peace he could sketch out the other land markers and chart a path for them to take. Every moment they wasted was one Yamini could use.

Arpiya made her way over to help Kunal and he looked at her gratefully, passing her a compass and a piece of chalk. This was the boring part of campaigns that Alok and Laksh had always hated, where you made your plans and checked and rechecked. He didn't want to take any chances this time.

Laksh bent over the table near Arpiya, leaning close to her and whispering something into her ear. She giggled, which was enough in itself to concern Kunal, but he figured she could take care of herself. And Laksh had seemed to keep his word. He had only his best self for Arpiya and she seemed to like him even at his worst. Kunal had overheard them speaking of the best ways to deceive someone at cards at dinner the previous night.

"How can I help?" Alok asked.

Kunal sighed and straightened, using the moment to stretch his aching hands. "I need all those scrolls organized and the distances confirmed so I can complete this map."

"On it," Alok said, surprising Kunal. How much they had all changed in these past six moons.

"Are you ready?" Alok asked, his voice quieting as he sorted the scrolls. "For tomorrow? I know Esha is anxious to leave, get to the city first."

"Ready as I'll ever be. I can't help but admit that I can't wait till this is all over."

"Me too," Alok said. "I miss my bed."

Kunal laughed at that.

Tomorrow, they would be one step closer to saving the land. And for the first time, Kunal could see the dream as a reality.

They just had to make it through.

CHAPTER 31

Esha woke to the noise of ringing bells. She shot up in her bed and threw off the covers, racing to the windows.

The palace was on fire.

Flames rose from the outer side of the southwest corner, near the western gate. It didn't seem to have reached the palace proper yet, but if it kept going unchecked it would certainly take over the gardens and the western wing.

Esha tugged her weapons out from their hiding place under her pillows and strapped them into her waist sash as quick as she could. A glance outside told her that everyone was rushing to the fire, to contain it most likely.

Esha took a sharp turn left away and ran toward the eastern part of the palace. She trusted her team. They'd soon realize that fire wasn't common at this time of year, especially with the amount of moisture in the air. That it was sabotage. They would contain the fire and they would deal with the threat to the palace's and its residents' safety.

She pumped her legs faster, willing them to carry her to the one place she suspected did need protection.

Esha veered sharply into the Great Library, spotting the small locked chest tucked into one of the shelves. She didn't move toward it, especially when she heard the shuffle of feet paces away.

"I was hoping to find you," a voice said from behind her.

Esha turned around, her hands at her weapons.

Yamini was decked in dark clothing, her trademark furs replaced by a loose linen uttariya thrown over her shoulders and head. It was a nice attempt, but the heir to the Yavar throne was not someone that could be easily forgotten. Her lips curved into a smile and Esha thought maybe she saw a glimmer of true joy at seeing Esha again.

There had been a moment when Esha had believed them friends.

She had believed a lot of wrong things.

"I won't let you—"

"Esha, it's not that I don't like you. But I can't let my people down, not when we have a chance to fulfill the promise of the ballads of Vasu. So I'll do whatever it takes to get that scroll. Including going through you."

The scroll? Esha blanched as she realized what Yamini wanted. Not the artifacts but the copper scroll. Their map to the City of Gold.

"Good luck," Esha said, standing her ground. "Going

through me won't be that easy."

"You Southern Landers never appreciated what you had," Yamini said. "You destroyed it for power and greed. And now you've finally discovered the City of Gold. You've been behind this whole time, bickering and fighting and destroying yourselves. Why should you find the city? Why should you remake the world?" Her words were bursting with deep-seated anger. But Yamini quickly recovered, her face once again placid as a lake.

"That's a nice little speech," Esha said.

She kept underestimating this woman. And if they already knew about the City of Gold, they were closer than she had thought. But it was also clear that Yamini didn't know *where* it was, not just yet. Otherwise she wouldn't be here trying to steal the copper scroll from them.

"Who let you in?" Esha demanded.

"Who said anyone did?"

Esha walked closer to Yamini, her whips out and ready at her sides. "I've known for a while something was amiss. You found Kunal and Reha at the mountain and then again in the jungle."

Yamini rose an eyebrow. "Perhaps."

"Have you been working with Vardaan?" Esha asked.

"No." Yamini's face was honest. "I haven't thought about him since he failed to deliver the princess to us."

"Then—" Esha racked her brain. Vardaan had mentioned a mole. . . .

A boom went off in the distance. A flash of panic crossed

Yamini's face, one that surprised Esha with its urgency. Something was going wrong.

"Clearly you have a contact within the palace, someone who told you we've been keeping to the east wing. That's why you set the fire to the west wing, didn't you? To draw us out? Who is it?" Esha demanded.

"I did as you said, Yamini. Now let's get—"

Zhyani walked into the room, carrying a long sword and a sack slung across her back.

———◄o►———

Kunal had sensed something amiss before the smoke had drifted into his room. In a minute he had donned his armor and run for Reha's room to ensure their queen was safe.

"It's an attack," she said when she saw him. She was already awake, her waist sash of knives tied around her hips. "Sulphur in those fumes."

Kunal nodded. "The army doesn't use sulfur; they use camphor. It's the Yavar."

They took off at a sprint toward the Great Library. Kunal's heart sped faster at the thought of Esha in danger. As they drew closer they heard the crack of Esha's whips— and voices.

They turned the corner to see Esha facing off with Zhyani and Yamini. "Zhyani?" Esha's voice wavered. "How could you do this? To the Scales?"

Reha pushed forward, but Kunal swung out an arm to hold her back and shook his head.

Zhyani gritted her teeth and swung her longsword

around. She took a defensive stance. "You don't understand, you'd never understand. Some of us don't have a choice to let go of our past," Zhyani said, standing her ground in front of Esha. She swallowed and stood tall. "Where is the copper scroll?"

"Doesn't matter if I understand. But will Reha?" Esha said, ignoring her question.

Reha stumbled back, bracing herself against the doorframe. "No," she whispered. "There has to be a reason."

Kunal squeezed her shoulder but didn't say anything. His eyes were on Esha, and the enemy who had been plaguing them. "Stay here," he said.

He slunk back and decided to approach from the shelves behind Yamini. He stayed as silent as he could be.

———<o>———

Esha still couldn't believe it.

Zhyani.

Esha noticed the flicker of pain in Zhyani's eyes and paired it with her previous words. Reha's oldest friend wasn't here by choice. Vardaan's taunts had held truth in them, even if he had bent the truth to suit his needs.

Not a mole for Vardaan but a betrayal nonetheless. Vardaan had known that Yamini had approached Zhyani. How?

The answer came immediately. He had overheard them together, much like Harun had overheard Yamini's plans, reminding Esha that yet again, it was easy to underestimate the powers of the royals when they were unseen. Esha knew they should've kept Vardaan in the blue-sapphire ropes—and put wax in his ears.

"Zhyani, what did they threaten you with?" Esha said.

"Nothing," Zhyani said back viciously. But she had given herself away with a glance out the window, at the citadel. Esha remembered she had left the city with her team—perhaps an attempt to escape?

"Your team," Esha said softly. "You don't have to do this." She stepped closer. "I'll get your team to safety. Reha—"

"Just give it to her and let this be over. Please," Zhyani said. There was a snarl of emotions in her voice. "The sooner you give it to her, the sooner we can get to the cistern. She caught me when I tried to leave, when I tried to stop all of this. I had just been so angry. . . ."

The cistern? Esha could think of only one cistern. It lay beneath the citadel, directly under the dungeons.

That must be where Zhyani's team was being held right now.

"Zhyani—" she said, trying to show the woman she understood, that they could work together.

"Enough talk," Yamini shouted.

She yelled and lunged forward, her spear out. Esha dodged out of the way, ducking under the swing of her spear. Esha lashed her whips against the ground, leading Yamini to a more open part of the library, away from where the copper scroll was hidden.

Esha dodged Yamini's spear as she walked backward, leading her away. Her whips met the spear, but something about the spear itself repelled the tips of her weapons. They weren't able to wrap around Yamini's spear, and for the first time, Esha was at a loss.

She began to aim for the woman instead.

Esha was able to lash Yamini and she cried out, almost dropping her spear. But her training was solid and she managed to keep hold of it, even as Esha spun around and unleashed her whip again. This time it caught Yamini's arm and the spear did clatter to the ground.

But Yamini grabbed hold of the whip itself and tugged.

Esha hurtled forward, falling to the ground. She let go of the whip and rolled out of the way as Yamini stabbed her spear down where Esha had been.

She was strong, just as Esha had expected, and craftier than she thought. If only Yamini hadn't turned out to be her enemy, they might have been actual friends.

As Esha got up, Yamini caught her with a jab to her face. Esha narrowly turned away, only catching the edge of the punch. Esha flew back and hit the table, the sharp edge of it slicing into her back.

Esha fell to the ground. She scrambled back on the floor, searching around for one of her whips, both of which evaded her.

There. With a swift movement she rolled and caught her whip again. She rose to her feet, slower than before, and wiped the blood from her nose.

"Why are we fighting, my lady?" Esha said, panting. "We could be on the same side."

"There is only one side. My own."

"That seems lonely."

"It's practical," Yamini said. "Served me well so far."

"Really?"

Esha was stalling now, but only because she had heard noises outside. She didn't know if it was friend or foe, but either way, she needed a few seconds to regain her balance. Fighting Yamini was like what Esha imagined fighting herself would be like. Hard. Brutal. Devious.

A Yavar soldier burst through the rows of shelves of the Great Library, followed by a growling, keening noise. Behind him was Kunal, phased into his talons and running at a supernatural speed. A few Blades had made their way to the library door and were fending off attackers as best they could.

Esha cursed and glanced at the shelf with the ancient chest containing the artifacts.

Yamini's eyes glinted in the shifting lights.

"Well played, Lady Esha," she said, before running for the shelf. Esha sped after her, but she was too late. "But no match."

Yamini grabbed the chest in triumph, but Esha scooped up her spear and threw it, lodging Yamini's uttariya into the wood of the shelf behind her. Like Kunal had trapped her, moons ago. Yamini fared as well as she did, struggling to unravel herself. Esha ran over and knocked the chest out of the woman's hands, grabbing it before it fell to the floor.

"Wrong," Esha said.

To her side, Kunal had managed to tackle the Yavar soldier to the ground and he held him in a choke hold.

She slid the chest across the floor into the stacks of shelves, and whipped back around to Yamini. Esha moved to wrap her whip around her neck and ease her into unconsciousness.

Yamini sprang forward, grabbing and twirling the spear around as she moved toward Esha. Esha dodged back but the spear tip caught her across the arm and she staggered back, searing pain shooting up her arm and shoulder.

Esha bit down hard, fighting back a wave of pain. She stumbled to the ground, opening the way for Yamini.

No. Not like this. Esha tried to crawl toward her. She couldn't let Yamini take the copper scroll. Everyone else was occupied fighting off the Yavar. Only Esha was open to stop her.

Kunal burst into view, throwing his body in front of the chest. He was wounded too, and slower than normal.

"I don't want to hurt you, Kunal," Yamini said.

"Then don't."

"I have to do this," Yamini said. "It's my duty."

Kunal hesitated, for only a moment's time. It was enough.

Yamini threw a perfectly aimed spear. It hit Kunal in the shoulder and he fell to the ground, to his knees.

Then she charged at him, her second spear pointed at the dead center of his chest.

Kunal wouldn't be quick enough. Even with his powers,

the second spear would skewer him.

Esha let loose a guttural cry, like Reha's, and it sparked something deep inside her, something that gave her the last bit of strength she needed to rush forward. Esha lashed her whip out toward Yamini's feet as she rammed into Kunal, knocking him over.

The spear thudded into the wood above them and Yamini went flying.

A cry lit up the room, a groan of pain that sounded too much like her lemon boy.

But he was alive.

———◄○►———

All Kunal knew was that he had hesitated for what could be his last time. He had closed his eyes. He had been ready for the end.

But the crack of a whip had rent the air and Kunal had felt himself go flying. And even now, through the haze and fog of pain, he knew that Esha had saved him.

Something cracked open in his heart, spilling forward until all Kunal could do was choke out sounds, ones that wished they were words.

Esha looked down at him, mistaking the noises. "Kunal. Are you okay?"

Her voice was frantic, desperate. She cupped his face, not realizing the trail of bloody fingerprints she left.

"I'm okay," he said.

Esha sat back heavily, cradling her face in her hands.

He reached out to caress her cheek.

"I'm okay," he repeated, softer. Slowly, she nodded. Her chest heaved with exertion, her breaths calming down as they both noticed the chaos around them.

"It would have to be the world ending to take me away from you," he said quietly. Her eyes lit up in recognition at the words he had told her before the Sun Mela chariot race.

"Then this isn't the end of the world?"

Kunal smiled and shook his head. He struggled up to a seated position despite Esha's protests, dragging himself over to collapse against a stone wall. He snapped the spear handle and pulled it out of his shoulder in a swift movement.

An armor-clad Laya burst into the library, searching for someone. "My lady!"

Esha's head bobbed up. "Yes?"

"The citadel," she said, panting and resting her hands on her knees. Laya must have run the whole way here from the citadel. "It's been attacked by the Yavar."

Kunal's head began to spin—from the onslaught of information and the rush of blood. That's what Yamini had needed from Zhyani. A distraction.

And something far worse. Kunal had a feeling Yamini had known exactly who was being kept in the citadel. Esha seemed to realize it as well.

"We need to get to the citadel and the cistern immediately," Esha said to Laya. "Go check on the dungeons. Now. We'll catch up."

Laya saluted and sprinted away.

Kunal looked to where Yamini had been standing, ferocity and steel, moments ago.

The spot was empty now.

He scanned the room, noticing the small jeweled chest still at the back of the room. Something was off, something was wrong. And then it hit him.

The chest was open and the ivory satin of its insides was empty.

Yamini was gone, and the copper scroll with her.

Kunal gripped Esha's arm, urgency suffusing his voice. "The citadel. Vardaan. I'll be fine. But . . ."

Esha didn't need to be told twice.

"Stay here," Esha said. "You better not move a muscle, lemon boy. I'll be back soon and then we can discuss how you seem to enjoy constantly putting yourself in danger."

She waved over a Blade, giving him short precise directives to Kunal's care.

Her face was grim as she left.

———◇———

The pathway between the palace and the citadel was deserted this early in the morning. Esha caught up with Laya despite the stitch growing in her side. She didn't have time to think about pain when so much was at stake.

If Yamini had released Vardaan . . . it could be disaster.

Esha cursed violently. Laya did a double take.

"My lady?"

"Please, stop calling me that. As you can tell, I'm not much of a lady."

They pushed through the gates that separated the royal pathway from the citadel and rushed down the remaining flights of stairs.

It was chaos.

Broken bars of wood and bent metal were strewn about the last landing of stairs and farther into the now-open entrance to the dungeons. Three mangled bodies lay at the foot of the door, long vicious cuts slashed across faces and bodies.

Esha's muscles tightened at the sight in front of her, her jaw clenching.

No. No, it couldn't be.

She sprinted to the cell at the end of the room where she had taunted Vardaan only a few weeks ago.

But she knew before she got there what she would find.

An empty cell, the bars bent and the room torn up. More injured soldiers littered the ground, their shields and weapons having proven useless. One of them rose to a seated position, a hand held tightly to the gaping wound in his belly. "My lady . . ."

Esha dropped to her knees and tore off the end of her sari. She wrapped it quickly around the soldier and cinched it tight. He winced but dropped his hand. Blood seeped into the ground below them, tinting the cracked stones a dark red.

"I'm sorry . . . the old king escaped," he said in a wheeze. "Vardaan escaped. We couldn't hold him back."

Esha wiped the soldier's brow. "It's not your fault. He had help."

"The Yavar knew he was being held here. They knew how many of us there were, where our posts were. It was over before it started." The soldier gasped, his eyes fluttering.

"Rest," Esha said. "It's not your fault."

If anyone's, it was Zhyani's.

But Esha couldn't hold that rancor in her either. Not fully.

Zhyani had tried to fix a choice made in anger and instead had put her entire team in danger. Had that not been Esha a few moons ago? Esha still remembered the rash decision she had made, the whip she had left behind. The moment that had unraveled this entire story.

"Laya, go to the cistern below. I think Zhyani's team might be held there."

Laya nodded and left her, taking a few Blades with her.

Esha got to her feet with a few shaky steps, balancing against the stone wall. The adrenaline from before fled her body, leaving her feeling like a husk.

The copper scroll, gone.

Vardaan, gone.

Everything was gone.

CHAPTER 32

Esha was sitting on the bed when Kunal woke up.

"How are you feeling?" she asked, drawing a hand over his forehead.

He groaned in response.

"Nothing's broken. Just a little hole in your shoulder. It's healing pretty well." She sounded as if she was trying to reassure him.

"Better than I would've expected," he said, wincing. He felt like someone had scraped eggshells all over his arms.

There was a moment of silence between them, alone together in the room in a way they hadn't been in a long time. Memories surfaced, ones which were plunged back down before Kunal felt a new sort of pain.

They stared at each other, both unsure what to say.

"Esha—" he started.

She held up a hand and he closed his mouth instantly.

The look on her face was like fire and brimstone, a decision made. Kunal hoped it wasn't an end. That this wasn't the end.

"No more throwing yourself in front of people to die. No more reckless risks, you hear me?" she said.

Kunal stared at her. Moons ago, before meeting her, no one would have ever put *Kunal* and *reckless* in the same sentence. Back at the Fort he had never stood up for anything real, a way to avoid risk—or failure.

"Hello?" Esha said, growing annoyed. "Does staring at me mean yes?"

"Why?"

"Why what?"

"Why no more risks?"

Esha huffed. "Maybe I just don't want you to die. Is that enough of a reason? You're not allowed to die," she repeated.

"I'm not allowed to die? And why is that?"

"You know exactly why."

"I want to hear you say it."

Silence hung between them.

"I don't regret it," he said softly, before he lost his nerve. "I know you might hate me for my choice to leave, but I don't regret it."

"I know." Her tone was wry, her mouth twisted into a half smile. "And I did hate you for it—not because you made the choice but because you left me out of it. Maybe next time just leave me a note?"

Kunal chuckled. "I tried, if you can believe it." He

swallowed hard. "I hope you can forgive me."

"I have, Kunal. Why do you think I'm so annoyed at you for risking your life?" Esha said. She reached a tentative hand out before pulling close to Kunal. He allowed it and nuzzled his face into her hair, letting the curls capture his smile. There was a hesitancy in her body, different from before.

"It'll never be the same, will it?" he said quietly.

"No," Esha said. "But maybe that's not a bad thing."

"I suppose . . ." Kunal stopped. Something niggled at him, a realization waiting to be discovered. "Wait."

"What?" Esha asked immediately, her hands going to her whips.

"Maybe change isn't a bad thing," was all he said.

"What do you mean?"

"Never mind," he said, shaking his head. "Just a thought. I am starving, though."

Esha looked as if she wanted to push him on what he had started to say, but instead held out a hand. Her eyes were bright, promising a new start, a new road. "Come on, the others are waiting."

He took her hand.

———◇———

The mood in the room had dipped lower than the sun outside.

Vardaan had escaped in the chaos of the Yavar break-in. Yamini had stolen the scroll. The team was gathered in one place, scattered about the room like planets in their own orbits. Kunal was suddenly uncertain of what to say to them all.

Esha squeezed his hand, at his side. A rush of affection flooded him at the sight of her next to him, her strong profile never wavering.

She stepped forward to speak to the room when there was a tap at the door. Aahal got up to open it, rubbing a hand against his groggy face. He straightened at the sight of the Blade on the other side.

"Laya," Esha said, her voice carrying a sigh in it.

"I'm sorry, my lady. You asked for a report a few days ago, on the status of the land and magic after the bond was broken." The girl shifted in place, clearly uncomfortable.

"Yes, yes. Has it only been a few days?" Esha asked to no one in particular. The aftermath of those days in question could be seen all around them, in the weary stares and heavy movements of their team. They had taken Zhyani and her team into custody until they could sort out the tangled loyalties. Esha had spent days questioning and talking to the woman only to realize how little prepared they had been for the Yavar.

Yamini had approached Zhyani during the Sun Mela itself, and when Zhyani had refused to help her anymore, Yamini had taken drastic measures. Still, Zhyani was helping Esha and their side now, laying out chains of command and giving them other information about the Yavar. But it felt like weeks had gone by. Not days.

"It has been only a few days, my lady," Laya confirmed.

"But you'll be pleased to hear this. The reports about the land's magic aren't that bad." She cleared her throat. "In fact, they're not bad at all, I would say."

"What?" Esha said. "What does that mean?"

"Really?" Alok said from his seat.

"That's what the reports say. The river is unpredictable without the bond, ebbing and flowing. But after its disappearance, most people are just happy to have their water and livelihoods back. They can handle the tides, even if they are new to them. They can relearn the rhythms of the river. Adapt. It's not a catastrophe."

Esha nodded. "I had hoped for that. People are slowly awakening to their connection with nature. But the magic?"

Laya looked uncomfortable. "Small occurrences, my lady. A man in Onda was able to speed up his crop growth with the water."

Kunal had stayed silent until that moment, unsure what to say or how to feel. But at the look of fascination on Farhan's face, he spoke. "How are people handling it? What are they saying?"

"That it is the return of the gods to our land. Or that it is an abomination. Two young men have died from attacks from a mountain lion that was magic crazed."

Harun pursed his lips in thought. "Of course. We will have to send out people to help."

"And up north?" Esha asked.

"The same," Laya said. "Nothing has changed. The magic has not touched the land past the Aiforas. I'm not sure the Yavar even know what has truly happened down here."

Esha thanked Laya for the report and closed the door after she left. She leaned against it, turning to face the silent room, each person digesting the information in their own way.

The Southern Lands were returning to an era bygone, feeling the constructive and destructive forces of the magic flooding back into the land, but the Yavar? They were closed off, again. They might not deal with catastrophe, but they'd be robbed of the benefits too.

It wasn't right. There had to be a better way and Kunal wanted to find it.

Esha caught his eyes, raising an eyebrow at him. He gave her a smile, shaking his head. He was fine.

Maybe change isn't a bad thing.

His words from earlier stuck in his mind, tangling with his other questions and thoughts until a new idea formed.

"Perhaps we've been wrong all along, trying to save something that needed to be put into the past," Kunal said slowly.

To her credit, Esha didn't immediately turn away. Maybe she had been thinking it as well. Maybe she had felt the tides of change brushing against her skin, like he had.

"We've been fighting so hard for a status quo that doesn't even serve the people anymore. And why are we trying to prevent the Yavar from having their bond? Yamini is not wrong in wanting a connection to the land and gods."

"How could you say that?" Bhandu said immediately.

"Listen. I'm not saying she's going about it right. It seems she sees it as a lose-lose situation. But what if there was a way for all of us to win?" Kunal said.

"There isn't."

"I beg to disagree, Bhandu," Laksh said. He stood up from his seat, taking in the scattered people in the room. "That's the kind of thinking that made the Blades and the Scales work at cross-purposes for moons. We need to think ahead, not cling to the past. Maybe Kunal has a point."

"Oi, are you calling me old, Scale?" Arpiya put a reassuring hand on Bhandu, but he shook her off. "Don't touch me; you're as bad as him."

Arpiya looked stricken, and Esha stepped in. "Bhandu, that's enough. We're discussing solutions and unless you have a good reason that this is a bad one, we're going to consider it."

"It? What are we even considering? Working with those horse thieves in the north?" Bhandu said, clearly flustered.

"No," Esha said. She looked pointedly at Bhandu. "I'm not saying we work with them. I don't think Kunal is either. But perhaps we can force their hand into an outcome that isn't a disaster to one of us. There's nothing wrong with wanting land and food for your people. Do you really disagree with that?"

Bhandu's shoulders slumped. "No, I don't. I just— My grandpa was killed by Yavar, during the War in the North."

"That's why we need to end this," Kunal said, speaking up. "Yavar kill our men, we kill Yavar men, I've killed

Dharkans, you've—" He looked at all of them. "Killed Jansans. It's a cycle, a vicious cycle that will continue to churn on and on if we're not willing to end it. If we stop it from spinning, we could end this. Don't you see?"

Kunal walked into the middle of the room and Esha followed. He gestured at all of them, at a loss for words. How did he explain this? Telling Esha was one thing. He had understood her pain and rage. He knew how to speak to her.

Esha stepped in for him. "I think what the soldier is trying to say is to look at us. We've all hurt each other in some way—"

"Not me—" Aahal said.

"—or threatened each other."

Bhandu nodded with a shrug.

"And yet, we're here together. We decided to leave the past behind and build a better future. But that future can't be built without taking a chance, without real change."

There was a beat of silence in the room, a breath of consideration. They might have fought more if not for another interruption at the door.

Farhan ran in and Alok jumped to his feet, moving toward the boy. "What's wrong?" Alok asked, looking at Farhan's face.

"Nothing," Farhan said. There was a look of such happiness on his face, it looked as if he'd swallowed the sun itself. "I think we have it, even without the copper scroll. The Drowned City of Gold.

"I took the map we had started to build—Kunal had

the great idea of tracing it out ourselves—and the information gathered from his scouting mission. It matches up here, do you see?" Farhan moved frantically, laying out the parchments over themselves into something that looked like a map.

"No," everyone chorused.

Farhan's brow furrowed, clearly irritated. Alok reached out a calming hand. "Let me help." He arranged some of the papers and let Farhan order him about.

"Now that's true love," Arpiya said softly. Laksh's head cocked to the side.

"Ordering someone around?" he asked.

"Letting someone order you around."

Kunal chuckled but leaned forward. He was eager to see Farhan's deduction based off his idea. Could it be true? Could they actually have the location to the City?

"Here." Farhan pointed. "It's transcribed."

Esha gasped from her corner. She shot up and whirled around. "The question is, does Yamini know where it is? Will she be waiting for us there? Or get there first?"

"She has the scroll, but it took us days to decipher it and our care in treating the old material ensured that we wrote nothing on it. None of our maps will be traceable on that," Farhan said. "That will certainly slow them down. Unless they already had part of it," he added.

Kunal's rising spirits sank at that thought.

"I checked the reports this morning," Aahal said from the corner. "There haven't been any Yavar troop movements in that direction, but we can keep an eye on it."

Esha nodded. "It won't be long before she discovers the location too. The copper scroll won't hide all of its secrets from her, not for too long, even without our findings."

"Now the question is, how do we get it back from her?" Farhan said.

"Send me," Aahal said excitedly. "I got a new weapon I'm dying to try out."

"Raid on their camp," Bhandu said.

"A knife to the heart," Arpiya said. Laksh gave her a look, but it wasn't one of disgust.

"I'm learning so much about you," he said. "I kind of like it." She shrugged, a faint blush on her cheeks.

"No," Harun said. They all turned to look at him. "She'll be expecting us to react like that. We can't try to steal the scroll back. We can only hope to get there first."

Farhan gasped. "We're not going to get the scroll back? Do you know how many centuries of information and knowledge are in that scroll, waiting to be discovered?"

"We'll get it back eventually," Harun said, trying to mollify the now-distraught Farhan.

Kunal looked between them, a curious look on his face. "I have an idea," he said. "A way to solve all of this. But it won't be easy." He looked out at all of them. "And we might have to awaken the gods."

Silence reigned for a moment, uncertain and heady.

Bhandu spoke first, as always. "What in the Moon Lord's name are you talking about, cat eyes?"

A knock at the door interrupted Kunal's answer. Laya pushed into the room without waiting.

"Laya, we can get the afternoon report later," Esha said.

"My lady, I think you'll want to hear this."

Esha's brow furrowed. "Go on, then."

"He's here," she said breathlessly. Sweat beaded at her brow. "Vardaan is here at the gates, with an army."

CHAPTER 33

The room descended into silence. It wasn't a calm silence, like Kunal normally craved, but full of terrible possibilities.

He couldn't believe it, didn't dare believe it. The faces surrounding him spoke of the same conflict. This was the last thing they needed after Yamini's attack.

"What do you mean he's at the gates?" Bhandu demanded, shattering the fragile atmosphere.

"Literally at the gates?" Aahal asked, eyes wide as he glanced at the window nearby.

Laya nodded, sending a nervous glance at Esha, who had still not said a word. "The army caught sight of something early this morning, but it wasn't until the sun rose that they saw it for what it is. They sent out scouts that just returned, and they let us know at once. Vardaan's army has us surrounded on the eastern and southern sides. Our western and northern sides are protected, even though the river is weak. We haven't spotted any ships yet, but the possibility can't be ignored."

"Has General Mayank been notified?" Esha asked finally. Laya nodded. "Good. Bring him and the Senap commander to the war room in ten minutes. We'll wrap up here."

Laya bowed and exited the room.

"How in the Sun Maiden's name are we going to get out of the city now?" Reha asked, running a hand through her hair. She looked as if she had aged years in a few days, especially after having to carry Zhyani off in chains. The past few days weighed on them all. "Surrounded. We won't be able to leave. We'll have to stay and fight."

She glanced at Kunal, question in her eyes.

But Kunal had no answer for her.

———◄◦►———

Kunal made his way through the palace, dodging servants and rebels carrying spears and moving buckets of tar and pitch.

Preparations for the siege were under way across the palace and the citizens of Gwali had been alerted to the danger that lurked outside the city gates. That morning had already seen one attack from Vardaan's eastern flank, which had left the wall standing but sustaining heavy damages to the guard tower. Lord Mayank had rushed extra troops to the eastern gates and the martial quarter was in controlled chaos.

Outside the palace ramp were masses of men and

women, those who had come to fight and defend their city. The Jansan army was turning no one away. They couldn't afford to. From the open windows of the palace, shouts could be heard, Senaps and footmen teaching basic defensive and attack positions to those who had no training. In the courtyard, the more advanced fighters were going through the army calls and practicing drills.

Kunal wished he was down there with the new soldiers, helping them prepare for the battle in front of them. But he had taken on a new role beside Esha, helping strategize and giving her and Harun as much information as possible.

Lord Mayank had proven to be more adept than Kunal had thought at battle strategy and had already drawn up siege plans for the city. Soldiers and volunteers were beginning to take up sentry shifts on the outer walls of the city, thickly built and fortified again during Vardaan's time.

If Vardaan had come looking for a fight, he was going to get one.

Dissent had been minimal and whatever existed had been handled by the citizens themselves. A number of Vardaan sympathizers had shown up on the palace steps, bound and gagged, trussed up like gifts. That was the power of a good story, Esha said.

Kunal thought it was more that the people of the city knew what they were fighting for now. Reha had given them hope—they had done the rest.

Kunal had just returned from a scouting mission out over the battlefields. He had counted about five thousand opposing troops, not a large force but enough to delay them from getting to the Drowned City of Gold in time.

That was what Kunal was truly worried about. Their time was running out. He had been meeting with the Blades every day and yet, they still didn't have a plan for getting to the city. While Kunal thought he might have a solution . . . he wasn't sure. He had considered simply flying everyone over as an escape, but they wouldn't get very far. And if they showed up and there was a force of Yavar at the location of the city, they would be outnumbered.

No, they would need something else. A distraction.

The war room was brighter than normal, every camphor torch in the hall ablaze. It spoke to how often this room was currently being used. Servants trailed in and out, refreshing pots of tea and plates of food.

Esha sat in a corner, shrouded in the half-light with open scrolls spread across her lap. She jumped up at the sight of him and he wrapped her in an embrace before the others arrived. She set her head against his chest for a moment and he thought he heard a sigh—or a sniffle; he couldn't be sure.

"How are you faring?" he asked softly.

"Fine," she said. "I'm not sure the servants agree, though. They keep offering me chai and biscuits, as if it will solve all my problems."

Kunal knew better than to say anything, but he had noticed how gaunt she looked, the shadows under her eyes and the slight tremor in her hand.

The others began to arrive and Kunal let go of her,

instead turning to the big map that was the centerpiece of the room. Harun was the last to arrive and the meeting started in earnest.

"Kunal?" Harun said. "You scouted today? How are we looking?"

Kunal hadn't spoken up at first because he was strategizing, going through the numerous options in his head. They were running out of time and they needed to make a decision today. He cleared his throat.

"They're running three flanks of troops. There might be wiggle room to escape, but not until we're able to knock out at least one flank," Kunal said.

"The army will be positioned to defend the city, but our main goal is to get through. Perhaps we can use some combination of coercion and a strike team to puncture through the southern flank," Harun said. He shrugged, but it looked more defeated than Kunal had seen before. "We'll have to see. I admit, it's going to be tough. We don't have enough troops for an assault, and even though my father says he can bring some of his own, we don't know when they'll arrive. In time for the siege, most likely, but not in time for this mission."

"How about—?" Kunal started out tentatively, until he remembered that out of everyone, he had the most experience here. Here, he could trust his instincts. Here, he had to. "Remember my plan from before? It can still work." The room shifted to watch him, the various Blades and Scales turning to him for a bit of hope. "We always knew Vardaan was going to come back and try for this city. It's all he has.

But we're fighting for something bigger than our individual desires. We're fighting together and we will make it through."

He didn't know if it was working, but the others were still listening, so he decided to continue. Esha was looking at him with an emotion he couldn't identify.

"We'll run a smaller team, split in two. Some of you will have to stay back and help defend this city, and the rest, it'll be dangerous, but it'll be worth it. We can beat a siege from Vardaan, but we cannot let Yamini win," Kunal said.

Bhandu nodded slowly from his seat. "Cat eyes is right. We all need to shake ourselves off and get it together."

"What do you suggest, soldier?"

"We'll take a play from everyone's favorite, the Viper," he said slowly. Esha cocked her head at him, her eyes questioning. "We tell a story that is hard to believe. We build a legend."

"Is anyone else not following?" Alok whispered to Laksh.

Esha seemed to understand. She walked over to the map and moved a few pieces around. "We make it look like one thing while we're doing another. A feint. So obvious it can't be anything but the truth."

"Hiding in plain sight," Kunal said, sharing a grin with her.

"If I'm following, and I think I am," Harun said, "we don't have enough people for that. We'll need at least two other squads and the Blades are already stretched thin."

"It's the Hara Desert play," Bhandu said, finally having understood. Arpiya rolled her eyes.

"I have no idea what happened in the Hara Desert, but just to confirm, you want us to try to trick one of the deadliest generals, one who helped build the defenses of this city?" Reha asked, her tone suggesting they all had been temporarily relieved of their sanity.

Esha shook her head. "We're already prepared for him knowing the city. We know it just as well, thanks to Mayank and the Senap commander. We've buried every entrance, fortified every weakness. Or did you think our squads were running around because they needed exercise?"

"And we're not trying to win, Reha," Kunal said. "We're trying to get to the Drowned City. That is the goal."

"Can someone please explain this to me?" Alok said, gesturing wildly.

"Still doesn't change the fact that we need more people, according to my dear brother," Reha said.

There was a commotion at the door and it swung open, revealing a tall man with salt-and-pepper hair.

The sight of King Mahir made Kunal's throat catch, if only because of the way it made Reha's entire being light up. King Mahir pointed out the tall windows to the water below—and the small fleet of ships and men that gathered around the cliffs.

"Will that be enough?"

———◇———

Esha and Harun spent the rest of the evening briefing King Mahir and his guard, preparing for the early-morning assault that Vardaan would begin just past dawn. King Mahir had ridden ahead of Dharka's army with his personal guard to join his children while the rest of the army would be arriving in a few days.

They didn't sleep at all, but as Esha made her way back to her room, the first tendrils of light threatening to reach out into the sky, only hope was in her chest.

This time they had a plan.

King Mahir's guard had numbers to provide two more squads, just enough to cover the harebrained plan they had come up with. Though those were Reha's words, not her own.

It was a solid plan in Esha's mind, just insane enough to work and for Vardaan to overlook. In any other case it would mean certain death for the squad to engage in a suicide attack, except that Esha had already briefed Mayank and gotten his word that there would be extra support for them: multiple teams of archers and reinforcements once she and the others had broken their squad through.

They would leave at sundown, launching their assault just as Vardaan's troops were tiring and readying for retreat. Hopefully, they'd catch them during the retreat itself, which would hasten their departure and ensure less casualties, but either way, their teams were ready.

Esha glanced outside as she slid into her room, hoping to catch even an hour of sleep. The sun was up, setting the pink of the palace aflame in the early light.

Far in the distance, a boom rent the air. Right on time.

———◁◦▷———

Esha awoke to a frightened whisper. She sat up straight in bed, her hand going immediately to her whips before she remembered where she was. The palace was filled with noise. She must have been exhausted if she had slept so deeply.

Laya held out a hand to her. "You're being called, my lady."

Esha took the offered hand and got to her feet. She dressed as quickly as she could and Laya turned away to give her privacy. Esha pulled on the comfiest sari she could find, attaching her knives and whips as well. "What's happened?" Esha asked.

"I don't know, just that the prince was asking for you, and he looked frantic." Laya opened the door as soon as Esha finished. It didn't bode well that the typically even-tempered Laya was almost running through the halls.

Esha picked up her pace, shaking the grogginess out of her head as best she could. A heart-wrenching boom thudded into the air and Esha skittered toward the nearest pillar before realizing the noise wasn't near them.

She turned a questioning eye to Laya. "That sounds new."

Laya nodded tightly. "I think that might be why you're needed. I don't know for sure, but I heard some of the sentries say they spotted ships for Vardaan."

Esha's eyes widened. That wasn't good. That would make their escape difficult, if not impossible.

They hurried through the palace until they arrived at the war room. Harun and Mayank were already there, and just outside an alert-looking Kunal ordered about a squad of archers.

"What did I miss?" she asked. "Someone should've woken me up earlier."

Harun shook his head. "You needed the rest, especially after staying up all night. Vardaan has ships. Not many but enough to cause problems."

Laksh appeared at Esha's elbow. "Normally I'd say we should wait it out—this city is built for siege—but we don't have the time. What do we know about the troops? Can they be coerced? With favors? Positions? Money?" There was an edge of desperation to his voice that Esha was positive they all felt.

"I think so," Arpiya said. "These men are not truly loyal to Vardaan, or very few are. These aren't hardened soldiers. We have a chance to convince them but no way to communicate with them—certainly not before they manage to blow a hole through the eastern gate."

"We could send out a messenger," Laksh suggested.

"Which might also be certain death," Arpiya said.

"What else, then?" Laksh's voice was sharp, frustrated. Arpiya put her hand over his.

"A herald," Harun said. "Vardaan would not dare to harm a herald."

"There is little Vardaan hasn't dared before," Esha said. She got up and circled the table, peering at the map. There had to be something they were missing.

The others continued arguing, but Harun walked over to her and bowed his head close to her. "What are you thinking?"

Esha glanced up at him. "There has to be another way for us to get out. If the men aren't loyal, it's true that money or new positions might appeal to them. But we don't know what Vardaan has already offered them. Maybe he's given them first crack at the city and its treasures, the right to loot the palace—it could be anything. If we had more time, we could find out more, strategize better."

"But we don't," Harun said softly.

"No," she said. Esha rolled one of the metal eagle figurines in her hand. The sharp point of the wing cut into the soft tip of her finger, drawing a tiny slash of blood. She hissed and lifted the finger to her lips but paused. And stared at the blood.

"That's it," Esha said, grabbing Harun's hand. "We have to draw first blood."

"First blood? What do you mean?" Harun said. "Esha, it's already been drawn. We've already run up a number of casualties."

"No," she said. "First blood. We need to get to Vardaan first."

Harun stepped back and stared at her. That had caught him by surprise.

"Esha, that's . . . ruthless. Think of what you're asking for," he said, shaking his head. Still, Harun hadn't said no. Esha knew that meant he was considering it.

There was no love lost between Harun and his uncle, especially after everything he had done, but still. Vardaan was Harun's uncle, the man who had taught him how to wield a sword properly. And she was suggesting they kill him outright.

"That's how we end this," Esha continued, placing a gentle hand on Harun's arm. "These soldiers have only a tenuous loyalty and it will sow immediate chaos if he is taken off the board."

"Esha, I can't— What would my father say?" Harun said.

"We could always ask him," Esha said. "If he says no, then . . . we won't."

She said the words, knowing she didn't really mean it. Vardaan had to go. His stars had been written the moment he had chosen the wrong path, but Esha knew it wouldn't be something that would be easy to hear for Harun or King Mahir.

Harun waved over one of the Blades and whispered to him, asking him to bring his father to the room. Heaviness descended upon Harun's shoulders as they waited. Finally, he turned to her.

"I think you're forgetting to mention something else. Another reason you want to do this." His words weren't harsh or cruel, merely a statement of fact.

Esha swallowed. "I want us to bring back balance. . . ."

"And?" Harun prompted.

Esha looked at him in question and he only stared back with that keen-eyed gaze.

"And I will have finally fulfilled my promise," she whispered.

Harun squeezed her hand but said nothing, lost in his own thoughts.

King Mahir arrived a few minutes later and Esha relayed the plan to him as well. The others had stepped back, realizing that this was a family matter.

The king sank into a nearby chair, his head in his hands. "I had hoped it would never come to this," he said quietly.

Harun placed a hand on his father's shoulder, squeezing. "I'm sorry, my king, but in war—"

"Yes, I know," King Mahir said sharply. Then he sighed, his voice turning resigned. "I know what must be done. But how can I think of anything but of Vardu, my little brother? It doesn't matter what sort of monster he's become. I will always remember him, who he used to be. I wish he had never left for Jansa so many moons again."

King Mahir hung his head

The quiet of the room was thick, heady, and filled with unspilled tears. Esha's own heart constricted at the pain she saw between them.

"Do it," King Mahir said. "But do not tell me any more about it, not until it's done."

Esha nodded, keeping silent until the king had left. The others gathered around again, each looking at each other with uncertainty, with hope.

"I know you might not believe me, but I'm sorry it's come to this," Esha said softly to Harun. He nodded, his lips a tight line.

"It is what it is." He cleared his throat and straightened. "What's our course of action?"

Esha was ready for this. "The Viper. Alone," she said immediately.

"It's risky."

"But will you stop me?" she asked.

Harun searched her face for something before placing his hands on both of her shoulders. She felt her resolve flicker for a moment as he continued to stay silent.

"No," he said softly. "I won't. But be careful, Esha."

Esha nodded, her grip on her weapons tightening. She and Harun turned back to the table and Mayank cocked his head at them.

"Are we still sticking to the plan?" Mayank asked.

Harun glanced at Esha. She hesitated. "Yes, but with a few modifications."

CHAPTER 34

Esha spent the rest of the afternoon planning for their escape and plotting out her own mission. It would have to be timed perfectly.

The plan required precision and teamwork, as well as Harun's and Reha's powers. Esha sent a prayer to the Moon Lord that all would go as planned—or at least somewhat successfully.

A messenger arrived and had to cling to a nearby wall as another boom shook the palace and the northern gate beyond it. They were safe from the assault on the eastern gate, but it was worrisome that the catapults were powerful enough to be heard even from here.

All Esha overheard were snippets. Eastern gate. Battering ram. Sunset.

They were enough to set her into motion.

She ran outside the war room and into the chaos that

was the main hall. Kunal was in the corner, talking to one of the Senap captains. Kunal glanced up and she waved him over.

He jogged over. At the look on her face he immediately dropped his voice. "What's wrong?"

"I need your help on something," she said, pulling him aside.

"Anything."

She raised an eyebrow. "Don't you want to know what it is before you make promises?"

"No," he said. "Should I be worried?"

"Possibly. But you already said yes," Esha said with a grin.

———◇———

Kunal and Esha arrived just as the army below began to set up for their next volley of arrows. They ran to the top of the guard tower, charging up the battlements.

Half of the eastern gate was falling apart and scores of troops were down. They wouldn't be able to survive a few more attacks and their line certainly wouldn't hold. Worse, if the battering ram got through . . . it would be over.

Soldiers ran to and fro, responding to sharp orders being shouted from tower to tower. The injured had been pulled together, faint groans and the smells of ash and burning wood filling the air around them. Another boom hit the air and the militia near her ducked, loose stone and rubble flying over their heads and to the ground below.

Esha had been in many fights but never a battle like this,

never a war that was senseless and brutal. Kunal's expression was stoic. This had been his life for years. Chaos and terror, everywhere.

If she could get to Vardaan first, she would end it. Finally.

For herself, for her parents, for everyone.

No more lives lost.

She grabbed Kunal's arm. "There," Esha said, pointing. "Can you fly me over?"

"Directly into the battlefield? Are you mad?"

"Only a little."

This was the best way. "He's there, Kunal. Can't you sense him?" Esha hadn't meant it so literally, but Kunal closed his eyes, sinking into that power of his.

His eyes flashed open, tinged with yellow. "Yes, he's there."

"Take me."

Kunal gave her an are-you-sure look and Esha held his gaze. He nodded once and she squeezed his forearm in thanks.

He wrapped her in his arms and they shot up into the sky, arching over the battlements and flying down into the inky spots on the battlefield below.

———◄◦►———

They crept over the ditches, inching away from the soldier a number of paces away and sinking into the back of the enemy's battle lines.

"Over there," Kunal whispered.

"If we get him," she started, "this will all be over. It can finally be over." Kunal seemed to hear the wistful note in her voice. He put a warm hand on her arm, the only affection they had time for right now. The scene at the gates had shaken her more than she wanted to admit.

"We will," was all he said.

Kunal glanced out and then back at her, quickly nodding and pointing two fingers ahead. She followed close behind, pulling her bow at the ready.

Vardaan stood on top of a dais in full bronze armor, a sword at his side. Esha notched her arrow and pulled the string back, aiming true.

She just had to let go. His back was to her.

But before she could release the arrow, he stilled and turned his head.

"I was wondering when you'd find me."

◄○►

Kunal jerked back at Vardaan's words, but Esha held steady, the fire in her eyes too bright to turn away. The Viper wouldn't.

But Esha wasn't the same Viper as before.

And Kunal wasn't the same soldier.

Years ago he might have found Vardaan to be a worthy idol as he stood there, tall, commanding, the pinnacle of what he had thought a soldier was.

But Kunal knew more now, he knew better.

"You've surprised me again, Archer," Vardaan said, turning to face him. "Tricked me, I'd even say. You are far more than you let on, far more than your uncle said. It's now clear to me why Setu never let us meet. I thought you were a disappointment, but you were a treasure." Something akin to pain flashed across his face. "The Scales were right. There was a lost prince. I should've known those old translations were so unreliable. But whose are you? Shilpa was an old crow, but she had been fun in her youth." He chuckled, looking unconcerned that an arrow was aimed at his chest.

"And the Viper. After our last meeting I looked into you," Vardaan said to Esha. "Esha Amara, the ambassador's daughter. I remember you, a little. You look just like your father. He was a good man, kind and noble, but in the wrong place at the wrong time. I didn't mean for him to die, really; he simply knew too much. Still, it is one of my regrets. One of many."

Esha's face had grown pale. "It doesn't matter. You killed him. You killed thousands. This is your justice."

Esha drew the bow back, fire on her face.

But there was a breath of hesitation. Kunal and Vardaan both saw it.

"And what about your soldier there? Do you know what he's done? How many people's blood he has on his hands? And what about you, Viper? You're no innocent either."

"I've never claimed to be," she spat out.

"Then do it. Kill me," Vardaan said. "You had your chance before and you stayed your hand." He let out a mocking laugh, his lips turning into a cruel smile. "What a charade. You're weak. Even now you can't end this." His voice turned mocking. "Are you weak, Viper?"

Esha stepped back, her hand still clenched around the wood of her bow, so tight that the etching cut into her palm.

"Weak, like the queens of before," Vardaan sneered.

She wasn't weak.

She wasn't weak, but something felt wrong.

Esha couldn't put her finger on it, couldn't place the ragged, staccato beat in her chest as her arm held the bow string back, her shoulders aching with the struggle.

She had been here millions of times before. This—this was it. This was all she had wanted for years. A desperate aching need for justice, for revenge.

Anything to fill the emptiness of her heart. Anything to answer her ghosts, those of her father, mother, those of so many more.

But it wasn't the finality of it.

It was his words.

Are you weak, Viper?

No, but this wasn't strength either.

Fighting, killing, avenging. If she did this, she'd never have a chance to be more than her revenge. She'd never have a chance to forgive, to move on. She would be the Viper forever.

And for the first time, she didn't want it. She wanted to be Esha.

She was desperate to be Esha again, to be the girl her father had believed in, that he had died for.

Her arms were heavy weights; she was drowning in this choice. Esha felt her arms drop from their position, saw herself opening up to attack, helpless to do anything.

Was this the price of forgiveness?

A soft click and then the slide of an arrow, loud enough that Esha couldn't ignore it.

She opened her eyes, ready to face whatever came next.

Kunal raised his bow and pointed at Vardaan's heart. His eyes were the color of a tiger's, fierce and focused. A hunter.

He moved so fast that Vardaan didn't even notice the arrow protruding from his neck until he looked down in shock. Vardaan slid a hand to his wound, trying in vain to stop the blood. His eyes flashed as he looked at her, looked at the man standing in front of her.

"You're—" Vardaan stepped back, recognition alighting his face. He knew what Kunal was, whose blood he was.

"Your song. It's so familiar." Vardaan's face grew peaceful as he slumped to the ground. "Payal. You're her son."

Kunal stood tall, letting the arrow drop to his side. "Yes. Kunal."

"She was my friend once. She had believed in me. At least she'll . . . never know what I became," Vardaan said, his eyes fluttering closed. The stream of blood from his wound made it clear his time on the earth wasn't for much longer.

At the slumped form of Vardaan, Kunal ran over to Esha, wrapping her in his arms.

"I would've done it," she whispered.

Kunal didn't say anything. He didn't need to.

He knew her, heart and soul, past and future, better than anyone. Even when the Viper had been all the world had seen, Kunal had seen Esha.

He had fought for Esha.

Vardaan looked between the two of them, at the unspoken words and familiar touch. His eyelids shuttered and his body stooped over. "I did it all wrong, didn't I?"

Those were his last words.

And like that, the Pretender King of Jansa was no longer a threat.

He was only a man.

CHAPTER 35

Kunal wrapped Esha up in his arms and flew them out as soon as Laya and the Blades arrived. Whether Harun had sent them as protection or insurance if they failed, he didn't know.

All Kunal knew was that for a moment he had thought he would lose Esha. He didn't think, didn't consider, didn't decide to kill the Pretender King of Jansa in that moment. The choice had been made for him moons ago, in a tree in the Tej, in the city streets of Gwali when he had fallen in love with a girl.

His duty had changed.

There was a lightness in his chest that he hadn't felt in years. Vardaan had never been his demon, but he had been the cause of so much pain. And in the end, no matter how he had once imagined speaking with the king who had been his uncle's friend, the king whose armies he had helped lead, this had been the only option.

After meeting Esha, there had been only one ending.

Esha was silent, dueling her own demons as they flew over the still-raging battle below. And Kunal didn't push. They still had an ordeal ahead of them. It wasn't over yet.

They landed and when Kunal put Esha down gently on the outskirts of the battlefield, he saw on her face that she knew the same.

One mission done. One more to go.

———◄◦►———

The Red Fortress was a silent monument, perched on top of the cliff like a sun-dappled ruby. They had sent a force to take the Fort after they had taken the palace. It was theirs now, though not without heavy losses.

It was fitting, really. Kunal didn't think he could ever see the Fort again without remembering its history of violence. Even though it had been used only as a military outpost for ten years, it was enough to shift perception.

The Blood Fort, as Esha had called it at first.

They had met the others quickly on the outskirts of the battlefield, their feint working as well as they could've hoped. Mahir's squads had managed to draw the southern flank away without much harm. Harun, Laksh, and Reha had snuck through the back, protected by the Red Squad, and now, they were here with them. The Red Squad was a half league behind, covering their approach.

Kunal and the others rode down the hill at a fast clip, their horses tired from the half-day's journey from Gwali.

Laksh and Reha were close behind them, Harun's horse running at their pace.

"Let's take a break," Esha said, waving them to a stop with her hand. "We can also take the time to scope out the location using Farhan's map."

They nodded, each splitting up into their functions.

Kunal would fly over the sea to confirm that he could hear the song of the city. Harun and Reha were to scout for the entrance, using their powers. Laksh was lookout, alongside Esha.

They had barely dismounted their horses when the ground began to shake. Kunal bent to the ground, running a hand across it. The stones were jumping as the hill above them rumbled. His hand tightened around one of the stones.

"Get back on your horses!" he yelled. "Retreat, go back!"

It was too late.

A horde of Yavar horse people rushed down the bank of the hill, their hooves thundering toward them.

Kunal shifted into his eagle form and swept up Esha just as Reha bounded over and grabbed Laksh. Harun had shifted as well and was roaring at the incoming Yavar. Some of the horses skittered back or turned away, enough to cause confusion. Kunal thought he saw the glimmer of a smile on the tawny lion's face before he turned around and ran.

Kunal picked up his pace and flew to follow Harun and Reha's trail.

They got to the edge of the cliff that held the Red Fort, the ocean a vast canvas of cerulean beyond.

Kunal landed near Harun, who slowed to a stop, Reha and Laksh not far behind. They had already shifted back and Kunal did as well, though he was loathe to let go of the protection of his animal form.

The Yavar weren't far behind.

"Do we have it?" Esha said, her voice urgent.

"Yes," he said. "The map. I have it here."

Kunal tugged it out of his bag as Esha paced around the edge of the cliff. "How do we open this dratted thing?"

"Maybe if we had decided to steal the copper scroll back, we'd know," Laksh said.

"Not the time, Laksh," Kunal said.

"What about in our copy, does it say anything?"

Harun stepped forward, reaching his hand out into the space that rested above the cliff. This was the spot, according to Farhan's calculations. This was where the door to the Drowned City of Gold would lie.

"Farhan said the door appears at sunrise to those who are seeking it," Kunal said.

"Could it be any more unhelpful?" Esha asked.

"And there's a key, a stone of rainbow hues. They exist where spirits live, and with the Drowned City of Gold, that shouldn't be a problem. We just have to look for a ratna."

"Oh, just look for a magical ancient stone that we've only heard of in tales?" Laksh said in a low voice. "I thought a ratna was the reason the Chariot of Dusk broke and was unable to continue the Lord of Darkness's reign over the earth."

"Actually—" Kunal said.

"We don't have time for a history lesson," Esha interrupted. "Let's move." They split up to look. Now that magic was back, the cliffs and the land near the Red Fort glittered and thrummed with vitality. Kunal didn't think it would be as difficult anymore to find the stone.

Something stuck out of the ground, a faint glimmer that punctuated the air above it. Kunal bent down and picked it up, brushing off the top.

In the faint distance, hooves could be heard again and Kunal got to his feet. "They're coming; we have to move. And I think I might have found one."

He turned to the others with a smile just as something came hurtling toward him.

Kunal didn't even have a chance to defend himself. He was knocked down and was only able to cover his head before everything went black.

————◈————

Three Yavar horse people ran toward them, yelling their battle cries. Harun shifted and Laksh ran to engage them as Esha and Reha held their ground near the edge of the cliff.

"Looking for this?" a voice called out, holding out the ratna that had been in Kunal's hand. Yamini's grin was wicked in its gleam.

Esha's rage rose like fire. If Kunal didn't get up in a few seconds, she would rip Yamini limb from limb. She wanted to run to Kunal but knew she couldn't. They had to get the ratna back.

Reha growled next to her, her eyes turning russet, claws lengthening out of her fingertips in warning. Esha wouldn't want to mess with Reha in this state, but Yamini clearly didn't know what was best for her.

Esha ran forward from her covered spot, rushing at Yamini. The woman dodged neatly. Esha skidded and turned around quickly to follow Yamini as she ran away.

But she was too fast and the downhill was to her advantage.

Esha whistled sharply to draw the attention of others and turn them from their own fights. Laksh and Harun whipped around and found her with their gazes. They ran after her, following through on their plan.

"She's getting away!" she yelled.

Their goal was easy. Separate Yamini from her soldiers. Then get her into the city alone.

Step one was already done. Now to get her into that city by herself.

Yamini ran to the rock with the notch and slotted in the ratna. It clicked in and a sharp, blinding pulse of light shot forward, pushing them all back and turning them into statues for a moment. The light faded as the last stone clicked into place and a massive door rose from the side of the cliff, opening into the sky.

The door was made of solid gold, etched with lions and eagles. It rose into the air and slowly expanded until it towered over the entire cliff, a dark cloud in its own right. As Esha looked closer she saw that the reliefs on the door told the story of the Chariot at Dusk, the last side of the Lord of Darkness before he faced defeat. The reliefs seemed almost alive, the artwork moving on its own.

It was awe-inspiring. It was incredible. It was myth come to life.

It was terrifying.

Esha almost skittered to a stop as she reached the door, fear taking over her heart at the massive drop that seemed to be behind the door. Yamini disappeared behind the door but not before throwing a triumphant glance at Esha.

Esha took a deep, centering breath and ran after Yamini, through the ominous gold door.

CHAPTER 36

Esha tumbled through the door, bracing herself for a great fall. Soft grass met her instead and Esha rolled to a stop. She bounced to her feet, instantly looking around for Yamini.

The girl's armor shined in the light. Hearing footsteps not far behind, Esha could tell there was at least one member of her team behind her. She ran after Yamini.

Now her only goal was to get to the center of the city before Yamini.

Esha pumped her legs, straining against the limits of her muscles.

The vast city loomed over her. Everything was made of gold, the city somehow taking on the opulent metal and making it its own. But there was more to it, hints of knowledge they had forgotten in the curved shapes of the buildings, the layout of the city. There had been something lost when this city had been struck down, a black mark on the name of humanity.

Esha had never wondered very much why it had been called the Blighted War. Now she did.

The buildings themselves were huge, circling around a tower in the center. The temple, where the gods could be awakened and where the artifacts had originally been created. The first temple where the Ayana had been performed by Naran and Naria.

Esha heard a noise to her right, and though it looked as if she needed to take a left to go into the city, she veered right.

If she could take Yamini down first, it would all end.

———◇———

Kunal's head was still ringing when he got up, but in truth, he had faced much worse blows before. This wouldn't take him down.

But it might slow him down.

Esha had already disappeared through the door and his only goal now was to follow. He couldn't leave her in there with no backup.

A short Yavar woman swiped at his head with a curved-blade spear and Kunal ducked just in time. She came at him, her blows relentless. He dodged each one, trying in vain to get in one of his own. These Yavar were good soldiers, likely Yamini's personal guard.

They had something, someone to lose. Kunal lunged to

the side and finally landed a blow, giving him enough time to run.

Kunal phased into his wings and launched into the air, but something was weighing him down. The Yavar warrior was still attempting to cling on to him, and despite his attempts at shaking her off, she somehow stayed on.

It took a roll through the air to get her to loosen her grip. She fell to the ground, but Kunal had been flying low enough that it wouldn't mean certain death.

He landed and shifted back into his human form, using his speed and senses to try and catch up with Esha.

There were a set of paths in front of him, and while from above they all seemed to go to the center of the city, Kunal felt there was more to it. Something whispered to him in the city and its streets.

He turned away, focusing in on Esha.

She was close, Yamini not too far ahead.

Kunal sped up.

———<o>———

Esha continued following the bright glimpse of Yamini's armor and soon found herself in the center of the city.

The temple loomed over them, tall and stacked with increasingly intricate layers, each showcasing another myth of creation. Esha reached the front entrance and unfurled her whips, on alert.

There was a flash, out of the corner of her eye, and Esha grinned.

She slowed down but continued following the noise she

heard above. "Yamini! Come out, wherever you are. Let's talk about this."

Silence followed, but Esha waited.

Footsteps padded to her side. Yamini appeared, copper scroll in hand.

Her gaze was hard as the metal in her hand, flinty and cold. Whatever warmth had once been between them had vanished in the wake of her goal.

"There's not much to talk about. Get out of my way, Lady Esha."

"You still call me that. Why?" Esha said, hoping to draw her into conversation, stall her.

Yamini didn't take the bait to talk. "I tire of your questions."

Esha had underestimated Yamini's desperation. Yamini moved so fast that even if Esha had been looking directly at her, she might not have been able to block her.

Yamini's knife was out, aimed at Esha's heart.

But it missed.

A huge lion, gold as the city around it, leaped in front of her. Harun roared as the knife plunged into his leg.

And a scream ripped out of Esha's throat.

◄○►

Kunal ran toward the scream, arriving to find Yamini facing off with Harun in his lion form. There was blood dripping from one of his legs, but the prince didn't seem slowed down in the least.

Yamini looked up and caught sight of him, a grim smile

on her lips. Kunal saw it first, the second knife in her hand.

"Duck!" he yelled. Harun heard him in time and it was enough to distract Yamini so that her aim was off, the blade lodging in the ground to the side of them.

Kunal rushed over, but Yamini took the moment to run off. She headed for the temple and there could be no mistaking what she aimed to do.

"She doesn't have the artifacts," Esha said, panting as she rose to her feet.

"She might not need them," Kunal said. "We have to move."

Kunal helped Esha to her feet as Harun shifted back. She ran to him, but Harun waved her off.

"It's nothing," he said. "I'll catch up." Kunal noticed the paleness of his face but nodded.

They ran toward the temple as fast as they could. The massive doors were already open.

Yamini knelt at the altar that took up the inner sanctum of the temple, light reflecting off her head.

"Oh, no she doesn't," Esha said, venom in her voice. She unfurled her whips and approached Yamini with deadly speed.

Yamini was chanting in the old tongue and the air around her had begun to shimmer, bend in the light. She lifted her hand to put something forward.

But Esha had caught up with her. Her whip flicked out and secured itself around Yamini's wrist.

Yamini whipped around, her lips turning into a sneer.

"I can commend you on not giving up, but this is futile. I will succeed," she said. Yamini tugged at her wrist, but Esha held her ground. Her muscles strained, but she didn't budge.

Kunal caught up to Yamini and drew his knife. Harun had already reached them, though. Yamini, one hand still caught in the whip, whirled around and aimed a kick at Harun's head. He dodged but barely.

Yamini was still formidable with one hand tied behind her back. Kunal wasn't surprised, certainly not after all he'd seen.

Esha struggled to hold on to her whip, trying to slow down the Yavar princess, but Yamini spun and struck Kunal across the chin. He staggered back before ramming forward and shoving her to the ground.

Yamini's head hit the stone with a thud, but still, she didn't stay down. She looked up at him, her eyes turning thoughtful. It was infinitely scarier than before.

"Kunal, the lost prince. What's your place in all this?" she asked, reminiscent of the words she had spoken to him in the forest. "What about our new world order?"

"I'm trying for one," he said, panting.

She chuckled in disbelief as she slowly got to her feet. To his right, the others arrived, hiding in the shadows. Kunal blocked her, serving as the barrier between her and the altar.

"Your father," Yamini said. "He's alive. Did you know that?"

"Lies," Kunal said. She wouldn't distract him. He nodded at Esha and Harun, who staggered forward to the altar. They had only a short time to make this work.

"Are you sure? Are you willing to bet on that?"

No, he wasn't willing to bet on that. But Kunal didn't know if he could believe her or believe Vardaan. They had seen a desire in Kunal and were twisting it against him—or they were telling the truth. It didn't change what had to be done.

Kunal looked into her face. It was the face of someone whose duty had turned to obsession. This was who he didn't want to be; this was what he wanted to escape.

He shifted ferociously, snapping his talons and wings as he dove at her. Her eyes flashed in confusion before she jumped out of his direction. He flipped around and came at her again. This time she was too slow and Kunal tackled her to the ground.

He held her down even as she thrashed against him. His sharpened strength was too much for her. If he hadn't been a royal, she would've been more than up to the task.

"Now!" Esha yelled.

Yamini struggled against him, her eyes wide and wild as he drew his talons closer to her, edging close to her throat.

"No," she said. "All I wanted was to—"

Laksh and Reha raced out of the shadows toward them. Kunal reached down, and with a single swipe, he cut across Yamini's arm. Blood pooled out of the slash and Kunal pushed her forward into Laksh's arms. Laksh grabbed her and shoved her arm down toward the floor.

One. Two. Three.

Three drops of blood fell into the ground.

Laksh blew the conch—a sharp, bellowing sound—at the same time as Reha lit the lamp.

Harun's voice rang out in the cold silence of the empty temple. He chanted the ancient invocation passed down from royal to royal—with a few changes, courtesy of Farhan.

The sound filled up the vast space of the ancient hall, bouncing off the gold to create an echoing sound that made the hairs on Kunal's arms stand on end. The temple itself began to shake, tremors racking its spine. Debris fell from the sky and Kunal phased his wings in to cover him and the others as best as he could.

They cowered, expecting the worst, but without warning the temple stopped shaking. It burst into a radiant light that was so blinding they all had to turn their faces away.

Two figures appeared on the dais, shadows in the blinding light, forming into otherworldly creatures.

The gods had arrived.

CHAPTER 37

Esha fell to her knees. The others did as well. Laksh managed to do it while keeping a firm grip on Yamini, who still looked dazed.

Esha sneaked a peek up at the gods, their figures like the outlines of a flickering fire: gorgeous, raw, and painful to look at directly. Neither held a full form and neither looked completely human.

"Who called us here?" the goddess demanded.

"We have," Esha said. "We who worship you as the Sun Maiden and you as the Moon Lord." She turned to bow to each god. "We've come to ask for your help."

"No," the goddess said, her voice terrible and thunderous. "Humanity is none of our concern. Not anymore."

"Please, goddess," Esha said. Someday, far in the future, she'd wonder how in the gods' names she had managed to find the courage to speak to them. "We require your help."

"You have broken your bond."

"Not on purpose, goddess. We seek another bond, another boon," Harun said from behind. His voice was steady, deliberate.

"You dare to bargain with us?" The shimmering lady's voice turned cold. "After desecrating our one gift to you?"

"We dare to ask for a new beginning," Esha said. She could feel the energy in her limbs lessen the more she looked upon the gods' faces. She had to turn away. The others noticed, each stepping forward in turn.

"One that includes all of us, no divisions," Kunal said.

"No lies," Harun added.

"No boundaries," Reha said.

"And no more pain," Laksh whispered.

"And what of her?" The goddess's shifting form reached out to Yamini, who was still on the ground, clutching her arm.

"She'll come around," Esha said confidently.

The goddess turned, the full force of her beauty and power like the rays of the sun. Esha could make out only the faint hint of a face, unrecognizable in its foreignness. "You're a strong one, aren't you? Pity you are one of his."

Esha's eyes flickered over to the god to her right, his form shifting between a crescent moon and that of an armor-clad giant.

"That's what we want to change," Esha said slowly, carefully. She heard the tremble in her voice and tried to steady it. It wouldn't do to anger a god. "I'm not his, Kunal isn't yours. We're all the same. We're all of the gods. Of creation."

Kunal went still at her side as the goddess shifted her attention to him.

"Yes, indeed. But is humanity prepared for what that means?"

"I don't know, my lady," Kunal admitted.

"I do," Reha said, stepping forward. Her mouth was set in a grim, determined line. Harun followed behind her.

"Ah, you're different, aren't you?" The goddess seemed intrigued. "You both have the magic of both of our descendants, the keepers of the blood. I can smell it on you."

She stepped back.

"What is your offer? What is your sacrifice?"

They each held out one of the original offerings for the ancients used in the first Ayana: flowers and fruits and milk of the land that they had carefully collected.

"We offer ourselves, we offer all of the people of all of the lands as custodians."

"That didn't work before," the god said. His voice rumbled like a crumbling mountain. "And magic is in your lands. Learn to harness it and leave us be."

"But it is not available to all of us," Harun said, stepping forward.

Yamini's eyes flew open and she struggled to her knees.

"By all the people of the lands, we mean all of them. Including Vasu's," Reha said.

The Moon Lord's ethereal form shifted like the tides, flashing into a red moon and waves that flooded the entire room and Sun Maiden's form glowed a deeper, dangerous burnished gold.

Kunal and Esha lurched back, ready to smash the artifacts and the connection if need be.

"You would risk it all for them?" the goddess asked.

The five of them looked at each other.

"For a new world," Esha said.

"A new world?" The goddess seemed to consider the concept. "A new bond will not solve your problems, young ones. You will still divide yourselves, still find ways to war and kill and steal. It is a vicious cycle."

"And yet, these humans are trying to break it," the Moon Lord said. He whispered a word so beautiful in sound that it made their ears hurt from the perfection of it. Laksh fell to his knees, covering his ears. The goddess's form flashed in response, as if he had called her name. "It has been some time since the last humans came through here."

"They're all the same," the goddess said.

"None of them are the same. We are steady, unmoving, observing. They are not."

Her form contorted ever so slightly as she looked out at them, still holding their lives in the palm of her hand.

He said that word again—the goddess's true, ultimate name—and Esha also covered her ears, unable to control herself. This final plea wore down the goddess, who accepted with a nod.

The Moon Lord stepped forward to Esha, fully manifesting into the form of a giant armor-clad human. She dropped her hands from her ears and fell to her knees.

"Get up, my child." She did as he said and felt the faintest of touches under her chin, like lightning had brushed her skin. The Moon Lord lifted her chin. "We will reforge the bond. To all of you. To my children, to the Maiden's children, and to Vasu's children. And to us you will pledge your every breath. You will accept this?"

Esha nodded and he turned to Reha and Harun. "You both have the blood of the ancient lines, and you will keep maintaining it. The last time the power was given to all of the people, it didn't end well. You will be the wardens of this magic. You will teach everyone, spread the knowledge of the land and your promise. And if you break this promise, mark my words, we will come back and collect our due. And we will not be so kind then."

A single flash of lightning shattered the darkness, striking a tile a few feet away.

They barely had time to respond before the room burst into a blinding gold light, illuminating every crevice in the hall, and then sputtered into darkness.

"Did it work?" Laksh whispered into the darkness.

Harun's breath hitched, audible in the slowly receding darkness.

"Yes. The magic, the music. It's everywhere." He looked down at Yamini. "And it's in all of us."

CHAPTER 38

The sun arched over the sky, unencumbered by clouds or the storms of the past few days. It was a glorious pink, the color of hope. A new dawn for the city of Gwali and Jansa beyond.

Kunal sat on top of the tallest rampart in the palace, looking out over the city and the ocean beyond. The battlements were being cleared below, with pyres of fallen soldiers on both sides. Kunal had fought for that. There was no need to disrespect the dead, regardless of which side they had been on.

The new *janma* bond could be seen everywhere, in the raging river to the west, to the fisherman boats that were now making their way down the river and into the mouth of the ocean. It was what they had hoped for.

But since then, people were also awakening to new powers they didn't recognize. Farhan said it would take some time for them to understand truly what they had awakened by reforging the bond. Scholars would study this new magic for years and there would need to be a proper census, protection, and training.

Esha had a few ideas already. She had been astonished when she had first felt the connection, sensed the soft twitter of a bird nearby before it hopped into sight and chirped at her. Since then, she had been diving into her magic, her connection to the land. Exploring it fully. Kunal was glad to share everything he knew—and to learn a few new tricks from her.

"Kunal," a soft voice called.

He turned around and smiled at the curly-haired girl standing across from him. Esha seemed younger than usual, maybe due to the fashionable sari Reha had forced her into for the coronation. Or the fact that peace had finally been achieved. Either way, there was a fullness and a joy to her face now that Kunal was desperate to keep there. Forever.

He had fallen in love with Esha, with the Viper, with all of her. But now, they finally had a chance to get to know each other without the labels of Fort soldier and rebel.

A new world.

"The coronation is about to start. We need the new prince of Jansa at Reha's side."

"Did she ask for me?"

Esha chuckled. "Not in so many words. You know our Reha."

She held out a hand to him and he took it.

———<o>———

Esha smoothed the silk of her new sari, a deep amber-and-russet geometric print that was edged in gold. The sun above them shone down as if the Sun Maiden herself was blessing the proceedings below. A warm, salty breeze drifted through the air, so different than before. Esha could sense that the ocean was happy today, content. The fishers would be happy with their hauls.

Reha walked up the ramp in the old tradition, an offering of fruit and flowers in her hands as she approached the palace. She wore a brilliant indigo sari of pure silk, embroidered with thick gold strands and a heavy border—a sari befitting a queen. They had been right to do the coronation in the old ways. Citizens had arrived from all over Gwali and were in every nook and cranny of the Queen's Road.

She met the councilors and high priestess, all newly instated under the rule of Queen Reha, at the gates of the palace. The ceremony was simple and ancient. Reha offered the fruit and flowers at the gate before touching her forehead against the ground, giving thanks to the Sun Maiden and the gods above and asking for blessings in return.

The high priestess's voice rose above the low chatter of the proceedings, soaring into a beautiful song and chant that had been banned during Vardaan's time. They told the story of Naria, the first warrior queen, and all the queens that had followed. The song told stories of the prowess and the follies of the Samyads. And at the end, Reha's name was woven into the song to become an eternal part of the chant.

"All hail the reign of Queen Reha, keeper of the blood-lines, oath bringer, savior," the high priestess intoned. And as her voice rose, the citizens of Gwali responded in kind. A swell of emotion rose in Esha's throat, fighting against her good sense.

She tapped the edges of her eyes before anyone could notice. The Viper didn't cry.

Esha apparently did, though.

A smile broke through and Kunal glanced down at her.

"What's that smile for?" he said.

"I can't smile?"

He lifted her hand and brushed over her wet fingertip. "I can't help it," she sniffed. "It's an emotional day."

"Indeed," he said, teasing. "I think your new position as the ambassador of Dharka allows for displays of emotion."

"And what about you, general?" Esha asked, tilting her head up. He bent his head and captured her lips in a quick kiss.

"They'd better get used to them. I plan on changing things in the army." His voice was light but resolute.

Esha didn't doubt it. She'd known it the day she had met him, eleven years ago in an orchard, that her lemon boy was destined for more.

And now, there was a chance for it.

Esha craned her neck around a tall nobleman in front of her, aiming to catch a glimpse of Reha as she crossed the gates and officially became queen.

Reha stood on the threshold, one foot hovering over

the step. She glanced back at the crowd, her eyes searching for something. Esha waved a little through the crowd and Reha's gaze snapped to hers, her face breaking into a smile.

The hint of worry in Reha's eyes melted away as she winked at the two of them, crossed over the threshold, and became Queen of Jansa.

———◄○►———

The cliffs below the Red Fortress of Jansa were the same and yet not.

A deep crevice slashed through the stone from top to bottom and the ruby cliffs had deepened into a red the color of garnets and old blood. A reminder of the cost of the past few weeks.

While most didn't know what exactly had happened, what had been sacrificed, whispers of it were everywhere, from the open market stalls to the back rooms of the inns they had stopped in on their way down.

Princess Reha was now queen. A new bond between the land and people had been forged. The gods were back, as were the spirits and old creatures. One man had found a lion eating his berry shrubs one morning. Another saw an air sprite dance along the water of a nearby stream.

More and more people were waking up every day with a newfound power in their veins, with ownership over their connection to the land and gods.

A duty.

Kunal shaded his eyes from the early-morning sun, looking up at the rampart that had been his favorite. A figure was leaning out of the open window, waving down at him.

Esha had gone up earlier that morning to let in the first round of people. It had been her idea to use the Fort as a rest area of sorts. A refuge for the remaining Yavar and as a training school for those whose magic was new and untested.

He grinned and waved back at her. It should have felt odd to be back at the Fort. In some ways it would always be difficult to come back here, to the place where his life had ended and where it had begun anew. It would always be the place that had molded Kunal, beaten him down, but it was also a reminder of how far he had come.

Kunal glanced back up at the rampart, but Esha was gone. The servant's door creaked open and he turned around just in time to catch her in an embrace and twirl her around.

He would never tire of this. The smell of night rose and the way she fit in his arms. Only a few were this blessed in life, and while he had done his cursed best to ruin what they had built at times, they were here now. Together.

She tilted her head up at him, assessing him. "Did you notice where I was standing?"

"My old station. Where I was the night we met."

Esha tapped his temple. "I knew you were a smart one."

"You don't belong here," he said, echoing the first words he had spoken to her.

"Neither do you, Prince." Esha traced a finger over the anguli he now wore, the sigil of the Samyad eagle emblazoned on it.

"But I do belong here," he said, wrapping his arms tighter around her.

"Yes." Esha laughed and Kunal reveled in the fact that it was for him, that her laughs would be his gift for the rest of his life.

"A soldier and the Viper? Really?"

"Ambassador and prince," she said. "Kunal and Esha."

He raised her hand to his lips, placing a kiss on her knuckles.

"A match for the ages."

"A match for the history books."

She clucked her tongue. "Now, that's taking it a bit far. We're not that special, Kunal."

"That's where you're wrong. Every one of us has a story. And each of those stories is a treasure," Kunal said.

Esha smiled at him, one of those smiles that he would spend the rest of his life unraveling, trying to understand how he had gotten so lucky that night, all those years ago.

"You really are a warrior poet," she said.

Esha cupped his face and pulled him close for a light kiss, one of many to come. Forever stretched in front of them, endless and hopeful.

They laced their fingers together and walked away from the Red Fort, their shadows fading into the horizon.

ACKNOWLEDGMENTS

I still can't really believe this series is at an end. I feel so lucky to have been able to write Kunal and Esha's story, and even more lucky to have found such fantastic and loyal readers. First and foremost, thank you. Your support and love have meant everything, and I'll forever be grateful that you let Kunal and Esha into your hearts.

To Kristin, my partner in crime: thank you for being my fearless copilot in the wild ride that is publishing. Always thankful to have you in my corner.

To Mabel Hsu: thank you for always fighting for the core of these books. I've learned so much from you, and this series wouldn't exist as is without your guidance and insight.

To the fantastic team at Katherine Tegen Books and HarperCollins: thank you to Katherine Tegen, Tanu Srivastava, Jon Howard, Robin Roy, Aubrey Churchward, David Curtis, Ebony LaDelle, Valerie Wong, Tyler Breitfeller, and all the tireless sales, marketing, and publicity people who have worked on this series. You all are the best!

To Amma, Nanna, and my Akkas: you've been my biggest fans since day one, no matter what crazy scheme I come up with. I wouldn't be here without all of you.

To Aakash: thank you for always pushing me to be my best, even when I don't want to be.

To Chelsea, Crystal, Madeleine, Rosie, Tanvi: you all are the absolute best, and I'm pretty sure I wouldn't have survived the past four years and certainly never would have finished these books without every one of you.

To Mayura, Meghana, Nikki: ten years of friendship and counting. Forever grateful.

To every single person who has read, reviewed, hand sold, promoted, or supported this book, thank you.

Thank you, thank you, thank you.

Glossary

Anguli—A sigil ring worn by all Jansans.

Chai—Indian tea, often heavily spiced with ginger, cardamom, or masala.

Crescent Blades—A rebel group based out of Dharka with the aim to bring down the Pretender King.

Cuirass—Armor for the upper body that includes a breastplate and backplate welded together.

Dhoti—A garment worn by men. It's a long, unstitched piece of cloth that is worn as pants by wrapping the cloth around the waist and through the legs.

Himyad—The royal house of Dharka.

Jalebi—Thin strips of fried dough drenched in syrup.

Janma Bond—The magical bond between humans and the Southern Lands, gifted by the gods.

Naran and Naria—Twin demigods who pulled the Southern Lands from the sea and founded Jansa and Dharka.

Samyad—The royal house of Jansa.

Sari—A garment worn by women along with a blouse. It is a long piece of unstitched cloth, often embroidered and printed with beautiful designs, that is wrapped around the legs with the end thrown over one shoulder.

Senap—An elite squad of soldiers in the Jansan Army, trained as trackers and stealthy warriors.

Uttariya—An upper garment worn by men and women. It is like a shawl and is typically made of cotton or silk. It can be worn over the shoulder or around the neck. The modern form of an uttariya is the dupatta.

Valaya—A steel bracelet worn by all Dharkans.